TAUCEITI INCIDENT

Intrigue in the Sarducretchen Temple

Paul D. Escudero

WORKBOOK PRESS LLC
187 E Warm Springs Rd,
Suite B285, Las Vegas, NV 89119, USA

Website: https://workbookpress.com/
Hotline: 1-888-818-4856
Email: admin@workbookpress.com

Ordering Information:
Quantity sales. Special discounts are available on quantity purchases by corporations, associations, and others.
For details, contact the publisher at the address above.

ISBN-13:   978-1-958176-48-1 (Paperback Version)
              978-1-958176-49-8 (Digital Version)

REV. DATE: 30/03/2022

Tauceti Incident III

Intrigue in the S,ardukretchen Temple

By

Paul D. Escudero

保羅・道・埃斯庫德羅

January 2022 ©

Chapter One
The Gamulin Mission

The moment of truth now unfolded. After many years of struggle and immense stress at times, the Gamulin Mission finally launched. The Caro Interplanetary Transport poised for this unprecedented journey sat motionless for a few moments as permission to deploy finally arrived.

The Chief-pilot looked over at his Co-pilot and nodded then glanced back at Doctor Metongy Zeugcha, a Mission Specialist and asked, "Are you guys ready to go?"

"I'm going on this mission, even though I didn't want to be onboard." Metongy Zeugcha answered.

"What made you agree to come?" The Pilot asked.

"I was forced to support this mission. It was either I go on this mission, or the Planetary Security Service would allow the Clerics to have their way and my head would be served on a silver platter."

"Alright then," the pilot then replied and turned back to the Co-pilot and said, "Since we are all ready and we've been cleared to go, it's time to leave the Space Dock."

"I'm ready for the start of the mission, Captain," the Co-pilot responded.

"Engage the Repulser's," The Pilot commanded starting the undocking.

"Repulser's engaged," the Co-pilot announced as he stated many times in Simulators back at the Three-Dimensional Mockup Training for this event.

Upon the Pilot's command the magnetic Repulser's slowly shoved the huge Interplanetary Transport out of the grip of the Space Dock. Within just the past few hours the Space Dock atmosphere had been slowly removed to almost a vacuum so that when the deployment area opened there was no drastic change in pressures placing the vessel at risk of a rapid depressurization event. This also allowed an air retention check to make sure no leaks existed, and it would be safe to launch the Spaceship into space.

"Uniform Motion maintained, the Interplanetary Transport is now moving one inch per second," the Co-pilot reported.

"That's a good velocity, but we should start to see it increase shortly," the pilot responded.

"It's a slow and painful process to carefully undock," the Co-pilot said as he glanced back at Doctor Provkovitev another Mission Specialist.

"Yes, but a Spaceship loaded full of fuel for a round trip is particularly a hazardous vessel," Doctor Provkovitev expressed his viewpoint like any neophyte would.

"Accordingly, patience and care are essential to ensure no damage is done by any unexpected movement that might result in undue stress on the High-Tech Hull designed for incredible speed," The Co-pilot said watching the display carefully which showed several undocking parameters such as alignment and positions relative to the Space Dock.

"Every foot we move away from the Space Dock is one foot closer to the launch point and away from the dangers of any Space-Dock incident," The pilot stated as he realized they were in one of the most hazardous phases of the mission.

"The upcoming launch will of course have its own risks," Metongy Zeugcha stated as he reluctantly sat there brooding because he was stuck onboard for the mission.

"In fact, this will be the first time the Interplanetary Transport Spacecraft will be tested in its final form," The Co-pilot stated which did not reassure Metongy Zeugcha.

Moments later, the Co-pilot announced, "The Interplanetary Transport is free of the Space Dock. We now have space between the Space Dock and the Interplanetary Transport."

"Mark separation velocity," The Pilot stated.

"Five feet per second," The Co-pilot responded.

"Secure Repulser's," The pilot commanded while not releasing his hands on the manual maneuvering control just in case he had to take some emergency action.

"Repulser's secured."

"Arm the Cyclonic Inverters and start the countdown to Cyclonic Ignition."

"Cyclonic Inverters are Armed," The Co-Pilot stated and

looked over at the Pilot (Captain) with a look of uncertainty and hoping his actions would not end up creating a gigantic fireball.

Planetary Security Service controlling and monitoring the ship from Caro and the Space Dock facilities transferred control of the Cyclonic Inverters to the ship's crew upon receipt of the Arm Command. The pilot watched the various readouts as the countdown to launch began. The launch process was fully automated.

The Pilot then said, "Engaging the launch sequence."

The Co-pilot entered and said, "Concurrence Code entered."

"All that's left to do is sit back and enjoy the ride," The pilot responded.

"These first few minutes should be interesting," Metongy Zeugcha stated trying to appear like he was not full of fear and concern.

"The crew is testing the limits of Caro technology," the brilliant Mathematician and Mission Navigator Marlneiker said in the most serious tone.

The final automatic systems reconfigurations and command executions now slowly painted the control board showing the point in the sequence and should anything malfunction, that indicator would start flashing red instead of turning green to signal completion of event and abort the ignition of the Cyclonic Inverters.

"All interlocks are closed, and indicators all indicate green indicating ready to launch," The Co-pilot announced.

The launch command initiated auto throttles control of the Cyclonic Inverters that created tremendous thrust that slowly increased to 10% power as they moved away from the Space Dock. In due time the auto throttles would ramp up to max power which occurred in flight after system health checks indicated it was safe to transcend to max power ranges. The Interplanetary Transport would not initiate max power until they reached the edge of the solar system where the hydrogen gases thinned out allowing them to exceed light speed.

"Launch status indicators indicate all green, auto throttles engaging," the Co-pilot announced as required by protocol.

"Here we go, any last thoughts of not wanting to go are too late," the Pilot said the obvious as they had just reached the point of no return. It didn't take long for the crew to feel the G Forces that 10% power created as the propulsion engaged.

The Interplanetary Transport increased speed steadily in accordance with the flight plan. Megawatts of power output was creating acceleration like none of them had ever felt before and the vibration they could feel from the enormous thrust served only one good purpose. It reminded them they were still alive.

"Nothing like flying on theoretical designs," Doctor Provkovitev stated.

"Yea, but I hate to be the test pilot," the Co-pilot responded.

The crew members in the control room of the Interplanetary Transport were all nervous. Anyone who would say he wasn't either lying or ignored the reality they were traveling in ways no Caro had ever done before.

Metongy Zeugcha, an action-oriented individual with an analytical mind seemed to have clairvoyance. His curiosity and strategizing inertia led to critical thinking resulting in pioneering designs now utilized in the latest adventure. His dedication and bravery helped determine the course of these recent events that were now unfolding. Metongy Zeugcha's Arithmetic Preconvolver was instrumental in perhaps the most important discovery in Caro history which then eventually prompted developing the Cyclonic Inverters and led to this mission.

An accurate assessment of the Caro's most ambitious plan gave the appearance this optimistic proposal destined to face enormous challenges and possibly a distortion of the space-time continuum where matter existed in ways that preserved the uniform motion of space in spite of the tendency to experience a mysterious deviation and naturally seeking postures that eventually might prove totally unacceptable to the time constraints they now faced.

~~~
~~~

Chapter Two
What led to the Gamulin Mission?

Metongy Zeugcha's flashback to earlier times long before the advent of Cyclonic Inverters enabled this current exploration. The vibrations from the propulsion made Metongy Zeugcha suddenly feel how impossible the task at hand would have been had his ingenuity not spawned the invention that now allowed for the first time to depart the Tauceti Solar System and attempt to reach a destination which was believed to be the source of numerous radio wave signals arriving. This mission to explore the star system approximately seven light years away unfolded rather remarkably.

There had been no prior motivation to seek out other worlds. The Grand Clerics had all the wisdom and knew the Caro's were the only living and intelligent creatures and that God had created them in his physical form, but for reasons nobody could ever determine why. The Caro's blind faith remained unquestionable until that fateful day many years prior when a sudden noise started interfering with terrestrial communications.

"The radio signal interference was small at first and not even an annoyance, but eventually it grew to the point the planetary communications directorate was tasked to discover what was causing all the noise that was starting to affect signal quality in communications around the planet during certain times of the day," Metongy Zeugcha stated as the volunteer assistant watched him analyze the newest radio intercept data.

"In effect the Mass Differentiator painfully and systematically over a long investigation keeps pointing to the possibility, the signals do not originate anywhere on the Caro planet," the assistant responded.

"The mere mention of Mass Differentiator localization intercepts to the Clerics would nearly spawn an Inquisition of us Scientific Heretics," Metongy Zeugcha added.

"Scientists are under increasing pressure because in due time the interference signals increased from intermittent in nature slowly to a periodicity of almost continuous broadcast over a several year period," the assistant added.

"The interference on planetary communications is suddenly creating more and more consternation from the Caro leaders because scientists are gradually getting to the point of refusal to state opinions of the origin of the signals let alone whether they were not of terrestrial nature to avoid the wrath of the Clerics," Marlneiker stated.

Unknown to the Caro, a convergence zone in space occurred in the signal pathway between the planetary source of the signals and the Tauceti system. Just like a Tsunami gaining strength as the waves approach land, signals that would otherwise spread out and diffuse to the point they would not be detectable recombined almost like a Tsunami gaining signal strength. In spite of the blurring effect of signal spreading and recombination, enough amplitude gain existed to give the appearance the radiator was a lot closer than it really was as the cosmic and gravity waves created this phenomenon.

"Eventually when the public as a whole, starts demanding action and explanation, the leaders and the clerics will suddenly be thrust into a new reality," the Assistant stated.

"The investigation will have to proceed without Cleric interfering because it's starting to get painfully obvious planetary communications may possibly require major redesign efforts to eliminate the interference that is now starting to become slightly debilitating," Metongy Zeugcha added.

"The interference problem gets so severe at times that communications are only free of the interference when the planet areas were pointing 90 degrees in relation to the Tauceti sun. When the planet rotated 270 degrees in relation to the path around Tauceti, communications started to break down," the Volunteer on the Staff noted.

Doctor Metongy Zeugcha concluded, "The interference is probably not terrestrial, and through the use of this new Arithmetic Preconvolver we can carefully detect the direction of the intercepts."

"At first there was no panic. In the early stages of the interference, it was just annoying signals that would sometimes mix in communications bands causing data corruption and rebroadcasts," the Mathematician stated.

"Which in turn sometimes added inconvenient delays in signal transmission," the Volunteer responded.

"In the early days there was no indication these interfering signals was anything more than space noise, possibly noises caused by cosmic events in the universe," Metongy Zeugcha noted.

"Sure, such noises are not unexpected and had arrived over thousands of years randomly in signal nature as well as random directions," the Mathematician Marlneiker emphasized.

"As the noise grew, so did my curiosity, and with far more people observing and analyzing, it did not take long before the obvious length of the noise duty cycles grew, along with the dynamic characteristics," Metongy stated. He then continued, "In the span of 5 years the signals grew from a few seconds in duration to suddenly 30 minutes or longer several times per day."

Metongy Zeugcha took a drink of his Chénzi tea then continued, "What nobody expected, especially with the

Clerics micro-managing scientists and government officials directing them to derive explanation that best fit the cleric's needs, a period where the increase of signals and duration increased to the point where they lasted all day long."

"What motivated you to design the Arithmetic Preconvolver?" Marlneiker asked.

"Initially there were only a few frequencies. But as time passed and when this increased burst in signals occurred, Scientists like us are suddenly faced with explaining the reception of hundreds of different frequencies," Metongy Zeugcha replied.

"Some scientists in their minds believe these signals contain intelligence because they had reached the point of dynamic characteristics that now patterns emerge," Marlneiker commented.

"Unfortunately for them because of disclosure, a few of the so-called Heretic scientists were executed for causing global strife by publicly suggesting the signals were of extra-terrestrial intelligence," Metongy Zeugcha replied.

Metongy Zeugcha observing scientists treated as Heretics

and upon hearing the rumors the clerics were causing them extreme grief for daring to suggest any signal was extra-terrestrial in nature informed the Volunteer: "This is what led me to secretly develop and operate this Arithmetic Preconvolver in my own lab here in the living space of my private residence."

"Is the Arithmetic Preconvolver the centerpiece of the Electro-Clarifier?" Marlneiker asked.

"In some ways yes, it allows for the Electro-Clarifier cataloging the intercepts and developing patterns so that Linguists can start piecing together a macro image of the language and attempt to derive some knowledge of the intelligence the signals contain," Metongy Zeugcha replied.

Before long, the Electro-Clarifier system developed to analyze the Arithmetic Preconvolver signal processing output, created a stir within Metongy Zeugcha's Volunteer who explained, "These results expose the essence of situational context influences building upon syntax and very precisely demonstrates these signals have to be from multiple sources and multiple languages!"

As Metongy Zeugcha further resolved Earth signal ambiguities he mentioned to his staff, "It's clear the possible syntax derived came from at least 20 different languages."

"What about the encryption?" the volunteer asked.

"Encryption is nothing new to Caro's World History that had numerous black periods where war, strife, and famine stretching over 150,000 years before planetary unification and globalization, caused warring parties to invest significant time and effort into the process," Metongy Zeugcha stated.

"Yes, but since the completion of globalization, the need for secrecy and massive amounts of encryption was significantly curtailed," the volunteer responded.

"That's true. However, Mathematicians and Historians often write and discuss the intricate nature of encryption devices and methods," Metongy Zeugcha countered.

Before long some of the results of the Electro-Clarifier necessitated help from additional Mathematicians as well as Historians to help come to grips with the everyday revelations growing at an alarming rate.

An encryption expert quickly reported, "I discovered an

encryption process was going on in multiple intercepts. Also, encryption techniques varied to which language and frequency used."

"That seemed to come about quickly," Metongy Zeugcha stated.

"Thanks in part to the Arithmetic Preconvolver it did not take long to establish pairs of communications surrounding a particular encryption," the Mathematician Ferdastad stated.

Initially the encryption was quite simplistic in nature. But thanks in part to Metongy Zeugcha's curiosity and Ferdastad's mathematical genius; long before they would be confronted by the clerics, a realization occurred.

"We have identified at least 20 pairs of signal sources using encryption." Ferdastad stated.

"Have you solved the decryption?" Metongy Zeugcha asked.

"Yes, we have. However, we have no idea yet what the communications mean," Ferdastad replied.

"One thing we can now see is this is a fairly advanced race of beings," Metongy Zeugcha stated.

"What's more interesting is that they appear to be using some sort of international coding system where the signals come in groups of bauds," Ferdastad stated.

"Yes, even though the languages are different the basic topology is the same," Marlneiker chimed in.

"Which means each group is more or less using the same technology, just applying different languages," Ferdastad noted.

"Caro had several hundred languages and dialects at the start of the Great War Periods lasting thousands of years, so discovering an Alien Planet is similarly dispositioned is not unexpected," Metongy Zeugcha added.

For the next five years the signal intercepts had grown to an astonishing number. And during certain peaks, the number of signals was impressive. Even though the signals were binary in nature consisting of long and short pulses, the repeating codes had numerical orientation. Then one day the unexpected happened.

"We have just started receiving sounds we demodulated that are clearly voice," the Volunteer reported.

"How's the quality?" Metongy Zeugcha asked.

"The raw signals are very dirty from cosmic interference and dilution, but after we clean them up using our Arithmetic Preconvolver we believe we will be able to derive syntax and hopefully match it to the vast number of coded messages we received." The volunteer stated.

"How well can we hear them?" Metongy Zeugcha asked.

The volunteer obviously animated with enthusiasm responded, "The Earth people voice utterances are now clear enough after we process them to start developing the structural linguistics."

"So, it's no longer an abstract phenomenon," Marlneiker noted.

"We need to build a Lexicography and compile an Alien Dictionary before the Clerics discover us and try to shut us down," Metongy Zeugcha explained in an almost emotional manner.

"I wish we knew more about this Alien race so that we could establish translation and interpretation," Ferdastad said.

"But we do know a few things now such as they have a Calendar System and a Numeric System that appears to be universal among the 20 or so languages, we have isolated," Metongy Zeugcha remarked with a hopeful look.

"Yes, that has been helpful in establishing events and a time history of events discussed in numerous communications," the volunteer responded.

"We should be able to now start determining the correct alphabet through the use of the audio as we compare the audio to the coded messages," Metongy Zeugcha suggested.

"Plus, it should more or less confirm all the decryptions were correct," Ferdastad commented.

<div style="text-align:center">~~~</div>

Chapter Three
Compromise from Within

A few years later information was piling up; however, the secrecy behind Metongy Zeugcha's Alien communication project precluded a large staff to sift through the information without the risk of being discovered by the Clerics.

Ferdastad's mate, Zurella Myco was growing increasingly agitated. Jealousy and preconceived notions caused by Ferdastad's frequent long departures by spending time with Metongy Zeugcha led her to start complaining to her family, and her brother who was a member of the Planetary Security Service, who then offered to help and get down to the bottom of what was going on.

"Do you think he's into some kind of illegal activity?"

"He acts normal in all ways, except it's not natural for a mate to be away from the family as often as he is," Zurella Myco responded to her brother Chomvik.

"Has he possibly come in contact with another Caro and has an infidelity issue?"

"No, his Brosting behavior hasn't declined, so I have no reason to believe he's Caroing somewhere else."

Some mates do go Caroing even though it was highly illegal. The Brosting did occur occasionally when curiosity and lapses of moral and ethical behavior led to the irrational behavior.

Zurella Myco could go to a cleric as a last resort, but that would result in some severe punishment of her mate, as society expected to make examples out of Brosting violators. Once the allegation was made, there could never be a repair or return to normal. The Clerics would then enter their lives and just like catching a disease you never wanted, it was well understood that taking your problems to the Clerics usually resulted in consequences much worse than the original complaint. The cure was always worse than the disease.

Since Zurella Myco had a close family member who could discretely perform the investigation, going to the Clerics would be a matter of last resort.

Agent Chomvik a member of the Planetary Security Service, very fit with an athletic build knew the art of investigation and penetration without tipping off the target.

Unfortunately, due to the mountains of information they were processing, Agent Chomvik could not break into Metongy Zeugcha's lab very easily because it was almost occupied 24 hours a day. Metongy Zeugcha and Ferdastad often overlapped their presence in their secret lab however Agent Chomvik didn't take long to put together a calendar and timeline of when he might be able to have access without tipping off the target, they were the subject of a serious investigation.

For the first couple of weeks installing bugs and hidden secret video equipment took up almost all available time. The insertion process was nearly impossible, and without the help of a good friend in law enforcement to warn Chomvik to leave the lab in time to avoid being detected, took a while longer. But he persevered and eventually had a network of surveillance equipment set up and operating.

Now the fun part began. In the first day of monitoring, Chomvik quickly ascertained why all the secrecy and then reported back to his sister, "It truly is scientific research that's going on at Metongy Zeugcha's home."

"Maybe I should ask a Cleric to talk with him and ask Ferdastad to start spending a little more time with the family instead of being gone all the time?"

"If you notified the Clerics, Ferdastad would be in very serious trouble."

Therefore, Zurella Myco begrudgingly continued her life privately agonizing over the disruption of their family that now seemed even more concern when her brother informed her, "If the Clerics ever caught Metongy Zeugcha and Ferdastad doing their daily routines, their futures would not be very rosy."

Zurella Myco realized she could not confront Ferdastad without him wondering how she came to know what he was doing in Metongy Zeugcha's secret lab. She also understood he would conclude there was only one possibility: *she had someone spying on him.*

Chomvik feared Zurella Myco's exposure to the Clerics and the negative consequences.

~~~

Several years after the first confirmation of possible extra-terrestrial signals, there was a dramatic decrease in signals and right after the voice transmissions became apparent, a new event occurred that caused great interest.

Within a new frequency band there were several signals superimposed. Soon Metongy Zeugcha's conundrum grew exponentially as he said, "I've isolated the voice component of this new signal."

"What about the rest of the signal?" Ferdastad asked.

"The other components appear to be some sort of data." Metongy Zeugcha answered.

"Using pure logic, if you ask the question, if you got voice why would you need data to go along with it, at a much higher bandwidth?" Ferdastad inquired.

"One could make the conclusion that if you had the voice recorded, the only other thing that would be needed, would be video," Marlneiker implied.

It took a while to figure out how the video was developed
~~~

with the complex waveform, but with the help of Ferdastad, Marlneiker, and others, the team was together when Metongy demonstrated the ability to show the video.

Suddenly they had crude video of these Aliens and now so did the government since Chomvik felt compelled shortly after observing the video to make a report to his superiors what he knew would possibly explode the clerics into action if this was revealed. He only assumed what the clerics might do, but he knew dam well the Planetary Security Service had their own agenda, and they would soon confiscate all of Metongy Zeugcha's materials.

The Clerics had their spies everywhere. They always feared losing control of the masses and during the thousands of years of turmoil as conquest and consolidation slowly evolved from a secular society to a more homogenous Cleric dominated one. It didn't take long for complete control corrupted the Clerics who imbedded themselves in every aspect of Caro life.

When Chomvik made his reports to his superiors, knowingly breaking the law with illegal surveillance and failure to report suspicious activity, he did not fully appreciate the extent to which the Clerics had penetrated the Planetary Security Service. Hence, the Clerics had the information on the same day as Planetary Security Service.

Metongy Zeugcha always fearful of discovery and confiscation had the wisdom of storing information and designs at several locations, so even when cargo haulers showed up with workers to cart away everything lock stock and barrel, he still had at these other secret locations, materials and electro-clarifier analysis and video's captured allowing him to slowly study the language and secretly continued to learn much about those major amounts of communications they intercepted but could not make much sense of it until now.

During the period that had an exponential growth rate in the Alien communications slowly unfolding, the intercepts indicated planetary strife existed where the signals originated. No different than the Caro who fought each other for thousands of years, these Aliens engaged in global violence during this dreadful era just like the Caro mass killing resulting in almost half the Caro population wiped out.

Metongy Zeugcha's information was of course suppressed in that none of his research the Planetary Security Service confiscated was ever made public. Cleric Gummartukchik had no tolerance for anything that ruptured the delicate fabric of Cleric dominance had great influence over the Planetary Security Service establishment who also feared the repercussions of public awareness. They especially knew that if they became aware Caro now had video images of the beings that were the source of the radio frequency interference that many now increasingly complained of.

It took a while to secretly rebuild the hardware Metongy Zeugcha required to receive and process the Alien signals and he knew only one other person had known all aspects of the operation, Ferdastad. Therefore, he felt he could no longer trust him for fear of another breach and potentially more serious consequences including dealing with the Clerics.

Working alone became far more time consuming, but the end result was no longer another possible incursion by the Planetary Security Service, Clergy, or anyone else. Without his operation of the Arithmetic Preconvolver, no useful intelligence could be derived, but the Planetary Security Service certainly didn't appear willing to upset the Clerics by continuing the investigation into the interference using Metongy Zeugcha's equipment.

~~~
~~~

Chapter Four
Caro Focus on Earth Begins.

In the years to follow, as Metongy got more and more involved in study and analysis and developed rudimentary understanding of several of the earth languages such as English, German, French, Japanese, and Russian, it was clear the distant planet was starting to go through seriously turbulent times.

Making routine measurements to determine the direction to the signals as Caro orbited around the Tauceti star, there was one solar system that clearly appeared likely to be the source of the intercepted signals. Caro astronomers had photographed the solar system that contained the planet and had no knowledge it was inhabited. Since the Planetary Security Service never shared with the scientific community Metongy Zeugcha's fantastic discoveries, they had no reason to study the solar system and it remained a very low priority to interested parties. It was a mere coincidence a Caro space telescope was pointing at the Gamulin solar system in what later was calculated the signal origination from the planet to be around July 16, 1945, that resulted in photographing a very bright flash coming from a particular planet within that solar system.

Then, because of the interest which also had information flowing into the Planetary Security Service by mere accident, a second bright flash occurred which 7 years later after the fact, was calculated to coincide with August 6, 1945. Planetary Security Service got even more concerned knowing the details Metongy Zeugcha had put together on the major struggle that appeared to have gripped that planet.

These huge energy releases were definitely not Asteroid impacts and now caused new increased interest. Planetary Security Service then met with the Clerics to address the possibilities and warnings this revelation could possibly mean because seven light years wasn't that far away.

Cleric Gummartukchik met with Planetary Security Service director Bazion the day after Planetary Security Service became aware of the 2nd bright flash from that planet indicating a larger energy release.

"We think now it's important to study this civilization because the energy release and radio and video signals we are now missing could warn us of problems we may face in the future from an extra-terrestrial race."

"Mr. Bazion, there is no such a thing as extra-terrestrial life."

"Dear high priest, you know, and I know we've already determined these people exist and you yourself saw the few videos we intercepted."

"I don't believe it came off the planet. Someone here created those videos."

"No sir, they are the real thing. We secretly recorded Mr. Metongy Zeugcha's operation for an extended period. We have all the recordings and information, it's fully legitimate."

"We'll never agree to it."

"These two energy releases on the planet are very troubling. It's an indication they may have developed energy weapons of a magnitude that would be a threat to us should they ever come our way."

"But there is no life elsewhere."

"Your holiness, you need to think hard about this because it's only a matter of time before the public becomes aware then your position will become untenable, especially if the public discovers you were hiding the truth and terrorizing individuals for telling the truth."

The discussion degraded from there and Planetary Security Service director Bazion silently calculated that Cleric Gummartukchik would soon attempt to silence him like he did anyone else that was ever a threat to him and the Clerics.

Unfortunately for Cleric Gummartukchik, 3 days later which equated to August 9th, 1945, on Earth, there was another bright flash in the same general area on the planet that exhibited another huge energy release, rich in gamma rays, X-rays and other types of radiation that is often attributed to a nuclear explosion. It was no doubt that planet was undergoing some type of nuclear war and eventually might become a serious threat to Caro should they be discovered.

Since Metongy Zeugcha had done measureable translations it was then easy for the Planetary Security Service analysts to determine the Earth War ended soon afterwards. Caro now had a serious problem. They were no longer alone in the Universe, and one of the nearest solar systems just had a nuclear war. Even though it was a small one and only 3 massive energy releases occurred, nevertheless it posed a serious question about disclosure and other aspects of the revelation. Planetary Security Service now changed their strategy.

~~~
~~~

Chapter Five

Dr. Metongy Zeugcha meets Planetary Security Service Director Bazion

The communicator tone alerted communications were arriving.

"Hello."

"May I speak with Doctor Metongy Zeugcha?"

"I'm Metongy Zeugcha."

"Doctor Zeugcha, this is Planetary Security Service Director Bazion."

"Good afternoon, Director Bazion."

"Doctor Zeugcha, I would like you to come by my office as soon as possible, I have an urgent matter to speak to you about."

"Am I in some sort of trouble?" Metongy Zeugcha asked with bitter memories of the abuse and strong-arm tactics the Planetary Security Service used when they confiscated all his equipment.

"No, you are not. But this is a serious matter, and we need to discuss it privately."

"When do you want to meet with me?"

"As soon as you can get here."

"You mean today?"

"Yes, as soon as you can get here. I can send an official skycar to pick you up and save a lot of time."

"I suppose that would work since we have a Skycar port on top of the building."

"This is a rather urgent matter; I'm going to send over a Planetary Security Service Skycar right away, should be landing on your building in 10 minute or less."

"Sure, I'll go up on the Skycar Port now and wait for the transportation."

The red Skycar could carry six people, was fully computerized and did not require pilots. All controls were voice activated or occupants could key in or say addresses and the Skycar which is linked up to worldwide Skycar networks would proceed to that location. Skycars had millions of invisible airway paths carefully regulated and controlled by the Global Skycar Administration. These Skycars which were utilized mainly by the Planetary Security Service or wealthy citizens were lately about the only form of transportation available that wasn't public rapid transit devices such as Tube Trains, Surface Crawlers, and long-range Atmospheric Gliders launched by electric catapults that flew above the atmosphere.

As he promised, Metongy Zeugcha was up on the roof in the passenger waiting area that protected them from inclement weather and wind gusts from the Skycar until they were directed to board. The red Skycar had Planetary Security Service markings on its bottom, top, and sides. This Caro image included the Planetary Security Service logo superimposed on the top of it in bright yellow over the red.

The Electric Motors driving the Skycars Turbo Thrusters

gave enormous lift and the energy storage allowed several hours of flying between recharges that had very fast duty cycles. While the Skycar remained on the top of the building on the Skycar parking area, the electric motors were shut down and telescoping contacts dropped down the bottom of the Skycar onto contacts which supplied high currents to give the skycars fast recharge boosts. On this roof top there were eight Skycar parking spots, each separated by a few feet to allow comfortable boarding by its passengers.

Only Planetary Security Service skycars, taxi skycars, and a few rare wealthy owned skycars would ever be seen on top of buildings. Accessing the skycars on the roof top eliminated the need to get down to the crowded street level where egress was problematic, and the Planetary Security Service always avoided it.

As soon as Metongy Zeugcha approached the skycar after the indicator by the entrance of the protective cover went green and stated, "safe to walk to parked skycars," the skycar's rear passenger side roof area which contained the door, pivoted upwards allowing great access to passengers. A person could step in and sit down. As soon as the skycars internal data terminal determined the passenger was sitting, the roof and door slowly pivoted down into the secure position.

The Skycar operator then spoke which the data terminal monitored and had voice print verification, "Proceed to Planetary Security Service headquarters," the Skycar then signaled the planetary global Skycar administration it requested permission to leave the top of the building and proceed to Planetary Security Service headquarters. Global Skycar Administration data terminals then validated there was no danger to any rooftop occupants (they were either in skycars or the protective station area) and once the interlocks were closed, the skycar's data terminal executed the Global Skycar Administration instructions which then vectored it out onto the Skycar airway system.

Had Doctor Metongy Zeugcha walked to Planetary Security Service headquarters, it might have taken him an hour. Had he boarded one of the city Crawlers, it might take probably 30 minutes. A Tube Train could get him there in 10 minutes but getting to and from the Tube Train would waste another 20 minutes. The Skycar had him delivered to Planetary Security Service in 5 minutes. As soon as the Skycar landed and interlocks were open and it was safe to exit the Skycar, the Skycar door roof area pivoted up and Metongy Zeugcha got out and was met with a couple Planetary Security Service agents, one of which happened to be Chomvik.

"I'm surprised to meet you here, Chomvik."

"It's one of my many tasks I do with VIP guests."

"I'm considered VIP now?" Metongy Zeugcha asked then added, "I thought I was still in disfavor with the Planetary Security Service."

"Apparently you are not in disfavor," Chomvik responded and said, "This way please, the director is waiting for you."

Chomvik along with Metongy Zeugcha, and another Planetary Security Service agent then walked into the skycar waiting area when the automatic doors opened and closed behind them. They walked over to the elevator, got in, and then went down 50 floors to Planetary Security Service director Bazion's office. The secure elevator would normally not allow someone such as Metongy Zeugcha in, but with his Planetary Security Service escorts, the computer chips in surgically installed in their bodies was scanned and since they were precleared and expected, facilitated taking Metongy Zeugcha to Planetary Security Service director Bazion's office where he anxiously awaited him.

As soon as Chomvik and his partner delivered Metongy Zeugcha to Bazion, they were politely asked, "Please wait outside."

Metongy Zeugcha could not help but notice a Cleric was sitting in a chair adjacent to Bazion's desk.

"Doctor Zeugcha, this is the Grand Cleric, Gummartukchik," Bazion stated and signaled with a hand movement.

The Cleric who was too self-important to be concerned about a low life such as Metongy Zeugcha, felt no need to acknowledge him or do any sort of greeting.

Metongy Zeugcha was immediately alarmed fearing he was in some sort of serious trouble. And it was easy to contemplate he might now be part of an Inquisition and this being the first phase of something he would seriously regret. He started thinking Ferdastad might have been tortured or compelled to reveal he had duplicated a lot of his research materials and still have significant ability to continue his research.

"I suppose you are curious as to why I asked you to come over here?"

"Yes sir, the thought crossed my mind."

"Cleric Gummartukchik is here because he has some serious issues with what has transpired."

"Well, my equipment was confiscated, I see no reason for being here now."

"I understand your anger, but under the conditions we found ourselves in, we felt it was prudent to avoid a public spectacle and possible public reaction that could be destabilizing should this become exposed."

"I wasn't discussing it with the public."

"We had no idea that you would or would not reveal it to public information systems."

"Under the circumstances, I felt it would be unwise to reveal it to the public and had no intentions to do so in any event."

"Do you still feel that way?"

"Yes. I do."

"Why is that?"

"With the news circulating about the bright flashes photographed from the planet located in the Gamulin star system, I would be afraid public reaction would make it very difficult for me to continue my research. I suspect curiosity would draw a lot of people towards my research team which then would disrupt our operations for a good deal of time."

"What is your opinion about the signals and bright flashes observed and reported by the news and your own research?"

"I've concluded the interference signals are most likely coming from intelligent life that exists in the Gamulin star system," Metongy Zeugcha replied.

"There is no life that exists outside this planet," Cleric Gummartukchik angrily countered.

"I know it upsets you Cleric Gummartukchik, but I

respectfully disagree," Bazion countered.

A new dynamic was evolving between these two men, ever since the third bright flash came from the planet. What Cleric Gummartukchik didn't know was Bazion had numerous scientists engaged in galactic inquiry, working at various observatories that had multiple wavelength measurements and when they witnessed the huge X-ray and Gamma-ray distribution from the bright flashes, they concluded it could only be one thing: nuclear blasts.

Of course, Metongy Zeugcha who knew far more than he was willing to admit, played coy and avoided any comments or confrontation that might suddenly place him as a target of an investigation with intensive interrogations that would follow.

"Doctor Zeugcha, what do you make of the three bright flashes?"

"Well director Bazion, since I was not involved in any of the observatory work and have no personal involvement, I could only speculate what it implies, so I would have to defer to your scientists who were actually photographing and measuring them to make their assertions."

Metongy Zeugcha had no appreciation for the level of spy networks and surveillance capability Bazion had at his fingertips. He assumed because they seemed to leave him alone that he got away with the biggest heist in world history, stealing his own work and preventing total confiscation.

What Metongy Zeugcha didn't realize was that Director Bazion was far cleverer and more ambitious than he or Cleric Gummartukchik could understand. Bazion didn't become the Planetary Security Service Director without significant political skill, and cunning and astute methods that were disciplined and irresolute. His guile even exceeded that of the Cleric Gummartukchik.

Part of Bazion's strategy was to kill two birds with one stone, and he did it in a way that neither the cleric nor Metongy Zeugcha would ever believe. First thing he did was take away all of Metongy's toys to satisfy the Cleric, then he put in place men such as Chomvik who were masters at infiltration and insertion of technology to follow his hunch: the scientist would not give up his life's work and would eventually secretly go about it somewhere else.

And it didn't take him long to figure out where "somewhere else" was located.

Furthermore, since Metongy Zeugcha no longer could trust a staff and feared detection and confiscation of critical information and designs that he no longer could hide elsewhere, the fact he had a significantly smaller staff made it easier to break in since the secret lab was abandoned for a longer portion of the day, due to the lack of bodies present and working there.

Director Bazion also over the years patiently vetted people that were not under the influence of the Clerics. As such he put together a Special Projects Intelligence Team that was extraordinarily "compartmentalized." He would only pick individuals who had spilled blood for him in the past whom he knew had more dedication to the Planetary Security Service than any Cleric would ever receive.

His unique instructions to Special Projects Operatives included, "Allow the doctor to continue working in his laboratory. Only report the most serious information directly to me to avoid Cleric's intercepting and causing us a lot of grief including possibly our own Inquisition."

Metongy Zeugcha really did not realize he only saw Bazion's poker face. And Bazion's didn't react when Metongy Zeugcha either lied or omitted a lot of information, which Bazion had already received from his Special Projects Intelligence Team.

Bazion also had decided having a nuclear capable civilization close enough to be observed using those weapons meant a real possible future threat to Caro. *Especially if they found us before we found them.*

Director Bazion didn't need Dr. Zeugcha's help now. He already had the information required to analyze the nuclear threat of a nearby solar system. However, he could ill afford to expose his Special Projects Intelligence Team to the Clerics now. Bazion knew the Team's vital resources might desperately be needed in the future. Therefore, he had to surface the revelations that Dr. Zeugcha had determined surreptitiously long after the fact. He now began that process adapting to the circumstances and realizing he had to protect his flanks from the Clerics by the strategic implementation which now unfolded.

"Doctor Zeugcha, if the Planetary Security Service were to

return all your equipment and records, how soon could you be operational again?"

As Metongy Zeugcha seemed suddenly amazed looked into Bazion's poker face, he felt suddenly elated, but at the same time was curious as to *"what caused Bazion to do this?"* Clearly there was a change of heart for some remarkable reason.

"I'm not sure how soon we could be efficiently providing results. We would have to gradually work up to the point we were gathering and processing information like we did in the past."

"Are we talking Weeks, Months, or Years?"

"It could be Weeks provided I could get some of my staff back right away."

"Why would that be a problem?"

"Well sir, when the cargo movers showed up with Planetary Security Service personnel, they really spooked my guys, I'm not sure any of them would want to come back."

"How about if you get your key personnel back right

away?"

"Well, if I could get back my Mathematical Genius, Ferdastad that would help out a great deal."

Knowing Chomvik triggered the confiscations, Bazion cleverly thought of a way to influence him to reconsider coming back suggested, "How about I send agent Chomvik over to talk with Ferdastad, his brother-in-law. Chomvik can explain the desires of the Planetary Security Service that he re-engage with you for the sake of the planet, do you think that would help?"

Cleric Gummartukchik, slowly getting angry then interjected, "Director Bazion and Doctor Zeugcha, you two are starting to sound like Heretics."

"With all due respect Cleric Gummartukchik, your religion fundamentals are not going to change, its best you cooperate now because thanks to the observatory folks, the public may no longer easily go along with another Inquisition. It also might be in your best interest now to start figuring out a new strategy, because we are quickly reaching a point of no return as we get more and more bombarded with the

Gamulin System radio waves, it will be increasingly harder to hide and avoid disclosure to the public."

"I see no point in remaining here, I have more important things to do," Cleric Gummartukchik stated as he stood up and spontaneously headed for the door to exit.

Bazion had growing confidence he could now handle the Clerics. He controlled a lot of firepower with Planetary Security Service and the few agents that have been exposed to Doctor Zeugcha's Alien Intercepts fully understood, they were on a threshold of change, and the Clerics may no longer be able to control. Especially now, with planets at a nearby star had been exploding nukes!

"Doctor Zeugcha, if you will agree to recommence work on the Gamulin Solar System signals, I will order the cargo haulers to your home and lab today to start bringing back all the material we confiscated."

"I would certainly like to have it all back."

"I will send it all back and provide you protection under one condition."

"And what is that condition?"

"Doctor Zeugcha, the Global Security Council will need time to determine how to make the public aware of these extra-terrestrial life forms that you have so eloquently discovered. That determination has to happen before you release any information to the public."

"I understand that."

"Good. I have a team set up who will be an interface to you. If you discover something important that you think deserves my attention, then I would expect you to send that information via one of these couriers."

"Understand."

"Very well doctor, the cargo haulers will deliver all your equipment and materials back to your lab. You will also have a dozen personnel we'll provide to help you move everything where it needs to be."

Bazion stood up and walked around to his desk and then escorted Metongy Zeugcha to the door and asked Chomvik waiting outside, "Please escort Dr. Zeugcha to the Skycar so that he may return to his residence."

"Right away, Director Bazion," Chomvik said then added,

"Dr. Zeugcha, this way please."

Three minutes to the roof top, one minute to board the skycar, and five minutes to fly back to his residence, and in almost ten minutes, Metongy Zeugcha was back at his home wondering, *how the heck all* this *Planetary Security Service business had changed so radically suddenly?*

~~~
~~~

Chapter Six

Ferdastad and Metongy Zeugcha Meet

Secret Lab Back in Operation

Metongy Zeugcha no sooner sat down relaxing, unwinding from severe stress of going over and meeting face to face with the chief Cleric Gummartukchik who initiated more *"Scientist Inquisitions"* than any other, suddenly heard the buzzer on his communicator.

"Metongy?"

Metongy Zeugcha instantly recognized Ferdastad's voice and replied, "Yes, Ferdastad?"

"I just had the strangest visit from Chomvik."

"Yes, I was aware he would be visiting you."

"Is this for real, they're giving you back all the equipment and files?"

"That's what they said."

"Does that mean we are putting the team back together again?"

"We sure are. Why you don't come over so we can have a little talk."

"Certainly, I'll be right over."

Metongy Zeugcha clicked off his communicator, and then slumped back in his chair wondering, *"what really was going on?"* He couldn't help but feel Bazion had a rift going with Cleric Gummartukchik whom he considered a ruthless and devious character. In his mind he was saying to himself, *"This is not going to end well."*

Ferdastad didn't have the convenient transportation that Metongy Zeugcha just enjoyed. Like most Caronians, Ferdastad's budget only allowed the Tube Train or the Crawler or both. He left his apartment building, hopped on the free Crawler that never stopped except for someone pressing the handicapped button at a Crawler stop, then traveled on it for about six blocks to the Tube Train station.

The Crawlers didn't have wheels. They had robotic legs. In fact, someone from earth might say it could easily look like a centipede or some insect looking creature. With over one hundred robot legs to support the weight of the mass transportation device, the long surface transportation device swiveled every twenty feet and could bend around crowded streets, especially in the narrow roads of the old town sections of Caro Cities.

The fifteen mile per hour average top speed didn't go too far very quickly, but it was designed to haul people with their shopping bags and personal goods along residential areas to transportation concentrators such as the Tube Train stations.

The Tube Trains were pneumatic powered by air pushing and a vacuum pulling the train at high speeds along major transportation corridors. Riders could feel the acceleration as well as the deaccelerating as it sped up and slowed down very efficiently since it never had air resistance flying into a vacuum being pushed along rather smartly from the back as the Tube Train car body conformed to the dimensions of the tube. Hence the Tube Trains were air powered. Express trains would run up to ten miles without stopping but the local service trains rarely went beyond two miles without stopping. They of course were the cheapest fares and Ferdastad was on one since he only needed to travel about seven miles.

Ferdastad didn't detect he was being followed. Nor did the Cleric following him realize he was also being followed by a Caro Special Projects Intelligence Operative.

The urgent matter of analyzing and making determinations about the bright flashes on the Gamulin solar system planet suddenly took on new emphasis because unknown to the Clerics who were still traveling down a prim-rose path towards illogical denial of susceptibility towards a nearby powerful Alien race, Bazion realized he had to be ahead of the power curve because the Clerics would fail to contain the release of information if the scientists felt further threatened and decided it was in the planet's best interest to lay the cards on the table and explain the forecast of what's to follow if they ignored this revealing new situation that found their existence near a nuclear capable planet suddenly thrust upon them without any preparations.

After a couple starts and stops the train arrived at the station where Ferdastad got off and momentarily hopped on another crawler that made its way through narrow streets that ultimately took him to Metongy Zeugcha's residence and what used to be their secret science lab.

Ferdastad hopped off the crawler then doing about three mph at the time and walked briskly towards the apartment building on Zhìhuì Street.

The elevator was crowded and slow since it was at the end of the working day and workers were returning home for the evening. It almost took as much time riding the elevator up as it did ride on the crawler from the Tube Train station.

As Ferdastad approached the entrance to the Metongy Zeugcha residence, the security system notified Metongy, and he pressed the button on the remote access on the small table next to the sofa where he sat. Ferdastad was notified by the metallic voice in the welcoming system to "please enter."

Ferdastad opened the door that had electric locks disengaged by the security system, then walked in.

As he walked into the all too familiar spacious apartment, Metongy asked, "Is there anything I can get you something to drink or a snack?"

"No thank you that will not be necessary."

"Please have a seat," Metongy said and gestured towards a chair.

"When do you think we'll get restarted with our project?" Ferdastad asked with tremendous curiosity because of the amazing change of plans.

"I would say that probably we'll get active as soon as the equipment shows up," Metongy Zeugcha responded also somewhat in a mental fog over these rapidly changing circumstances.

"Now that Planetary Security Service is now allowing us to operate, does that mean we can go public with our findings?"

"No. business as usual. We still have to worry about the Clerics and the public is not ready to hear what we have found."

Suddenly the security system announced an arrival, "There is a visitor at the entrance."

Metongy Zeugcha looked at the security screen which filmed live via video the person at the front door. The person on the video monitor appeared energetic and friendly and was wearing a cargo hauler uniform.

"It looks like the cargo hauling professionals are arriving now with our equipment."

"Things are moving quicker than I anticipated." Metongy Zeugcha stated then stood up and walked over to the front entrance where he opened the door and greeted the logistics handler employee.

"Hello, are you here with the equipment and boxes?"

"Yes sir, we are bringing all the equipment, instruments, and apparatuses up now on the freight elevator."

"Very well, come on in, I'll show your guys where to put everything."

In the matter of eight hours all the materials previously

confiscated by the Planetary Security Service were brought back and Metongy Zeugcha and his team soon had no excuses why not to proceed with further scientific investigation and inquiry into all the signals arriving from the Gamulin Solar System.

The problem that Metongy Zeugcha now faced was that he knew far more than the current records would show. How he should channel the amount of data to Ferdastad without informing Ferdastad that another cache with intercepting and processed data existed elsewhere was Metongy's next challenge.

~~~
~~~

Chapter Seven
Despair and Irrational Transcendence

Just as Zurella Myco feared, over the subsequent days, Ferdastad appeared to be distracted more and more and he was away increasingly more often, ostensibly at Metongy Zeugcha's residence. Zurella in due course contacted her brother Chomvik via her communicator.

"Chomvik, I need to talk to you."

"About what?"

"Not over the communicator, can you come by here where we can talk privately?"

"Sure, I can be there in a little while."

Unlike Ferdastad who had no option but to take public transportation, Chomvik was senior enough in the Planetary Security Service that he could take a skycar from headquarters during the day and go just about anywhere without anyone asking too many questions. Ferdastad lived in a building that had skycar ports and Chomvik was able to get there within about 10 minutes.

"What's the problem?" Chomvik asked shortly after arriving in Zurella Myco and Ferdastad's residence.

"Ferdastad is making numerous trips to Metongy Zeugcha's residence again and spending more and more time away from home."

Chomvik could not divulge to his sister that *Metongy Zeugcha had recently been brought to Director Bazion's office and during his visit there, Cleric Gummartukchik was apparently alone with the two during a very private meeting.* Whatever Metongy Zeugcha was doing, it had to be quite serious if the top Cleric was privately meeting with him. But he also knew the surveillance on Metongy Zeugcha was also exposing he systematically provided Planetary Security Service Director-Bazion, vast amounts of information on the Gamulin situation without knowing he had been infiltrated.

"I'll look into it. I'm sure Ferdastad and Metongy Zeugcha

are back performing important scientific research like they were in the past."

"Maybe I should go see a Cleric?"

"I would not advise it. I doubt they can help you," Chomvik responded knowing Ferdastad might be in over his head and the Clerics would only cause a lot of trouble for him if his sister sought their help.

Chomvik left soon after the conversation and went back to his office thinking he convinced his sister to stay away from the Clerics. He was up on the roof top in about four minutes and the Skycar departed and within another six minutes was landing on top of the Planetary Security Service building where Chomvik got out and went back to his office and there examined more of the secret surveillance video and audio tracks from all the sophisticated surveillance devices he had planted in Metongy Zeugcha's residence.

One thing Chomvik knew for certain is Metongy Zeugcha for some strange reason did not trust Ferdastad it seems as he was never seen in any of these surveillance videos taken from the backup facilities. Chomvik could not help but wonder, "Have the Clerics been tipped off about all this which Metongy Zeugcha thought he was hiding from everyone?"

~~~

Paul D. Esdudero

wonder, "Have the Clerics been tipped off about all this which Metongy Zeugcha thought he was hiding from everyone?"

64
~~~

Chapter Eight
Zurella Myco and the Clerics

Ferdastad's partner Zurella Myco accommodated him for a while, but in due time, slowly grew unhappy and slightly bitter when he spent more and more time away from home. As far as Zurella was concerned Ferdastad was abandoning his family, while pursuing these irrelevant activities with Metongy Zeugcha. When she mated with him, he seemed so idealistic. Ferdastad the Mathematician was a brilliant man, a *Visionary*, and had been semi romantic. Now he was simply gone most of the time and his income barely kept up with family needs because all the time he could have been spent on Commercial Mathematical Projects were consumed with Volunteer work for Metongy Zeugcha. In due time her desperation overruled her common sense and she suddenly felt compelled to stop following her brother Chomvik's advice.

Late one morning when Zurella had made up her mind,

she left their residence after finishing up all her homework and tidying up the place, walked out building then stepped onto the Crawler loading conveyor that matched the speed of people walking with the Crawlers that came by every few minutes. She got off the conveyor and into the crawler and found a seat easily since it was at a time when commuters were not expected. The Crawler slowly made its way to the nearest tube station where she exited and found a train that would take her near the Sardukretchen Temple where she would seek advice from one of the Clerics whom she might get to intervene and try to keep her mate at home more often, plus he would have more time available to work on well-funded projects to build up their credits.

When Zurella Myco got off the Tube Train, she only had to walk five minutes to the Sardukretchen Temple. This seventy fifth century relic of more prosperous times could best be described as gaudy, even though the spiritualistic environment was enhanced by the unusual architecture and design long forgotten by modern Caro. Because of the mysteries in the building construction, it was unlikely the Clerics could entertain attempting building a similar structure in the present period.

When the Sardukretchen's originally built the Temple, the world was still in strife as the globalization had not materialized and the seven warring parties often inflicted massive numbers of casualties. Because of all the death and destruction, the design was influenced by progressive minds who wanted to commemorate the last defense by the Caronians who saved the Eastern Hemisphere from the wrath of the Taucetian's; whose imperialistic goals otherwise might have ended in an extinction event for them not too different than the end of the ancient Martians they would one day discover.

Hence, the spirit of the Caronians sacrifice was indelibly etched in the unusual architecture that exposed the genius as well as the intellect behind the designers and the planners that completed the construction in less than one hundred years with inferior tools and materials. Already the building had out lasted almost all others built at the same time or afterwards during the past seventy-five centuries.

Entering the Sardukretchen's Temple was a somber experience since it was a memorial to the masses that were slaughtered and to the last stand of the Caronians who prevented the rest of them from experiencing similar fate.

This time of day, it was somewhat unexpected for worshipers to arrive at the Temple. Though from time to time a few who had personal issues came to meditate or seek council from the Sardukretchen's seemingly humanitarian Clerics. The Sardukretchen Clerics gave the impression they always had the most practical solutions to their worshipers' problems if they could be solved.

When Zurella Myco found the courage to enter and proceed down the aisle to where she observed a Cleric laying out essential materials for services that would begin in a couple hours, she was quickly noticed. The Cleric looked up at her and being an expert in body language knew another woman with family problems had just arrived.

The type of issues people sought advice could stem from numerous varieties. The Cleric would never presume what worshiper's problems might be and would simply listen really well then figure out a way to intervene if it were possible.

"Good morning," The Cleric said very softly as he didn't want to cause the worshiper any more stress than the woman most likely felt.

"Good morning to you as well," Zurella Myco responded in an upbeat manner obscuring her emotions that brought her to the Sardukretchen's Temple.

"How may I help you?" The Sardukretchen Cleric asked.

"I need someone to talk to," Zurella Myco said in a manner which instantly signaled to the Cleric his deduction: this woman had a problem.

"Let me see if I can be of some assistance," the Cleric responded looking very concerned, hoping this would not be another emotional tragedy, like he just dealt with yesterday. Often people didn't seek their council until situations suddenly manifested, like yesterday when he was confronted with the challenge of helping the woman whose relatively young husband was just diagnosed with a rare form of cancer that not only wasn't treatable but was usually fatal.

Because of so many dead and dying people entered the

Sardukretchen's Temple over the seventy-five centuries, many claimed to have experienced paranormal activity, and some claimed their relatives communicated to them here. The Clerics never abused their positions to reinforce those perceptions, but at the same time their actions facilitated the natural tendency for them to grow and nurture in a place that had such architecture that could easily conjure up thought processes some felt triggered such irrational behavior.

"Do you want to sit down?" asked the Cleric as his hand waved towards one of the long congregation pews for the Sardukretchen worshipers next to the woman.

"I suppose so, thank you," Zurella Myco replied then sat down near where the Cleric stood but the Cleric remained standing.

"Since nobody is here but us, I think you can go ahead and tell me what it is that you would like to discuss."

"It concerns my husband."

"Does he have some kind of health issue?" The priest asked now leading the woman to expose the essence of her troubles.

"No, nothing like that."

"Do you argue and fight often?"

"No, we never fight or argue."

The Cleric was going through a flow chart in his mind, which he had memorized for such occasions. It was craftily designed, peeling the onion so to speak one layer at a time until he drilled down to the essence of her problem. Knowing he would have to trigger something to get her to divulge the root cause that precipitated her presence in the Sardukretchen Temple, he went to the next question in the mental flow chart.

"Is he having a Brosting or Caroing another female? "

"No, he would never have any infidelity, I totally trust him in that regard."

The next obvious possible problem the mental flow chart hit upon then triggered the next question: "Is he having financial problems?"

"Not really, though if he spent less time volunteering with Doctor Metongy Zeugcha he could conceivably make more money and our family would have more disposable income."

"Is this problem about money?"

"Oh no, not at all."

The Cleric then decided to drill down from the comment the woman said concerning Doctor Metongy Zeugcha, "It sounds like the problem is he spends too much time with Doctor Zeugcha and not enough time with you?"

"Yes, that's most of it."

"How much time does he spend with Doctor Zeugcha?"

"Every day, he often spends eight hours or more at Dr. Metongy Zeugcha's residence and on weekends even more."

The Cleric instantly understood the woman had a valid concern. He wasn't sure what he could do about it but offered, "Would you like me to visit your home and perhaps talk with your mate?"

"I'm not sure he would be ready for that."

"What's his name?"

"Ferdastad."

"Have you had discussions with Ferdastad concerning his frequent absence?"

"Yes, but he's so idealistic, his eyesight is clouded with the noble idea of assisting his friend with a large project."

"What kind of project?"

"He's a mathematician; he does a lot of numerical calculations for his friend."

"I have an idea, why don't you talk to your husband and ask him if it would be possible if I visited and talked with the two of you together?"

"Sure, I will do that, but he'll probably have a lot of excuses that he's too busy."

"Well, we have to be available for our Families. He's probably spending too much time away from home."

"That's how I feel about it."

"Okay, let me give you one of my appointment cards, talk to your husband and call me back one way or the other."

Zurella looked down on the appointment card just handed to her and saw the Cleric's name Zrebrek.

"If Ferdastad agrees to meet with me, I'll be happy to come by your home, otherwise call me back and we'll think of some other ways we can possibly help you."

"I really appreciate that."

"What is your name by the way?"

"I'm Zurella Myco."

"Okay, Zurella, give me call if I can be of further assistance to you."

"I will, thank you."

Zurella Myco took the appointment card, then turned around and walked out of the Sardukretchen Temple.

What Zurella Myco did not realize, her husband was often being observed by Cleric spies and operatives. Zurella Myco seldom ventured from home, but nevertheless Ferdastad and she were both under Cleric and Planetary Security Service surveillance. So, when Zurella Myco ventured to the Sardukretchen Temple, Cleric spies held surveillance on her.

Reports were made immediately and shortly after Zurella Myco departed the Sardukretchen Temple. Cleric Zrebrek had visitors and Zrebrek received special instructions.

~~~

When a database the size that Metongy Zeugcha developed, with the help of a mathematician such as Ferdastad, combining pieces of information eventually creates a synergistic situation that increases the data reduction rate, hence providing more reliable analysis and determination is made much easier. But what Ferdastad didn't know is Metongy Zeugcha already had a lot of answers he couldn't divulge without exposing the fact they had already ventured down this path and correlated and corroborated information in ways to provide clear and compelling evidence on various events and scenarios that occurred seven years ago on planet Earth. What was happening now would not be known for that same period. But the one critical piece of evidence that became crystal clear with the help of the video and the numerous encrypted messages they intercepted; planet Earth had just had a
~~~

nuclear war. And even though it appears there had only been 3 explosions prior to the Japanese capitulating, what could have happened subsequently in the next seven years?

That evening when Ferdastad returned home around 11:00 p.m. local Caro time which had 26-hour days, his mate Zurella brought up the absence issue again.

"Is there any way you can start spending more time at home instead of always being at Metongy Zeugcha's?"

"I'm involved in a really tough project now and for the next few weeks I really need to do a lot of calculations."

"Would it be possible for you to talk with a Cleric about this and see if he has some guidance for you?"

"I don't have time for that now."

"You are being gone all the time really is a burden on us."

"I'm sorry but this is a very important project."

"You will not talk with the Cleric?"

"No, not now."

Zurella Myco dropped the subject but called Cleric Zrebrek

in the morning using the communicator number posted on his appointment card.

"Ferdastad's not willing to meet you now."

"Perhaps I can arrange to be there sometime when you know Ferdastad will be home?"

"Well, like last night he did not reach home until eleven p.m."

"Ask him when he thinks he can be home, I can get there easily enough."

"Okay, I will."

Cleric Zrebrek now involved was a strong supporter of Cleric Gummartukchik, and with his special instructions, Zurella Myco had no knowledge she was now nothing more than a pawn in a very sophisticated game of subterfuge. Cleric Gummartukchik's worst fears were the stark reality that Alien disclosure may happen any day, and the Clerics were more than ill prepared to respond to the most likely outcome on planetary society. His goal and that of the other Clerics such as Zrebrek included their desire to avoid disclosure for at least a few more centuries, because that is how long it would take to craft a new story as to not illegitimatize their scriptures.

The very last thing they wanted was to lose control over the masses.

~~~
~~~

Chapter Nine
Surveillance

Metongy Zeugcha made frequent trips over to the library which was within range of the Crawler to get him to and from the library. He would have opted to walk, but that might take him 3 times as long especially since Crawlers always had the right of way at intersections and pedestrians and any other surface transportation means was stuck at the crosswalks because the Crawler advanced across the roads in front of them.

No sooner than when Metongy Zeugcha exited the building a Crawler was advancing directly in front and there was the conveyor to board the Crawler directly ahead. Metongy stepped on the conveyor which slowly raised him up to the main Crawler entrance level at approximately 1.5 miles per hour and onto the platform so that when the Crawler came by, he simply stepped inside and worked his way forward into the covered area.

The one hundred or more robotic legs of the Crawler hydraulically powered gave off a low modulating hum as they systematically moved that would propel the Crawler maximum speed up to around 15 miles per hour, which it maintained unless it had to pause for a handicapped person. A person in a wheelchair could go up the ramp with everyone else or take the chair lifter at the front of the Crawler where the driver could maintain eye contact with the individual and get them safely aboard. The chair lifter appeared to slide from under the Crawler and positioned on the yellow painted square people in wheelchairs would then drive onto, and then get lifted to cab level so that people could then drive onto the handicapped entrance of the Crawler. A similar operation occurred as they offloaded at their destination.

Metongy Zeugcha did not detect he was followed as he got on the Crawler. Several people got on about the same time he did, and even though they did not look familiar, it was a busy city, and he had no reason to assume they were anyone of interest.

The Cleric operative, who reported directly to Zrebrek,

sat down directly in a chair facing Metongy Zeugcha and avoided eye contact. Within 15 minutes, while the Crawler passed by the loading ramp at the library, Metongy Zeugcha got off. The Cleric operative wearing a disguise, waited until Metongy was nearly off the Crawler before he stood up and followed him.

Metongy Zeugcha made a bee line into the library and walked down several rows of bookcases where he made several loops as if he were looking for publications. Meanwhile the Cleric walked over to the nearest book shelve which happened to be in the History section, grabbed a randomly picked book, and proceeded over to the dozen tables laid out for readers, where he sat near the librarians and the location gave him a commanding view of the premises.

After Metongy Zeugcha made a couple loops around bookshelves and convinced himself he was alone and safe, he then proceeded over to a research area that had obscure ancient micro-film cabinets that were usually only half full. He pulled out the drawer he knew he wanted to seek the contents and under "Tables for Modern Analytical

Geometry," a group of extra Mylar sheets existed with an index label that would be useless to most people and ignored. He then found index-222 sheet removed it and replaced it with a similarly labeled Mylar sheet. Nobody was around to see the switch and to most individuals if they had been present would have not seen the switch and assumed the person was doing some very innocuous activity.

Metongy Zeugcha then walked about ten feet to the microfilm reader where it was possible to read over one hundred thousand document pages on this single Mylar sheet thanks to the micron-microscopic reproduction techniques perfected generations ago. Modern day scientists no longer used this technology, but it was one that Metongy Zeugcha used since it was the least expected and light and compact thus avoiding detection.

After confirming the sheet had the information he wanted, he shut off the microfilm reader machine and put the sheet into his notebook, then walked out the front entrance of the library.

Metongy Zeugcha departed the library, got back onto another Crawler heading in the opposite direction from the one he had just used to get to the Library and was back at his residence in about 15 minutes. He then took the sheet and fed it into a scanner that had the ability to read the documents in much greater detail than what the library machine could. After scanning and placing the contents onto the data cube, he then verified his reader had a good replica of the information, and then sat it aside.

Ferdastad arrived a while later as expected to perform some mathematical calculations on the datasets contained on the data cube. This wasn't the first time this data was processed, but begrudgingly. Metongy Zeugcha had to do it again as to not tip off Ferdastad and others he had already processed the data and knew the answers, as to avoid disclosing one of his unique hiding locations for reams of data already acquired in past intercepts.

~~~
~~~

Chapter Ten
Doctor Provkovitev, The meeting.

Breaking the crypto of this dataset was difficult even for Caro abilities which were most likely several thousand years advanced compared to Earth. But this was an important document because it was communications between Franklin Roosevelt and Winston Churchill concerning the Manhattan Project. Because of the seven-year time delay, it took information to get to the Tauceti solar system; Caro horror had not yet begun by the revelation Earthlings had just exploded a Hydrogen Bomb. And when 7 years after 1954 information arrived, the knowledge that two nations had now exploded atomic weapons clearly painted the picture that Earth was on a course of self-annihilation.

Suddenly there was a sense of urgency, and Metongy Zeugcha understood, it would take months of painstaking efforts to spoon feed Ferdastad all the massive amount of data already processed and understood so that he could move that information up to official channels while avoiding exposure to their hidden archives.

After a couple more weeks of work Metongy Zeugcha unexpectantly heard his communicator signal indicating someone was calling.

"Hello."

"Metongy Zeugcha, this is Planetary Security Service Director Bazion."

"I wasn't expecting a call from you. Is there a problem?"

"Actually, there is an issue we need to discuss. I need you to come by my office. A Skycar is being sent over to pick you up."

"Understand Director Bazion. I'll go up to the roof skycar Parking area now."

In a brief amount of time the Skycar picked up Metongy Zeugcha and after a short Skycar ride, landed at the Planetary Security Service Headquarters Building. Doctor Metongy Zeugcha and his Security-Escorts were once again at Director Bazion's office in a brief period of time.

This time no Clerics were present and Metongy found himself sitting in front of Bazion's desk with one other man he never met before.

"Doctor Zeugcha, this is Doctor Provkovitev."

"Please to meet you Doctor Provkovitev."

"Likewise, Doctor Zeugcha."

"Gentlemen, I'm going to get right to the point, with all the reports we've received from Metongy Zeugcha's group lately, it may be time for Caro to venture into space and confirm the location of the signals and ascertain a little more about their capability and evaluate the threat."

"The most likelihood the signals are from the Gamulin Star system, and at seven light years distance, it would be centuries before they could be of any threat because of the distance and time it would take to get here," Doctor Provkovitev stated.

"How would we be able to travel there?" Metongy Zeugcha asked.

"We do not have the means," Doctor Provkovitev

responded.

"That was true until just recently," Director Bazion asserted.

"Has there been a new development?" Doctor Provkovitev asked.

"That's why I asked you both to come here."

Metongy Zeugcha looking slightly bewildered wondered just what exactly Bazion meant by that and was soon informed.

"It would take us twenty to thirty years to get there," Doctor Provkovitev stated and continued, "There is no way we can carry enough food, water, and air for such a long journey."

"I'm going to send both of you to Yarneos to meet with Professor Qwrezzella who is leading the effort to give us the ability to travel there in a shorter time frame."

"When are we going?" Metongy Zeugcha inquired.

"Now. I'll have a Skycar take you over to the Preznium Air Transportation Center and there's an Atmospheric

Glider waiting for you. You'll have a few hours to meet with Professor Qwrezzella, and then we'll have you back in Preznium a couple hours later."

The two men were escorted to the roof and put on a Skycar within five minutes. Ten minutes later the Skycar had the two researchers at the Preznium Air Transportation Center, and it landed next to the atmospheric glider they were immediately put on.

Things moved along very rapidly. The Planetary Security Service had incredible resources, including their own Atmospheric Gliders that flew at One Hundred Fifty Thousand feet above the Caro atmosphere and traveled long distance very quickly. Even though Yarneos was seven thousand miles away, they would arrive in a little over an hour.

Once the two passengers inside the Atmospheric Glider a few minutes later, the Atmospheric Glider doors were secured, and an Air Tug pulled the Atmospheric Glider that was essentially, battery powered over to the launch ramp.

The Planetary Security Service wasted no time getting the

Atmospheric Glider airborne. They were given priority in the flight line and shortly the Air Tug pulled the Atmospheric Glider onto the electric catapult that was 3 miles long on a ramp that sloped up to 500 feet above the runway at the launch end. Toroidal electric magnets that energized upon takeoff on the Atmospheric Glider would remain locked to a sliding magnetic field on the catapult system as it gained velocity moving to the launch end of the ramp.

Just like a MAGLEV train on earth, the MAGLAUNCH sequence began as the magnetic fields gripping the atmospheric glider along with constant acceleration. From the time the atmospheric glider started to roll, the passengers in special designed seats felt 8 G's not only during the catapult, but because the craft went almost vertical shortly after launch. The G forces would remain strong until they approached 120,000 feet when less gravity was felt. Soon afterwards, they leveled off at 150,000 feet where they would coast for thousands of miles, no G forces were felt.

Even though at 150,000 feet the air is very thin, the atmospheric glider was traveling at a fast enough velocity where control surfaces still worked with the help of miniature rockets to alter flight profiles when necessary. The data terminal control activation then heeled the nose of the Atmospheric Glider over and they were suddenly on a 45 degree down angle on final approach. Just like body lift craft, they dropped quickly though remaining in supersonic flight.

As the Atmospheric Glider approached Yarneos Air Transportation Center, the airframe angle of attack slowly decreased, and at 10,000 feet they slowed below supersonic speed and soon were down below 1000 feet on a landing pattern to the Yarneos Air Transportation Center. Data terminals carefully guided the Atmospheric Glider to the ramp where the magnetic grippers soon locked up the toroidal electric magnets on the catapult system that were used to slow and stop the Atmospheric Glider right after it slowed and turned off the main runway. An Air Tug then hooked on and pulled the craft to the parking apron adjacent to a Skycar parked next to it.

~~~
~~~

Chapter Eleven

Visit to Yarneos Center for Advanced Study

With Caro efficiency, the two gentlemen were off the atmospheric glider and aboard the Skycar and in two minutes airborne to Yarneos Center for Advanced Study to meet Doctor Qwrezzella.

Yarneos Center for Advanced Study was more of a think tank facility, ostensibly set up for graduate students to advance their knowledge in targeted research in areas the government deemed lacking skills and knowledge in various subject matters. Interplanetary travel happened to be such an issue, since up until recent years the Clerics had done an excellent job of scuttling any attempts to truly build Interplanetary Transport Spacecraft.

From the Skycar the Yarneos Center for Advanced Study Campus looked very well maintained and the luster of the foliage, aside from appearing parklike, did not give the slight appearance of urban sprawl one would observe back in Preznium. The very nicely laid out campus abounding in flora and almost appeared like a botanical garden gave a deceptive appearance. The beauty and spender of the campus did a great job of obscuring the fact tension was brewing and the business-like climate in no way conveyed a laid-back atmosphere.

Just outside the main administration building, several Skycar parking spots existed. From the air looking out the window of the Skycar, Metongy Zeugcha could see a couple people standing nearby apparently waiting for them. As soon as the electric turbo's shutdown, the door access tilted up and the passengers stood up and stepped out of the Skycars and approached the waiting individuals all wearing white lab coats.

"Doctors Zeugcha and Provkovitev, I'm Doctor Dabler Qwrezzella."

"Pleased to meet you Doctor Qwrezzella," Metongy Zeugcha said then bowed slightly, Caro style.

Doctor Provkovitev also bowed slightly and said, "It's an honor Doctor Qwrezzella."

"This is my assistant, Grable Reagal." Dr. Qwrezzella said while his hand gestured towards the research associate.

"Pleased to meet you Grable," Dr. Provkovitev said and bowed along with Metongy.

"Let me take you to my office, gentlemen," Professor Qwrezzella said then led them into the building down a hallway, up a set of stairs and down a few doors to a spacious office, which appeared to be a supervisor's office with his own private conference table with room for twenty plus attendees.

There were drinks and snacks already laid out on the table and Professor Qwrezzella said, "Have a seat Gentlemen."

Professor Qwrezzella nodded at Grable Reagal who then went over and shut the door then came back and joined the group.

"I wasn't expecting your visit today, but a few hours ago I had an interesting communicator exchange with Director Bazion," Professor Qwrezzella explained.

"We didn't know we were coming here until about an hour and half ago," Metongy Zeugcha responded.

"Thanks in part to your fine work, Dr. Zeugcha, it appears the Planetary Security Service is concerned we have some potential vulnerabilities, and a new reality is beginning in spite of the Cleric activity."

"Did Director Bazion brief you professor Qwrezzella, what we have done with the signals we detected?"

"Dr. Zeugcha, yes, I'm briefed on what you discovered and quite frankly I'm not the least bit shocked because the teachings the Clerics have given really never did seem logical to me. I was always a skeptic to their beliefs."

"It's clear that Cleric Gummartukchik is not willing to back down on his assertion there is no extra-terrestrials."

"Gummartukchik probably understands that as soon as the public believes extra-terrestrials exist, the Sardukretchen's will lose control over the masses."

"Which also means they will also lose a lot of power and control?"

"Undoubtedly, that's why they are all over society now, watching everyone."

"Which means, we have to keep a low profile."

"I don't think that matters."

"Why not?"

"For starters, the Planetary Security Service is in bed with them. We can't protect ourselves from them."

"It will become hard to hide our developments."

"Which brings me to the point, what is our development?"

"The Planetary Security Service wants a space craft that will get to the Gamulin star and back in a few years."

"That seems rather impossible to do."

"I believe it's feasible," Professor Qwrezzella responded.

"We currently do not have the propulsion system capable of such a journey." Doctor Provkovitev stated most emphatically.

"Not yet anyway, but I think we are close to a prototype we might be able to try." Professor Qwrezzella then put up a briefing showing a proposed Interplanetary Transport Spacecraft.

"This looks interesting," Metongy Zeugcha stated as he looked at the artist conception that certainly had a very futuristic look at it.

"How large is that craft?" Doctor Provkovitev asked as he tried to ascertain the essence of what this remarkably interesting looking craft exhibited.

"It's a couple thousand feet long," Professor Qwrezzella replied as he soon saw disbelief on the other's face.

"How can we possibly build such a huge craft?" Doctor Provkovitev asked thinking this was most likely just academic wishful thinking.

"The secret to construction for such a large space vessel will rely on construction in space using modular construction techniques."

"How do we get the materials up in space and the workers and who would volunteer for such a task and project?" Metongy Zeugcha asked.

"We'll utilize our existing Atmospheric Gliders to ferry cargo in launch vehicles up to near space to one hundred fifty thousand feet just like cruising for long distance transportation. Once the Atmospheric Gliders reach the correct flight profile, the cargo vessels will launch off the backs of the Atmospheric Gliders utilizing chemical rockets for own propulsion and sent up to the planned distance for planetary orbit," Professor Qwrezzella explained.

"What about Space Workers?"

"Initial launches will include habitability modules that will be bolted together to create a space station to work on our interplanetary craft."

"Then what?" Metongy Zeugcha asked.

"Eventually major assemblies and components will arrive where Space Workers will integrate those sections into a complete ship with its own internal power plant allowing it to proceed to the Gamulin Star System," Professor Qwrezzella further explained.

"Will this huge ship become capable of landing on the Alien planet?" Doctor Provkovitev asked.

"No, it's only designed to support the mission in the vacuum of space. A planetary lander will have to be carried as part of its cargo and used to go from the mother ship to the planet's surface and back if deemed safe to do so."

"What if the planetary lander space craft has a malfunction, any reason why the mother ship couldn't take along a backup lander?"

"The reason why this thing is almost half mile long is precisely that reason, all systems will have backup plus some number of spare parts will be included."

"What types of defenses will be installed on the Interplanetary Transport?"

"We obviously are not visiting with any war like intentions, but just in case the Earth people exhibit hostile intentions, there will be some kinetic weapons launched by electromagnetic catapults. We also will have a cache of chemical rockets as a backup to avoid using the Kinetic Weapons."

"Why do you have the reluctance to use the Kinetic weapons?"

"The projectiles will be sent flying at incredible speeds and will be a hazard in space, without knowing where it could impact."

"What size of crew will be necessary to fly this spacecraft to the Gamulin star system and back?"

"Maximum would be around twenty-four crew members, minimum around twelve personnel."

"Why do you plan for so many personnel?"

"To operate the Interplanetary Transport around the clock, monitoring sensors, communicate back to Caro, and perform corrective maintenance as required and perform damage control in the case of casualties."

"How soon will this ship get built?"

"We have already started."

"Incredible, how much is built?"

"Forty Five percent of the final craft modularized sections are complete and ready to start moving out into space as soon as we get the habitat set up. In fact, we have a Three-Dimensional Mockup already in place. Would you like to see it?"

"Definitely."

Professor Qwrezzella stood up and said, "Will you gentlemen please come with me." He then moved towards the door and opened it to everyone's surprise.

Professor Qwrezzella then led them to the hallway then out to an elevator. He then pressed a button that said B2 which suggested to Metongy Zeugcha, it might mean basement number two floor.

Security personnel monitoring the individuals in the elevator knew that Professor Qwrezzella was cleared to go into B2 and gave the authorization for the elevator to continue down to B2 as he and Grable Reagal were escorting the 2 guests that were identified as Planetary Security Service sponsored VIP's.

When the elevator opened, the hallway had a security guard which they walked past nodded at Professor Qwrezzella the director of research at the Yarneos Center for Advanced Study. Metongy Zeugcha realized there was more here at Yarneos Center for Advanced Study than anyone would assume. *Was it such a secret to keep the Clerics away from it?*

After they walked down the short hallway, they walked through another set of doors into what appeared to be some type of transportation center. Moments after arriving on what looked like a train platform, a Tube Train pulled up and stopped directly in front of them that was entirely empty and only had a couple passenger-cars.

"Gentlemen we need to take this Tube Train to the space craft facility which is ten miles away."

Metongy Zeugcha felt rather astonished learning that *Yarneos Center for Advanced Study had its own private Tube Train system!*

"It's rather impressive you have your own Tube Train system," Metongy Zeugcha commented.

"We have some dangerous facilities that we do not want close to the campus or population, so a lot of that is built into local mountains and is left over from the Tauceti War IV."

"The government gave the Tube Train system to the University?"

"During Tauceti War II, III, and IV, Yarneos Center for Advanced Study did principal research on a lot of technology the military used, so in order to protect the research and avoid disclosing people or products to possible warfare and become a target to Tauceti drones, it was decided to build these complexes. They have remained secret even though we now have globalization."

"Why keep it a secret?"

"Those who have determined the need for secrecy should remain, set the policy."

"Who made that policy?"

"Planetary Security Service."

"Do you have any idea why?"

"I could only speculate the Planetary Security Service has some reservations about the Tauceti revolting and also since the Clerics came from the Tauceti, there might be reasons to be extra careful."

"Even though eight centuries have gone by since the Tauceti's were defeated, and we have Globalization?"

"Planetary Security Service has continued this policy and I see no change coming soon. This latest revelation coming from the Gamulin Star System probably will delay any changes scheduled any time soon."

The Tube Train accelerated very rapidly and at the frictionless speeds obtained, it seemed like they were already slowing down as Metongy Zeugcha felt the negative G forces caused by the deceleration.

~~~
~~~

Chapter Twelve
Gamulin Mission 3D Mockup

The train came to a Tube Train terminal and stopped. The group exited the train and went through a hallway with a security guard and proceeded into the main underground complex.

They entered an access door and suddenly Metongy Zeugcha was in total awe. The huge undergrown cavern was massive. They walked over to what appeared to be a railing as if they were looking down into a dry-dock looking at a Spaceship. And in the bottom of this endless pit was what appeared to be a ship. In fact, it was a Spaceship, though for now just a Three-Dimensional-Mockup of the Interplanetary Transport.

The mockup was required to perfectly fit all the parts and build the ship on the planet, then disassemble sections and prepare them for launch into space where they would be assembled into a real interplanetary vessel.

Aside from the Interplanetary Transport Three-Dimensional Mockup measuring over a half mile long, the cavern it set in was almost twice as big. Metongy Zeugcha had never seen anything like it in his life. It was an understatement to say he was overwhelmed at first. Doctor Provkovitev was equally elated as this revelation eclipsed anything he had seen in his lifetime and that included the Sardukretchen Temple!

"Shall we walk inside the 3D mockup and take a look?"

"Sure, why not?"

Not far from where they were standing appeared to be a walkway going from the balcony platform on over to the mockup sitting in a makeshift dry-dock.

No doubt this event was a humbling experience for Metongy Zeugcha as well as Doctor Provkovitev.

"Just building the mockup is a monumental achievement, especially since it has been kept totally secret and unknown to the public," Metongy Zeugcha stated.

The first observation gave the impression the Three-Dimensional Mockup basic design work was complete and all work on the Three-Dimensional Mockup looked as if it was in a fully finished state.

Inside the Three-Dimensional Mockup was no different than looking at it from the outside. A sense of completeness created an atmosphere in awe. All the control consoles and operator consoles were fully operational, and personnel were performing checks. Essentially the Three-Dimensional Mockup had two purposes: first was to fit all the parts and verify they all mated properly together. Exact duplicate parts used in building the mockup were also built for the actual space craft and moved to storage facilities to be later taken out into space where they would be used to build the actual ship destined to travel to the Gamulin Star System.

"Does this mockup have a power plant prototype?"

"Actually, yes, for the internal generation of electrical power."

"Is that Power Plant operational?"

"It certainly is fully operational and in fact is providing all the electricity used to power the Interplanetary Transport Systems that you see the technicians working on."

"What are all these people doing here?"

"They're actually running scenarios to evaluate all the control mechanisms."

"Why are they doing that?"

"Even though most of the results are simulated, we can at least assess the controls to verify they engage exactly the way we planned."

"So, this is sort of like a simulator used to train pilots flying the Atmospheric Glider?"

"It is for that purpose, but it's also built to train the entire crew and make sure we have no manufacturing mistakes before we ship parts out into space."

"Since most of the travel through space will have artificial gravity, people training here will more or less feel gravity not much different than what they experience working here."

"How did you produce the artificial gravity?"

"We took an anti-gravity machine and reversed the process. So instead of canceling the gravity we add to it."

"Is this the crew who will fly the mission?"

"Not quite, we are missing a couple that are not yet training with us."

"When will they start training?"

"As soon as you and Doctor Provkovitev interview with Director Bazion and sign the agreement to go on the mission."

Metongy Zeugcha did not know if Professor Qwrezzella was joking, and if not, it's a surreal discovery he never planned on before.

The men slowly did a walk-through of the ship including the power plant spaces.

"How are you generating the electricity?"

"We are using nuclear fusion."

"What are you using for fuel?"

"We are using liquid hydrogen and just like we will in

space we discard the Helium we produce."

"Are you dumping the Helium into the atmosphere now?"

"No, we are capturing it and selling it commercially."

"How about, when the ship goes out in Space?"

"We have no choice; we'll dump the Helium into space."

"No uses for it?"

"We use liquid helium as coolant in our fusion reactors, but we produce far more helium than required to sustain the reactor energy transfer function. We do not have any other uses at this time, perhaps in the future we may create some new uses such as cooling long duty cycle lasers and not discard what is now excess helium in space."

As they walked through the engineering spaces, the first thought that Metongy Zeugcha had was all the machinery seemed so immense which prompted, "You really think you can build all this out in space?"

"Actually, no. That's why we are building modules we'll bolt together in space because you are looking at a million-Caro years' worth of effort."

Metongy Zeugcha also thought, *it's hard to believe the Clerics didn't know about this project.*

"Consequently, it's going to take more than seven years to travel to the Gamulin Solar System?"

"No, it will only take a year."

"How can that be? Speed of light is only three hundred million meters per second?"

"Well, that's not entirely true."

"Please explain."

"Within the solar system where hydrogen and helium exist in large abundance, there is a cloud of those elements that are slowly sucked into the Tauceti star, but out in space a few hundred million miles away from our sun the space gets much thinner and instead of a few hydrogen atoms per cubic meter, it thins out to a few hydrogen atoms per one thousand cubic meters. Within the solar system, spacecraft will slow down simply by running into photons and hydrogen atoms. But a good distance away from a solar system where the vacuum of space is far greater, there is nothing to slow a body down. Hence a craft can accelerate to no limits, though we believe at around eight times light speed a ship might experience a quantum jump, therefore we would avoid going over eight times light speed."

"It might sound strange but during the acceleration phase the Cyclonic Inverters would be pushing against the solar system vacuum of two hydrogen atoms per cubic meter, plus the plume that creates a gravity cloud which normally would not provide much traction but since the plume will grow to one million miles long and intensified by solar winds, it will actually provide good traction to facilitate further acceleration. Since the space craft is traveling in the direction of reduced atoms in a more complete vacuum, eventually it loses all friction allowing unlimited speeds."

"Is that theory or fact?"

"You are not cleared high enough for me to answer one way or another, since you would demand an explanation of how we know this actually works."

"When do you plan on having the rest of the components complete in order to start assembly of the spacecraft?"

"We will begin launches within 90 days to lift habitability

units and eventually sections to build a Space Dock."

"Explain, what is the Space Dock?"

"It will look remarkably like what you see here. The Space Dock provides a controlled atmosphere where people can work and breathe normally."

"Any welding or hot work in the Space Dock?"

"No welding, everything is in a kit bolted together or in some cases glued on."

"What kind of glue?"

"We have this substance we call Xiéjiāo [歇脚]activates and bonds to materials for fastening purposes in the absence of air."

"That couldn't be nearly as strong as bolting or welding sections together?"

"Atmospheric Glider wings are glued on with Xiéjiāo. No bolts are strong enough to endure the stress the catapult launches put on those air frames."

"That's probably something the public doesn't want to

know. But, how do you know it will harden properly in the vacuum of space?"

"Doctor Zeugcha, with the importance of this mission, we have to make maximum effort to be successful. All processes including testing Xiéjiāo applications in space have been completed."

"Did you evaluate Xiéjiāo in some kind of pressure chamber on the planet?"

"Yes, we did. However, for quality control purposes and application science, we sent a few Caro Astronauts into space to do fabrications. Stress tests were performed on the objects they created using Xiéjiāo without ever encountering the planet atmosphere. The amount of strength the Xiéjiāo demonstrated matched what we found on applying Xiéjiāo to Atmospheric Glider wings to attach them to the body of the glider fuselage."

After walking about seven miles through the three-dimensional mockup, Metongy Zeugcha and Doctor Provkovitev were both feeling slightly fatigued and both indicated, "We have seen enough."

The men then retraced their steps to the Tube Train and back to Professor Dabler Qwrezzella's office at the Yarneos Center for Advanced Study.

Back in the office they went over the milestones and goals, and it became quite obvious why Metongy Zeugcha and Doctor Provkovitev were picked for this mission to Gamulin Solar System, to facilitate communications and if a meeting happens, make any sort of preliminary agreements that were feasible, as well as size up the terrestrial beings there.

In time, they went back to a Skycar and flew to Yarneos Air Transportation Center and put back onboard an atmospheric glider which quickly took them back seven thousand miles to Preznium. Expecting they might travel back to Planetary Security Service Headquarters; they were both surprised to find they flew to their private residences. Director Bazion did not want to press the two Doctors on this day for any commitments to travel on a mission to the Gamulin Star System.

~~~
~~~

Chapter Thirteen

Zurella Myco a Sardukretchen's Recruit?

Zurella Myco was starting to get on Ferdastad nerves as she started demanding increasingly, he stay home and come home earlier. On some evenings, his communicator signaled him 30 times, to which he just turned it off and put it in suspend mode.

"Metongy, would it be ok if I take some of these data cubes home and work on them there? Zurella is really starting to get on my nerves. If I work on them at my apartment, it may quiet her down a bit."

"Sure, I don't see why not, since Planetary Security Service now gets everything, we produce."

"Thanks for the consideration. I'm going to leave early tonight, perhaps take her out someplace nice for a delicious meal, then after she goes to sleep which, she usually does around 21:00 I can work on them for at least three hours."

"Fine, we'll see you in the morning, Ferdastad."

Zurella Myco went to the Temple again and hoped to find Cleric Zrebrek there for another discussion. Zurella was relieved and elated to discover Cleric Zrebrek was in the Sardukretchen Temple doing exactly what he was doing the last time they met.

"Good afternoon, Cleric Zrebrek."

"Good afternoon to you as well, Zurella Myco is that right?"

"Yes, that's my name, thanks for remembering."

"What did your husband say about me coming over for a visit?"

"Ferdastad's response was he's too busy, and he's over at Metongy Zeugcha's residence right now."

"Perhaps you need to talk with him more and find out a little more about what he's doing."

"He thinks I'm too dumb to figure out all that stuff he

works with."

"Well maybe it's time you prove to him you are not so dumb after all."

"I'll do that. You made my day Cleric Zrebrek."

"Keep asking him to set some time aside, it's no problem for me to visit your home."

"I will. Thank you."

"Next time call on the communicator."

"I needed to get out of the house, the exercise did me some good, and coming here to the Sardukretchen Temple gives me great feelings."

"I'm glad you feel that way. Many others tell me the same thing."

"Okay Cleric Zrebrek, I must leave now, I will call you soon."

"I'll be waiting to hear from you."

Zurella Myco, walked out of the Sardukretchen Temple, walked five minutes to the Tube Train station and was back to the residence moments before Ferdastad arrived home unexpectantly.

"You are home early, is your project finished?"

"No, I thought I would bring some of the work home so I could be with you more."

"That's nice. Perhaps you can show me a little of what you are doing?"

"I would like to, but this information is highly proprietary, I've more or less promised I would not reveal this project to anyone."

"It's not as if I'm going to go blabbing it to anyone."

"I think it's best you do not get exposed to the information."

Zurella Myco remembering what Cleric Zrebrek said a little while ago said to herself, *"I'm going to find out exactly what it is."*

<center>~~~</center>

Metongy Zeugcha did not divulge anything about his trip to Ferdastad and didn't plan on disclosing any information to anyone else. He now saw the big picture. Planetary Security Service was not really playing ball with the Clerics. This whole operation was now very delicate. Such a vast enterprise hidden from the public, was operating out of a university, which is known to be full of radicals and sources of leaks. *How they kept this secret for so long, is probably one of the top five mysteries of the Caro civilization.*

The Yarneos Center for Advanced Studies was somewhat different than other Universities in that there were very few undergraduates. As the name implied it really was a research center. People involved in the Gamulin Star System Project were most likely handpicked and admonished what could happen to them for revealing information to people not associated with the project.

Ferdastad had a routine. He would work past midnight then crash and sleep until 8:00 a.m. usually. The 26-hour days of the Caro planet were just too short. Ferdastad could easily use another 4 hours per day to get done all he needed.

Today was no different, except instead of working over at Metongy Zeugcha's residence, he had what he needed and worked really late. It was already two hours past midnight when he finally could go no further, he felt like collapsing, just left his data cubes next to the data terminal and went into the bedroom, undressed, and climbed into bed, and soon was semi-comatose sleeping in a way that it would take a lot to awaken.

Zurella Myco was an early riser. She rarely could sleep past 7:00 a.m. got up sometimes showered or waited until Ferdastad left for work then she would clean up. This morning however, she was in a sour mood because it really upset her that Ferdastad was so condescending last night acting if she was too dumb to figure out what he was up to. She took matters into her own hands, walked over to the data terminal that still had the screen up. Ferdastad assuming he could just continue where he left off when he woke up, severely underestimated Zurella Myco who immediately started reading the document he had prepared and looked down and saw several data cubes. She then walked over to her own private data terminal with one of the data cubes and since it was not password protected, copied it, and started viewing it. She suddenly felt dumb because she didn't have a clue to what it all meant. But she didn't care, she was going to learn!

After Zurella Myco copied all the data cubes onto her private data terminal, she took the data cubes back to Ferdastad's terminal and arranged them as she found them. She then started reading the document again. It was about places and persons she had never heard of. It was quite extensive and being somewhat immersed in history while she attended the University knew she had never read any of this before and she thought, *I was well read.*

But since Zurella was a History Student, she knew some technical things used in the past such as encryption and other technical matters that were seen throughout the document including nuclear devices, which had not been used on Caro in 30 or 40 centuries. Names such as Roosevelt, Churchill, Stalin, Hitler, Mussolini, and Hirohito just did not show up anywhere in Caro history.

Then as Zurella read on, she discovered more. They were decrypting this information with an Arithmetic Preconvolver and comments such as received most likely from the Gamulin Solar System. None of it made any sense to her, but she had plenty of data cubes to go through. She would take her time. She also wondered if Cleric Zrebrek could somehow help her make sense of all it. Perhaps this was her chance to finally turn things around and eventually get Ferdastad make her a big part of his life again, instead of an auxiliary person in the household increasingly becoming *a domestic engineer.*

Zurella watched the time and when it was around 8:00 she went to the food processor in the other room and programmed in a meal that would start cooking shortly and if all worked out correctly, Ferdastad would have his morning meal ready as soon as he was up and about.

Zurella then went back to her data terminals and slowly peeked at samples of the documents she pirated off Ferdastad's data cubes.

Even though Zurella didn't have a handle on what all the information was about, it was now clear why Ferdastad was gone all the time, he had mountains of data to work on. *Some of this data was intercepted years ago and they still had not processed it. Lack of help was evident.*

Eventually Ferdastad was awaken, had a morning meal,

dressed, got all his data cubes together and said, "I have to leave and will try to get home earlier tonight."

"Thanks for coming home earlier last night, I appreciated it."

"You're welcome." Ferdastad then departed and went back to Metongy Zeugcha's secret lab and got new downloads in a similar fashion as before.

Not long after Ferdastad departed, Zurella Myco put on some fresh clothes and made herself look a little prettier, then called Cleric Zrebrek on his communicator.

"Hello, this is Zrebrek how can I help you?"

"Good morning, Cleric Zrebrek I'm Zurella Myco. I talked to you yesterday about my husband being gone all the time."

"Yes, I remember you quite well Zurella."

"Ferdastad brought home some of his work last night and while he was sleeping, I copied the files so I could figure out what he's been up to."

"Did you find something that disturbs you?"

"It doesn't disturb me, but it makes no sense at all and has vast amounts of information that has nothing to do with Caro."

"I see."

"I was wondering if I could bring over a data cube and have you look at it and tell me I'm not totally dumb for not knowing any of this stuff."

"I'm sure you are not dumb."

"Well thank you I appreciate your viewpoint."

"Sure, bring it over, and let me take a look at it."

"I will do that, thank you so much."

"See you soon."

"Bye."

In the back of her mind, Zurella Myco would not be upset if Cleric Zrebrek made a pass at her. She had heard stories of Clerics making lonely housewives happy again, especially when husbands didn't pay enough attention to their spouse. *Perhaps I put on too much makeup?* Zurella Myco asked herself as she looked in the mirror for the final time before departing.

In about an hour Zurella Myco entered the Sardukretchen's Temple. She didn't know what to expect but she knew she felt a strange attraction to Cleric Zrebrek.

No sooner than Zurella went inside the Temple she spotted Cleric Zrebrek and walked toward him. He too simultaneously spotted her and met her halfway up the aisle. The Temple was empty, just the two stood there.

"I brought a data cube I hope I'm not taking up too much of your time."

"No not a problem, why don't we go to my office where I have a data terminal and we can look at it."

"Sure," Zurella said as she felt apprehensive not knowing what to expect.

Cleric Zrebrek led Zurella Myco to his office and said, "Please have a seat," and gestured towards a chair sitting right in front of his desk which was often used by temple goers who came in with their own problems.

She handed him the data cube and said, "Here's the files."

Zrebrek took the data cube, mounted it on his data terminal and started looking at the documents. It would be nonsense to him except for the fact he had a special briefing by Cleric Gummartukchik. What Zurella Myco just did to her husband would one day be considered the ultimate treachery in that she had just handed the Clerics "the Rosetta Stone" of Earth intercepts. Zrebrek was utterly astonished. More importantly, the Clerics now had a bird's eye view on what really was going on in Metongy Zeugcha's secret lab!

A desperate woman, now all dressed up seemingly teasing the Cleric, but most likely possibly wanting more than implied, was not the key to Zrebrek's success. Their ability to complete the goal to keep the extra-terrestrial information hidden from the public indefinitely, just improved greatly when Zurella walked into his office with fresh makeup on, semi evocatively dressed and no doubt a willing to be a collaborator.

Zrebrek just needed to figure out how to tweak Zurella Myco slightly to get her fully engaged as a Cleric unwitting agent. On this one data cube alone was more new intelligence than the huge and costly intelligence apparatus the Clerics ran combined. And instead of paying out a vast fortune, they got it for free!

"Zurella, this is all very interesting, I need some time to go through it all, may I suggest we meet for lunch tomorrow, and I'll be able to discuss it better after I know what's in it."

"That sounds good, I appreciate your help. Do you think I'm too dumb for not knowing much about what's in those files?"

"Zurella, don't be too concerned, very few people know what's on this data cube."

"That's reassuring."

"One other thing I must warn you about."

"What is that?"

"This could backfire on you if your husband finds out you gave me this information. So please do not discuss it with anyone."

"All right, I understand."

"Keep this matter totally confidential between us. Otherwise, it could cause problems not only for you but me as well."

"I will."

"Fine, let me walk you to the door."

Zrebrek walked Zurella to the Sardukretchen's Temple front entrance and opened the door for her.

"Thank you for seeing me Cleric Zrebrek."

"Not a problem, I want to do what I can to help solve your problem."

A little later as Zurella sat in the Tube Train car going home, she felt exhilarated. She had great vibes from Cleric Zrebrek and even possibly some seedy thoughts and knew her days of being taken for granted were nearly over.

Cleric Zrebrek contacted Cleric Gummartukchik immediately after Zurella Myco left the Sardukretchen's Temple.

"Your Excellency, Gummartukchik, I need to talk with you right away."

"Does this pertain to the Metongy Zeugcha operation?"

"Yes, it does."

"Please, come right over."

"I'll be there shortly."

The Sardukretchen's Temple had immense wealth. Because of donations and Caro's leaving their estate to the Sardukretchen Temple, the amount of wealth in their treasury continued to grow rapidly. As such the Sardukretchen Temple owned several Skycar's, one of which was slated for Sardukretchen's Temple support and operations. Since Cleric Zrebrek was the Cleric on duty and had a ceremony to perform in two hours, made haste and went directly to one of the skycars parked in Temple parking next to it.

Gummartukchik lived in a mountain retreat twenty minutes away by Skycar, otherwise it would be almost six hours taking a combination Crawler and Tube Trains to get to the mountain top resort like retreat.

The journey took them over the congested City of Preznium for a while. The Skycars were stacked up in a three-dimensional sky freeway with probably several hundred Skycars forward of them in their view. It was a busy time of day. Even with the traffic, Cleric Zrebrek still beat the surface transportation by at least five and a half hours.

The Skycar landed down on the oval driveway near the front entrance. This would be a short stay.

"Here's a data cube with a lot of files on them which came from Doctor Metongy Zeugcha's lab."

"How did you get this?"

"Zurella Myco brought this in a short while ago. She is afraid she might be considered dumb to her husband and didn't understand the information, nor had she ever seen anything like it."

As soon as Gummartukchik started reading Metongy Zeugcha's "the Rosetta Stone" of Earth intercepts, he quickly surmised the significance of this finding and started formulating in his mind how they would deal with it. Cleric Zrebrek would soon undergo additional special counseling about how to deal with Zurella Myco moving forward. The stage was set. The Clerics now had the upper hand since they had their own spy apparatus fully immersed into this Earth Communications business.

~~~
~~~

Chapter Fourteen

Journey to the Great Hefoxia Desert

In due time Metongy Zeugcha and Doctor Provkovitev, were summoned back to the Yarneos Center for Advanced study. Professor Qwrezzella received them as they were escorted into his office by Grable Reagal.

"Good afternoon gentlemen," Professor Qwrezzella said as he stood up from his desk and walked around to greet the guests.

"What's the reason why you wanted us to come here?" Metongy Zeugcha asked as he wondered if they were in for another huge surprise such as looking at the three-dimensional mockup and simulator on their last trip.

"Today is another huge milestone in the Gamulin Mission."

"What does that mean?"

"Why don't you gentlemen follow me, I'll take you there so

you can see with your own eyes."

In the span of a few moments, they were aboard the Yarneos Center for Advanced Studies Tube Train. Metongy assumed they were going back to the three-dimensional mockup, but when the train got up to speed of nearly 300 miles per hour it did not slow down and stop at the expected station near the three-dimensional mockup.

This trip took a little longer. Metongy Zeugcha didn't look at the time, but it seemed to him the train travel to a total of 30 minutes. That meant they were probably 150 miles from Yarneos when the train suddenly slowed down and came to a stop. They followed professor Qwrezzella out of the train, into a nearby elevator that took them up to the surface where they got out, into very bright sunlight.

"Wish I had worn some sunglasses."

"Don't worry we are going over to a platform that has a roof on top of it, you'll be in the shade shortly."

It was noticeably hot and looking around they appeared to be in a desert.

"Would it be proper for me to ask you where we are at

now?"

"This is a secret location but as you probably may have guessed, we are out in the middle of the Great Hefoxia Desert."

"Why are we here?"

"If you look over there, you will see a ramp."

The long ramp went up several hundred feet in the air.

"How long is that ramp? It must be more than a couple miles?"

"It's four miles long, actually."

"Why do you have a ramp out in the desert?"

"That is what you will see in a few minutes. Look at the distance you can see something down at the far end of the start of the ramp."

"Yes, I can't make it out, but I can see something there."

"Keep watching."

Professor Qwrezzella nodded at Grable Reagal who then said over his portable communicator obviously to someone in the control tower nearby, "Commence the launch sequence."

Moments later Metongy Zeugcha noticed undulating waves like looking down a hiway on a hot summer day and the small object he had been observing at the far end of the ramp several miles away suddenly growing in size and appeared to be coming this way. As it got closer, he could see it was a huge atmospheric glider, much larger than any he had ever seen.

Excitement grew as it came closer and the strange sound of a traveling magnetic wave pulling the Atmospheric Glider along accelerating it and about the time it went past the observation platform that had a glass panel a major shock wave hit them and it continued on and in a brief few seconds, hit the end of the ramp and appeared to have been flung upwards, reaching 10,000 feet in just a few seconds.

"How can people withstand G forces like that?"

"There are no personnel aboard the Atmospheric Glider, its fully robotic."

"What's the Atmospheric Glider transporting?"

"That's our first payload into space for the construction of the Gamulin Mission habitability modules."

"The Gamulin Mission is really beginning?"

"Yes, it is."

"What's the latest date for the start of the Mission?"

"Our goal is to have the planetary transport leave our planet Caro within a year from now."

"How long before all the habitability modules and Space Dock will be ready to assemble the transport?"

"Right now, we are planning to start ferrying up personnel within the month that will start bolting pieces together. The Keel will be laid in Space Dock probably a month from now."

"Amazing," Metongy Zeugcha said as he thought about it.

"That's the show for today; let's go back to my office where we can discuss this more, there is much to address."

Right after they took the elevator back down to track level, the Tube Train was still sitting there, obviously dedicated to their trip today. It took about 30 minutes to get back to Professor Qwrezzella's office.

"Planetary Security Service Director Bazion asked me to discuss with you the Gamulin Mission and what he's requesting from you."

"And what is that?"

"As I stated in your last visit, he visualizes the need to send the two of you, Metongy Zeugcha and Doctor Provkovitev along on the Gamulin Mission."

"We are not trained astronauts."

"You are Mission Specialists and do not require the astronaut training course."

"But what if something goes wrong with the space craft?"

"It's really simple, if the astronauts onboard are not able to deal with it, you might be in trouble."

"That means we are considered expendable beings."

"Precisely."

"Why us?" Doctor Provkovitev asked.

"We need someone with your communications expertise to be able to communicate with the people on that planet."

"What is it I'm specifically required to communicate about?" Doctor Provkovitev asked.

"Over the next year as you prepare to go, we'll lay down all the possible scenarios and the types of agreements you should make with those Earth representatives that you will meet."

"What are you implying is that I'm going to act as the ambassador from the Caro Civilization? "

"Yes, and that's why we took special care to select a few individuals that will nominally represent this planet in the most proper fashion.

"What if I decide I don't want to go?" Metongy Zeugcha chimed in.

"You will not have the luxury of that choice."

Metongy Zeugcha appeared stunned at Professor Qwrezzella's statement and the planned timeline for the mission.

"Doctors Provkovitev, Zeugcha, and Grable Reagal you are part of the short list identified to go on the Gamulin mission,"

Professor Qwrezzella stated most emphatically.

"Now comes the tricky part, teaching individuals who might come in contact with Earth people the languages," Doctor Provkovitev suggested.

Metongy stated, "The crew or a good portion of the crew should learn at least one of the major Earth languages so that when or if they arrived there, efficient communications would allow an exchange with the Earth people in a reasonable fashion."

Professor Qwrezzella asked, "What will be the main issues of Caro learning Earth Languages?

"One factor that seemed overwhelming at first was the voice sounds. But Earth languages are not too different than Caro global language that was introduced upon the final globalization period," Metongy Zeugcha stated.

"Why is that so important?" Doctor Provkovitev asked.

"It means their vocal cords and the ability to create sound is similar to the way we form words. Also, the video we obtained from the intercepts gives the appearance of these Earth people not too different than Caro, even though dress is quite a bit different," Metongy Zeugcha replied.

"The fact these Earth people were not reptilian, amphibian, or non-mammals at least gave pause they would not be confronted with horrible looking beings that would cause psychological issues with many," Professor Qwrezzella noted.

In setting up the language classes and communications experiments, Planetary Security Service Director Bazion got involved and due to fear of security and prevention of disclosure, Planetary Security Service decided the language training and experimentation using the vast simulator capability of the Three-Dimensional Mockup would give a realistic training capability as they practiced several scenarios, which reinforced their language ability. Eventually all twenty-four prospective crew members were trained primarily in English, but were also given some brief training in Japanese, Russian, German, and French.

As the ship's crew practiced the Earth arrival, they did scenarios where the Earth Shuttle Craft simulator communicated with the mother ship three-dimensional mockup simulator.

Not long into the training period, Metongy Zeugcha and Doctor Provkovitev were taken by Professor Qwrezzella back out to the desert to watch another launch. Today was different. The atmospheric glider didn't seem to be passing by as quick as they witnessed previously, plus the glider didn't seem quite as large.

The shockwave when the atmospheric glider passed by didn't seem quite as intense as the freight lifters. Nor did it almost instantly get up to 10,000 feet as previously observed.

Metongy Zeugcha knew it was going fast but not quite as fast, when suddenly there appeared to be a separation of parts of the atmospheric glider. A cylindrical shaped structure left the glider and a chemical rocket engine ignited.

"That's interesting," Metongy Zeugcha said as he was suddenly surprised at the revelation.

"What you are observing gentlemen is a personnel carrier, delivering workers up to the Space Dock and habitats."

"Why is there a rocket engine?"

"We can't subject the people to the same amount of G forces you witnessed with the robot ships. We only use about half of electromagnetic lifter acceleration, so we have to use the chemical rockets to get the people up to the Space Dock orbit."

In a few minutes out of nowhere came an atmospheric glider. It was the same one that just launched the worker shuttle. It touched down on the ramp in front of them and the electromagnet catapult used for landing in reverse, slowed it down to a crawl in almost 1.5 miles.

Professor Qwrezzella then said, "Gentlemen, please get in the land car, I'm going to take you to the hangers where you will be spending some time in the future."

Doctor Provkovitev, Grable Reagal and Metongy Zeugcha all stepped up the ladder to the Hovercraft that would take them down the cement roadway to the hanger complex observable several miles away.

"This well disguised hanger complex was left over from the Tauceti conflict and as you can see look like a series of hills until you approached closely, and with the hanger doors open it was easily identified, however when they are shut, the camouflage looks like a hill side," Grable Reagal noted.

The Hovercraft whined as the gas turbines that operated

the air pumps to raise the cushions and fans to move the Hovercraft came up to speed. In a brief period, the Hovercraft accelerated above 170 mph as it moved towards then slowed and pulled up near one of the open hangers.

The hill complex contained an impressive facility, now obsolete, but due to the security it provided through the isolation of the vast desert it now was ideal for the development of all the support craft and missions needed to build a Space Dock and fill it with sections of the Interplanetary Transport.

The turbines shut down and the Hovercraft cushions deflated as the craft slowly settled down on the parking apron in front of the hangers. Tents and temporary buildings were scattered around, and workers appeared unloading a group of cargo haulers parked at loading docks. Supplies were pouring in.

<div align="center">~~~</div>

Chapter Fifteen
The Interplanetary Transport

"This way gentlemen," Professor Qwrezzella said as he led the group through the huge doors that were wide open exposing the huge underground cavern teaming with activity.

In the distance they could see welding and grinding behind areas with clear plastic like skirts.

Metongy Zeugcha looked around and soon asked the obvious question: "What is the basic material used in construction of the Interplanetary Transport?"

"What you are looking at is parts made from Krastron," Professor Qwrezzella noted.

"What is so special about Krastron?" Doctor Provkovitev asked.

"The Krastron material used in the construction of the

Interplanetary Transport hull and major assemblies has incredible strength and is somewhat lightweight. It also was free of magnetic properties which were desirable in avoiding magnetic storms or provide an element of safety from solar flares," Professor Qwrezzella noted.

"How large is this facility?"

"From the entrance it's hard to see just exactly how large this underground cavity might be, but one might assume 30 to 40 acres."

An electric powered cart was waiting for them directly ahead along with the manager Nymstrom Purgatraceous.

"Greetings Gentlemen," Nymstrom Purgatraceous said in a friendly fashion.

"How are things going here at the Interplanetary Transport assembly complex?" Professor Qwrezzella asked in a most professional tone.

"Right on schedule Professor Qwrezzella."

"When will the Space Dock be completed?"

"We anticipate the main dock will be ready in a month.

The Airlock will start testing two weeks afterwards."

"Yea, the airlock is the critical feature in that it allows us to bring a lot of material into the dock and allow people to work inside the dock enclosure without breathing apparatus or protective clothing."

"Would you guys like to take a look at the facility?"

"Yes. I'm sure it will be interesting to see," Metongy Zeugcha stated in a positive manner.

"Hop on the cart and I'll show you around." Nymstrom Purgatraceous said as the group immediately got on the cart which carried up to eight people.

"This first section here is the foundry, where we cast and produce parts using Krastron."

"Do you produce the Krastron here locally?"

"No, we transport it in from the mills located 105 miles due east of here."

"How do you cast the parts?"

"We heat up the Krastron using an oxygen furnace then

pour it into molds."

The electric cart pulled forward and they came up to a section where some smaller parts were stamped out of large half inch thick sheets of Krastron.

A short distance further there were men welding parts together. Nymstrom Purgatraceous explained, "This is where we fabricate larger components that require welding."

"Will there be any welding in space?" Doktor Provkovitev asked in the most inquisitive fashion.

"We'll do welding in only for emergency repairs or reconfigurations and sparingly. All sections are bolted and glued on."

"Glue seems to be something not strong enough."

"Actually, we developed a glue called "Xiéjiāo" that cures in the absence of air and ends up providing fastening stronger than bolts. We just use bolts to hold the sections together until the glues cure."

"Interesting. I think Professor Qwrezzella explained all about Xiéjiāo back in his office." Then Metongy Zeugcha recalled the discussion with Professor Qwrezzella back at the 3D mockup/simulator.

As the electric cart drove through the factory like complex, they came across people doing wiring harness and building various equipment's that would be mounted in the Interplanetary Transporter.

People working all wore dark blue uniforms with name tags and Interplanetary Transporter patches. In some areas they saw people wearing lab coats.

"Is this where most of the construction of parts is done?"

"This is only a small portion of the facility. Probably 80% is beyond walls ahead."

The electric cart approached two large doors and stopped. Nymstrom Purgatraceous got out of the electric cart, walked over to a scanner on the wall that had visual face recognition software and additionally he put his palm on a scanner pad. Suddenly the double doors split open and slid sideways to allow access. Nymstrom Purgatraceous got back into the electric-cart and continued driving forward. Due to motion detectors, the doors started closing as soon as the electric cart was clear of the doors. Within a few seconds the doors moved back into the shut position, Nymstrom Purgatraceous soon made a hard right turn drove down a hall that appeared to be a driveway, then made another left turn and then he continued his tour.

"Gentlemen behold: The Cyclonic Inverters."

"Impressive looking!"

The three huge devices had an evil look to them. They stood almost 3 stories high.

"Does the Interplanetary Transport use three Cyclonic Inverters?"

"No, it uses just two Cyclonic Inverters. The third Cyclonic Inverter is spare part in case there is a problem delivering them up to the Space Dock."

"Are these Cyclonic Inverters the best propulsion systems available?"

"Yes. Never has thrust devices been developed with Cyclonic Inverters capability.

"When will the Cyclonic Inverters be delivered to the

Space Dock?"

"We plan to launch them around a month from now. Would you like to come see the shipment?"

"Sure, why not?"

The shiny metallic structures gave someone the appearance of a device that dwarfed their imagination.

"I notice we are behind a security boundary."

"That's correct, only crew members and the few construction personnel associated with the Cyclonic Inverters are allowed in this area."

"Why is there such secrecy? Since we had globalization there should not be any need of secrets."

"We are worried about sabotage."

"Why is that?"

"There are Clerical Fanatics who do not want us to travel to the stars."

The cart then turned around and went out the door it previously entered. Sensors in the hallway opened the double doors as the cart approached. The cart made a few more passes through portions of the Interplanetary Transporter facility while these visitors observed numerous activities and components that were appearing a completed appearance.

"I notice a number of the parts are painted in differing colors?"

"That's correct. It makes sure those components are delivered to the right construction zone in the Space Dock to avoid getting parts mixed up."

Finally, they came to a large open area that had a large cylindrical shape device with huge hatches on it open and a crane lowering machinery into it.

"This gentleman is one of our cargo bays that we'll be loading up on one of the atmospheric gliders today to transport up to the Space Dock."

The electric cart drove on and then out the large access doors and right in front of them was one of the Planetary Gliders with a crane lowering one of the cylinders into it.

"Here's the next flight due to go up and deliver

components."

The cart then drove over to the Hovercraft and stopped.

"I hope you enjoyed the tour."

"It was very insightful," Metongy Zeugcha said as he pondered the trip, he didn't want to go on but realized Planetary Security Service Director Bazion would soon apply the appropriate pressure to force him to go on the Gamulin Mission.

"Us get back to the Tube Train, and to the Three-Dimensional Mockup, we have a session planned today simulating conversations with Earthlings."

~~~
~~~

Chapter Sixteen
It Starts in the Simulators.

The men exited the electric cart, climbed up the ladder to the Hovercraft and inside its cab. The Hovercraft operator flipped on switches and the turbines came online and the cushions were suddenly inflated with the Hovercraft main body rising about 6 feet into the air as the cushions were inflated. He then initiated movement with the data terminal-controlled propulsion and guidance system, then steered the Hovercraft onto the cement road leading back to the end of the launch ramp where they got out and took the elevator down to the Tube Train platform. The men then boarded the waiting Tube Train then traveled back to the Three-Dimensional Mockup and simulator. The Tube Train traveled the 150 miles through the underground tunnel in less than half an hour. Moments after arriving at the Three-Dimensional Mockup and Simulator station, they were in the control room of the Interplanetary Transport with the crew all manning their stations.

Before the simulation started, they had a brief discussing their goals and expectations. Metongy Zeugcha who coordinated Earth communications training began the pre-simulation brief.

"We are going to rehearse this with a number of scenarios, since we do not know how we'll be received, and whether they detect the Interplanetary Transporter before we make contact with them."

"How do you think we'll be received?" A crewmember asked.

"After observing a number of grainy television video's and observing the behavior, a rough estimation of the humans showed the complexities and emotional side we will have to contend with."

"And what did you determine their probable behavior might be?"

"Observing Earth's World War Two film footage on News Releases exposed a very lethal and dangerous side to these warlike creatures. However, there were also video's that painted a completely different picture of redeeming qualities."

Another crew member asked, "How do you think we'll be received?"

"It all depends on who we first contact."

"Why is that?"

"Certainly, with diverse personalities we see in their video, it will make a huge difference."

The scenarios were observed, and people communicated with a control booth next to the Three-Dimensional Mockup simulator happened to also be crewmembers practicing their English.

Metongy Zeugcha then laid out the simulation plan:

"We'll simulate arriving in orbit around the planet, wait for a prescribed time to see if they spot us first and try to communicate. While we observe them, we'll orbit around the planet using our space telescope and try to identify cities based on the radio intercepts we are now getting."

"Which radio intercepts are you referring too?"

"We have detected amplitude modulated signals that come from what appears to be entertainment stations broadcasting both music as well as news. In those station broadcasts they identify their cities."

"What use will we make of that information?"

"Once we get into Orbit around planet Earth, we'll be able to slowly plot the positions of those cities and based on this INTEL, make a determination of where we might land, such as a nation's capital."

"Will we get a chance to train with the Shuttle Craft today?"

"Yes, in fact that is all part of the plan. We'll make a couple simulated orbits around the planet, then man the shuttlecraft and simulate going to the planet's surface based on what we determine mapping the cities."

"Everyone man your stations, we will now proceed with the simulation."

The first simulation included Earth detecting the Interplanetary Transporter upon reaching orbit around planet Earth. The scenario plays out like this:

Russians detect the space craft first.

CIA intercepts Soviet communications which convey they were tracking a spectacular UFO.

The United States of America has NASA find and start tracking the sudden arrival. This constitutes the first living Aliens detected. All others were killed in crashes before a meeting.

USA attempts communicating with the Space Craft and the scenario unfolds:

"This is the United States of America wishing to contact Space Craft in Orbit around the planet."

"United States of America, we are the Caro visiting from our planet in another solar system. We have learned your languages and can communicate. Can you hear us?"

"Caro Space Craft, we hear you loud and clear."

"United States of America, we would like permission to visit the planet and request you give us locations to land. We have mapped your major cities and can figure out where you wish us to land."

"Caro Space Craft. Please stand by, we will provide you those instructions momentarily."

Metongy Zeugcha then said to the Interplanetary Transport Captain (chief pilot), "Sir I recommend the landing crew get aboard the shuttle craft and prepare to launch to the planet while we wait for coordinates."

"Very well, away teams proceed to the shuttle and prepare to launch on my orders."

Within a few minutes the landing teams were seated and ready to launch the shuttle craft.

About that time the Americans communicated, "Caro spaceship, we will start a beacon from a runway transmitting at 150 Megacycles, use that signal to navigate to designated landing zone."

"United States of America, we understand 150 Megacycles beacon, standing by to receive the beacon."

The sensor's operator suddenly reported, "Captain I'm picking up the 150 Megacycles beacon, feeding the RDF values into ship's navigation data terminals to establish track."

"Very well, sensors operators, let me know when to engage the Shuttle Launch."

Within a couple minutes the sensor operator reported, "Captain, we've downloaded the coordinates into the Shuttle's Navigation Data Terminals, they are ready to be launched."

"Very well," the captain stated.

Everyone including the shuttle occupants had real time audio and video fed from the Interplanetary Transport's control room area and the captain's image.

"Shuttle, you are cleared to engage the launch sequence."

"Captain, this is the Shuttlecraft, understand Permission to Launch."

The shuttle operator then hit the auto-launch switch that signaled to onboard data terminals to commence launch.

The shuttle bay hatches suddenly opened, exposing the shuttle craft, and clearing the way for its launch. Restraint clamps were disengaged freeing the shuttle craft.

The shuttle's electromagnetic Repulser's activated, as

well as the Interplanetary Transport's Repulser's and the combined electromagnets pushed the shuttle craft simulated moving out of the shuttle bay slowly setting it in motion. Initially moving at one inch per second gradually increased rate of movement to approximately three inches per second and eventually hit ten inches per second until the Repulser's were shut off because they didn't have much more effect. As soon as the shuttle was approximately 100 feet away from the Interplanetary Transport, its propulsion kicked on and it started moving towards the planet.

Inside the shuttlecraft all the displays gave a simulated appearance as to exactly how they would see it in a real mission.

Unlike Earth re-entry, the Caro Shuttlecraft could control its re-entry profile much more accurately and simply pointed directly towards the beacon they were tracking. As such it did not hit the ionosphere traveling at extreme speeds such as Earth spacecraft did, hence didn't have nearly the heat problem.

The Interplanetary Transport had assumed a geosynchronous orbit and reported to the planet,

"American's this is the Caro, our Shuttle is now entering the atmosphere, should be down to your level momentarily."

On the displays video of the planet was shown appearing as if they were getting closer. The video was developed on speculation and reenactment based on observing video's intercepted from earth.

Using the Caro space telescope, the mothership could see the shuttle was heading for a desert area someplace North of Los Vegas Nevada as shown on their navigation display which looked like American navigation displays on their jet fighters 50 years later.

Soon the shuttle made it to the surface of the planet where the Caro exited in protective clothing and breathing apparatus which was needed until they established air analysis to determine it would be safe.

The desert area they were landing had air temperatures currently at 95 degrees Fahrenheit (35 degrees Celsius) which was not too different from their own Caro deserts.

As the Caro exited the shuttle, they were suddenly met by dignitaries.

"Welcome to Earth."

"Thank you, we come in peace."

"We are so glad you speak English which helps out our situation."

The current simulation then ended, and soon other scenarios were practiced.

Metongy Zeugcha later returned to Preznium, where he processed further earth segments and observed the development of the earth's history.

~~~
~~~

Chapter Seventeen
The Phone Call

Zurella Myco called Cleric Zrebrek and after he answered the telephone she asked, "Cleric Zrebrek do you have time to see me today, I would like to discuss with you the contents of the data cube."

"Zurella come on over to the Sardukretchen Temple I'll be here."

"Okay, I'm on my way."

With Metongy Zeugcha gone a lot lately, much of the work fell on Ferdastad which took him away from home even more. The situation with Zurella was now reaching a critical point. Cleric Zrebrek intended to capitalize on that and now she was his pawn, he would soon take more control of her, and soon she would involve into the useful idiot that would give him powerful unrestricted access.

In 30 minutes Zurella Myco arrived at the Sardukretchen Temple, showing a gradual improvement in her personal attire from previous visits. Her behavior was betraying her and Cleric Zrebrek an expert in dealing with human behavior, a master in psychology, body language reader, and master manipulator perceived the willingness about to unfold. Zurella was on the edge of a cliff and all Zrebrek had to do is give her a little push.

"Why don't you come with me to my office where we can discuss the data without others overhearing it?"

"Certainly."

Cleric Zrebrek led Zurella to his office and after the entered he closed the door so there would be total privacy.

"Did you figure out what the data is on the data cube?"

"I certainly did, and I want to caution you on a few things if I may?"

"Sure."

"The discussions we have must be kept very confidential and private between just you and me. Otherwise, there could be some serious consequences. Do you understand?"

"Yes. I understand, Cleric Zrebrek."

"All right. Your husband is processing information from an alien world. If your mate were to attempt to go public with this information, I sincerely believe very bad things would happen to him."

"Such as?"

"He could easily permanently disappear."

"It's that serious?"

"Yes, it is."

"What can I do?"

"One way you can protect yourself and your mate is to only provide this information to me. I can give it to the right people and keep you out of any visibility."

"I understand."

"When was the last time you were in a Skycar?"

"I've never been in a Skycar."

"I'm going to take you someplace now in a Skycar where we can talk about what's on the data cube without anyone able to hear us."

"Okay."

Zrebrek led Zurella Myco out the side door of his office which opened into a courtyard a short distance away from ground floor Skycar parking. Rarely in the cities are ground level Skycar parking spots because land is too priceless. Zrebrek pressed a couple buttons on the Skycar which opened both passenger and controller's doors which pivoted upwards all must looking like gull wings, allowing them easy access.

The Skycar under Global Skycar Administration control was sent up 5,000 feet into the air which gave a great view of the horizon. The short ride to the magnificent estate exemplified the essence of a rare thrill in Zurella and made a lifelong impression that would alter her for the rest of her life. And the best was yet to come as the Skycar slowly glided down to the area of the estate and it veered off the main Global Skycar Administration corridor into an axillary stream of 3D groups of Skycars slowly dispersing into the surrounding areas where the more affluent lived.

The Skycar slowly descended into a Skycar parking spot inside the estate behind 8-foot-tall walls that gave it immense privacy as well as protection in the event civil unrest occurred.

As soon as the electric powered turbos were shut down, the driver and passenger side doors pivoted up and the two occupants got out. Cleric Zrebrek led Zurella Myco through the covered entrance to the main hallway leading into the main building in the estate. Several guest houses surrounded the main structure that was made available to people the Clerics wanted to manipulate and influence. Planetary Security Service Director Bazion had spent time in one of those guest houses, and if it had become publicly aware what Cleric Gummartukchik had provided him, there no doubt would have been a public outcry.

As they walked through the main hallway, Zurella Myco marveled at the fabulous artwork that decorated the main estate building that seemed more like a castle than a retreat.

"Are all those works of art from the real artists?"

"Yes, these make up one of the most priceless Art Exhibit Collections."

Some of the works were identifiable from Zurella's memory from art classes she took long ago.

Cleric Zrebrek then went into a well decorated room that had very comfortable furniture and some video equipment set up for private briefings for distinguished Clerics.

The mystery started to unfold as Cleric Zrebrek had a data cube with him he took out of his pocket. He then put it into the machine which brought up a complete briefing presentation he started going over with Zurella.

"This is communications between these Aliens which Caro's Planetary Security Service is studying to better understand them."

"They live on another planet?"

"Yes."

"How far away?"

"About seven light years."

"And you believe it's true?"

"Certainly."

Cleric Zrebrek could tell by Zurella Myco's body language she was now struggling and exhibiting a serious and remorseful behavior. Zurella Myco would not be the only person to have a tough time after exposure to all this, which is more of a reason why the Clerics wanted to delay exposing the public to all this.

After they went over many details Zrebrek realized he was getting hungry suggested, "Zurella, why don't we go to the dining room, I'm sure there is something there for us to eat."

"Sure."

The dining room was also very well laid out filled with untold treasures. And places were set as if they were expected.

Zurella was in for a treat from a world class Chef. And they were immediately seated. Almost instantly the food started rolling out, servants started waiting on Zurella Myco and Cleric Zrebrek as if they were celebrities. In a sense Cleric Zrebrek was a celebrity because he often officiated over services at the Sardukretchen Temple. Thousands of people knew him and 10 times that many knew of him.

As she prepared for this visit, Zurella Myco dressed up the best she could without looking too gaudy. As Cleric Zrebrek analyzed her he thought she was a good-looking Caro female. He also had determined that despite her husband's neglect, there was nothing wrong with her intelligence. If it were not for the fact, he had such tremendous visibility and most likely was spied upon in his current mission by Cleric Gummartukchik's henchmen, he could see how he might be influenced to violate his ethics and allow himself to enjoy the obvious luster of this woman in a different framework. But that would be far too risky. The thoughts nevertheless were tantalizing.

As Zrebrek silently observed Zurella while she was eating, he felt confident he had reached a point where he could manipulate her for the Clerics purposes. Any other collateral functions would only complicate matters and possibly risk the loss of a well-placed asset for critical information. The Clerics needed to have all the information that Director Bazion had so they could predict his next move.

After the meal finished, Zrebrek knowing Zurella had not enjoyed the serenity of the palatial botanical gardens in her life suggested he would give her a treat.

"Would you like to go for a short walk before I take you home?"

"You mean back to the Temple?"

"No, I'll take you to your residence. You have Skycar landing zones on the roof of your building I assume?"

"Yes, as most do these days."

The two stood up and Zrebrek said, "Come this way with me I'll show you the gardens."

Cleric Zrebrek led Zurella Myco out of the building and down a long sidewalk that allowed them to approach the Botanical Gardens main entrance. As they walked through the gardens, they both observed the wonder and the splendor of the often rare and almost extinct plant life that was nearly wiped out in the long-protracted conflict between the Caro and the Tauceti.

Even though planet wide arborists were slowly recovering

much of the plant life, partly thanks to the Sardukretchen's who managed to preserve many samples of these, many cities lacked much of it including the few city parks left over from the urban sprawl due to mismanagement and slow recovery from global conflict. Because of poor planning and the priority to provide ample housing and public transportation to the masses, esthetics was left out by planners by necessity.

Contaminated land had to be reclaimed; the job was just too enormous. A species, of trees for example, had almost been wiped out: only a small sample of them remained, and huge efforts to reforest scorched earth were actively ongoing. Some arborists made a career of it, and it was generally believed that too much had been consumed for new buildings, although some instances of the synthetically produced substances facilitated much of the reconstruction. Sadly, during the many periods of conflict, desperate souls plundered much of the remaining forests for temporary shelter and heat during the frigid winters which created a barren landscape not too dissimilar to what Zurella Myco experienced in her everyday life.

This botanical garden fascinated Zurella Myco who had

a growing affection towards Cleric Zrebrek. And he could sense it as her cheerfulness and eagerness, betrayed her.

Color from strange flower petals and leaves totally unfamiliar created that surreal atmosphere that blended the tapestry of her emotions to her transcendental feelings that for a brief period escaped the turmoil associated with a neglectful Ferdastad.

Zurella Myco was now fully trapped by Cleric Zrebrek's spell. If it were not for the fact, he knew the high level of surveillance on him at this moment, and in the future any time he was to be near the woman, he might have succumbed to Caro passions without restraint. Her figure and alluring features and no doubt her pheromones pouring out like a tropical rain could mysteriously stimulate most enthusiastically. Cleric Zrebrek's discipline determined his actions as he creatively manifested this unwitting disciple and inspired her idealistic mannerisms that would facilitate the ultimate transformation. Even though it seemed there was some awkwardness as Zurella's body language betrayed her emotions, Cleric Zrebrek applied his talent in a clever but compassionate way.

As they walked through the Botanical Garden, much of it was shaded and out of direct sunlight which provided a very pleasant atmosphere. Soon they walked over a small bridge with a slow running creek through it. The water appeared crystal clear just like a typical mountain stream with the random sounds they make.

Another amazing event suddenly unfolded. Zurella Myco saw for one of the rare times in her life small colorful birds flying through the gardens. This truly was a natures paradise, and her strange feelings had a growing attraction to Cleric Zrebrek to the point she knew she was very vulnerable. Zurella Myco didn't know if she could control herself if Cleric Zrebrek were to suggest Brosting.

They slowly came back full circle to where they started and Cleric Zrebrek then said, "I think it's time I take you home, I need to get back to the Temple to prepare for the next services."

"Ferdastad's not going to get in any kind of trouble from what that information I gave you?"

"No absolutely not. However, you should keep giving

me the information so I can look at it and advise you, if necessary, to council him so that he doesn't get himself into trouble."

"I understand that's important."

"Most importantly, he needs to insure he never divulges any of this Alien business to the public, otherwise I'm afraid there would be no way the Sardukretchen's could protect him. The Planetary Security Service absolutely do not want any kind of Alien disclosure, that I'm absolutely assure of."

"I don't know how I can bring the subject up without tipping him off that people are interested in what he's doing."

"That's how I can help you. If he ever seems like he's going to divulge this information, then call me right away, I will personally come visit him, and I'm sure with my contacts I can find Dr. Metongy Zeugcha and explain to him the repercussions. They may have done an incredible job discovering this information, but now is not the time to bring it to the attention of the public. To do so would mean they would suffer the wrath of the Planetary Security

Service."

"All right, if I hear something I will contact your immediately."

"Day or night, don't worry about waking me up, this is very serious."

"I promise, I will."

"Thank you."

"No, thank you for helping me."

"It's been my pleasure."

The two walked to the Skycar parking area and got on and soon were airborne, flying to Zurella's residence, and landed on the Skycar landing pad on the top of the building. As soon as the electric powered turbo lifters shut down, Cleric Zrebrek pressed a door button and the door roof area over the passenger side tilted upwards allowing Zurella Myco to get out.

"Thank you for the most pleasant experience."

"You are welcome, I enjoyed it too. More than you can

imagine."

Zurella walked promptly to the passenger waiting area that was empty as few skycar's ever landed on this building. If they did, it was usually for emergency purposes for some medical condition. In a few minutes she was home at her residence looking at semi-empty walls and Ferdastad was gone as expected. That made her memories of the recent trip with Zrebrek even more satisfying.

~~~
~~~

Chapter Eighteen

The First Cyclonic Inverter Goes to Space

Metongy Zeugcha and Doctor Provkovitev were again seated in the Hovercraft as it glided effortlessly down the cement road towards the Interplanetary Transport assembly area. They were back after relatively short notice. Another big milestone was upon them.

Professor Qwrezzella had the driver pull up near the huge Atmospheric Glider.

This Atmospheric Glider reminded Metongy Zeugcha of the first one he had seen but appeared to have some strange added hardware making it somewhat strange looking.

"I notice the Atmospheric Glider is already on the ramp."

"That's an astute observation. Yes, it is. We have a very heavy load today and had to have it up there before we started loading."

A huge set of cranes were lifting an extremely large cylinder onto the back of the atmospheric glider.

"You can't see it because it's enclosed in that transport body, but this is the first Cyclonic Inverter."

"The Interplanetary Transport is finished to the point the Cyclonic Inverter's can be added?"

"Actually, we have to put the two Cyclonic Inverters into the Space Dock before most of the hull is assembled because everything else will fit through the air lock."

"How do you get this into the Space Dock?"

"Until the Cyclonic Inverters are placed at their key positions in the Space Dock, the deployment area will not be covered, and the two Cyclonic Inverters will be eventually placed by Space Dock movers, space cranes, and arms at an exact spot and secured and will be bolted and glued onto the Interplanetary Transport rear housing."

Each crane was attached to one end of a large lifting device attached to the cylindrical shape device holding the

Cyclonic Inverter. With Caro and robot efficiency the heavy looking cylinder slowly steadied out on the bowls of the atmospheric glider. A third crane lifted a work cage onto the lifting device that now had slack as the cylinder was now mounted on the atmospheric glider and restraints attached. Workers with safety harness stepped out of the cage and slowly unbolted the lifting device from the cylinder.

After all the lifting bolts were in containers inside the cages, personnel moved back into the cages and were lifted back to the surface where they carried containers full of lifting bolts out of the basket and placed them in a service cart next to the crane. The 2 cranes then lifted the lifting device up and out of the way. Both tracked cranes then backed away from the atmospheric glider.

Professor Qwrezzella then led Metongy Zeugcha's group over to the Hovercraft where he ordered the Hovercraft driver, "Take us back to the observation booth."

Moments later the Hovercraft sped up and arrived at the viewing stand in a brief period. After the Hovercraft turbo's shut down and the cab slowly sank to the surface of concrete roadway, the men stepped off it and followed Professor

Qwrezzella behind the glass shield of the observation platform.

Grable Reagal in communications with the atmospheric glider crew suddenly said, "The glider is departing now."

In a few minutes the glider soon approached them screaming along giving off a huge sonic boom and as it hit the end of the ramp shot upwards and reached 10,000 feet in a couple seconds, then suddenly rocket boosters lit off assisting with the acceleration. Within another couple minutes as the atmospheric glider slowly diminished in size the boosters shut down and suddenly, the huge cylinder appeared to separate from the atmospheric glider and its own rocket engine ignited and left a plume behind as it slowly moved out of site for the naked eye due to its distance.

As the men talked for a few minutes the atmospheric glider with its booster engines suddenly came from nowhere down the ramp and was slowed by the electromagnets in the glider and built into the ramp. As it slowed and eventually stopped it was several miles away, nearing the Interplanetary Transport construction site.

"When will the next Cyclonic Inverter flight go?"

"It should be about the same time tomorrow."

"Then what after that?"

"The airlock is already installed on the Space Dock and the deployment area will be covered up and sealed airtight and pressurized."

"Work on the hull commences then?"

"Yes. We have already prepositioned major hull sections there, ready to start bolting together and gluing where required."

"So, all the major pieces are already up there?"

"Yes. Only piece left to put up there now before we put the cover on and seal it is the next Cyclonic Inverter scheduled to lift tomorrow."

The men held another meeting and more training sessions at the 3D mockup and simulator, and then returned home.

~~~
~~~

Chapter Nineteen
Living with a Spy

Metongy Zeugcha was relying more and more on Ferdastad and after he departed on the Gamulin Mission, Ferdastad would have to take over all the work since he would be gone.

Because the training was taking him away more and more and greater requirements were placed on Ferdastad, he naturally took more and more of his work home on data cubes. Since he had a regular routine, Zurella Myco systematically was able to continue copying much of his work. And it became much easier for Zurella to hand off the data cubes to Cleric Zrebrek, as he now flew the Skycar directly to her building, picked her up and to avoid public notice, took her to Cleric Gummartukchik's luxurious retreat where he copied the data cube and studied it and discussed it with Zurella.

It didn't take Zrebrek long to figure out that this engagement and studying the intercepts with Zurella helped them both to understand the significance more fully of what they were reading.

Ferdastad did fabulous analysis of the data. His decryptions were ultimately flawless. His track record was about one million times faster than Bletchley Park in reading the Shark Crypto from the German Enigma machine. Likewise, the Japanese Purple Code and the Japanese Admiral Level JN25 Crypto, though elegant design by the three Polish Crypto experts the Japanese hired long before the war started, was dissected, and broke apart just as efficiently as he did the German Submarine Shark Enigma Code.

They could have spent hours and hours together pouring through the data. On this day as they read the decrypts of enigma and the Allies rerouting of Convoy SC 127 on April 1943, they were captivated by the story of this incredible venture taking place on that planet. It was almost an eerie feeling reading and learning all about the Earthlings without them knowing they were being observed. Granted this was all information received after it traveled through space seven years, so it was time delayed. The one conclusion easily determined is the Earthlings had not counter detected the Caro.

The Caro were very fortunate. The convergent zone that made it possible for the Caro to receive strong signals from earth did not work the same in the opposite direction. Because of the way the gravity and cosmic waves caused the radio waves to bend in space also caused Caro signals to go somewhere other than Earth. Earthmen would not know anything about the Caro until they initiated the first contact. And since they would have no way of knowing where the Caro world existed, they would not know where to look.

After several months, Zurella Myco and Cleric Zrebrek became the most informed persons on the planet next to Dr. Metongy Zeugcha and Ferdastad.

The greatest achievement of a spy is to do the espionage without ever being caught or the enemy ever knowing what they had lost. In the vast conflicts between the Caro and Tauceti, spying was common, and the Clerics were truly the backbone of the Tauceti spy network. That fact was never realized by the Caronians because the interface between the Tauceti's and the Sardukretchen's was so thin, it was virtually impossible to detect. Even though globalization had long been finalized, the art and skill of the Sardukretchen's spies were simply redirected elsewhere, mainly to manifest the predominance of them. Hence the trade craft was alive and well and Cleric Zrebrek was a Master of it all.

Even though Zurella's body language and pheromones were signaling willingness and desire, Zrebrek proved to be one of the best of the best spies as he did not allow his emotions to interfere with the work at hand.

Today, Cleric Zrebrek arranged for them to eat their lunch out in the Botanical Gardens in a small picnic area. The meal was modest, Plastnybalkon salad sandwiches. The Plastnybalkon farm raised fowl had beautiful feathers and looked almost identical to pheasants on Earth. In fact, a lot of things on Caro were so earthlike. If the Gamulin Mission made it to Earth they would discover the likeness and ponder the question: "Did, we all come from the same place?"

In another 500 years the Caro would discover they and Earthlings both had Martian DNA. But then where did the

Martians come from?

Cleric Zrebrek had a habit of feeding the birds. He loved birds and when he had picnics out in the Botanical Garden, they didn't take long to discover him and knew he would throw food scraps at them.

Zurella Myco felt it slightly annoying having the filthy birds flapping around near them; nevertheless, she did admire their beautiful colors. It was rather ironic the birds seemed to love the taste of Plastnybalkon meat as they picked at the portions of the sandwich he threw to the birds.

"I hope you enjoyed your lunch?"

"Yes, it was very delicious." *But it also seems to be helping my grocery bill* Zurella thought as she spent far less lately. Ferdastad seemed to always take his meals at Metongy Zeugcha's residence, as now Planetary Security Service was paying Metongy Zeugcha as a member of the Gamulin Mission.

Metongy Zeugcha feeling somewhat responsible for disrupting Ferdastad's life, insisted on feeding him and any other staff person who worked there. Because of this strange arrangement for the family, their disposable income was slowly improving. So was Zurella's disposition.

Even though Zrebrek was not about to risk his spy business by "dipping his pen in company ink," he nevertheless enjoyed Zurella's company. He kept a healthy distance between them emotionally. Today like many other days, he took Zurella home in the skycar.

Today, Ferdastad arrived home unexpectedly. He noticed the Skycar coming in and landing on the rooftop of their building. He knew that was extremely rare, and even thought on a given day he could see several Skycars, the novelty never wore off.

Zurella got out of the Skycar, took the elevator down to the floor of their residence and was home about one minute before Ferdastad arrived.

Zurella was dressed nicely and seemed very pleasant upon Ferdastad's arrival. He assumed that since he was trying to spend more time at home she was reciprocating with much more appreciative behavior. Her affection was authentic, and her gratitude seemed genuine. Her industrious behavior and her humor often done in an intelligent manner gave Ferdastad a sense of inner peace. No doubt she was an independent woman and her ingenuity often left Ferdastad feeling rather self-assured. And moments like now when she seemed so energetic and often entertaining, there seemed to be a spontaneous transcendence that would lead them to eventually erupt into a passionate embrace.

Ferdastad was now living with a spy, who was now more dangerous for his survival than anything else in his life. The female he loved the most was quickly developing and compiling a vast knowledge of all his work. The Coaching that Cleric Zrebrek did in a team-oriented fashion, created the synergism for practical espionage, even though no world powers were involved like on earth where countries like America, Germany, and Japan were embroiled in a fight for survival.

But now there were three entities on the Caro planet, the Sardukretchen Clerics, the Planetary Security Service, and the Globalization Government. All three interplayed and all three spied on each other.

<div align="center">~~~</div>

Chapter Twenty
Sabotage

The next day Metongy Zeugcha and Doctor Provkovitev traveled to the Three-Dimensional Mockup and Simulator. They worked on more scenarios and trained the crew on a variety of possible Earth receptions.

Professor Qwrezzella was near the ramp to watch the next Cyclonic Inverter lift off into space to be delivered it to the Space Dock. This was the expected final delivery prior to closing the Space Dock top and pressurizing it. Once the second Cyclonic Inverter arrived in the Space Dock and was secured in its transport fabrication position, and after to the pressurization of the Space Dock, workers could build the interplanetary transport without requiring protective breathing apparatus and space suits.

Pirsrgyo was a Cleric 'operative' mole. As a long-term mole, it took them 20 years to fully infiltrate him into

Planetary Security Service Space Operations. Pirsrgyo could not pick any particular assignments, but as fate would have it, on that most auspicious occasion, he was chosen to work on the atmospheric gliders. This didn't seem like a target of opportunity until necessity deemed otherwise. Getting key components into the Interplanetary Transport construction facility was virtually impossible because security was tight.

A lot of material existed on the site and unfortunately for the Planetary Security Service didn't do a good job of sealing off all the extraneous underground passages that were left over from the last Caro-Taucetian's conflict. Only 25% of the original underground complex was utilized for the piece part construction of the Interplanetary Transport construction.

Pirsrgyo spent a lot of time identifying an innocuous tunnel that had an obscure entrance from the main complex. He needed a place to take materials and assemble what he needed to do the sabotage necessary to keep the Interplanetary Transport from getting completed.

The big problem was that the manufacturing of the parts was so widespread, and a lot of equipment and components were being supplied from elsewhere. That didn't make this complex a good target. But there was one thing here that wasn't built anywhere else that was a key piece and a critical component and that was the Cyclonic Inverters.

Pirsrgyo only knew of the Cyclonic Inverters, and not entirely what they did but it was going to be his job to help get them up to the Space Dock.

Pirsrgyo figured out his plan. He would make sure the first Cyclonic Inverter successfully made its way up to the Space Dock, then sabotage the next one. That way there would be less suspicion. He barely had enough time stealing materials to build his device before the 2nd Cyclonic Inverter was due to takeoff.

Pirsrgyo had unfettered access to the flights. The stage was set. Part of the strategic planning to delay or eliminate the Interplanetary Transport centered on wrecking the weak link, the Cyclonic Inverters, because without Cyclonic Inverters, space journey was impossible.

Professor Qwrezzella stood watching; unexpecting anything significant observed the atmospheric glider get closer as it was approaching the end of the ramp where it would be thrown up into the air.

The atmospheric glider hit the end of the ramp and flung upwards 10,000 feet, lit off the rocket boosters and after 5 seconds there was a huge explosion!

CRACK! BOOM! Thunderous sounds then followed for several seconds as if a summer storm was in progress.

As the huge fireball erupted and within moments pieces and parts started crashing down all around them. Professor Qwrezzella stayed in the best possible location as the roof of the observation platform was designed for this special purpose.

It now became obvious why certain parties demanded a 3rd Cyclonic Inverter built just for this reason. But what just happened?

"Was it a manmade disaster? Grable Reagal asked.

"I'm not sure but contact Nymstrom Purgatraceous and inform him that anybody who was associated with this launch is not allowed near the next Cyclonic Inverter, including the loading and launching."

"Also get a list put together of anyone who had access to the Cyclonic Inverter or the atmospheric glider in the past month. Pull all surveillance video and confirm the list."

"When will we attempt to launch the 3rd Cyclonic Inverter?" Grable Reagal asked.

"We need to do it really soon. We have 4 more C-Class atmospheric gliders available and backup booster rockets so a launch vehicle should not be an issue."

"How soon do you think Planetary Security Service investigators will be here?"

"I think they may already be here." Professor Dabler Qwrezzella stated knowing for a fact a secret surveillance group was here *and if it in fact was a case of sabotage, and how did they miss it?*

Planetary Security Service Director Bazion was of course extremely agitated, but at the same time Cleric Gummartukchik was all smiles as he knew the likelihood of the Planetary Security Service ability to successfully conduct this Gamulin Mission was highly unlikely. The mole working for Cleric Gummartukchik would simply sabotage the next atmospheric glider and it would take several years to build another Cyclonic Inverter, by then they will have squelched Bazion and killed the program.

Bazion's curiosity peaked, and he did not discount anything including mechanical failure, sabotage, or plain negligence. Despite the stringent quality control checks, sometimes due to distractions or misapplication of torque specs or some other reason, unexplained events occurred.

When word of the disaster reached the Three-Dimensional Mockup and Simulator, Metongy Zeugcha reacted quite calmly exhibiting self-control. His critical thinking and sagacious perspective summarized in a comment he made to Doctor Provkovitev:

"Anything could happen in a space development like this."

Doctor Provkovitev on the other hand appeared more choleric in his assessment responded, "Someone doesn't want this mission to go off, and it would not surprise me if the Clerics were somehow behind all this."

"You could be right; they definitely are firmly opposed to

disclosing anything possibly extra-terrestrial in nature."

The following moments, Planetary Security Service Director Bazion in contact with his special liaison at the Interplanetary Transport construction site communicated, "Go to Nymstrom Purgatraceous and direct him to initiate Two-man rule throughout the complex, and except for those individuals we clear for Cyclonic Inverter launch preparations, all workers are to be removed from the complex except those directly involved in the launch until its completed."

The thought of sabotage infuriated Bazion as in his heart he knew the Clerics had just struck. He would have to avoid a direct confrontation which could easily trigger a civil war, so he would have to proceed very delicately. The fact that he in his own mind had concluded it was a Cleric operation allowed him to win the next round. The Clerics had no idea the extreme he would now go to protect the launch site and the only remaining Cyclonic Inverter he must protect, or it would set this whole project back perhaps as many as 4 or 5 years, which he concluded would be just long enough for the Clerics to achieve their agenda *to prevent any venture deep into space.*

Next Bazion ordered General Napp via communicator, "General take the Rapid Deployment Force to the Interplanetary Transport construction site. I want you to set up complete security; your men are to enforce two-man rules throughout. I don't give a dam if they have to send two people to the toilet at the same time; nobody is allowed to travel alone."

"Should we send them via Atmospheric Gliders to the site?" General Napp asked.

"No that would tip off potential adversaries and they might attempt to escape before we can apprehend them. This is what I want you to do: Fly your troops in civilian clothes to Yarneos Air Transportation Center, then shuttle them to the Yarneos Center for Advanced Study. Professor Qwrezzella's group will then send them to the Interplanetary Transport construction site via Tube Train, once there they have plenty of surface transportation."

"I'll make that happen right away."

"One other thing, make sure your men search all incoming

freight."

"Understand, Director Bazion."

"I want a full accounting of whose there now, and who comes and goes and when."

Meanwhile Nymstrom Purgatraceous had already started implementing an order from Director Bazion; nobody was allowed to leave the area including Cargo Haulers.

Pirsrgyo joyously celebrated his achievement. He knew the Clerics would reward him handsomely. That included access to Cleric Gummartukchik's visitor housing and good amount of time enjoying the Botanical Gardens, the large swimming pool that had gorgeous swim coaches that rumors had it did far more than just swim training, an enhanced diet, and future credits that would extend his disposable income to five or ten times more than the average Caro.

Now he was just waiting to begin the next sabotage job that would take care of the third Cyclonic Inverter which would indefinitely suspend the Gamulin Mission the Clerics did not want to commence.

"Hey Pirsrgyo, did you see that fireball?" Romgen

somewhat a novice machinist and neophyte asked.

"Yea Romgen it was tremendous."

"Damn! It littered the tarmac with all kinds of debris; I hear a few guys got some severe injuries as some of that junk came down on them."

"Poor guys," Pirsrgyo responded in a most persuasive manner.

The Rapid Deployment Force didn't like wearing civilian clothes in conducting their assignments, but when General Napp ordered Colonel Gujane to do so, she knew her knuckleheads knew better than to grumble to her. Throughout her career Gujane was considered the "toughest bitch in the outfit." Her martial arts skills were second to none, and as a sharpshooter, hitting a wild Plastnybalkon at 400 yards for dinner, growing up in a sparsely populated mountainous region was considered typical ability for those semi-hardened people yet far different than what any city slicker could do.

Several atmospheric gliders with no special markings lined up on the launch ramp which the rapid deployment force loaded up in, each carrying a bag which had their uniform and boots in it. Once they got aboard the Tube Train at Yarneos Center for Advanced Study they would change into their uniforms and the first site of them would be as they poured out of the elevator at the Interplanetary Transport launch site.

Colonel Gujane observing the loading adjacent to the lead Atmospheric Glider barked, "Okay dog faces, get the hell on these Gliders, us get going!"

The Rapid Deployment Force, consummate professionals didn't need any encouragement, but they somehow enjoyed hearing the bitch scream at them. She was the fire in their belly as they were long overdue itching for a fight somewhere. The continual training in simulators and using computerized rounds to simulate taking out the bad guys just did not feel the same as shooting at real people. Globalization tore the heart out of their souls because it meant no more wars and no need for the Rapid Deployment Force. Then suddenly this mission sprang on them out of the blue. They had no idea what their mission was until they got on the Atmospheric Glider and were briefed in route what to expect and what to do. Guard duty just didn't seem like the sorts of excitement they were hoping to see.

One after the other, Atmospheric Gliders launched and soon traveled the 12,000 miles to the destination at Yarneos Air Transportation Center. After they arrived and deplaned, shuttle Skycars took them directly to the Yarneos Center for Advanced Study. These Skycars were quite different in that they were delivery vans used for expensive merchandise delivered to distribution centers from high tech factories. Each one could haul 20 dog faces plus their bags. Since there was only a half dozen of them, they relayed the troops from the Air Transportation Center to the Center for Advanced Studies. Since it was a relatively short trip of five minutes, it didn't take long to ferry the troops over. Soon they all were systematically led down to the Tube Train station.

Cargo haulers also deposited several large boxes to the Tube Train Station as well. Senior non-coms opened the boxes and as dog faces boarded the train, they were handed their weapons and spare ammo. In short order all the dogfaces were on the train changing and cargo haulers removed the empty boxes, most likely destined to recyclers.

After Colonel Gujane received word, all troopers were on board the train and switched into uniforms, she gave the conductor the word and the train immediately left the station and didn't take long to get up to 300 miles per hour, which took around 30 minutes to reach the Interplanetary Transport Construction site.

The bottleneck was now the elevator that could only handle about 20 troops at a time. Soon enough the troops were forming above near the observation platform when a half dozen hovercraft suddenly appeared and shut down their turbines next to the formations of troops.

The officers provided with detailed maps didn't have much time to plan for the disposition of troops, had mapped out systematically the assignments and the shifts.

Civilians who were not deemed necessary for the next week and not immediately required for the Cyclonic Inverter launch were shuttled to the Tube Train and taken to the Three-Dimensional Mockup and Simulator site which had ample housing so they could be sequestered until after the launch and brought back to continue their work. Since they were gone in large numbers from the Interplanetary

Transport Construction Site, the temporary housing (trailers in most cases), was suddenly made available to the rapid deployment force troops that just arrived.

The dog faces very quickly got on the Hovercraft which had to make a couple trips to transport the entire battalion. As soon as everyone was aboard, their turbines whined and away they went racing down the side of the launch ramp towards the Interplanetary Transport Construction Site Complex. As the Hovercraft pulled up next to the large doors of the facility, the turbines shut down and the dog faces piled out of the Hovercraft and members then deployed to the areas carrying copies of maps explaining their assignments.

The Civilians who were rounded up soon replaced them on the Hovercraft and went back the opposite direction in route to their new makeshift homes.

This relocation of civilians almost turned the place into a ghost town. However, there were still several personnel left there to facilitate the next launch. All the remaining personnel were gathered in a glob of people adjacent to where the rapid deployment was standing in formation awaiting further instructions.

Nymstrom Purgatraceous was asked by Colonel Gujane, "Mr. Purgatraceous, I would like that list of names Director Bazion required you to provide that includes those who were involved in Cyclonic Inverter number two launch."

"Here it is Colonel Gujane."

Colonel Gujane looked momentarily looked at the list then handed it to Major Finkster and said, "Major, call these names out and have the designated military police escort them to our special handling facility."

"Right away Colonel."

Major Finkster walked over to where a stepladder to a six-foot platform was set up so he could get up high enough to look at all the crowd and with audio speakers so they could all hear the instructions.

"Ladies and Gentlemen, as I call your names out, please proceed to my left here, you will be escorted to the Hovercraft and will be taken to temporary quarters for approximately one week."

"Romvick, Sedgecak, Grastopher, Pirsrgyo …"

Soon all the names were read off and away they went. Pirsrgyo suddenly felt alarmed, he was with the group now on the Hovercraft and one thing he knew for sure, every single one of them were part of the launch team!

"Am I a suspect?" Pirsrgyo asked himself as he suddenly started to contemplate his fate.

Furthermore, he did not have time to get the package into Cyclonic Inverter number three before he was nabbed and directed to report outside the building. The security detail did a very fast and spontaneous sweep. No sooner than the last bit of debris hit the airfield that it seemed they were already rounding everyone up. As he was walking out the huge double doors, he overheard the man wearing the sunglasses ask the other guy wearing a suit, "Is anyone else left inside?"

"As far as infrared scanners go, we think we got everyone, there is no movement in the building."

"Ok, seal it off."

One thing that surprised everyone is the two huge doors suddenly started closing. Nobody present, had ever seen the facility with the doors closed!

As soon as the doors were closed, anyone observing or flying by would think it was just a hill, the facility was very well camouflaged.

Suddenly the turbines kicking in raising the Hovercraft yanked Pirsrgyo out of his thought process and soon watched as the Hovercraft sped up traveling down the cement road parallel to the launch ramp.

Another security measure was then implemented. All communicators except encrypted Planetary Security Service communicators were disabled. Only Colonel Gujane and Nymstrom Purgatraceous had the ability to communicate to outside entities.

Any civilian that was left now was paired up with a rapid deployment force soldier. The two-man rule was thoroughly explained and since the remaining civilians were all part of the Cyclonic Inverter group, none were left that had not been thoroughly vetted and now as a separate measure had a set of eyes on them with instructions to report via their walkie-talkie's anything they deemed important which an officer would immediately investigate.

The stage was now set to get the last Cyclonic Inverter up into the Space Dock. They would be somewhat shorthanded, but as Nymstrom Purgatraceous explained to the workers, "It will be tougher now since we have fewer bodies, so I expect it will take a little longer to get Cyclonic Inverter loaded aboard an atmospheric glider. Our launch date has been set for five days from now. Everyone will just have to work harder."

The men exhaustively worked and one added bonus of sending away the rest of the workforce is they were not limited to nighttime movement of the Cyclonic Inverter when reduced staffing was on hand. By working in daylight hours, it made some of the tasks a lot easier because the visibility was much better.

Inside the cave like structure the Cyclonic Inverter was slowly slid on big steel rollers into the cylinder currently mounted on a huge flatbed which had 200 wheels under it so that it could haul an extremely heavy load. As soon as the Cyclonic Inverter was positioned with the correct center of gravity, mounting struts were inserted inside the huge cavity to make a ridged and safe mounting that would prevent tipping over or movement in transport, as well as provide some mechanical shock prevention. The end of the cylinder was then dropped in position at the end of the overall device where it was now bolted and glued onto the end of it. Part of the Cylinder was liquid oxygen tanks and petroleum-based fuel tanks for the rocket engines attached. Because of the extreme weight, the combination booster rockets and Cyclonic Inverter carrier rocket, as well as the magnetic launch ramp, enough velocity would be obtained to get into orbit. The cylinder carrying the Cyclonic Inverter with its propulsion ability would fly directly above the Space Dock where robotic arm grippers would attach to special lifting pads installed right after the lifting device was removed during prelaunch.

In space the cylinder would rotate so that the robotic arms could snag the Cyclonic Inverter and slowly position it in the Space Dock. The robotic arms would then be used to shut the huge cover over the top of the Space Dock. Men in space suits would then be sent within the Space Dock using back packs that had built in rockets that would slowly take them across the roof area where they would thread the self-locking mounting hardware and after they were all engaged most of the way, torqued down by a special torque wrench to proper specifications. As soon as that was accomplished, they would fly to the air chamber and once inside habitability workers would begin pressurizing the Space Dock to 14.7 pounds per square inch.

At the new required launch date, the Cyclonic Inverter was all set to be sent up to the space dock. Cranes lifted the Cyclonic Inverter up onto the back of the atmospheric glider with booster rockets mounted and fueled up. No irregularities were discovered, the launch countdown began.

Metongy Zeugcha, Doctor Provkovitev, Professor Qwrezzella and Grable Reagal were standing at the review stand when the launch order was given.

"Here it comes."

"Looks impressive, definitely." Everyone knew this was the do or die launch. Without a successful conclusion the program would most likely falter as it would give the Clerics time to dismantle it piece by piece.

Just like before with the heavy lifts the shockwave when the atmospheric glider came by was impressive and everyone in advance had their hands over their ears ready for it.

Just like before the glider shot up to 10,000 feet in the span of about two seconds, then the booster rockets kicked in lifting it rapidly as it slowly reduced in size flying downrange. And just barely before they lost sight of it the cylinder released from the atmospheric glider and after it was a short distance away ignited its own rocket engine that continued it on up into space leaving behind a large plume until it fully exited the atmosphere. Caro technicians monitoring the launch continued to report good results. When Director Bazion heard the flow of information, he felt great relief because he was able to get the 2nd Cyclonic Inverter up to the Space Dock where it would soon be in position and the hull construction would commence in large measure.

"Now it was time for the security detail to go over the complex with a fine-tooth comb," the chief "spook" asserted when he called up discussing the situation.

Director Bazion responded, "Get ahold of all the plans for the site, I want it searched completely. If there are any sealed off tunnels, I want them searched as well and if any dubious materials are discovered, bring in the forensic teams and try to get some evidence and protect any crime scenes even if we have to delay work."

Records were hard to find, but eventually detailed plans were discovered. They were immediately sent to Colonel Gujane and Nymstrom Purgatraceous. Some of the sealed off caves were hard to break into and special equipment was flown in to check air for dangerous gases 75 tunnels required entry. Nearly 100 acres of abandoned underground caverns needed investigated. In a matter of time, complete machine shops and other facilities were found, but due to the condition they were discovered, often with an inch of debris covering most of the equipment, they quickly determined they had not been tampered with and were immediately resealed and security cameras installed.

Tunnel by tunnel it was a laborious process and after exploring well over 50 tunnels they discovered one that had been unsealed and someone had ingeniously resealed it in a manner where it would appear nobody had tampered with it. Once inside this particular tunnel they quickly discovered modern tools and equipment that did not exist long ago when this tunnel was sealed. There was leftover equipment from the last Tauceti conflict but much of that was covered with dirt and debris from earthquakes, seismic activity and airflow through a forced air ventilation system that recirculated air even though entry was closed off.

Nymstrom Purgatraceous and Colonel Gujane visited the tunnel and by the time they arrived the forensics' team was well at work dusting for fingerprints and getting any clues as to what was going on in there.

"Did you find anything interesting?" Nymstrom Purgatraceous asked the chief forensics' officer that happened to be a rapid deployment officer working for Colonel Gujane.

"Yes sir, whoever was operating in here was taking materials used in the Transporter construction and using them to develop bombs."

"Did you find any additional bombs?"

"Yes sir, it looks like one we found completely assembled was ready to be installed aboard a ship real soon."

"No doubt the Cyclonic Inverter that just launched."

"Whoever it was, either got removed when we sequestered the facility, or they were too scared to come in here to get the device to install it with so much visibility."

"All right, let me know as soon as you find out if there are any fingerprints or other evidence to identify the person."

The men who were with Pirsrgyo's group were taken to Preznium directly to Planetary Security Services headquarters where they all slowly were interrogated by the finest Caro criminologists.

~~~
~~~

Chapter Twenty-One
Assassination

By now Cleric Gummartukchik understood that Pirsrgyo who was expendable and was no longer an asset, hence was now a liability. Gummartukchik met with Zrebrek and others in an emergency meeting at his mountain retreat where they planned their next move. It was clear they had to do damage control.

"Scuttling the Interplanetary Transporter will have to go on the back burner," Cleric Gummartukchik announced as he pondered the recent events.

"Perhaps we underestimated Planetary Security Services Director Bazion."

"Not really, he just got lucky that he suspected sabotage immediately and took those steps we didn't perceive he would take."

"How are we going to stop the Interplanetary Transport now?"

"We'll have to somehow sneak a bomb aboard the Dry-dock or the Spacecraft and destroy it."

"So that's our next move?"

"No, we first need to deal with Pirsrgyo."

"Do you think the Planetary Security Service will identify Pirsrgyo, as the saboteur?"

"Our man inside the Planetary Security Service headquarters will tell us shortly if that is the case."

"What will we do about Pirsrgyo?"

"We have no choice but to eliminate Pirsrgyo immediately."

"How will we do that?"

"We'll have to assassinate him."

"Who can do that if he's under confinement at Planetary Security Services Headquarters under heavy surveillance?"

"It will have to be an insider do the job."

"An insider who does the assassination will want some large compensation."

"No doubt, but we don't have any other choice. Pirsrgyo knows too much and can identify people in our organization who then might betray us to save their own skin."

"The Rat-Fink Law is really detrimental."

"Do you think that was enacted with us in mind?"

"Absolutely I do. It's another one of Bazion's moves that caught us by surprise."

"This seems rather urgent. When do we assassinate Pirsrgyo?"

"As soon as possible, contact our man on the inside and give him his marching orders."

~~~
~~~

Chapter Twenty-Two
Caro Space Shuttles

Work slowly moved ahead under tight security. People, who were housed at the Three-dimensional Mockup and Simulator site, were slowly brought back in groups based on priorities of their need for near term requirements. As they left the Three-Dimensional Mockup and Interplanetary Transport Spacecraft Simulator, they first arrived at Yarneos Center for Advanced Study where advanced machines designed to measure human behavior and most specifically advanced lie detector processes were used. One by one they went through the process as they were separated from the group and after the vetting process loaded back up on Tube Trains to transport back to the Interplanetary Transport construction site.

It was most fortunate for the sake of time that Space Dock construction crews were already in place and nearly two or three months of materials on hand for hull construction preventing huge delays. Most significantly the shuttle craft were designed and built elsewhere on the planet.

Metongy Zeugcha, Doctor Provkovitev, the Interplanetary Transport prospective Pilot and Co-pilot as well as the backup Pilot and backup Co-pilot, Grable Reagal and a few other crew members were flown via Atmospheric Glider nearly 14,000 miles to Nimbocratus, a provincial industrial center to train with the shuttle craft.

They first had classroom training which Professor Qwrezzella was on hand to organize as well as critique the instructors as this was particularly important since their lives would be at risk, not only from possible Earth response, but also the orbital re-entry had numerous complications even though they had designed a low-speed re-entry that was geosynchronous while descending vertically towards a projected landing site. The days of re-entering at 17,000 miles per hour were over. Heat shields became far less complex and thus would be more durable and allow frequent use.

The instructor showing design data on the overhead projectors' images right from data terminal memory was explaining the last portion of the design review when asked the question: "So the reactor and artificial gravity device is powered by a fission process with U115?"

"That's correct."

"Why U115?"

"Mainly because it doesn't have the radiation problem that using uranium, plutonium, or hydrogen isotopes do."

"How much U115 fuel does the shuttle carry?"

"We have calculated you could probably make 100 trips to the Earth's surface and back before it was depleted."

"Can it be refueled?"

"Not after it leaves Caro. The methods and processes to insert the fuel rods require laborious techniques and ultra-clean environments, and at our manufacturing facility here is the only place we know of that has all the requirements met to insure we don't introduce some flaw that might put the crew at risk."

"How does the flight controls work?"

"The basic flight controls are based on Skycar technology.

Instead of Global Skycar Administration sending navigation coefficients the Interplanetary Transport will or if it goes into internal autopilot, the shuttle can do what's necessary with its own onboard data terminals, but we stress that is just a backup mode since it does not have all the numerous features available if flown from the Interplanetary Transporter which has a far more robust program since it can use the firepower of the onboard data terminals the Interplanetary Transporter can provide."

"That rather interesting," Metongy Zeugcha responded.

After a brief break the instructor stated, "Today is your lucky day Gentlemen."

"Why is that?" Metongy Zeugcha asked.

"The first phase of the Shuttle test program has been completed, the craft is now certified for planetary operations and we are going to begin space launches from the planet today, and after a few touch and goes we'll ask for some of you to fly it up to the Space Dock, mate with the Space Dock, then if you would like a short tour, we'll let you see it, then return."

The instructor looked over the group and then asked, "Any volunteers?"

There was an eerie silence in the classroom. Nobody stirred.

The instructor quickly surmised none of them wanted to become the test pilots, so he went on to say, "In case some of you are afraid to go up now in space on the shuttle, allow me to explain a few things."

The crowd offered no response as the instructor continued, "First of all, the Shuttle has been up to space and back several times, it just did not take any live Caro with it. We carefully instrumented the flights and can guarantee the habitability aboard the Shuttle is robust to the point we don't even suggest there be a requirement to wear a space suit."

The instructor paused for a moment checking all the individuals present for the training to see if there was any indication of willingness to be the first to test the shuttle.

"Still no volunteers?"

The prospective Interplanetary Transport Pilot then responded, "I'm not a test pilot but I would be happy to go if you can convince one of these pollywogs to go up with me."

"That should not be a problem since nobody presently gets to leave until everyone has made at least one trip up and back."

"I would preferably not go," Metongy Zeugcha stated then continued, "But if I have to go, I might as well get it over with right away."

"Outstanding. It's always good when we get volunteers."

The co-pilot spoke up next, "I have no objections of going."

The instructor then asked, "Doctor Provkovitev, would you consider going up with the Co-pilot?"

"Sure, why not?"

"Okay you four guys follow me, and I'll get you started, then come back and set up a schedule for those remaining."

The small partial group walked out into the hallway, took the elevator down to floor B2. Like Yarneos Center for Advanced Study, Nimbocratus design bureau had a Tube cart system that went between this office building and launch site 25 miles away. This distance was far enough so that an inadvertent disaster would not harm the large industrial city that had a growing pollution problem that would reduce visibility below minimum necessary for the test flights.

The launch pads were just east of the nearby 8,000 feet high mountain peaks that not only reduced the pollution flowing in the direction of the space base, but also obscured it from the Nimbocratus community which had been necessary during the Tauceti conflicts in the past before unification.

The group got off the Tube Train, took the elevator up and discovered they had entered a research facility that had hangers and buildings necessary to support the research and the test flights.

"The space base appeared to have had better years," Metongy Zeugcha had said to Doctor Provkovitev when he saw it inside the open bay of the large hanger they walked out of and were led to a Hovercraft waiting for them.

As soon as they got aboard the cab of the Hovercraft, the operator turned on the turbines and the cushions soon filled with air, and it rose six feet in the air and soon afterwards scooted down a concrete road to their launch area a couple miles away. Soon they approached the waiting craft and technicians doing last minute checkouts.

The Hovercraft turbines then shut down and the cab slowly settled down onto the road allowing the passengers to easily disembark. Their instructor led them over to the craft, which looked exactly like the model in their classroom training documents and projections and for some of them, exactly like the shuttlecraft back at the three-dimensional mockup and simulator.

"Instructor, we don't have to wear any kind of space suits?"

"No. Our environmental controls are well designed to eliminate the need for space suits allowing more flexibility to egress when necessary."

"Not even protective clothing in case the Earthlings have diseases that are deadly for us?"

"On the return trip from Earth if you do happen to get infected with a fatal disease you will most likely die aboard the ship, otherwise you will simply be isolated for a while in a biosphere shelter upon your return in which key medical researchers will do all necessary tests to medically clear you."

"Will the doctors and nurses live with us inside the biosphere?"

"Yes, they will, there is no other alternative. We have a number of volunteers willing to sacrifice their lives, if necessary, to enlighten "Carokind" when you bring home lots of evidence of extra-terrestrial life."

The pilot and Metongy Zeugcha had both flown the shuttle simulator a dozen times and were very familiar with its layout. The real machine they now boarded was an exact replica of what they had simulated in, but this one had one other feature, this Caro shuttle flew.

The instructor then advised the first two, Metongy Zeugcha and the Interplanetary Transport pilot, "For your first flight, we are going to control it from the ground. There will be no requirements of you to control anything. It will be flying just as if it were in autopilot which is our main goal for your mission as well."

"That's not fun," The pilot stated as he quickly made a mental note to scratch the joyride, he wanted to do that might make Metongy Zeugcha slightly air sick.

Both men sat down in the forward seats.

"All the other seats in the back have instrument racks mounted in them."

"Yea that must be for data gathering."

"That's why only two of us at a time would be flying."

"Where are the headphones?"

"You will not need headphones; we have designed a quiet cab and all communications will go over speaker systems and your microphones are mounted in the dash directly in front of you."

Technicians checked their seat belts, did some last-minute settings on the equipment racks then said, "Okay gentlemen we will be launching in about five minutes. Countdown will commence in four minutes."

Just like the Interplanetary Transport cockpit, the shuttle had similar displays to look at for indications and system reports. In four minutes over the intercom, Metongy Zeugcha and the pilot heard, "Commencing countdown to launch in 60 seconds."

Lights on the control panel were shifting colors and layer by layer slowly turning green. When most of them had turned green the control tower reported to Metongy Zeugcha and the pilot, "Interlocks are closed commencing launch sequence."

Within about 15 seconds all the indicators were green and launch permission granted ostensibly from the mothership as it would be in real life, nevertheless today that permission came from the control tower.

Just like in the simulator there was not a lot of noise.

"I can feel some vibration."

"Yes, I can feel we are starting to move."

In a few moments they could see the altitude of the shuttle increasing and about five minutes later they were not only going vertical they had changed aspect to an angle and were speeding up. The city just west of them was now fully observable from the air as it slowly shrank in size. They could also notice G forces now as the shuttle apparently increased velocity. Soon the shuttle attained an angle and sped up. Before long they were up at 150,000 feet and could see the curvature of the planet just like they were on an atmospheric glider.

Neither man had been up in space before. This was a real treat and the further they moved away from the planet the darker the space appeared. Already they were now starting to see stars they could not see before. Looking at the control panel display, they were soon passing 250,000 feet when it shifted to a mile's scale showing they were now at 47.3484848 miles above the planet.

One of the control console displays showed a graphic which now displayed the Space Dock in relation to own ship's position offset from the planet. The Space Dock was in geosynchronous orbit about 500 miles away from the planet. Every second the distance was updating, and they were currently 600 miles away. The shuttle speed increased steadily as it got further away from the planet's gravity and the closure rate was increasing to the point, they were now closing the Space Dock by 15 miles a minute and increasing eventually to 25 miles a minute that quickly reduced the distance, then suddenly, they started slowing down.

It didn't seem long before they were only 50 miles away from the Space Dock and they could feel the negative Gs as the shuttle appeared to be breaking and slowing down. They watched the speed slowly decrease and at 25 miles from the Space Dock they were now closing at three miles a minute. At 10 miles they had slowed to a closure rate of two miles a minute and as they crossed over the five-mile distance, a display popped up a warning, "5 Miles to Destination."

The craft continued slowing and at one mile to destination the closure rate was down to yards per second and slowed down from there till finally at 100 feet with the huge Space Dock looming in front of them, they came upon a docking platform. They slid into very slowly and it was apparent to them soon that magnetic grippers were carefully positioning them into the hanger when they suddenly came to a complete stop observing the hanger wall a mere few feet in front of them. A door then shut sealing the shuttle in. For a few minutes they could hear a strange random noise. What they were hearing is the hanger was being pressurized. The control panel could see "Outside Pressure Indicator" that had recently read 0.0 pounds per square inch while they were in the process of docking, now read, 14.4 pounds per square inch.

Then over the intercom they could hear the operator in the booth observing the shuttle through an observation window say, "We are now equalizing the shuttle pressure with the hanger bay, you will be allowed to leave the shuttle momentarily."

Unexpectedly right in front of them a couple men walked out of a hanger door, into the shuttle hanger bay, approached the shuttle and turned a handle that released the door and opened it.

"This way gentlemen."

Metongy Zeugcha and the pilot followed the men through the door which was shut behind them and secured and they proceeded to walk down a hallway that was congested with equipment with all kinds of systems and controls that eventually led through some isolation hatches, most likely designed to seal off compartments in an emergency and eventually to a control room that overlooked the Interplanetary Transport in the Space Dock. From this vantage point the entire port side of the Interplanetary Transport could be observed.

"Mother of all spacecraft," the pilot stated as he looked on in awe.

"To look at it on a projection is one thing but to personally eyeball it is another."

"I'm so surprised it's so far along."

"The modular construction and routine flights got a lot of sections up here fast."

Down at the end of the rear of the Interplanetary Transport those malicious looking Cyclonic Inverters added immensely to the optical illusion of something nobody could ever conjure up.

Metongy Zeugcha felt a tingling sensation as it created an everlasting image that he would never be able to forget in his lifetime.

Captain Kambalner approached the men and said,

"Welcome aboard Caro's first Space Dock. I'm Captain Kambalner the Officer in Charge (OIC) here."

"Please to meet you Captain Kambalner."

"You look familiar," Captain Kambalner said looking at Metongy Zeugcha.

"Come to think of it, Capitan Kambalner, I think I saw you a few times at the three-dimensional Model und Simulator," Metongy Zeugcha responded.

"Yes, I spent some time there studying the mockup so I would know where all the components go and how it's supposed to look when installed."

"I was training at the three-dimensional mockup and simulator off and on, Captain Kambalner."

"I'm the designated prospective pilot for the Interplanetary Transport," the pilot stated and added, "I'm Captain Nuuk."

"Please to meet you Captain Nuuk. It's a real honor to meet the very first pilot who will take a Caro ship out of the solar system."

"Captain Kambalner, it's also a privilege for me to meet

the very first Space Dock Captain." The men bowed towards each other and smiled.

"Shall we go aboard the Interplanetary Transport and take a look around?"

"Sure, why not?"

Captain Kambalner led the men down a hallway that intersected with the bridge tunnel to the spacecraft. They went through an airlock compartment that had interlocks preventing entry in the next area before closure behind them. Inside there were emergency breathing apparatus with face masks hanging on the wall all in a convenient carrying bag.

"Take one of these with you. It's in case we have a rapid decompression event." They watched the captain strap on his pouch, which they had done back at the Three-dimensional mockup, but did not appreciate the realism it truly conveyed.

As soon as they all had their Emergency Breathing Apparatus strapped on their backs, Captain Kambalner turned the manual airlock handle which allowed the door to open. After everyone stepped through, he then secured and tightened the door. They then were at the ship's door lock, where again they opened it and closed it behind them.

"We are nearly reaching the point we can pressurize the Interplanetary Transport."

"When you pressurize the Interplanetary Transport, is that a significant milestone?"

"Yes, when we can pressurize the Interplanetary Transport, it will add a complete level of safety for workmen we currently do not have in the event of rapid decompression."

Looking inside the ship they could see a lot of "equipment." Some of the Data Terminal Consoles ready to be installed were still in shipping containers inside the Interplanetary Transport Control Room.

"How do you get all this material inside the Interplanetary Transport?"

"The Interplanetary Transport has cargo doors and currently we have a housing unit attached there bolted to the hull which we sealed which acts as an air lock. We also have a major air lock for cargo delivery. Exterior robotic arms take the cargo out of the transport cylinders, places them in the air lock. The external door is then shut and sealed, then we pressurize the air lock, then open the internal door and use robotic arms to move the material out of the airlock and into the bottom of the Space Dock where we figure out where it needs sent aboard the ship."

Captain Kambalner led Metongy Zeugcha and the Pilot through the control room and other parts of the Interplanetary Transport where they could look around.

"It looks identical to the Three-Dimensional Mockup."

"It certainly does since everything you see here was first mounted in the mockup for fitment."

After a brief walk through some of the spaces and ships living quarters, then back to the power plant that was soon coming online, Captain Kambalner escorted them back to the control room of the Space Dock and they conversed a short while about the problems and lessons learned they discovered thus far. Then when it appeared there was no further any reason to remain, the Pilot and Metongy Zeugcha were escorted back to the Shuttle, where they boarded. Technicians then shut the door and locked it for them then exited the hanger bay and secured the door behind them.

The Space Dock Shuttle Hanger operators then notified the Pilot and Metongy Zeugcha via the intercom, "We are now depressurizing the hanger and we are monitoring the shuttle internal pressures."

In the beginning of the depressurization which included air compressors sucking the air out of it to almost a vacuum the external pressure indicated 14.5 pounds per square inch. That number slowly declined and in a few minutes was down to just one pound per square inch. To avoid wear and tear on the compressors, it was cheaper to ship up containers of canned air than to try to save one pound per square inch worth of air, so the residual air pressure got dumped to space as it equalized.

Soon the readouts indicated external air pressure was 0.0 pounds per square inch, a vacuum.

"Shuttle crew, the hanger bay is equalized to space pressure vacuum. We are now opening the hanger door." Once the hanger door was moved upwards and out of the way in a safe storage profile, they were ready for launch.

"Space Dock, understand," The Shuttle Pilot responded.

"Shuttle, turn on your repulser."

"Space Dock, the shuttle repulser is energized."

The electromagnet of the shuttle bay quickly moved the shuttle out of the hanger where it silently glided a distance away. When it was nearly 100 feet outward, propulsion cut in and the shuttle craft banked away from the Space Dock and then moved in the direction of atmospheric re-entry.

The flight controls and unique propulsion allowed casual penetration of the ozone belt that eliminated superheating the shuttle and eliminated the need for a heavy heat shield which allowed much heavier payloads. Since they were traveling vertically through the ozone layer, it did not take long to get down to the 150,000-foot level where standard atmospheric glider shielding was more than sufficient for safety. Ground controllers continued flying the shuttle for this particular mission, but in future evolutions the shuttle crew would be doing all the flying in autopilot from the on-board data terminals.

Just as it seemed like they had just got started they were

approaching Nimbocratus Space Port for a landing. Little winglets expanded outwards from the bottom of the shuttle to give more control as it flew near the speed of sound approaching the landing zone.

Shortly the Shuttle was at 1000 feet a mile from the landing zone doing 200 miles per hour and slowly decreasing speed as it angled down for the landing. At one quarter mile from the landing zone the shuttle went horizontal and slowly decreased altitude and slowed down for a landing speed around 50 miles per hour that was dropping off until it got directly over the vertical descent area where horizontal velocity reached 0.0 miles per hour and began a soft vertical descent directly on top of the cross hairs of the landing zone. By the time it was one foot off the ground its vertical velocity was one inch per second and sat down at ¼ inch per second terminal velocity.

~~~
~~~

Chapter Twenty-Three

Infiltration and Assassination

It didn't take long for the Clerics to figure out their plan to infiltrate Planetary Security Service and take care of Pirsrgyo. Cleric Zrebrek decided he could use his new disciple he had under his spell. If situations warranted, he would go so far as seducing her if he had too but hoped it did not come down to that. Just because they were Clerics did not protect them from the Planetary Security Service. It would not be the first nor the last time a Cleric was arrested for some serious crime.

In many cases it was the Temple worshipers themselves, who ratted out the Clerics, especially when internal strife required dethroning a top Clerical figure with immense powers such as Cleric Gummartukchik. Cleric Gummartukchik knew that if Pirsrgyo was subject to the brutality that Planetary Security Service could administer someone, especially since their new lie detector equipment had reached a point of 95% accuracy. There would be no way Pirsrgyo could sustain interrogations for long.

Ferdastad had just stepped on the Crawler as he looked up and saw the Skycar land on his building. *"I wonder who the big shot is that lives near me going on those Skycar rides?"*

He quickly lost interest as the Crawler moved on as his mind was running in huge speed thinking about some new information he had just decrypted. *This Earth business is getting quite interesting* he said to himself. The latest decrypts concerned communications between Great Britain and the United States concerning the VENONA transcript with the most relevance to the Hiss case #1822, sent March 30, 1945, from the Soviet's Washington station chief to Moscow. The Signal-Intelligence yield included discovery of the Cambridge Five espionage ring in the United Kingdom.

The minute Ferdastad left the residence, Zurella Myco quickly changed out of her plain Jane domestic engineer garb, into more fashionable clothes and because of her natural beauty didn't have to spend a lot of time doing makeup to help her look attractive. She looked at the clock and knew that Cleric Zrebrek would be picking her up any minute and he seemed to have some important business they needed to attend.

Chomvik had no idea the extent his sister had gotten involved with Cleric Zrebrek. As far as he was concerned Zrebrek was the devil's Bishop. The second most evil person on the planet next to Gummartukchik. It was bad enough he himself had gotten embroiled into performing espionage for the Clerics acting as a double spy for Planetary Security Service but soon, he would almost feel despair as it all unfolded to include his sister. He then found himself alone with the Cleric's agent recruiting him for another assignment:

"I'll agree to do it as long as you provide the injection equipment and I want 50,000 credits on 5 credit cubes," Chomvik stated in the frankest manner.

"We agree, we'll have a courier give you the materials and credits by special courier sometime today. We want the job completed as soon as possible."

~~~
~~~

Chapter Twenty-Four
A Spies Sister.

At the same time Chomvik was making the deal, Zurella Myco made it to the rooftop Skycar parking a moment after Cleric Zrebrek arrived. She walked out to the Skycar, and the passenger door roof area tilted and Zurella stepped inside and sat down. The door/roof section tilted down and secured, and the electric powered turbo lift soon raised the Skycar and soon had it in Skycar traffic heading for Gummartukchik's mountain retreat.

"Do you have any interesting materials today?"

"Oh yes, very much so. It's amazing what this other planet is doing. The spy business is really huge there."

"I see," Cleric Zrebrek politely said then thought, *if you only knew what goes on here on Caro.*

Soon Cleric Zrebrek and his new disciple were in an office

looking at the data cube information together. Zurella Myco had received a tremendous education in a brief period. Even though similar events did not take place on Caro, the abstract nature of them offer ideas and methods that could be applied on Caro. However, there currently were no warring parties since Globalization completed years ago after the great Tauceti purge.

Cleric Zrebrek then decided that now was the time to bring up a chore that he knew his disciple would easily perform.

"Your brother is Chomvik right?"

"Yes, how did you know?"

"He mentioned you to me recently," Zrebrek lied.

"I'm glad you know my brother."

"Sometimes we hire Chomvik to check out information for us when he's off duty."

"I hope he does a good job for you."

"Chomvik always performs in an excellent manner."

"That's good to know."

"Could you do me a favor?"

"Sure, why not?"

Zrebrek pulled a package he had waiting there out and handed it to Zurella and said, "Give this to your brother. He'll fly to the Skycar parking area on your building in his skycar just after I take you back."

"Sure, no problem."

"Shall we go to the Botanical Gardens for lunch?"

"I would love to."

Zrebrek smiled and led his disciple to her favorite place in Preznium. Nowhere else in the city, was there such beauty and splendor.

As Cleric Zrebrek walked with Zurella Myco towards the Botanical Gardens they passed by Cleric Gummartukchik who acted as if he was ignoring them, but Cleric Zrebrek nodded to Cleric Gummartukchik who saw Zurella Myco holding the package his operatives had just bundled for the mission.

While Zrebrek took Zurella out to the gardens, one

of Gummartukchik assistants called Chomvik on his communicator and said, "The package will arrive at 2:00 p.m. at Skycar landing pad at this address..."

The most amusing part of that communication to Chomvik was he instantly recognized the address as the building his sister lived in. Perhaps he would pay her a visit after he picked up the package.

Today Cleric Zrebrek laid on the charm. Zurella Myco was feeling moist and ready and even with the slightest suggestion she would lose control. Cleric Zrebrek knew this but also knew he would keep his distance because desire was always a stronger emotion than gratification. The minute gratification comes, the desire and control often release. Cleric Zrebrek's success as a master controller and manipulator was far more important than cheap gratification that was easily obtainable from numerous sources.

After they finished eating and talking like two good friends would about nonsensical things, Cleric Zrebrek looked at his time piece and suddenly said, "I need to take you home; we made an appointment with your brother for 2:00 p.m. He'll be expecting you at the landing pad area."

"I'm ready to leave."

The two made their way to the Skycar got in and flew to Zurella's residence and landed on the skycar parking area.

"Zurella, you might want to wait up here a few moments; your brother should be along at any minute."

"All right. I'll wait up here for Chomvik."

Cleric Zrebrek's Skycar then took off after Zurella made her way into the protective covering for passengers. Just like Cleric Zrebrek suggested, another Skycar with official Planetary Security Service markings came in and landed where Cleric Zrebrek Skycar had been just moments before.

From a distance Chomvik had seen a woman get out of the Skycar he knew had to be Zrebrek's helper based on the rendezvous time and the woman remained in the passenger protective area when he landed. Soon the Planetary Security Service Skycar turbos were shut down and safe to precede sign lit up, so Zurella Myco nonchalantly marched like a good disciple out to the Skycar. The door top swiveled upwards and Chomvik was momentarily stunned! It was his sister Zurella! His heart raced then he felt the world crashing down on him.

And to make matters worse, Chomvik potentially ruined his own life, but now he had his sister Zurella's involvement.

"Hello Chomvik. Cleric Zrebrek asked me to give this to you."

Chomvik knew he had to keep his composure until he figured out what to do simply asked, "Do you know what's inside the package?"

"No, he didn't tell me what it is, just asked me to give it to you."

"You're not working for Cleric Zrebrek are you?"

"No, I just went to him to get help with Ferdastad."

"I thought I told you to stay away from the Clerics?"

"I was getting desperate."

"Ok, whatever you do, do not get near Cleric Zrebrek again. This is very serious business. You may be in over your head."

Chomvik then did some fast thinking. "Do you know

where Metongy Zeugcha lives?"

"Sure, I've been there a couple times."

"Is Ferdastad there now?"

"He said that's where he's going."

"Please follow my instructions very carefully. Leave the landing pad area, go directly to Metongy Zeugcha's residence and tell Ferdastad the two of you are to remain there until I can make arrangements for you. If you go back to your residence now, someone may find you and your husband dead there in the morning."

"This isn't some sort of joke, is it?"

"No Zurella, you are now way in over your head because you got involved with the Clerics. There are many things going on now you don't know about. Your personal safety is at huge risk now. You should have stayed away from the Clerics like I asked you. Your life is now at risk and if you don't do exactly what I just told you, your life will be very short."

"You are in danger right now. I'll do what I can to protect

you to allow you to get to Metongy Zeugcha's residence. I can loiter in traffic patterns because I'm law enforcement. As soon as you leave, I will fly above the Crawler to make sure you get on and as soon as you get on the Tube Train, call my communicator. Now get going."

Zurella Myco had no idea she was involved in very serious espionage. In addition to the Clerics making their move now to eliminate Pirsrgyo, Planetary Security Service Director Bazion was making his own arrangements. It was about retention of power and world domination. The Clerics had left a lot of skeletons behind in the past, Zurella would be no different. Chomvik's mission just got more complicated.

True to her word Zurella now fully confused and semi distraught made her way onto the Crawler that in a short while transferred to the Tube Train and called her brother Chomvik who was orbiting overhead now in his Planetary Security Service Skycar.

"Chomvik, I'm on the Tube Train."

"So far so good, when you get on the Crawler that goes by Metongy Zeugcha's residence, call me again, but do not use my name."

"Understand."

Chomvik orbited around above the Crawler connection he expected Zurella to soon arrive. As expected, moments later she called again.

"Okay, I'm on the Crawler that goes by Metongy Zeugcha's residence."

"I'll see you when you get off in front of the building. Go directly to Metongy's residence. Once you get inside, contact me and let me know how many people there are in case we need to send in some protection."

„Understand," Zurella said now fraught with emotion. Her prince charming Cleric Zrebrek was using her for some nefarious purpose and now her personal safety was questionable at best.

The Crawler pulled up in front of Metongy Zeugcha's residential building and Zurella got off. Her heart was beating fast as fear was gripping her. Zurella had no idea how close she came to danger. A short while after she had taken the elevator straight down from the roof to street level at her residence allowed her to avoid the cleric operative that was positioned near her apartment entrance to permanently silence her. She would have appeared simply as the victim of another criminal who would have snatched her purse to make it look like a burglary.

Nobody was near and the elevator was instantly available, she got in alone and took it up to Metongy's apartment, walked out of the elevator and promptly walked over and rang the doorbell which was quickly opened. Ferdastad was almost shocked to see Zurella Myco. Zurella immediately reported to her brother: "I'm inside the apartment with Ferdastad. There are six men in here."

"Okay, stay there for now. Do not leave for any reason, I'll try to get you help."

Unknown to the half dozen men inside working in Metongy Zeugcha's apartment, one of them was a Planetary Security Service undercover security agent who could provide them all with an amount of protection. Today might be one of those days they might easily need it.

Ferdastad saw how Zurella looked frazzled and suggested

she sit down on the sofa, and they began a quiet conversation.

Before Ferdastad could start asking why she came, Zurella said: "My brother told me to come here for my personal safety."

"What happened?"

"It's a long story, I made some serious mistakes."

While Zurella Myco slowly and quietly informed Ferdastad much of the story, his anxiety also grew. Chomvik immediately flew to Planetary Security Services Headquarters where he landed the Skycar and immediately took the elevator down 50 stories and approached Director Bazion.

"We need to talk."

"Sure, come on in."

"Cleric Zrebrek contacted me. We now know who the person of interest is in the Cyclonic Inverter case."

"Oh really?"

"Yes, and he's detained here in the building now, a man

named Pirsrgyo."

"Ok we'll have him interrogated right away."

"Here's the bribe money and weapon Zrebrek sent me to do the inside job of assassinating Pirsrgyo."

"Excellent, now we got more evidence to nail Cleric Zrebrek with."

"Sir, under the circumstances, you need to put Pirsrgyo under immediate protective custody, because if I do not report back in a couple hours, he's been assassinated they will send in some emergency mole to finish him off."

"Good idea, but I have a better place to take him. Somewhere that I know they can't get to him."

"After you make the arrangements, there is another part of the case I have to tell you about that affects me personally."

"Ok, one minute, wait here I need to take care of Pirsrgyo first."

Bazion walked out the door and over to the next office where his right-hand man whom he fully trusted and gave him directions of where to take Pirsrgyo where his loyal agents were stationed in a rapid deployment like posture. Pirsrgyo would be untouchable there. The clerics just lost a major battle and didn't know it yet.

Bazion's assistant walked out of his office with Bazion and it automatically shut and locked behind him and he then took an elevator a number of floors above and grabbed a half dozen men who were on his trust list, and together they went to the detention center and took custody of Pirsrgyo and they immediately left in two Skycars to Preznium Air Transportation Center where they all boarded an unmarked Planetary Security Service atmospheric glider which flew 12,000 miles to Nimbocratus where Planetary Security Service had a special center hidden in the midst of a lot of design bureau buildings that obscured them really well.

Four of the Planetary Security Service men accompanying the special agent were expert interrogators and by the time they arrived at their secret facility, the full picture had materialized at what was in store for Pirsrgyo.

"If you cooperate with us, we'll give your life back to you."

"I have nothing to say."

"The Clerics have already hired a hit man to kill you. They will not stop at anything to get to you."

"I don't believe you."

Director Bazion had given the package to his special investigator who then opened it in front of Pirsrgyo and showed him and said, "You would have been assassinated in a couple hours with this device had we not intervened."

Pirsrgyo looked on without comment.

"Here's the bribe money."

Cleric Zrebrek always paid him with the same type of credits as soon as he saw the 5 credit tokens, he suddenly started getting nervous.

"Cleric Zrebrek paid someone to kill you, to silence you."

"I don't believe you."

"Right now, you are safe, but if we return you to Preznium I'm absolutely sure Cleric Zrebrek's people will get to you within a couple hours."

"You are staring at 50,000 credits. You blew up the Cyclonic

Inverter for only 5,000 credits."

The investigators knew Pirsrgyo would not last long and within a couple hours the crime lab had matched his fingerprints all over the materials found in the tunnel back at the Interplanetary Transporter. The interrogators now had more to use on breaking Pirsrgyo.

"The crime lab matched your fingerprints on all the materials in the cave. Here are some pictures of what we found with your fingerprints on them."

Pirsrgyo seemed to realize he was now in serious trouble.

"There is nothing the Clerics can do to save you now. In fact, all they will do is having you killed at the soonest time possible. They have a huge footprint within Planetary Security Service. If we take you back to Preznium you are a dead man, and I doubt you will survive a day."

"What do you want from me?" Pirsrgyo asked.

"Sign this confession."

Within an hour after Zurella not going to her residence, the Clerics knew something had gone wrong. In pure panic they contacted their deep mole inside Preznium Planetary Security Service headquarters and asked him to investigate Pirsrgyo and find out what his disposition was. When it was reported he was no longer in the building and nobody knew where he went, other than interrogators took him somewhere for questioning, the pressure mounted.

~~~
~~~

Chapter Twenty-Five
Finding the Mole

Director Bazion was having a good day because nobody had any reason to go looking for Pirsrgyo. At his request the crime lab sequestered the report and made no official report to tip off anyone potentially involved in a conspiracy.

Bazion had alerted the custody coordinator to inform him of anyone requesting access to Pirsrgyo for any reason. Towards the evening, a phone call came in.

"Director Bazion?"

"Yes, what can I do for you?"

"Hello, this is agent Occa; I'm the custody coordinator for the evening shift."

"Any updates?"

"Yes sir, just wanted to report as you requested, Agent Merriak was here a little while ago making an inquiry as to where Pirsrgyo was detained.

"Ok thanks for the information, and as I explained earlier, do not discuss this with anyone, it's of vital importance."

"Understand sir."

"Thank you."

After Bazion shut off the communicator, he then almost blew a cork. *Agent Merriak was Chomvik's partner!* He needed to contact Chomvik right away before Chomvik informed Merriak where his sister was hiding out.

The communicator sounded and Chomvik sitting next to his sister at Metongy Zeugcha's residence saw that Director Bazion was calling and said, "Excuse me for a minute I need to talk alone with my boss."

Chomvik got up walked into another room that was empty and answered the call.

"Agent Chomvik here."

"Chomvik, this is Bazion. Hate to tell you this but your partner Merriak is a Cleric agent. I hope you haven't told him where your sister is?"

"No, I haven't."

"Good. I've been thinking on what to do about this."

"What's your plan?"

"Get your sister and her husband and take them in your Skycar to Preznium Air Transportation Center. You will receive instructions from there. Be there in 15 minutes."

"Understand, on my way."

Chomvik walked back into the living room observing Zurella smiling and looking full of life sitting next to her husband whom he knew she truly adored. He then approached them.

"Zurella, you and Ferdastad need to come with me right away."

They both looked up at Chomvik whom they knew was very decisive and very astute and instantly had a look of horror on their faces and understood vividly compliance was not optional, stood up and followed him out.

In another 2 minutes they were up on the roof getting into Chomvik's skycar. The doors soon afterwards quickly pivoted down and closed and Chomvik then commanded the Skycar. Moments later the Skycar egressed into traffic but soon deviated for police action as he was allowed to do and took the short cut to Preznium's Air Transportation Center. About the same time Merriak and three conspirators stepped into the elevator, the Skycar was a distance away from the building.

A person at the Planetary Security Service INTEL section monitoring Chomvik's secret video links observed the four men get out of the elevator, walk over to Metongy Zeugcha's residence ring the doorbell, and then as people inside opened the door to inquire what they wanted they were shoved aside, and the four men entered as if they were looking for someone. The video easily identified Merriak. The undercover Planetary Security Service guy swung into action and when the men started beating on the occupants, he quickly disabled a couple of Merriak's men leaving just the two of them to deal with. Some of the scientists focused on Merriak's assistant, leaving the undercover man in a one-on-one fight with Merriak who was also one tough SOB. The fighting was fast and lethal.

One of the scientists not involved in the slugfest remembered Metongy Zeugcha was a blaster collector and similar to Earthly pistols, he also had some illegal ammunition. The scientist loaded the gun and then returned to the melee in the other room. Merriak had temporarily disabled the undercover man who was lying almost lifeless and Merriak and an object in his hand and appeared to get ready to swing it and most likely kill the guy when the scientist pulled the trigger several times. He hit Merriak twice in the middle of the chest which caused him to immediately form a facial expression then as blood started coming out of his mouth, fell forward mortally wounded into a pool of blood next to the undercover agent.

The other man was on top of one of the scientists beating him to death and would probably have killed him in another minute heard the gunshots and suddenly looked up spooked seeing the blaster pointed directly at him and watched Merriak hit the floor.

"Don't move or I'll kill you too."

Knowing the man knew how to operate the blaster as Merriak had crumpled to the floor from the gunshot wounds, the agent slowly raised his hands and immediately started to plan an exit strategy. Planetary Security Service operatives were taught several egress techniques so he knew in a little bit he would make good his escape.

Unfortunately, he didn't realize the level of surveillance going on in this residence, and the Planetary Security Service INTEL man had already sent a task force over to the building not long before the gun shots, the first Skycars were already on the roof and agents were coming down by both elevator and stairway.

The door to the entrance was wide open with the two Planetary Security Service agents unconscious laying in front of the door which kept it open. Luckily the undercover agent was coming too and one of the first men that entered knew this man and his assignment.

"Drop the blaster!"

"Don't shoot him; he's one of the good guys."

The scientist slowly sat the gun down on the floor as the room quickly filled up with agents.

The undercover agent looked up at the INTEL operative

and said, "Restrain him." He nodded to Merriak's partner.

Before Merriak's partner could execute his exit strategy Planetary Security Service Intel Agents had hand restraints on him, as well as the other two that were starting to become conscious again.

The building was quickly sealed off and other residents on the floor were notified by officials to stay inside their residence until further notice as police action unfolded. Within an hour all Planetary Security Service assets were gone, Metongy Zeugcha's residence was empty except for a couple Planetary Security Service guards inside preserving the crime scene waiting for forensics.

~~~
~~~

Chapter Twenty-Six
Witness Protection

When Chomvik arrived at Preznium Air Transportation Center, Planetary Security Services Director Bazion was there waiting for him next to the parking spot for the atmospheric glider that would be soon taking them to an undisclosed location.

"I'm sending them to a safe house at Nimbocratus. They will remain there until we work all this out."

"Perhaps I need to go with them?"

"Not to worry, they will be in good hands; I need you here to assist me tomorrow, when the fireworks start."

"Understand."

Chomvik walked over to Zurella Myco and Ferdastad and said, "The Planetary Security Service will be taking you someplace safe until all this gets worked out."

"I appreciate you looking out for us," Ferdastad said as he barely knew the half of what was going on.

"I suppose I should have listened to you," Zurella Myco said as she faced Chomvik with huge regret on her face.

"We all make mistakes. Now you know."

Director Bazion who had pressing business said: "Okay, you guys get on the atmospheric glider, we have some important business to attend."

Ferdastad and Zurella climbed aboard the Atmospheric Glider and within five minutes were on the ramp accelerating to their destination.

"Let's go back to the office. Much needs to be done tonight."

"I'll be right there," Chomvik replied as he then walked over to his Skycar and got in and flew to Planetary Security Services Headquarters.

~~~

A Planetary Security Services agent approached Metongy Zeugcha and informed him: "You have a couple friends that will be visiting you soon. Their whereabouts is to be kept
~~~

guarded, as we'll explain why later."

"Who's coming?"

"Ferdastad and Zurella Myco."

"Why are they coming here?"

"Protective custody."

The Planetary Security Services agent then informed him, "There was a homicide at your residence. Police have it roped off. We advise you to not return home for a couple weeks. Director Bazion has asked me to inform you that he wants you to spend all your time here or at the 3D mockup until further notice."

"What about my data collection."

"We'll just have to put that on hold."

Director Bazion felt that Ferdastad and Zurella would feel more comfortable if they knew Metongy Zeugcha was nearby, and thus arranged the rendezvous. They were briefed by the Planetary Security Service not to divulge their safe house even to Metongy Zeugcha.

~~~
~~~

Chapter Twenty-Seven

Arrests

By morning the 6 trusted men who delivered Ferdastad and Zurella to the safe house in Nimbocratus were back in Preznium at Planetary Security Service headquarters with Planetary Security Service Director Bazion and signed confession from Pirsrgyo. They had no evidence to go after Cleric Gummartukchik, but Director Bazion had ample evidence for Cleric Zrebrek's arrest.

Chomvik and the six other Planetary Security Service agents got into Skycars and flew to the Sardukretchen Temple. They landed and parked in empty Skycar slots adjacent to the Temple. A couple men guarded the rear of the temple and the rest walked briskly to the front. Two men waited outside to prevent anyone from entering or leaving. Meanwhile Chomvik and two others entered the grand cathedral which had seen

much history in 75 centuries. Today was another one of those memorable moments that left a dark mark on the Clerics. As the theory states, complete power corrupts completely. Once the Sardukretchen's recoiled from this scandal, they would clean up their act for a while until powerful figures like Gummartukchik and Zrebrek come along and focus on power struggle and control of the masses.

Cleric Gummartukchik who always operated through a surrogate never placed himself in a position of compromise. He never had any direct connections to any felonies and knew it would take a very long time to replace Cleric Zrebrek whom he knew would soon take the fall and never implicate him.

There were about 20 people in the Temple. Cleric Zrebrek just concluded services and the worshipers were standing and leaving, so Chomvik quickly exited the Sardukretchen Temple to inform the guys outside to let them exit. He then went back inside and waited for the place to clear out before he approached Zrebrek.

"We need to talk," Chomvik calmly stated as Zrebrek looked on realizing this was his *Swan Song* since **Chomvik or** Merriak had not reported back. And now suddenly here was Chomvik. None of the Clerics had information on the whereabouts of Pirsrgyo nor did they know the noose was slowly closing around them.

"What is it you want to discuss?"

"It would be best if you came with us, to our offices where it can all be done in private as to not have a spectacle to tarnish the image of the Sardukretchen Temple."

"Am I being charged with a crime?"

"Please come with us, we would like to ask you a few questions."

Since Cleric Zrebrek thought Chomvik was on his payroll, and now he wanted him to go to Planetary Security Service headquarters, it meant that all along he had probably been a double spy and there really was not much point in resisting simply replied, "As you wish," and followed him out of the Temple over to the

Skycar which he was invited to sit in the back between two agents.

In 5 minutes, Cleric Zrebrek was landing at Planetary Security Service headquarters, and in 10 minutes he was in an interrogation room. Zrebrek's role as a Cleric was now ended. All the criminal charges were now read to him including his involvement with Pirsrgyo and attempted assassination plot.

Pirsrgyo and defrocked Cleric Zrebrek were soon on an atmospheric glider and taken all the way over to the Eastern Hemisphere where the most secure prisons in the formerly Caro area exists. Prior to unification and globalization any Tauceti born Cleric captured and taken to the Eastern Hemisphere would be hanged immediately. Any present day Sardukretchen's could not help but have some tension arriving in a land that was not long ago avoided at all costs.

~~~
~~~

Chapter Twenty-Eight
Final Shuttle Testing and Loadout.

Security at the Interplanetary Transport construction site did not let up. Colonel Gujane the task master kept the troopers on their toes, and there would be no letup until the Interplanetary Transport was long on its way. Then and only then would they stand down.

The Interplanetary Transport slowly came together. Each week spelled more milestones met without any further injuries or disasters. Quality control remained high and careful attention to details led to high quality and prevention of delays.

A time slot finally arrived where the Space Dock would be depressurized, cover opened to allow actual shuttle operations for a couple weeks. During this time, both shuttles and shuttle bays were operated. The

Transport's power plant was up and operating. The only thing that wasn't operating on the Interplanetary Transport was the Cyclonic Inverters propulsion. Whether Cyclonic Inverters would be reliable and provide the thrust calculated, unfortunately would not be known until the main event while these brave Caro were on their way out of the solar system.

"Everybody ready?"

All the shuttle operators were on the main and backup Deployment Shuttles now going up to land on the Interplanetary Transport and do a few touch-and-goes.

"Looks like we are all set," Metongy Zeugcha said as he sat there contemplating his recent rendezvous with Ferdastad and Zurella Myco.

The first shuttle launched. The second waited one minute to give some separation. Onboard data terminals oversaw flight controls, the pilot and copilots were simply system monitors but could conceivably fly the shuttle in manual control if required. There was no conceivable plan to fly in manual control on this mission. That capability gave crew members some unrealistic feeling of comfort but in reality, planet re-entry required computer control, otherwise they might come in too quickly and burn up penetrating the atmosphere.

"This should be a fun ride, ride the shuttle up, do a few touch-and-goes in the shuttle bay, then come home on another backup shuttle."

"Well, this is the official loadout on the two Mission Shuttles."

"Yea once their onboard the hatches are shut, the Space Dock gets sealed back up and pressurized for final loadout and checkout."

The shuttle lifted off and soon approached the Interplanetary Transport that now had the forward shuttle bay opening.

The Mission Pilot and Co-Pilot were aboard the Interplanetary Transport to communicate and command as if they would on a mission. As part of the procedures, while on the Mission, they were not to ever leave the Interplanetary Transport. The only time they would leave would be if the Transport was in some sort of peril.

"Caro-1 this is shuttle #1 request permission to land."

"Suttle #1 permission to land granted."

The shuttle now approached the shuttle bay and soon slowly lowered into the shuttle bay. Repulser's turned into pullers as the electromagnets on the ship and the shuttle suddenly had mutual attraction.

"Energize the retractors."

"Retractors Status Indicates Activated."

"Mark Shuttle velocity towards docking position."

"Current approach velocity is two inches per second."

"Distance to the docking position is 10 feet."

"Keep this velocity until we get down to two feet from docking position then slow to one inch per second."

Moments later the Shuttle Pilot announced, "Crossing two feet from the docking position. Slowing to one inch per second and going to fully automatic."

At six inches the velocity would be further slowed and by touchdown on the docking position, the computerized target velocity would be one-fourth inch per second.

Shortly a slight bump was felt as the magnetic grabbers secured the shuttle.

"Shuttle#1, this is Caro-1, we have indications the Shuttle is stowed correctly at the docking position. Closing hatch in preparation of pressurizing Shuttle Hanger Bay compartment."

In about two minutes the shuttle bay hatch was closed and sealed followed by pressurization. Since the shuttle fit snugly in the bay a lot of air volume was not wasted so it only took a brief period to pressurize.

"Shuttle #1, shuttle bay pressure appears to be 14.5 pounds per square inch, you can now equalize the shuttle and open shuttle entry hatch."

Shuttle #2 copied the recent actions of Shuttle #1 and then they both launched and relanded on the shuttle bays doing shuttle touch and goes. In the final time they were stored for the mission. They would not be activated again until preparation to drop down to planet Earth.

One of the backup shuttles flew up to the Space Dock and retrieved the crews so they could spend some time on the planet and get their personal lives situated before they left.

Metongy Zeugcha had a slight mess to clean up and some carpet to replace from the pools of blood caused by gunshot wounds. And after the clean-up he had to hire a caretaker to look after his residence until he returned.

Once Cleric Zrebrek was convicted and sent away, Planetary Security Service Director Bazion felt it would be safe to return Ferdastad and Zurella to their home. With Zrebrek arrest, Clerics who might otherwise attempt brash moves were suddenly less active and many were semi-hiding and avoiding the Planetary Security Service.

As the crew members trained in the Interplanetary Transport Three-Dimensional Mockup and Simulator, the time quickly passed and eventually another milestone was met. The first fuel tanker arrived to the Space Dock to fill up the Interplanetary Transport fuel tanks. Most of the Space

Dock was evacuated for safety during the initial fueling in which Planetary Security Service delivered liquid oxygen, hydrogen, and petroleum.

A lot of Interplanetary Transport construction crews were systematically returned to Caro as their fabrication jobs completed. In due time the Space Dock manning shrank considerably since the Interplanetary Transport was mostly built and required no further efforts. Water and food were lastly brought aboard and after great study, the crew was reduced to a minimum which gave them ample duration to Earth and back.

Finally, after all checks were complete and final security sweep of the Space Dock and Interplanetary Transport, the crew flew on several shuttles up to the Space Dock then boarded in preparation to launch.

~~~
~~~

Chapter Twenty-Nine
On the way to Earth

Metongy Zeugcha's thoughts of the past quickly ended and suddenly he was back to the future as the Interplanetary Transport gradually increased its velocity when the Cyclonic Inverters ramped up their power.

"At seventy five percent Cyclonic Inverters power output, it will not take long for us to reach the edge of the solar system," the Pilot stated as he watched the Navigation screen that highlighted planets and stars used to plot their position.

"We'll finally discover what happens when we approach light speed," the ship's official Navigator, Doctor **Marlneiker stated.**

In due time they left behind all the planets and upon

the edge of the solar system the Cyclonic Inverters performing as envisioned accelerated them past the speed of light. With an emptier vacuum of space had such distance between hydrogen atoms they were essentially flying almost friction free in space, nothing slowed them down.

The crew developed standard routines. One of the major tasks that unquestionably remained a serious matter was the safe operation and maintenance of propulsion, electrical systems, and recyclers. Only so much water could be carried. As food was used up the resulting human waste added to the megawatts of energy released in the propulsion systems. Helium from the fusion reactors also left the ship in the plume created by the Cyclonic Inverters. The plume was readily observable while they traveled in the solar system, but once out into deep space it was no longer visible.

The Interplanetary Transport had exterior lights that blinked on and off at a definite rate. That rate appeared to change in frequency and duty cycle as the ship distanced itself from the planet and increased speed. Telescopic observation of the blink rate allowed scientists making observations with telescopes to conclude based on the Doppler associated with the speed change, they could accurately determine when the Interplanetary Transport went above light speed. It was a tense moment because there was real fear the ship would transcend into a different dimension or possibly blow up. No explosions were seen but the image created by the ship traveling above light speed left the scientists in a state of awe because it appeared they started seeing a "folding" of light information requiring special techniques to allow focus. Eventually the further the Interplanetary Transport traveled, the blinking light tracking ability faded.

The potential landing parties studied the major Earth languages and had a variety of video and audio to use as samples to emulate. Based on vast amounts of INTEL derived from the intercepts, Metongy Zeugcha's present and former teams had pieced together a significant translation and thanks in part to the video they now had some idea what the discussions meant. In many ways there were a lot of similarities to Caro, and in particular physical appearance. That major aspect would go a long way towards a more peaceful arrival and ostensibly possible future cooperation. Any possible form of trade and real time communications was out of the question due to distance.

Traveling above light speed in deep space was only a theory, they had yet to prove. If they didn't make it there in a year's time as planned, there would be some serious consequences, including most of the crew perishing. The mere thought of possible cannibalism, a distinct possibility in the event the theory didn't hold true, clearly was mildly disturbing.

Performing star fixes for navigation allowed them to accurately plot their position and at the same time calculate true velocity. The Cyclonic Inverters lost traction the further they got into deep space, but since the friction of almost a complete vacuum decreased appreciably the little traction that remained pushing against a plume continued to accelerate the Interplanetary Transport. Their destination was dead ahead, the Gamulin Star which had planet Earth circling it. So steering was simple when you had a significant marker like a star to point and approach.

When they achieved the breakthrough of light speed the only noticeable effects were the blurring of any image not directly ahead. Also, the light from the Gamulin star seemed to intensify as no doubt more photons were arriving quicker.

After the first month by plotting the blurred stars that got even more blurry along the beam, the realization was starting to form; *they would achieve their destination in about a year as predicted.* Consequently, the horrible thoughts of being marooned in space and forced to Cannibalization for the few remaining crew members that would be the last to die off no longer existed. The only risk now was getting hit by an asteroid on the way to Earth or receiving a nasty reception that might result in their inability to return home.

The plan was to obtain Earth Orbit and study the planet a while before exposing their presence to the civilization on the planet. Along the way, Metongy

Zeugcha and Doctor Provkovitev spent many hours in the analyst's room where they could continue study and decipher more incoming information.

~~~
~~~

Chapter Thirty
Earth and Caro Signals are Lost

About the one and a half month mark out in space Metongy Zeugcha noted, "The signals coming from earth were showing a remarkable decline in signal strength."

"Nothing changed on earth, life was as routine as possible, so nothing happened on earth, only the signals became weaker, and it became more difficult to receive and clean up and process with the onboard Preconvolver and the Electro Clarifier" replied Doctor Provkovitev.

"We know our systems are working because Caro signals arriving now that were broadcast a year ago though declining as we ventured out in deep space were more than adequate to receive and process and prove the equipment is not malfunctioning."

"What do you think is happening to the signals?" Doctor

Provkovitev asked.

"The only way adequate signals could have gotten to Caro must have been because of a convergence zone. We simply are now out of the convergence zone and soon may not be able to receive any Earth signals until we get a lot closer."

"As expected, signal strength eventually decreased below our ability to process as the signals were buried so deep in space noise, reconstruction was virtually impossible," Metongy Zeugcha stated a few days later after spending several hours in super Caro effort to pull out the most minute signal decibel levels.

As they continued the voyage, safe operating and recycling continued. As time passed, they switched weekly from using recycled water to using fresh water. However, bathing and food preparation only used recycled water.

The artificial gravity only achieved slightly more than weightlessness, so showers were not appropriate until they got near a planet again. As an alternative, they stepped into a bathing suit about once a week. It filled and vented at the same time capturing any possible water that might otherwise overflow. Temperature was nicely controlled. Everyone spent typically 30 minutes in the bathing suit soaking and then drained it which sent the water to recyclers.

Soap was not used, and everyone wore a shaved head using electric razors with built in vacuum to keep air particles out of the atmosphere. People expected to go to the planet surface stopped cutting their hair off in the last month to look more natural to the Aliens.

Urination and bowel movements required another sort of equipment which also had unique collectors. In essence due to stringent policy of personal hygiene to help prevent or contain any possible disease, the crew remained relatively physically healthy.

Mental health was another issue, but since they were able to limit the voyage to one year, that concern was highly diminished from what it could have been.

When all contact from earth was lost, Metongy said, "There was plenty of information already obtained which allowed them to further study and figure out conditions on earth."

Doctor Provkovitev noted: "By the time of the loss of Earth

signals, it was apparent the planet was slowly evolving into another period of international strife."

"In many ways the Earthlings parallel the Caro in the way we had similar periods over a 150,000-year period."

For the following 9 months nothing much changed other than shortly after losing Earth signals, Caro signals also diminished and thus they received no external signals other than images of the stars themselves which they used to update their navigation.

~~~

Then approximately one month out from Earth as the Gamulin star was growing noticeably larger and brighter, they finally started receiving weak Earth Signals.

"These signals are kind of hard to process; we can only get spotty hits now and then." Metongy Zeugcha noted.

"Yea when we get good signal, it usually lasts only a minute or two before its signal level is just too low to process."

"I would estimate they will improve as we get closer."

And as predicted in a few more days they did start getting
~~~

better, even though lots of holes in data streams, they were at least getting sixty percent of the content they could read and analyze.

"They're holding a major election in America."

"When is the election results?"

"The date is tomorrow which means at our velocity we'll know in a few hours."

The novelty of the election captivated several crew members.

"Earth's political systems are nothing like the Caro."

"Yes. Elections on Earth appear extremely obsolete."

"They're probably a lot like how we used to be."

As events unfolded election results were being announced on audio and visual channels, the Earthlings commonly referred to as radio and television.

"It appears a man named John F. Kennedy, is America's new leader."

Within hours they observed Kennedy's acceptance speech.

"He sends an inspiring message."

"Too bad he's not a world leader; his disposition would benefit the planet."

"Unfortunately, that's the way Caro used to be."

"And we lost almost half the Caro population because of it."

~~~
~~~

Chapter Thirty-One
Arrival to Earth

As the Caro approached the solar system approximately what Earth men would measure as four Astronomical Units (149.6 million kilometers) from the Gamulin star, the Navigator Doctor **Marlneiker** informed the Pilot, Metongy Zeugcha and Doctor Provkovitev all gathered in the control room for the expected activity: "It is now time to reorientate the Interplanetary Transport to slow down."

"Right about now is the time the hydrogen levels in space near the solar system increases would be the point we can get good traction for effective breaking," the Co-pilot added.

"We'll feel that traction real soon," the Pilot added.

"We run the risk of being spotted from Earth," The

Co-pilot noted.

"They will know sooner or later we are here; it might be the sooner is better for us anyway," Doctor Provkovitev responded.

The pilot made an announcement over the intercom system, "Crew, this is the captain speaking, in a few minutes we will be spinning the ship around so that we can use the Cyclonic Inverters to slow us down. We plan on using the large planet to obscure our view and will apply major thrust at that time. You will feel some vibration when that occurs."

The ship had been without any major vibration for a while since once they reached the cruise velocity, they no longer had to operate the Cyclonic Inverters until now.

At the proper moment just as the pilot promised, the ship was spun around right when Earth vanished behind planet Saturn in relative motion. The Cyclonic Inverters powered on, the crew could feel vibration but not much G forces, because the vacuum was still relatively thin.

However, at their velocity that would soon change as they were now entering the solar system.

Making star plots and observing the planets in the solar system they quickly determined the velocity of the ship was slowing. By the time they passed Saturn they would be one half-light speed and could then reorientation the ship, flipping it 180 degrees to point the bow of the Interplanetary Transport in the direction of their heading. At the slower speed and thicker hydrogen content in the vacuum of space, the Cyclonic Inverters had reversers which at the slower speed would further slow the ship which they would not do until they were past the distance of Jupiter that would take them down to one quarter light speed.

About this time technicians started performing checkouts of the two shuttles and diagnostics which had gone on monthly indicated that no faults were detected.

Communications were monitored carefully, and signal strength now was excellent to where they now achieved receiving many radio frequency radiators from planet earth. Later they reached a point when the

Cyclonic Inverters were reversed and added greatly to the breaking. Crew Members could feel the negative G Forces as the ship slowed down and gradually curved towards and Earth orbit.

"Here we are, we made it." Metongy Zeugcha said joyously as they now realized the chances of being marooned in space were long over and they had two operational Shuttles to get them to planet surface.

Doctor Provkovitev then stated the obvious, "We proved all the theory, now its fact and history."

"It took some effort to get here," Metongy Zeugcha replied and at the same time remembered the entire decisive and bitter struggle back on Caro that it took to make all this possible.

"Think about what our presence will soon have on all these earth people."

"No doubt our arrival will shake the foundation of their beliefs."

"Most likely their own Clerics will have a bad day real soon."

"Especially if they are caught perpetuating lies, myths, and conjecture."

"I hope we don't have to experience the same from their Clerics as we did our own."

"That's why we only deal strictly with their government and not get involved in any local politics or religions."

The Interplanetary Transport gradually curved into Earth orbit about 500 miles above the planet. From this distance, the space telescope could see population centers and they systematically mapped all the radio and television stations as well as detected military radars and communications equipment including mobile systems on ships and aircraft.

"The electronic macro picture of Earth is quite impressive for a primitive society."

"How far advanced compared to them do you think we are?"

"Most likely we are thousands of years more advanced."

"What makes you think that?"

"Their low altitude aircraft we've tracked, the slow-moving surface rail cars, and tremendously slow ships point to a primativie culture."

"Just because they do not have 160 miles per hour ocean going shipping is not a big deal."

"Well, there is clearly one other element, they do not have the millions of communicators in use that you would observe at any given moment on Caro."

"I suppose that's a good example."

"Especially since we do not see the use of any communicators."

"Well, they do have some radio communications."

"Certainly, that's what we'll have to rely on when we attempt contacting them since we've not heard from them."

"It's as if they don't know we are here."

"It's quite possible they do not know."

"The question now is, when would we start contacting the planet?"

"I think we need a couple more orbits to get more data

as we map the planet. We still have many areas we haven't fully mapped."

"Ok let's get the crew together for a discussion before we proceed."

It didn't take long before the general consensus was, "We came and found what we were looking for, now us head home."

"Our Mission is to meet people from Earth and establish a basis for future contact, and possibly cooperation."

"The planet is too far away to have any meaningful trade," a crew member stated.

"We need to leave them with the feeling we are not a threat to them and have no design on their solar system," Doctor Provkovitev responded.

"You can't predict they will believe us. This could actually backfire and make them into an adversary," the crewmember angrily countered.

"Our mission milestones are clear; we have an obligation to Caro to fulfill. After all, let me remind you, this is the very first discovery of Alien life outside our planet. We have a moral obligation to the people of Caro to send a peaceful message to them because if they discover us before we convince them we are peaceful creatures; they might actually become a serious threat to our planet." Doctor Provkovitev replied.

"It would take Earth centuries to develop Cyclonic Inverters necessary to reach our planet," Metongy Zeugcha added.

"What if they come up with something as efficient in the meantime?" the crew member asked.

"Looking at all their primitive equipment that is highly doubtful," Metongy Zeugcha responded.

~~~

At that same moment, a Colonel walked into General Curtis Lemay's office in the Pentagon, "Sir we have some kind of an Extra-terrestrial Alien spaceship orbiting the
~~~

planet now."

The General looked up at the Colonel and responded, "You can't be serious Colonel?"

"General, we have received reports from NORAD at Ent Airforce Base out in Colorado Springs. At first they thought it might be a Russian Space Craft until staff members claimed they traced the object arriving from way outside earth's orbit."

"So, where is this supposed space craft now?"

"Apparently it's now in Earth Orbit approximately 500 miles above the planet."

"Who's in charge out at Ent Air Force Base?"

"Ent is actually detachment of Peterson Air Force base."

"Who's in charge at Peterson?"

"Major General West, sir."

"Ask Major General West to call me right away."

"Yes sir."

The first thing that popped into General Lemay's head

was, *"Do we shoot it down or do we try to communicate with it?"*

The sudden appearance of the Caro Interplanetary Transport arrived just in time to justify the construction of Cheyenne Mountain that had already started in 1961.

General LeMay, a major figure in World War Two, and not well liked and remembered by the Japanese in Tokyo, had been instrumental in upgrading the Air Force as well as strategic forces. LeMay was not initially the head of the Strategic Air Command. That honor fell to General George Churchill Kenney.

Kenney enlisted as a flying cadet in the Aviation Section, U.S. Signal Corps in 1917, and served during WW1 on the Western Front with the 91st Aero Squadron. He was awarded a Silver Star and the Distinguished Service Cross for actions in which he fought off German fighters and shot two down.

Kenney's ability to get along with MacArthur and Sutherland in many ways resulted in the success he manifested in the SWPA in particular, places such as New Guinea.

In 1948 President Truman requested Charles A. Lindbergh review Strategic Air Command operations which Lindbergh wrote a scathing report concerning Strategic Air Command (SAC) operations in the air and at six SAC bases which resulted in General Kenney removed as Commanding General on 15 October 1948 and replaced on 19 October 1948 by Lieutenant General Curtis Lemay.

Kenney had known Charles Lindbergh from the war when he had him teach his P-38 pilots how to extend the range of their aircraft. Lindbergh's success in doing so, not only extended the range of the fighters, but allowed daytime bombing when escorts were able to stay with the B-17's all the way to the target and back which had a huge impact on subsequent battles.

General LeMay took a troubled SAC and in a few years remolded it into an incredible force that not only the Soviets respected but feared gravely.

Now suddenly thrust upon General LeMay was an event that tested every moral fiber and challenged his inner strength like nothing before including dealing with the Soviets and the Japanese.

Not since General Curtis LeMay initiated the Berlin airlift, then reorganized the Strategic Air Command into an effective instrument of nuclear war, was he suddenly challenged to such a major event when the Caro arrived.

Throughout his career, LeMay was widely and fondly known among his troops as "Old Iron Pants," and the "Big Cigar" which he always seemed to have in his mouth. LeMay had a reputation of emphasizing training as the key to saving lives. "You train as you fight"; was one of his cardinal rules.

General Curtis LeMay believed that while experiencing chaos, stress, and confusion of aerial combat, airmen will perform successfully, only if their individual acts are as second-nature, performed instinctively. Repetitive training in the midst of their actions allowed them to no longer require consciously reflecting upon what they are doing allowing them to simply do what they were required to do.

It was LeMay's second nature actions that now guided his reaction to the seemingly impossible revelation that some Alien ship was arrogantly orbiting the Earth.

General LeMay also did not underestimate the Soviet's propensity to pull stunts to embarrass the United States and waited patiently for the phone call.

The Colonel walked back into his office and said, "General LeMay, I have General West on the phone, line three."

General Lemay nodded, grabbed the black telephone receiver, punched in button number three, and said, "General West, glad you called me."

"General Lemay, I apologize for not calling you direct, we have a lot of information we are sifting through to figure out what we have on our hands right now."

"That's alright General West, you at least had your men call Colonel North and give him heads up for me. What's the latest?"

"General LeMay, we are sending up some reconnaissance aircraft now that have telescopes on board, we use to photograph Soviet Satellites flying at 65,000 feet to eliminate atmospheric blurring. We expect to get some pictures back in 30 minutes."

"No sign of communications from this Alien Spaceship?"

"Nothing yet sir."

"Do you have this thing on any radars?"

"We are only able to track it on one NORAD radar we developed to track ICBM's."

"General West call me back when you get the pictures and fax me a good sample of what you get."

"We will do that right away General Lemay."

~~~

The United States Air Force RB-57D was a high-altitude reconnaissance version of the B-57 Canberra Nuclear Bomber built by the British which the United States Air Force acquired to use as a stop gap until the U2 spy planes were completed. Considered a failure as a nuclear bomber due to lack of speed, it had most redeeming qualities as a photo reconnaissance plane because of the high lift the long wings provided.

The United States Air Force RB-57D reconnaissance plane with tail number 33977 was currently waiting for the upcoming mission inside a restricted hanger at Peterson Air
~~~

Force Base at Colorado Springs. This special purpose RB-57D was refueled and ready for another mission real soon as the CIA had forecast a new RORSAT launch out of Russia.

The RB-57D had a range more than 2000 nautical miles that could operate at altitudes of 65,000 feet which would be the case today.

Soviet Naval RORSAT' reconnaissance satellites often launched to coincide with major NATO and American Navy maneuvers.

The U.S. Pacific Fleet did an exercise once every few years with its Asian Allies to practice Naval Warfare in case the unexpected happened and the Soviets attacked.

RORSATs exhibited large radar antennas used to bounce signals off the ocean to monitor ship movements. These radars required substantial signal strength to work effectively. Because of the relatively backward state of electronics technology in the Eastern Bloc, Soviet designers adopted an innovative solution. They installed a small nuclear reactor in the RORSAT to power the radar.

Although prototype RORSATS's in the early-1960s flew

with only chemical batteries, the CIA had discovered a test model powered by reactors would soon be launched. The RB-57D remained in a readiness condition for that purpose when General West ordered the mission to get it air born but instead of looking for a Soviet satellite, they would be searching for an Alien ship.

The conference room where the Pilot, Co-Pilot and Telescope operator for the mission waited for the briefing, had an element of electricity in the air.

Air Force people had heard rumors about Roswell New Mexico and Aztec New Mexico UFO crashes, but those rumors had been squelched by a huge disinformation campaign, so the pilot looked in disbelief when he was given his mission.

"We expect you will be Airborne in 15 minutes. Here are some rough coordinates of where we want you to look where we expect you to see the space craft."

"Is this the RORSATS satellite with the new liquid sodium cooled reactor we expected the Soviets to launch any day?"

"No, that project is now on the back burner, we got bigger

fish to fry."

"Major Riley, and crew members, you will consider the following information is TOP SECRET and Q Clearance level information. You are already covered by non-disclosure agreements, so that will not be necessary at this time, but be aware, you are not to discuss this matter with anyone not in this room for any reasons unless IAW Q level direction you specifically are permitted in writing, signed by the Secretary of the Air Force to discuss it."

"Understand Sir."

"Gentlemen, this is possibly a UFO."

"We'll be looking for some type of Alien Spacecraft?"

"Yes, we think it's an Alien Spacecraft that did not originate on this planet."

"You have ruled out a possible Soviet or Chinese Spacecraft?"

"No. We can't reveal how we discovered it. This is a sensitive technology that you are not cleared for."

"That's pretty amazing."

"Ok Gentlemen, this concludes the briefing. You are to man your plane, get up to 65,000 feet and get those pictures as soon as possible. We'll give you the best coordinates we can while you are in flight. Try to remain over Colorado Springs so that when we give you angular positional data your camera will be pointing as close as possible to the object to help you find it."

"Understand all," Major Riley responded, then stood up followed by his crew and walked the short distance to his plane.

A tow rig was attached to the front wheel of the plane. As soon as all the crew members were aboard and the ground crew was informed via sound powered phone hookup directly to the pilot, "We are ready to move out of the hanger."

The RB-57D was slowly pulled out and turned sideways so that the Jet Engine exhaust would not directly hit the hanger so that crews would not have to shut the hanger door. About that time the pilot started up the Jet Engines and went through an abbreviated check list, since the plane was in the constant state of readiness, it was checked several times per day by the crew.

As soon as everything was sat, the tow rig was disconnected, and the plane was now able to continue on its own.

The plane slowly made its way to runway 31 which pointed to the Northwest directly into the wind. The long wings of the RB-57D and the very capable jet engines would have really good lift and get up to altitude quickly. On board Navigation equipment such as the Loran C would allow it to keep near Colorado Springs in an overcast day. However, today the snow-covered Pikes Peak would allow visual flight for station keeping way above commercial traffic.

The pilot shoved the throttles forward and the Martin RB-57D rolled forward promptly and the crew could feel the G forces in this very capable aircraft. With its powerful jet engines, today the crew would experience max takeoff capability as the pilot lifted and held level until even with the control tower then pulled near vertical for approximately 3000 feet then nosed over just a bit, to a 60–70-degree climb.

The telescope mounted just forward of the wings was currently in its stowed position and would not be raised vertical until they reached the thin air above 50,000 feet. With only half the fuel onboard the plane was lighter and could climb faster. They didn't need the extra fuel since this would be a short flight.

The plane continued in a corkscrew fashion like somewhat of an oval track gaining altitude remaining within 10 miles of Peterson Field. At 50,000 feet the pilot directed the telescope operator to deploy the scope which was more of a manual operation by a large hand wheel connected to a gear train. Once they got the scope near the target, the telescope operator had a positioning indicator system tracking the target on the X, Y and Z axis which would signal the pilot which direction he needed to position the plane. The process was fairly simple and for tracking satellites it allowed high resolution photographs while the satellite passed over head.

The Alien ship was coming over for another pass, timing was perfect. It would be almost directly overhead about the time they reached 65,000 feet with almost no turbulence whatsoever.

"Smooth as a baby's ass," the telescope operator said all smiles as he loaded the film package on the telescope barrel, flipped a couple switches and soon saw a green indicator signaling the film was positioned to take a series of photographs.

The pilot said over the intercom, "NORAD says the object should be almost directly overhead."

"Looking for the spacecraft sir," the Telescope operator replied.

The air crewman had some control with the large hand wheel to reposition the telescope and even some canting with a second wheel, but for the most part the pilot would have to re-orient the aircraft. By getting headings from ground controllers, they could take at least one angle out of the calculation which allowed the necessity to only have to work the big hand wheel until contact was made.

Because of the angle of the sun, the Alien ship was bathed in light and made it easy to find. Unlike finding a small satellite, the telescope operator nearly crapped his pants when the image came in focus.

"I'll be god damned!" The telescope operator said then started clicking pictures.

The Telescope Operator had photographed numerous objects in space at approximately the altitude of the Alien Spacecraft. He had never seen anything so large and strange looking like what he now observed.

"This is a huge Son of a Bitch." The Telescope Operator said which instantly made other crew members nearby instantly interested in the observations. It was obvious that as soon as he finished taking pictures, they wanted to look through the telescope as their curiosity was peaked like never before!

The Telescope Operator was forever changed. His moral and ethical values now were modified unlike any other event in his life including marriages, funerals, births, and tragedies he had seen flying over Korea almost 10 years before.

After taking what must have been 100 pictures and letting his buddies such as the radar and ESM operators look through the telescope at the Alien ship, the Telescope Operator notified the pilot, "I think I have enough pictures, you can return to base."

The pilot didn't have to fly very far, just point the nose

down 60 degrees and deploy some flaps. In less than 15 minutes he was rolling up to a stop parallel in front of the hanger and shut down the engines.

The photo reconnaissance technician was the first one off the aircraft and had two military police escort him over to the photo reconnaissance lab where developers were standing by. General West and Colonel Schmidt were standing there patiently waiting for the results.

Everyone in the room was read security requirements as technicians started developing the film. As the first pictures came out of the chemicals and the image was perfectly developed, General West stared at it knowing he had a piece of dynamite in his hands.

Absolute secrecy was necessary and people above him would have to determine the following course of events. He would soon have an INTEL officer explain to him that based on the altitude of the aircraft and distance established by radar of around 500 miles, the true dimension of the space craft was somewhere around possibly up to one half mile long. Calibrated measurements would soon come in by a few cleared scientists who would first do some fast calculations with their slide rules, and when they didn't like the results, keyed some numbers into their new Sperry Univac computer that would do a sanity check for them, but nevertheless return almost the same results they got off their slide rules using Trig and log tables.

General West took the first photograph and put it in a yellow envelope and said, "I will take this to my office, the rest of the pictures, you take custody Colonel Schmidt. Lock them up in our safe until we are directed what to do with them and the negatives."

From the photo reconnaissance lab to General West's office was a short walk. He went into his office, shut the door, and then called General LeMay.

"General LeMay, I'm ready to send a photograph of the Alien ship to you."

"General West, do you have a Finch Facsimile machine?"

"Yes, I do, General LeMay."

"Alright General West, give me five minutes to get my FAX machine all set up and you can start sending."

In a few minutes the stylus arm in the Finch machine was oscillating back and forth slowly burning an image onto the thermal paper in General LeMay's office.

If this revelation wasn't bad enough, General West called back in a few minutes to inform General LeMay that based on the size of the object at the telescope magnification levels and distance; *they believed it was possibly one-half mile long.*

General LeMay having firsthand witnessed massive destruction during World War Two, could easily surmise the sophistication and capability an Extra-Terrestrial Alien Civilization that had the technology to arrive here from a long distance away, felt a sudden frightening emotion. He seriously doubted the world could defend itself from these Aliens.

"Why are they here?" he wondered.

Good thing General LeMay was at the Pentagon, he didn't have to walk far to see the Joint Chiefs.

The American joint chiefs were happy they were three steps ahead of the CIA who had not found out about the Alien ship, so they were able to brief President Kennedy before Dulles and his gang could swoop in and take credit for the discovery. After the Joint Chiefs concurred on the Presidential briefing, Lemay was on his way.

The Pentagon's air traffic controller contacted the secret service and received permission for General LeMay's helicopter to land at the White House helicopter pad. Two miles away from the White House the helicopter pilots were given permission by the secret service to land as LeMay's appointment with Kennedy had been just confirmed by Kenneth Patrick "Kenny" O'Donnell, Kennedy's appointments secretary. The secret service then had the grounds keepers move the three removable aluminum discs which accommodate the helicopter's individual landing gear out on the South Lawn. Such actions were reserved for rare visits from the Joint Chiefs and the Head of the CIA and usually during urgent matters.

At a mile out the helicopter pilot saw the three aluminum disks being put into position and he slowed the speed to make sure they had enough time to get them set properly and then get out of the way of the helicopter.

Only five minutes lapsed from notification until the

Sikorsky S-61L helicopter touchdown. This was a rather large helicopter, but LeMay needed the accommodation for his staff he sometimes had to fly to Andrews Air Force Base to hop on Lockheed L-1049 Super Constellation Transports to inspect bases around the world. Since only he and his bodyguard were on the helicopter it would appear excessive, but LeMay preferred the Sikorsky S-61L helicopter reliability compared to all others. Plus, it had an outstanding range of nearly 500 miles and could fly at 165 miles per hour.

Shortly after the helicopter touched down on the South Lawn, LeMay and the Colonel stepped off the Helicopter and were met by a Marine Captain who saluted and a couple secret service agents to escort them into the White House from the South Lawn entrance which was normally reserved for world leaders and significant dignitaries. Moments later they were escorted into the Oval Office where everyone except LeMay, the Colonel and Kennedy's brother Robert were asked to leave the room.

"When did this Alien UFO arrive?"

"The best we can determine was about four hours ago."

The President stared at the facsimile which had pretty good detail in spite the fact it was a replica of a picture created by stylus running over the thermal paper.

Nobody knew anything about the ship or its motives, but Kennedy understood the implications: *The world situation just got a lot more complicated.*

"Any indication the Russians know about this ship?"

"Not yet, but we anticipate amateur astronomers will soon find it and they will certainly know about it shortly afterwards."

"Thank you for bringing me that picture, can I keep it?"

"Mr. President this is Q level clearance material, you don't have proper storage in the White House, and we need to take it back to the Pentagon. We can bring it back if you need to see it again."

"Okay, thanks."

LeMay and the Colonel were quickly escorted out of the Oval Office back to the waiting helicopter which was airborne and not allowed to fly over the white house moments later. LeMay was back in his office 10 minutes later with the picture.

In the Kremlin, Khrushchev was being advised by one of the GRU men, "The Americans have evidently launched another space craft now orbiting the planet."

"Did they show the launch on TV?"

"No, not a peep out of them."

"Must be some kind of military craft they are keeping away from public knowledge."

"We are attempting to find out; thus far we have not got any reports from our agents."

"That's odd."

"It certainly is."

"Keep me informed if you find out something."

"Certainly."

<p style="text-align:center">~~~</p>

Chapter Thirty-Two

The Caro Acquire Vast Amounts of Earth Data

After about four hours Earth time, Doctor Provkovitev reported, "The Interplanetary Transport crew has photographed or through the use of direction-finding radio intercepts, identified and mapped most of the cities in the northern hemisphere database."

A computer graphic showed up on the console Doctor Provkovitev was sitting at which had labels now showing on the data terminal screen.

"Are we above Denver, and Colorado Springs?" Metongy Zeugcha asked.

"That's pretty close, yes."

"Maybe it might be good to establish a geostationary orbit here, that way we will only have to deal with the

English language?"

"Since we've mapped the rest of the Northern Hemisphere, I see why not," the pilot responded.

The Caro Interplanetary Transport pilot then punched in a couple controls on the automation processor and orders were given to the auto throttles controlling the Cyclonic Inverter which did a series of some miner thrusts to get the ship into that geosynchronous orbit.

The advantage of the geosynchronous orbit was soon discovered. Several radio stations in Denver and Colorado Springs were soon picked up. Doctor Provkovitev monitoring the radio intercept receivers discovered some very pleasant music he isolated to a frequency. He then said to those crew members in the control room, "I'm going to put some music on the speaker coming from a Denver Colorado radio station, I think you will be interested in hearing it."

The crewmembers quickly took a liking to the nice sounding music that played for a while and when it finished a narrator discussed some current events, then more music was played.

~~~
~~~

Chapter Thirty-Three
CIA – AIRFORCE TURF BATTLE

Allen Dulles was quite surprised when his spy from over at the pentagon gave him a sudden phone call.

"Allen, this is Jerry."

"Hello Jerry. I'm surprised to hear from you this time of day."

"Well, it's kind of an emergency."

"Please explain."

"Air Force has just briefed the President about a UFO."

"That happens all the time, no big deal."

"It is now, Air Force just showed the President a photograph they took an hour or so ago."

"Where was the UFO?"

"It's in orbit 500 miles above the planet."

"How did they get the picture then?"

"They flew the Martin RB-57D out of Peterson Field in Colorado Springs that was on standby for Soviet RORSATS's."

"If the UFO is 500 miles above Earth, it must not be much of a picture?"

"It's a huge ship, probably a half mile long."

"Does General LeMay know about this?"

"Yes, he's the person who briefed the President and has been in contact with General West out at Peterson Field."

"Okay, thanks for information, Admiral."

"No problem, Allen."

Dulles hung up then called Curtis LeMay.

"LeMay here."

"General this is Allen Dulles; I would like to come by and talk with you."

"I'll be here most of the day, come on by."

"I'll be there shortly."

Dulles then buzzed his secretary, Mary Perkins and said, "Come into my office for a minute."

"Yes Mr. Dulles, what can I do for you?"

"Get Richard Bissell and Tracey Barnes and have them come to my office right away, they will be going over to the Pentagon with me in a short while."

Dulles knew that Bissell had good working relations with LeMay, and Tracey Barnes was one of the DD/P's best special projects man, would go with him to speak to LeMay *and help figure out why the Air Force just sand bagged him with the President.*

~~~

The Interplanetary Transport had not received any communications from the planet. Timing was somewhat lucky for them because the United States had just performed High-altitude nuclear explosions and would not have any new weapons available until 1963. Otherwise, it was
~~~

feasible they could have either destroyed or damaged the Interplanetary Transport.

Perhaps their salvation stemmed from them not making any sudden moves and patiently waiting for the Earth to make its move, so they showed great restraint and it began a game of who's watching who. The Caro were seemingly nervous to make the wrong move and were hoping they would be contacted first.

"Is there any indication we've been spotted by Earth Forces?" Metongy Zeugcha asked.

"So far no communications or chatter or threatening moves," Doctor Provkovitev responded as he continued to monitor communications channels.

"Life appears to be going on down on the planet without any knowledge or concern of us being here. I would think we'd hear about it if we were spotted."

"I've been monitoring Denver TV channels, life there appears interesting. Those people certainly have a lot more area to live in."

"Yes, not congested like Caro."

"I was tracking some of the contrails from their aircraft."

"What's their velocity?"

"The fastest seem to be around 550 miles per hour."

"Their slow transportation probably requires a lot of time to go great distances."

"Nothing like our Atmospheric Gliders."

"Their trains are not fast either, maybe 70 or 80 miles per hour on the average."

"They have such vast agriculture zones."

"That's one advantage they have over Caro. I bet it's nice not having to eat synthesized food all the time."

Metongy Zeugcha looked at the Pilot and said, "Captain, I suggest if they do not contact us by tomorrow, we should initiate communications to them."

"We've identified some military communications frequencies. We might want to start with them."

"What if they don't answer?"

"We have provisions for turning on strobe lights when

we are on the dark side of the planet. That should get their attention."

"We don't want to cause any chaos; I hope we can avoid that."

"It's part of our operation plan just in case we had problems communicating."

"If we use their amplitude modulated or frequency modulated communications links, we should be able to establish high quality communications."

"I have no doubt that once we start communicating to them, they will respond immediately."

"I'm surprised they have not spotted our ship?"

"Perhaps they have, they are just figuring out how to respond. No doubt they have people on the planet similar to our Clerics who want to control the masses and are figuring out a proper response."

"I'm sure they are just as afraid of losing power and control as our Clerics have been."

~~~
~~~

Tracey Barnes showed up first at Allen Dulles office followed by Richard Bissell a few minutes later.

Allen Dulles office was essentially part of a SKIF commonly referred to as a Sensitive Compartmented Information Facility. Inside there when the door was closed it was cleared for Q level information and communications. This was going to be an interesting event.

"The reason why I called you guys over here, I think this fall under the DD/P preview and what I'm about to tell you may cause you to think I'm nuts, I don't care, but we need to take care of it."

Bissell who had gotten to know Allen Dulles quite well during the U2 spy plane project and now the A12's being designed and built, and a few test-flights already successfully occurred, they were ready to deploy them to Okinawa. Hence, Bissell was seeing more of Dulles lately. The Bay of Pigs was right around the corner and Tracey Barnes who assisted Frank Wisner in planning that mission including training the B25 bomber crews, was also quickly becoming one of Dulles fair haired boys. Frank Wisner unfortunately had a mental breakdown under enormous pressure he had been in the late stages of the Eisenhower administration. Bissell who inherited the plan and had nothing much to do with it, was eventually held responsible by Kennedy and fired. But those days were yet to come.

"Well Allen we often have some of those strange stories in the DD/P, I'm sure it's something we can handle."

"I got a call from one of my top sources in the Pentagon, a well-placed person very close to the joint chiefs. He informed me that NORAD out in Colorado detected an Alien UFO and is currently tracking it."

"We've heard all those stories before."

"What you didn't hear before is they sent up an RB-57D they use to photograph Soviet Satellites and it came back with some very impressive pictures."

"Is that so?"

"That's why I called you guys over here. We are leaving in a few minutes and will be going to General Curtis LeMay's office to confront him about sandbagging us with the President."

"How did he do that?"

"He took the picture over and showed Kennedy a couple hours ago."

"I thought LeMay is one of our friends?"

"He is but he's also self-serving."

"So why do you want us to go with you to the Pentagon?"

"I want you to help me size up General LeMay and if we don't get the answers out of him like I want, I'm sending you guys to Colorado Springs to pay a visit to General West who's in charge of the photo reconnaissance group at Peterson Field."

"What if West blows us off and refuses to cooperate?"

"Well then you just have to explain to him what the *Cash in Advance Boys* in the DD/P does to people who do not want to play ball."

"We can certainly help him or hurt him."

"His maintenance budget probably sucks as well as a lot of other things we could help him with, such as getting his name moved up the promotion ladder so he can jump ahead of some of his West Point classmates, since he was originally with the Army Air Corp."

"I'm sure he would appreciate that."

"Ok, shall we?" Allen said as he opened the door and nodding with his head to signal to come along.

They walked 30 feet past a security door, then a short distance to the elevator and rode it down from the 5th floor.

Allen Dulles didn't walk to any cars, they followed him right out to the lawn where his private helicopter was waiting.

The Bell UH-1 Iroquois had a capacity to lift 3,880 lb. which could haul 14 troops, or six stretchers, or equivalent cargo. The pilot and co-pilot both carried submachine guns, and there were seats set up in the back to carry six passengers for CIA business which happened frequently, as this chopper went between Langley, White House, Pentagon, Camp David, Andrews Air Force Base, and on occasion Norfolk Virginia usually to an Aircraft Carrier either coming or going.

From Langley to the Pentagon was a short helicopter ride. Had they gone through traffic, then maybe it might take one hour or more depending on road congestion.

The chopper pilot and co-pilot were both Army majors assigned to the CIA. From time to time, they would have to fly other kinds of missions including plucking agents out of harm's way, such as they had done at least a couple times with Tracey Barnes in places like Guatemala and various Caribbean Islands.

The Bell UH-1 Iroquois helicopter touched down at the landing pad right next to the Pentagon. The men got out and were immediately escorted to the main entrance of the Pentagon and in a short period of time into one of the inner rings where General LeMay had his office. In this area, security was tight, but they knew dam well who Allen Dulles was. As such he was quickly escorted into LeMay's inner office with Tracey Barnes and Richard M. Bissel.

"Hello General LeMay."

"Director Dulles, good to see you again."

"Thank you."

"Can I get you guys some coffee or anything."

"No that will not be necessary," Allen Dulles replied as he knew General Curtis LeMay most likely wanted to stall.

"Please have a seat."

The General's Aid, a nice-looking female blonde, took LeMay's nod, left the room and closed the door to give the men privacy.

"What brings you here, Director Dulles?"

"General LeMay, I was extremely disappointed that you took the picture of the UFO and briefed the President."

"I thought it was an urgent matter."

"As you know General, it's the CIA's responsibility to brief the president, your job is to provide the CIA with the information so we can vet it and select what the President receives so he doesn't get overwhelmed down in the weeds reading too much information that will distract him from other important work."

"As you can probably appreciate, the information was highly classified and we were worried about leaks and wanted to restrict dissemination not only to Q clearance holders, but also those who really have the need to know."

"Okay General, I said my part, and hope that in the future you see where I'm coming from and attempt to cooperate."

"I always cooperate."

"General, can you tell us about the UFO? Do you have a photograph we can examine?"

General LeMay took the yellow envelope off his desk and pulled out the facsimilia and handed it to Allen Dulles.

Dulles stared at the UFO picture for a while then handed it to Bissell who looked who then handed it to Tracey Barnes.

"It's hard to gauge the size of the Spacecraft in that picture."

"That's a big spaceship. The picture was taken from 500 miles away."

"How big do you think the Spacecraft is?"

"Our photo interpreter experts think at least half a mile long."

General Lemay could see the body language on Allen

Dulles shift as he recoiled from the UFO picture.

"Has the UFO contacted us or have we attempted to contact it?"

"There have been no communications from the Alien Space Craft. I'm waiting for President to make a decision on how he wants to deal with this situation."

The meeting soon broke up and the CIA men soon left the Pentagon, went back to Langley by the Helicopter.

"Ok Richard and Tracey, I want you guys to take the corporate jet to Colorado Springs and pay General West a visit and find out everything he knows about the UFO."

"Understand." Richard Bissell said assuming the lead as his role in the DD/P overshadowed Tracey Barnes who thought he should be the man because he was closer to Frank Wisner.

"One last thing, when you talk to me remotely; use the code word BUFFALO to indicate the UFO."

"We will address the subject by the name, BUFFALO," Richard Bissell stated.

Allen Dulles got out of the Bell UH-1 Iroquois helicopter which soon took off again and flew Bissell and Barnes to Andrews Air Force base. At Andrews inside a high security hanger where only Presidents or CIA planes parked, sat a Swiss American Aircraft Corporation SAAC-23. This forerunner to Lear Jets was the beginning of the private Jet Era. Swiss American Aircraft Corporation eventually sold out to Lear Corporation which moved the company to Wichita Kansas where it blossomed into the first successful private business jet company.

Before the buyout and transfer, SAAC was unable to sell enough jets to make it a viable financially successful venture. The design by Swiss, German, French, and British engineers was sound, but it was reported later that Swiss workers were lazy, and the failure of the company was solely based on a poor production schedule.

The Cash in Advance boys quickly saw the advantage of flying covert ops people around the world in private business Jets to avoid airport terminals and allow penetration without a lot of visibility. A lot of targeted countries focused on the Airport Terminal assuming the U.S. Government would not waste such incredible sums to transport low level intelligence operatives around. It took them many years to understand the error in their ways. CIA succeeded in doing just that for a dozen years until spies that betrayed America alerted them to the real modus operandi.

The early success of the SAAC 23 quickly evolved into Learjet 23 and 24 which were a remarkable success, not only because people like Howard Huges saw the advantage of such jets, but also the Cash in Advance boys expanded the use as well as Texas Oilmen who had cash to burn and loved to show it.

The SAAC 23 had 6 very comfortable passenger seats plus dual controls for a pilot and co-pilot. CIA pilots who were on loan from the Air Force and wore civilian airline pilot uniforms were ready to go. A flight attendant who wasn't on board for their comfort, was the chief security officer for the plane and remained on board while the plane was parked at destination during trips. She would be stuck on the plane unless relieved by another CIA agent to maintain security to prevent ground crews from tampering with the internal compartments including installing bugs, which were becoming increasingly sophisticated.

As soon as the Bell UH-1 Iroquois helicopter landed 30 feet away from the hanger, Tracey Barnes and Richard Bissell got out of the helicopter and walked through the open double doors that exposed the plane and the tow tractor already hooked up.

The Helicopter pilots had their orders and immediately returned to Langley where they would wait for their next mission.

Tracey Barnes and Richard Bissell approached the SAAC 23 where Maryanne stood by the self-retracting steps. The men boarded the plane and Maryanne followed them up and pulled up the stairway into the jet and shut the access door.

"Just before you got here, some air force guys arrived with a package to send out to Colorado that's in the cargo hold of the plane."

"Any idea what it is?"

"Here's the manifest and paperwork," Maryanne handed to Richard.

Bissell looked at the paperwork and saw some information that he instantly understood. He then turned to Tracey Barnes and said, "It's some rolls of that new special film we are putting in the Corona Satellites."

"I wonder why they are sending that special film out to Colorado Springs?"

"I would imagine they plan on using it on the RB-57D to get enhanced photographs of that UFO."

"Does it require a special process to develop?"

"No uses the same chemicals, it just has better ultra-violet and infrared capability."

"Does that mean they can blow up the photograph to larger magnification?"

"Yea maybe 10 times as much."

"They also are sending another toy along."

"What's that?"

"It's one of those new lasers signaling devices."

"I guess it was a good thing I brushed up on my Morse

code when I was down in Guatemala in 1955," Tracey Barnes said.

"But are you proficient?"

"I can tap messages out in my sleep if I have too."

Maryanne ignoring the conversation walked up to the cockpit and informed the pilot and co-pilot they were cleared to leave. Maryanne like a railroad conductor was legally in charge of the plane and as a consummate professional delivered a lot of CIA personnel around the globe. Until recently she rode on propeller driven planes including the Lockheed Electra's and Constellation aircraft. Those were propeller driven craft, significantly modified, and carried fewer passengers than an airline but a lot more fuel so they could go non-stop to clandestine activities. Sometimes they were painted with airline colors and markings such as TWA to disguise their true purpose.

The pilot gave the thumbs up signal to the operator of the tow tractor who immediately began pulling the Jet out of the hanger. As soon as the Jet was clear and ground crew gave the signal, the large double doors shut hiding the other aircraft parked inside, some of which were painted black and only flew in dark hours.

"Would you guys like any coffee?" Maryanne asked knowing they were on another one of the numerous serious missions that often put their lives at risk and took them away from their Families.

"No thanks, I'm going to try and take a nap," Tracey Barnes said as he simultaneously tilted his seat backwards and raised the leg rests.

Richard Bissell responded, "Thanks Maryanne, I would appreciate a cup with a little cream and sugar in it."

Maryanne got to know Richard Bissell well flying him out to Area 51 numerous times in the past including on those Super Constellations where he observed some of the test flights of both U2 and A12 prototype. The following year A12 went into production and 12 planes were quickly built which ended up in Okinawa and spent much time flying over China.

Richard Bissell, who had a satchel with him, had some papers concerning the A-12 program he wanted to review.

This "Oxcart" program had delivered 11 other Archangel aircraft including the U2 spy plane Bissell had overseen and would soon serve to be one of America's most important assets during the Cuban Missile Crisis.

"Here's your Coffee Richard," Maryanne said moments later in a very pleasant manner as the plane was taxying out on the runway getting ready for takeoff.

Maryanne had immense respect and admiration for Richard Bissell, he was a very hard worker and often brought documents with him on the plane and sometimes was given documents by Maryanne sent from CIA headquarters to read then shred on board before he departed the aircraft.

Because of the massive amounts of documents that got shredded on the plane coming to and from destinations, Maryanne logged them in the destruct log. Only the document number was recorded which was usually in the form of a date, serial number, and the agency code number who owned the document. There was no useful information on what the document contained. Sometimes it was the master document, that was also annotated in the log and if the master was destroyed, there usually was never a trace to what it contained.

The plane soon turned North on Runway 01 Right and the pilot moved the throttles forward and the plane started rolling for takeoff. By this time Maryanne was seated with seatbelt on. The plane did a normal takeoff and as soon as Air Traffic Controllers directed them, the plane turned on a course of 265 degrees which it would maintain for a while. In due time it would fly over Cincinnati, St. Louis, Kansas City, then arrive at Peterson Air Force Base, Colorado Springs.

About Two hours into the flight, Bissell handed Maryanne the 20-page document he was reading and said, "I'm finished with this document, please shred it."

Maryanne smiled and said, "I'll get right to that Richard." She then walked up to the cockpit and warned the pilots, "I'll be operating the shredder in a couple minutes."

The IBM shredder was the very best, good for TOP SECRET documents, but it rigidly mounted and did vibrate a little, and because of the new nature of the SAAC 23, pilots were still learning the plane, and any vibrations usually got them worried. After a couple incidents, they requested Maryanne notify them every time she was running the shredder so they would not think the plane was developing a vibration problem which usually was a precursor to very bad things were about ready to happen.

Maryanne went back to her service bench, opened a drawer, and pulled out a green logbook, copied down the document serial number information in the destruct log. She then separated the papers from their fastener and fed them into the shredder one by one then turned the shredder off when she completed the task, then walked forward and notified the pilots, "I'm done using the shredder."

"Thanks for the heads up," the pilot said and appreciated it since he felt the vibration the shredder caused.

"Would you guys like some coffee?"

"I would love some, make it black."

"Make mine black too," the copilot stated.

Maryanne served them coffee and they would need it because this might end up as a long day.

The plane's phone rang. It was an experimental phone they

could remotely call from all over America and throughout Western Europe, but often they were limited to 10 minutes before they flew beyond range and the circuit died and had to be called again.

Maryanne picked up the phone. "Hello, this is DASH-1," reporting their call sign.

"DASH-1 this is Director Dulles, please put Richard on the line."

The telephone had a long cord that would reach his chair, and Maryanne walked over to Richard and handed him the phone and in a low voice said, "It's Allen Dulles."

"Yes director," Richard stated as soon as he had the handset next to his face.

"Richard, you by now must have learned you got some special equipment in the cargo hold."

"Yes sir, I'm aware of that."

"I've been authorized to have you use the toys to attempt contact with BUFFALO."

"Roger that."

"Also, there is some special film we put on the plane, turn that over to the Air Force and tell them to use it on the next flight. I know it will be a tight fit but I want you and Tracey on that flight to direct the operation."

"Understand all."

"We will be in touch." The phone then went dead as Dulles hung up.

Flying West made this long day even longer. The time to travel 1,490 miles from Washington D.C. to Colorado Springs went by quickly and they were landing at Peterson Air Force Base in Colorado Springs three and a half hours later as they managed to maintain 560 miles per hour over the ground. Because of the time difference they only lost two hours of daylight.

General West expected visitors because of what had happened. He just didn't think it would be this quick when he got a phone call from the tower saying a VIP jet was coming in requesting permission to land and was about 70 miles out over Eastern Colorado just passing Limon Colorado on their descent to Peterson.

West immediately left the building with Colonel Schmidt and hopped in an Air Force car and drove over to the hanger where VIPs routinely got out to avoid exposure at the main terminal since many times they were traveling incognito.

By the time the General pulled into the parking spot in front of the building and walked through the hanger past the two large open sliding doors, the SAAC-23 was in the process of landing on runway 17R heading south. It didn't take long for the plane to arrive at the hanger where it turned parallel to the building which would facilitate its departure later without requiring a tug to move it around.

The engines shut down and soon the door opened, and Maryanne stepped down the ladder to the tarmac where she waited beside the ladder as Richard Bissell and Tracey Barnes immediately deplaned and walked towards the hanger where they knew they would find General West.

"Hello Richard, good to see you again."

"Hi General, I bet you like your digs better here than you did out in Area 51?"

"You got that right, can actually go for a swim here or play tennis during the daytime."

"This is Tracey Barnes; he works with me."

"Glad to meet you Mr. Barnes and this is my exec, Colonel Schmidt."

"Greetings Colonel Schmidt."

"Welcome to Colorful Colorado," Colonel Schmidt responded.

"I have a car; let's drive over to my office."

"Certainly."

In a short while they arrived in his office and General West asked, "Can I get you guys a soda or some coffee?"

"I'm fine, thanks anyway."

"I suppose I know why you guys came out."

"Those facsimiles that General LeMay showed us were a little grainy so we thought we would like to see the originals."

"I'll unlock the safe General," Colonel Schmidt said then went across the room where he started manipulating the combination lock."

"What's the status of our visitor?"

"It's in an amazing geosynchronous orbit, barely budging in position."

"You would think that if they can travel this far from some other solar system, they would have the technology to hold their position in space."

"Apparently they are showing they can do precisely that."

"Here are the pictures," Colonel Schmidt said as he sat the box down on the desk and contained a stack of photographs in it.

Richard Bissell took the first photo out and stared at it momentarily, then handed it to Tracey Barnes.

"Nice picture but since the object is too far away there is not enough detail in it."

"That's kind of what I thought too, but we are operating at the limits of the film we have to use."

"Not anymore," Bissell smiled.

~~~
~~~

Chapter Thirty-Four
Showdown at the White House

Allen Dulles and President Kennedy were not the best buddies in the world by any stretch of the imagination. Dulles loathed the Kennedy family and felt from FDR onwards, every time America had a Democrat in the white house, bad things happened.

Going over to the Oval Office was not something he looked forward to, but it was an evil necessity because when General LeMay bypassed the CIA and went directly to the President, he fractured a long-standing agreement the CIA had with the Armed Services as *coordinator of information.* Part of the visit was damage control; the other part was to reclaim supremacy in intelligence coordination.

Allen Dulles also had to deal with this UFO situation that could easily get out of hand once amateur astronomers found it and started photographing it since some of them had some very powerful telescopes. In fact, some were so good they could make that UFO appear full size on a movie screen.

"Good to see you again Allen."

"Thank you, Mr. President."

"I assume you want to talk about the UFO?"

"That's correct Mr. President."

"What's the CIA doing about it?"

"We just flew a couple agents to Colorado Springs and their meeting with General West about now, getting ready to begin the next phase of the mission."

"And what precisely is that?"

"With your permission sir, we wish to attempt making direct contact with the Aliens."

"Do you think they came here under peaceful terms?"

"We have no way of knowing that, but the sooner we establish communications, the likelihood is we'll find out."

"Do you think there is any possibility we will meet them?"

"It's possible."

"Will there be some kind of quarantine so they don't accidently introduce some deadly disease that could wipe out the planet?"

"We'll try to limit their presence in a bio-sphere with glass barrier, then when they leave, we'll burn it thoroughly to make sure no virus or bacteria possibly left behind will survive."

"Thanks for coming by and keep me informed if there are any new developments."

"We will send over a special briefer immediately if new details emerge."

"Who will be the briefer?"

"I'll probably send Joe Hudson."

"I'm looking forward to hearing from Mr. Hudson."

"Thank you, Mr. President."

Allen Dulles stood up walked out of the oval office and

was soon out to the temporary helicopter pad on the south lawn often utilized by Marine One Presidential helicopter where the CIA Bell UH-1 Iroquois sat with its Lycoming T53-L-11 turbo idling and waiting for immediate takeoff.

352

~~~
~~~

Chapter Thirty-Five
Photographing and Making Initial Contact

The two CIA men soon found themselves in a briefing room with General West, Colonel Schmidt, and the crew of the RB-57D reconnaissance aircraft. Also laying on a table in the room was a box of film and another box that had the laser communicator.

Like most Air Force reconnaissance planes, the RB-57D reconnaissance aircraft were staffed and manned to fill all the available space on the plane so some heavy discussions went on to kick off crew members to make room for the two CIA agents.

"The best we can do is leave one guy behind, the rest of the men are essential unless you want to risk leaving the co-pilot behind."

"No, that will not be necessary. I think I know how to proceed. We need to do at a minimum two more flights. First to take the film up and shoot another series of photographs, and then another flight to attempt using the laser communicator after we modify the Telescope."

"You mean gut the Telescope."

"That's about the best way to describe it."

"So, you'll send up one of you on each flight?"

"Yes, I will go up on the first flight, since I'm more experienced in the aerial photography aspect of it, and Tracey will go up on the next flight with the laser communicator mounted to the barrel of the telescope to attempt communicating since he's an expert on the use of Morse Code."

"What makes you think the Aliens can decipher Morse Code?"

"If they have been monitoring us for 60 years, they have had plenty of time to fully learn Morse code as well as our languages."

"What if they think the laser is a weapon?"

"We'll be shooting the signals offset to them they will know we are not trying to hit them. Plus, it has low power; it's not capable of any damage."

Richard Bissel was provided a flight suit and soon followed the Air Force men out to the RB-57D where they loaded the film aboard and mounted the first roll of film to the camera mounted on the telescope. The Jet was soon airborne and climbing to 65,000 feet.

The camera operator positioned the telescope right on the UFO then started taking pictures. They shot half the film they carried on board as the pilot slowly made lazy 8's in the sky to old position and help keep the camera at a decent angle where the operator didn't have to move the telescope large increments.

Richard Bissell who had a lot of common sense, realized they had more than enough pictures said, "Okay secure taking pictures, let me take a look through the telescope."

The Air Force telescope operator removed the film

canister and put the eye piece back on. It was a sobering experience when Richard Bissell looked at the Alien space craft. In addition to the Alien Spacecraft looking gigantic, it also had a very strange hull appearance that conveyed the message they had traveled a long distance just to see Earth.

Richard Bissell being a religious person was now having his faith tested like never before. It would take him great efforts to reconcile it and deal with his emotions. Then he remembered he was not alone; the crew was in the same boat he was in with their faith being tested likewise.

The plane soon landed and pulled up to the hanger and was soon met by a fuel truck. Technicians went aboard the plane to modify the telescope to essentially gut it and install this communicator that was designed to fit in the barrel of a scope like this as they anticipated future communications with satellites and space craft would require a communication device like this for encrypted data transmissions so they could avoid the Soviets monitoring during classified missions the Air Force was planning.

A less powerful eye piece was built into the communicator to help find the target which would be about 10 times smaller image than what the normal telescope gave them but would be good enough to site the target when they would be sending the laser pulses near the Alien craft.

Tracey Barnes was suited up, and the laser communications system was fully tested. With the evening approaching the Rocky Mountains were now blocking the direct sunlight. Testing of the laser was easy to do as the ground crew could easily see the powerful laser shoot its beam up in the sky.

~~~
~~~

Chapter Thirty-Six
First Contact

The Caronians monitoring earth with their ship orientated upside down in relation to the planet could observe the area down in Colorado quite well.

The Caronians spotted the test firing of the lasers that were shot off to the distance but were bright enough for them to see the laser communicators with their advanced multiband optics.

"Sir, we are receiving strong light from possibly a signaling device," the sensor operator reported excitedly.

The Pilot approached the sensor operator's computer console and observed the elaborate display that captured the captured image in memory allowing operators to analyze the image over a period without losing the information.

The sensor technician informed the pilot looking over his shoulders: "The Earth lasers show up really strong in the ultraviolent bands."

The Caro quickly figured out it was indeed some kind of signaling equipment as the testing on the ground continued and immediately swung into action. Conditions aboard the Caro Interplanetary Transport now intensified as reality struck home, their mission was now reaching a critical stage where one of the most important events in all of Caro history was just about to happen. Likewise, the same could be said for planet Earth.

"Do you think the Earth people are attempting to signal us?"

"Yes, but why are they doing it with the light signals? They have overwhelmingly large number of radio transmitters?"

"They probably have the same problem we have back at Caro, keeping the information from the public because the Clerics are scared, they will lose control if the existence of Aliens were known."

"Are our signal lights ready?"

"Yes, they are."

"Where do we aim the signal beams?"

"The most logical is right at who signals us."

"Should we test them now?"

"Wait until they signal us again."

"Do you think they will be using that code they appear to be abandoning with the other forms of communications?"

"Yes, that's my guess, which is good since we are ready to use that code." The Caro didn't know the name for the process was Morse-Code, but they knew everything else about its use in radio communications including how to read and transmit it just in case it was required.

~~~

The Air Force RB-57D slowly climbed up to 65,000 feet while Bissell watched the Air Force photo reconnaissance
~~~

team back at the base, develop the film he used when he photographed the UFO a short while previously.

"How do we develop this film?"

"Same way you normally do. The only difference is the properties of the film to give us better pictures we can expand to much greater detail."

In a brief time, the negatives came out and the photographers knew right away this film was something special. One of the photographers took the first print over to a microscope and started looking and noted, "I've never seen such detail like this before on pictures taken 500 miles away.

"Remember this film is TOP SECRET, you are not allowed to discuss it with anyone," Richard Bissell reminded the Air Force Lieutenant.

"Yea I could see why the bad guys would want to be able to steal this technology."

"In about 10 years they will most likely develop their own."

"If not sooner."

~~~

The RB-57D finally got up to 65,000 feet and the same camera operator was there to move the telescope barrel around on to target.

"The image of the Alien ship is a lot smaller, but I can still track him pretty good."

Tracey Barnes suddenly came up with a great idea, "I'll tell you what. You track the contact and when I give you the warning shut your eyes and I'll transmit the message."

"That works for me."

"Tell the pilot we are starting communications and to keep flying straight and level for a few minutes."

The camera man relayed the message and said: "Pilot's notified, let's begin."

Tracey Barnes prepared for tapping out dots and dashes in a slow conservative manner that would equate to 20 words per minute.

"Okay close your eyes."
~~~

"Eye's shut ready."

He tapped out on the transmission key the first word as a normal word:

".... . .-.. .-.. ---" [hello]

"You can open your eyes, monitor for response." After a delay with no response Tracey Barnes then said, "Close your eyes, getting ready for the next transmission."

"I'm ready," the Air Force tech replied.

Next Tracey tapped the letters out one at a time with a break in between:

".... / . / .-.. / .-.. / ---"[h space e space l space l space o]

The Aliens did not respond so after a delay of 30 seconds Tracey repeated the process and began tapping out the next sequence of dots and dashes for Morse code:

".-- . / .- .-.. / .- -- . .-. .. -.-. .- -. ..." [We are Americans]

He delayed another 30 seconds and still no response, and after the Air Force Tech was ready typed again:

".-- .... --- / .- .-. . / -.-- --- ..-" [Who are you]"

The Air Force tech then said, „I see blue pulsed light from the Alien, I think it's Morse code!"

Tracey had a note pad and said, "If you can read the dots and dashes, read them out to me and I'll write them down."

"I missed the first part, but they are repeating it again." He then started reading the dots and dashes which Tracey wrote down and could translate them in his brain instantly and verbally repeated what he had written down:

".-- . / .- .-.. / - .... . / -.-. .- .-. ---" [We are the Caro]

Tracey had written down a few questions in advance so he would be armed with the proper questions to ask the visitors. The process then continued.

".-- .... -.-- / -.. .. -.. / -.-- --- ..- / -.-. --- -- . / .... . .-. . ..--.."
[Why did you come here?]

".-- . / .-.. . -.-. . .. .- . -.. / .. .- .-. - .... / -.-. --- -- -- ..- -. .. -.-.
.- - .. --- -. ... / .---- -.... / -.-- . .- .-. ... / .- --. --- / .- -. -.. / -... .
-.-. .. -.. . -.. / - --- / -.-. --- -- . / .. -. / .--. . .- -.-. . / .- -. -.. / .-..
. - / -.-- --- ..- / -.- -. --- .-- / -- . / . -..- .. ... -" [We received
Earth communications many years ago and decided to come in Peace and let you know we exist.]

Before Tracey could think of what to respond, the Aliens continued transmitting:

".-- .... -.-- / .- -.-. . / -.-- --- ..- / ..- ... .. -. --. / - .... / -.-. ---
-.. . / .. -. ... - . .- -.. / --- ..-. / ...- --- .. -.-. . ..--.." [Why are you using this code instead of voice?]

Tracey responded:

"- .... / .--. .-.. .- -. . - / .. ... / -. --- - / .--. .-. . .--. .- .-. . -.. /
..-. --- .-. / -.-- --- ..- .-. / .- .-. .-. .. ...- .- .-.. --.-- / -- . / .- .-. . / -.-
. . .--. .. -. --. / -.-- --- ..- .-. / .--. .-. . ... . -. -.-. . / .... . .-. . / -.-. --- -.
..-. .. -.. . -. - .. .- .-.. .-.-.-" [This planet is not prepared for your arrival, we are keeping your presence here confidential.]

The Aliens then sent a chill up Tracey's spine:

".-- . / .-- --- ..- .-.. -.. / .-.. .. -.- . / - --- / ...- .. .. - / -.-- ---
..- / . .- .-. - .... / .--. . --- .--. .-.. . .-.-.- " [We would like to visit you Earth people.]

Tracey then quickly thought he needed some support on the ground and responded:

".-- . / .-- .. .-.. .-.. / -- .- -.- . / .- .-. .-. .- -. --. . -- . -. - ... /
- .... . -. / -.-. --- -. - .- -.-. - / -.-- --- ..- .-.-.-" [We will make

arrangements then contact you.]

The Aliens responded:

".-- . / .- -.. . / ... - .- -. -.. .. -. --. / -... -.- / ..-. --- .-. / -.-- --- ..-
.-. / .. -. ... - .-. .. .- -.. - .. --- -. ... .-.-.-" [We are standing by for your instructions.]

Tracey realizing, he had a logistics nightmare offered:

".. - / .-- .. .-.. .-.. / - .- -.- . / - .. -- . / - --- / ..-. .. -. -.. / .- / .--.
.-... .- -.-. . / - --- / .--. .- .-. -.- / -.-- --- ..- .-. / ... . --. / ... .. -.
-.-.. . / .. - ... / --.- ..- .. - . / .-... .- .-. --. . .-.-.-" [It will take time to find a place to park your ship since it's quite large.]

The Aliens responded:

"--- ..- .-. / ... . --. / .-- .. .-.. .-.. / -. --- - / -.... . / .-... .- -. -.. ..
.. -. --. / --- -. / - .... . / .--. .-.. .- -. . - / .-- . / .... .- ...- . / ...
.... ..- - - .-... . / -.-. .-. . .- ..- - / - --- / ... . -. -.. / -.-. .-. . .. -- / --. .
-- -.... . .-. ... / -.. --- .-- -. / - --- / - .... . / .--. .-.. .- -. . -" [Our ship will not be landing on the planet, we have shuttle craft to send crew members down to the planet]

Tracey then advised:

".-- . / . -.- .-- -.-. . -.- . - / - --- / .... .- ...- . / .. -. ... - .- .-. .- -.-. - .."

--- -. ... / .. -. / .- / ..-. . .-- / .... --- ..- .-. ... .-.-.-" [We expect to have instructions in a few hours.]

The Aliens replied:

"..- -. -.. . .-. ... - .- -. -.. --..-- / ... - .- -. -.. .. -. --. / -... -.-- .-.-.-" [Understand, standing by.]

Tracey then asked the Air force technician to instruct the pilot, "Return back to base immediately."

In 30 minutes, Tracey had his notebook out repeating the conversation to Richard Bissell and General West along with Colonel Schmidt and the crew in debriefing that included the General's staff Air Force Intelligence Officer.

In the room Bissell grabbed the telephone and called Allen Dulles who answered right away and informed him, "Buffalo wants to visit us. Do you have a location we can have Buffalo visit?"

"Only one place I can think of cleared high enough, Area 51."

"My thoughts exactly."

After Bissell explained to Dulles how they communicate

with the Aliens, he instructed Bissell, "Probably the best way to handle this is have the Air Force fly you and Tracey aboard that RB-57D to Area 51 and have the Aliens follow you there and land there. The meeting will be there at Area 51."

Dulles then informed Bissell something he didn't know existed now became part of the operation.

"Richard, we have an Alien Arrival Team made up by a few scientists from NASA and Princeton Center for Advanced Study with Oppenheimer just for this type of event. We will be flying them out to Area 51."

"When will they arrive?"

"It will take 5 or 6 hours to get these scientists to Area-51."

"Are we allowed to meet them, shake hands?"

"Absolutely not. Consider them a bio-hazard."

"What kind of arrangements or meeting do we do?"

"We'll direct the Area 51 staff to set up a biosphere for the Aliens to enter to avoid contaminating this planet accidently with virus or bacteria our immune systems are not prepared to handle."

"Understand all."

"How soon do you think you can be Airborne?"

"Wait a second, let me ask the General."

After a quick back and forth between the General West, Colonel Schmidt, and the pilot they agreed in 30 minutes, Bissell reported, "Allen, it looks like 30 minutes from now."

"Alright, plan on landing in Area 51; we'll decide our next moves there."

"Will do."

The phone line went dead, Dulles had hung up.

"You heard CIA director Dulles, Tracey and I both need to be on the plane the next time up."

"The RADAR and ESM operators are not essential for the mission; they will be left behind so that you and Mr. Barnes, and the Telescope operator would be on board for this next mission," General West informed the CIA men and the crew.

It didn't take long for the RB-57D to get up to 65,000 feet

and were soon able to contact the Aliens with their laser communicator.

".-- . / .... .- ...- . / -.. . - . .-. -- .. -. . -.. / .- / .-.. .- -. -.. .. -. --. / ... .. - . / ..-. --- .-. / -.-- --- ..- .-.-.-" [We have determined a landing site for you.]

".-- .... .- - / .. ... / - .... . / .-.. --- -.-. .- - .. --- -. ..--.." [What is the location?]

"- .... . / .- .. .-. .--. .-.. .- -. . / .-. ..- .-. .-. . -. - .-.. -.-- / -.-. --- -- -- ..- -. .. -.-. .- - .. -. --. / .-- .. - .... / -.-- --- ..- / .-- .. .-.. .-.. / - .-. .- ...- . .-.. / - --- / - .... . / .-.. .- -. -.. .. -. --. / --.. --- -. . / .- -. -.. / --. .. ...- . / -.-- --- ..- / - .... . / -.-. --- --- .-. -.. .. -. .- - . ... / ..-. .-. --- -- / - .... . / .-.. .- -. -.. .. -. --. / .-. ..- -. .-- .- -.-- .-.-.-" [The airplane currently communicating with you will travel to the landing zone and give you the coordinates from the landing runway.]

". ... - .. -- .- - . -.. / - .. -- . ..--.." [Estimated time?]

".- .--. .--. .-. --- -..- .. -- .- - . .-.. -.-- / ..--- / .... --- ..- .-. ... / ..-. .-. --- -- / -. --- .-- .-.-.-" [Approximately 2 hours from now.]

"... - .- -. -.. .. -. --. / -... -.-- .-.-.-" [Standing by.]

When the Air Force RB-57D finally arrived at Area 51 it then communicated:

".-- . / .- .-. . / .- -.-- ... --- .-- . / - .... . / .-. .. .- -. -.-- .-- .- -.-- / .-- . /
.-- .. .. / -.-- --- ..- / - --- / .-.. .- -. -.. / --- -. .-.-.-" [We are above the runway we wish you to land on.]

".-- . / ... .- .-.. .-.. / -.... . / .- .-. .-. .. ...- .. -. --. / ... --- --- -. .-.-.-
.- / - .... . / ... .- - - .-.. . / -.-. .-. .- .- ..-.- / -.. --- . .... / -. --- - / ....
.- ...- . / .-.. .. --. .... - / -.-. .- .-. .- -.... .. .-.. .. - .. . .-.-.- / .-- . / -.-.
.- -. / -.-. --- -- -- ..- -. .. -.-. .- - . / ...- .. .- / -. --- -. -- .- .-.. / ..- ....
..-. / .-. .- -.... .. --- .-.-.-" [We shall be arriving soon. The shuttle craft does not have light capabilities. We can communicate via normal UHF radio.]

".-- . / ... .- .-.. .-.. / -.... . / .- .-. .-. .. ...- .. -. --. / ... --- --- -.
.-.-.- / - .... . / ... .- - - .-.. . / -.-. .-. .- .- ..-.- / -.. --- . .... / -. --- - /
.... .- ...- . / .-.. .. --. .... - / -.-. .- .-. .- -.... .. .-.. .. - .. . .-.-.- / .-- .
/ -.-. .- -. / -.-. --- -- -- ..- -. .. -.-. .- - . / ...- .. .- / -. --- -. -- .- .-.. /
..- .... ..-. / .-. .- -.... .. --- .-.-.-" [Alright, when you communicate UHF use the call sign "Triangle" and we will use the call sign "Square"]

"... --.- ..- .- .-. . / - .... / .. ... / - .-. .. .. .-. -. . .-.. . --..-- / ..- .-.

-.. . .-. ... - .- -. -.. / -.-. .- .-.. -.. / ... .. --. -. ... .-.-.-"[Square this is Triangle, understand call signs.]

Doctor Metongy Zeugcha and Doctor Provkovitev and four others boarded shuttle #1 and departed the Caronian's Interplanetary Transport. The mothership had already downloaded navigation coordinates to the Shuttle's data terminals, so it knew exactly were to land. And when it finally landed there was a welcoming committee.

The Air Force RB-57D reconnaissance aircraft landed on the 17,000-foot-long runway before the Aliens arrived and pulled up to the series of hangers as directed by the control tower. The crew and the two CIA men exited the plane after the engines were shut down.

Bissell who knew the Marine General Short from U2 and A12 flights walked up to him and said, "Evening General."

"Hello Richard, good to see you again."

"How's the security situation?"

"Security at Area 51 is very tight today," the base commander noted as the Alien shuttle approached and they could all see it coming down.

"I'm sure this sight will be hard to explain."

"In the past few hours, we rounded up all non-essential personnel and bused them to Tonopah where they would be spending the night in hotels there and not allowed back on the base until further orders."

"That's good."

The Alien Shuttle was eerily quiet. It made no apparent noise. It looked far different than any type of craft ever built on Earth.

The Shuttle Pilot said, "That looks like the welcoming committee." He then and took manual control of the craft to set it down near the crowd.

"There is a large white tent besides them lit up and marked with a large red "T" in the middle of the bright area," The Pilot said.

"That's probably where they want us to land," The Copilot commented.

The Caro had studied film of the Earth people and as such designed clothes to wear for this encounter that would appear in the realm of style and reality earth people would expect. That included hair styles and other outward appearances. They thought when they finished designing and trying on the clothes and looked at themselves verses numerous sample pictures; they felt they had replicated the essence of humans on Earth who appeared in the video's they observed.

It was getting dark, so the lights set up around the landing site, turned this part of the base almost into daylight.

The shuttle touched down with a final velocity of ¼ inch per second, an almost flawless soft landing.

Tension mounted as everyone waited with huge expectations, then suddenly the shuttle's door tilted upwards, and the Aliens started climbing out.

Their friendly attire looked comfortable and not too different than what people often wore on earth. They simply fit in immediately.

The welcoming party was of course stunned. In one regard they were gratified they didn't look like lizards of something horrible that one might see in the prevailing motion pictures that were now shown at movie halls.

The next moment of interest began when the Alien introduced himself and his people. "I'm Metongy Zeugcha; this is Doctor Provkovitev, and our Caro Ambassador for this exchange. This is our navigator Doctor Marlneiker." The Pilot, Co-Pilot, and others were also introduced.

"My name is Richard Bissell, I work for the United States government, this is my colleague Tracey Barnes, and this is the base commander General Short of the United States Marine Corp."

Richard Bissell went on to say, "We would like you all to step inside this tent set up which is a bio shield to help prevent biological contamination."

"Certainly." The Aliens showed no objections to the reception preparations.

Once inside the tent with microphones and speakers set up, they sat down and started discussions and exchange of some information. Metongy Zeugcha had a cloth star map which he unfolded from his pocket to show where they came from which had an overlay of Earth planets to indicate and idea of direction.

"Our main welcoming group is not here yet. They should be arriving soon by aircraft. They are bringing in some experts to meet you," Richard Bissell stated.

In the meantime, that did not stop Richard Bissell and Tracey Barnes to engage in a friendly conversation with Metongy Zeugcha, Doctor Provkovitev, and the other Caronians.

By the time the "experts" arrived, Richard Bissell and Tracey Barnes had established a rapport with the Aliens and had insights that the experts soon to arrive would not really exceed.

As promised, in a few hours a CIA Super Constellation landed on the 17,000-foot runway near them and taxied over to the hanger complex and shut down their engines. The base provided a ramp for the passengers. The plane was full up of CIA officials and NASA types. Not a spare seat was left on the plane when they took off from Langley Air Force base located in Hampton, Virginia, adjacent to Newport News.

Some of them had to carry their equipment on their laps for the entire flight. An outside observer would note a circus like environment.

Allen Dulles of course was amongst them, and he quickly approached Richard Bissell and Tracey Barnes and said, "Congratulation's, you guys did a hell of a job."

Bissell who brought with him a box of pictures handed them over to Dulles and said, "Here's your eye candy you wanted to see."

Dulles was clearly humbled looking at the space craft pictures and then when he walked into the tent on the human side of the glass barrier where he could look at the well-lighted tent thought, *the Aliens look just like us. Thank God! Things would be far more complicated if they showed up looking like lizard freaks.*

Dulles stood back and observed the NASA, and the Princeton folks move in and meet and talk with the Aliens. As the discussions evolved the interviewers came to some very interesting information that seriously troubled Dulles which evaluated as lessons learned for the planet in the event some other world that might come here wasn't so friendly: *"They had been studying us for a long time."*

Another very interesting aspect of these Aliens is they said, "We have never detected any other living creatures anywhere in the galaxy." Only by a freak of nature, a space convergence zone, allowed them to hear Earth.

The Caronians stated, "We expect on our trip home we will lose reception from Earth for a while and not pick up our own planet Caro until we get close to the planet."

"Can you hear your planet from here?"

"No, we lost reception months ago as we got out of range and the signals diffused."

Along the glass window separating the Aliens from the Americans, desktop chairs right out of a test pilot classroom at Area 51 lined both sides. There were ample chairs with desktops for each Caro Alien and each had a note pad and several freshly sharpened new pencils they could take notes on or make drawings.

The Americans had insufficient number of chairs for the numbers of scientists and researchers brought in from NASA and Princeton Center for Advanced Studies. Therefore, most of the Americans were left standing but that seemed alright because they were too thrilled to worry about the inconvenience of standing for a while.

Metongy Zeugcha and Doctor Provkovitev were sitting in the center of all the Aliens gathered by the middle of the glass barrier. The NASA heavy hitters and a couple Nobel Laureate's from Princeton attempted right away to take command of the seats almost directly in front of Metongy.

~~~
~~~

Chapter Thirty-Seven
Sophia Kuznetsov

Sophia Kuznetsov normally was not high up enough in standing to deserve the front row center seat, but had it not been for Allen Dulles wishing to stand and the Director of NASA manned space flight who aspired for Sophia, she would have been one of those standing.

Sophia, a child prodigy, immigrated to America with her Jewish Russian Parents when she was very young, just before Hitler invaded Russia in 1941. Their journey was an epic story which included migration from near the Polish border through most of central Russia via the Trans-Siberian Railroad where they managed to get off and make a pilgrimage South from Lake Baikal into Mongolia. As they made their way to Harbin China, they soon fell into an area controlled by the Japanese South Manchurian Railway company fortified with regular Japanese Army units. When they were obtained by Japanese military who looked upon them as refugees, they were soon vetted by an officer who had to make the decision whether to send them back to Russia, which more or less meant slave labor or death, an auspicious moment occurred when the officer interviewing them happened to be Japanese of Jewish decent.

Captain Suzuki the grandson of a Russian POW who requested to stay in Japan after the Russo Japanese War in 1906, like a few thousand others, attended the synagogue in Tokyo. He knew by the way the Russian man dressed and acted; he was well educated. Both men could speak English, and Suzuki knew a little Yiddish, which allowed them to communicate. Few of the other Japanese understood English, so the conversation was quite confidential.

After Captain Suzuki determined Mr. Kuznetsov was upper class, and most likely a former aristocrat prior to the Stalin purges, had an emotional sensitivity towards this Jewish family that made him to decide to allow them to pass through the checkpoint.

As he watched the poor meager family trudge on looking

obviously famished and physically exhausted, Captain Suzuki who was the duty officer at the border crossing told Sargent Musashi, "I'll be back in a while, I'm going into town for a short while, got some business to attend to."

"Yes sir!" Musashi replied and saluted, then gave a slight bow out of respect.

Captain Suzuki walked out, got into the Kurogane Type 95 the world's first mass-produced four-wheel-drive automobile, and headed down the road to the nearby town about 5 miles away. As he passed by the Kuznetsov family, he stopped the car and asked, "Mr. Kuznetsov may I give you a ride into town?"

Almost with disbelief, Mr. Kuznetsov smiled and replied, "That's very generous of you sir, thank you."

As they drove into town there was some minor chitchat but Captain Suzuki knew these poor people were in terrible need.

"Where are you going?"

"We are hoping to make it to Port Arthur so we can catch an ocean steamer to Shanghai or Hong Kong to catch a ship to San Francisco or somewhere in America."

"Do you have the funds for the fare?"

"Probably not, I'll try to hire on as deck hand and take the fee as passage for my family."

"That might be doable."

Captain Suzuki pulled up to the train station and the family got out. Suzuki got out as well and walked with them as they went to the ticket office to purchase a train ticket 3rd class down to Port Arthur. He felt sorry for the family when it took their very last coin to purchase the train tickets. They were now totally financially broke.

Smell from the food stuffs sold at the train station permeated the air and Suzuki could see the pain on the Russians faces, knowing they had not had much to eat for a while and were not going to get food any time soon, suggest, "Mister Kuznetsov if you would please permit me to buy you and your family a meal."

"You are most kind, sir; I don't know how I could ever repay you."

"Maybe one day this will produce positive Karma for me."

In a short period of time the family was eating when their train pulled in. Suzuki watched them grab the remnants of their meal and meager belongings and climb up into the rail passenger car. As a little girl, Sophia remembered the young Japanese Officer and as she was looking at Metongy Zeugcha, she could see similar characteristics in his face, almost as if he were a ghost from her past.

Sophia Kuznetsov's father was a brilliant mathematician and his departure like many Russian Jews had a staggering effect on the country's future. Many of them ended up in countries that turned out to be Russia's enemy during the cold war which was soon to reach a near calamity in the Cuban Missile Crisis. All through the 1960's and 1970's over one half of all new military intelligence information about Russia was provided by Jews. Stalin had made a significant blunder when he victimized the Jews.

Sophia maintained straight A's throughout school, was considered a mathematical genius and eventually was discovered and offered a full ride scholarship to CAL Tech. In due time she was involved in the man space program and helped design parts of the Mercury space craft and was also very pleasant person to look at.

Sophia did not telegraph her Jewish heritage, nor did she place it as a requirement for future possible mates, but she respected her father immensely and felt Jews had many redeeming qualities and added much to America's success in many ways. Few people in NASA knew she was Jewish, though most of them knew she was Russian, and probably one of the many white Russians who were direct descendants of the white Russians who fled Russia as Stalin crushed them.

Caronians were nowhere near as fashion conscious as their Earth human counterparts. Sophia's minimal makeup and clothes exceeded the lure and inspiration that any Caronian might offer. After a year in flight without seeing women, with an all-male crew, Sophia's appearance had significant evocative influence over Metongy Zeugcha, ultimately influencing his personal emotions. That more than subtle change in him ultimately led to a significant event in human experience.

"My name is Metongy Zeugcha from the Tauceti Solar

System. Our inhabited planet is called Caro and we are Caronians," he stated assuming that was a question likely to be asked real soon.

"My name is Sophia Kuznetsov, I work for NASA and I'm an American. It's a privilege to meet you."

"Thank you."

"Your ability to speak English is rather impressive."

"I spent the past 15 years learning it. Studying English took some effort and now I'm glad I put the effort forward to learn it."

"What does the Caro language sound like?"

"Here's an example: "Hěn gāoxìng xiànzài lái **dào** zhège shìjiè **yùjiàn** nǐ." [It is a pleasure to come to this world to meet you now.]

"It sounds kind of difficult."

"Caronians think English is far more difficult to learn."

"Tell me about your journey here to Earth."

"We left the Space Dock nearly a year ago and traveled

directly here."

"How far did you travel?"

"The distance is seven light years."

"How did you get here in less than seven years since nothing can exceed the speed of light? "

"Speed of light restrictions only occurs inside a solar system where ample random hydrogen gasses exist, but away from the solar system where the hydrogen atoms become few and far between the hydrogen atoms do not slow us down, so we can accelerate beyond the speed of light."

"You traveled seven light years in the span of a single year?"

"That's correct."

"Do you have a significant other?"

"You mean spouse or wife as you people on Earth refer to them?"

"Yes."

"No, I do not. How about yourself?"

"No, I do not have a husband yet."

"Do you plan on a mate?"

"When I meet the right person."

Metongy felt very attracted to this woman. But he like the other Caronians felt exhausted and then said, "We have not had much sleep as we were orbiting waiting to hear from Earth or contact you for a couple days. We need to leave soon, go back up to the Caro Interplanetary Transport and rest. Then we can come back."

"Alright, I assume you know the coordinates to come back directly to this spot?"

"Yes, our ship's data terminals have all that information programmed in them now."

"Are your data terminals similar to what we call computers, and are they advanced? »

"We have observed some of your Television signals showing your computer processing on Earth. Most of your data input and output is with your electric typewriters and what you call punch cards. Our data is presented on screens like your television sets and our data input is via a number of methods including voice."

Sophia Kuznetsov observing Metongy Zeugcha could see he appeared stressed and tired but was very open nevertheless.

"While observing Earth technology, your society broadcasted on your Television channels, we see that here on Earth you have separate cabinets full of the electronics to perform the numerical calculations. We did the same thing many generations ago. Since then, we have miniaturized significantly, and all the data processing is done withing the data terminal because of the small compact nature of how our technology is situated. Yes, the data terminals are very capable."

"Will you be coming back with a group after you rest?"

"Yes, I'm the main translator and Doctor Provkovitev is our ambassador. Doctor Marlneiker is a mathematician and chief navigator for this mission; he will be coming back as well. Some others will come down the next time to give everyone a little exposure to Earth and feel real gravity."

Metongy Zeugcha stood up and the others followed him as he walked out the back side of the tent and directly over to the shuttle craft that was surrounded by armed guards to keep everyone away. Even though only invited scientists were at this grand arrival, they seemed to be multiplying by every hour.

The NASA and Princeton scientists were highly disappointed but recognized the stress these poor souls must have probably been through and concurred they would be most happy meet again in a few more hours. This also gave NASA more time to send in more experts and materials.

The Caronians got back in their shuttle, and it took off with the crowd looking on. It had no noise which greatly agitated the aerospace experts among the NASA crowd. Since it was late at night and dark, it only took moments before the shuttle was invisible in the night sky as it headed for the Caro Interplanetary Transport.

During the time the Aliens were away, more tents, generators, lights, air conditioning units, and supplies were sent here to help deal with a growing number of people arriving to get their few minutes with the Aliens.

It was fine and dandy more people were brought in, but it also posed a huge crisis for the base commander. As he led the CIA men into the hanger he said, "We still have a lot of super top secret "equipment" housed in Area 51."

"Where did all these guards come from?" Richard Bissel asked.

"We ended up having to bring back half of those sent off to Tonopah simply to be used as armed guards around the base to ensure nobody got exposed to some of the secret research craft."

"You mean such as the A12 that is sitting inside Building 28?"

"Exactly."

~~~

Hours later, as the Aliens promised out of nowhere came their shuttle.

"Looks like there are a lot more people down there now," Metongy Zeugcha stated as they were about 500 feet off the
~~~

runway that was nice and lit up even though it was in the evening long past sundown.

"Must be four times as many people down there today," Doctor Provkovitev added.

The shuttle which seemed to cause great interest in the Americans because of the lack of noise was dropping fast until the last 500 feet where it seemed to slow down exponentially as it got closer to the runway. Just like yesterday the terminal velocity was ¼ inch per second.

Next to the Runway was a new object it appeared as a white tunnel with clear sides leading to the tent they were in the previous day. As they got out of the shuttle, Marine Corp General Short stood nearby and said to Professor Provkovitev, "Would you all mind walking through that enclosure to the interview tent, we are trying to set up better biological isolation?"

"Sure, no problem," Professor Provkovitev responded then said in Caro to the other Caronians:

"Wǒmen xūyào chuānguò tòumíng de sùliào wéilán dào huìyì shì dào cǎifǎng zhàngpéng. Tāmen yǐjīng jiànlìle shēngwù gélí." [We need to walk through the clear plastic enclosure to the conference room to the interview tent. They have set up biological isolation.]

The same school seats with desks were set up with microphones and speakers at the glass wall such as yesterday. The Caronians took the same seats they had the day before. Metongy Zeugcha was slightly disappointed the beautiful woman was not sitting down in front of him.

Like most academia, MIT and Harvard professors found out via their spies in the Pentagon about something unique going on out in Area 51. They knew some of the CAL Tech and Princeton people and when they called to make inquiry, discovered none of them could be located. They then used their political influence through members of the Joint Chiefs to get authorization for a trip out to Area 51.

Since some of the newly arrived scientists were Q level cleared and had worked with Vannevar Bush and Edward Teller on the Manhattan Project and were associated with the Lawrence Livermore radiation lab, they had carte blanche and not only got their invite as requested but free delivery via the Super Constellations the Air Force operated for the

CIA just like arrived the day before.

Long before the Aliens were scheduled to arrive, a semi-obese researcher from MIT who knew there was going to be some fantastic action sat down several hours before they anticipated arrival, with his soda and a roast beef sandwich and a stack of books, notepads, and other paraphernalia before others realized they better grab the seats before the crowd started going insane to get front view seating. General Short and Allen Dulles had not yet set up a reservation system, but that was soon to follow.

Sophia Kuznetsov had been spending the day sometimes on conference calls with NASA officials at Langley, but also conferring with other scientists and did not make it to the habitat tent until the feeding frenzy to gain control of the up-front seats had already began and every single seat which was now 6 rows back was filled, and the standing room was limited.

Metongy feeling very disappointed stood up and walked out of the tent and to the tunnel like entrance which was guarded by several military policemen who were somewhat surprised to see him return so quickly. One lieutenant in charge wearing a side arm and carrying a sub machine gun asked, "Sir are you leaving already?"

"No, I would like to talk with the American who's in charge of this facility."

"Yes sir, one moment please." The Lieutenant then turned to Sargent Hess and said, "Go get General Short immediately, tell him it's an urgent matter."

The Sargent knew the basic area the General would be in, the interview tent and went there right away and interrupted him talking with some Harvard people that were complaining "We have no seats and feel we should be up close."

"Excuse me General," Sargent Hess interrupted then continued, "You are wanted by the entrance for the Aliens. One of the Aliens is there and wishes to speak with you."

The general raised his eyebrows a second and said to the Harvard people then threatening to use their Kennedy Trump cards, "Excuse me gentlemen I will be right back and see if I can find you some seats."

General Short walked out of the tent and over to the side

where the tunnel like entrance had been installed for the Aliens that led immediately to the runway next to the shuttle parked there.

"What can I do for you. I'm General Short."

"Hello General Short, I'm the Caronian Metongy Zeugcha, I would like your assistance in a matter."

"Certainly, if I'm able to do it, I would be delighted."

"Yesterday while we were here, I was having a discussion with a NASA scientist by the name of Sophia Kuznetsov. I was not completed with my discussions but had to leave because my colleagues said they were exhausted. Would it be possible for you to remove the gentleman that is sitting directly in front of my chair and ask Sophia Kuznetsov to sit there so we can continue our conversation?"

"If I can find her, certainly."

"General, I saw her standing near the back of the room. She's the blonde headed lady wearing the light blue dress."

"Alright, let me see what I can do."

"Thank you General."

"You are most welcome."

General Short walked into the tent and near the back of it struggling for basic room was the young lady he instantly spotted, and she was the only person in the tent with a blue dress on.

General Short said to a couple of his security men wearing business suits and quietly said to them, "See the Alien in the middle who just sat down across from the chubby guy in the middle?"

"Yes General?"

"There is a lady in the back of the Tent in the blue dress. Her name is Sophia Kuznetsov, she works for NASA and has a NASA badge on, take her up to the front and put her in the seat the chubby guy is sitting in, have the chubby guy come see me, I'll be outside the tent."

"Right away General."

One of the Security men said to the other, "Go grab the lady, I'll get the man have her there when the seat is empty."

"Roger that boss."

The security man approached the woman and asked, "Excuse me, are you Sophia Kuznetsov?"

"Yes, what can I do for you?"

"General Short who's in charge of the base and this meeting, has asked that you be seated up front directly across from one of the Aliens, please follow me."

About that time the other plain clothes security guy, an Army CID officer, approached the heavy-set guy and said, "Excuse me sir, General Short who's in charge of the base would like to see you outside the tent, please follow me."

"That's absurd, I can't leave now, the Alien just sat down and I need to ask him a lot of questions."

"Sir, you must follow me now, this is a serious matter."

"I'm Hank Rogers, director of MIT physics department, I must remain here."

"Hank, I'm not sure why the General wants to talk to you about, but he said it's a serious matter so you must come with me now."

"This is bullshit, I'll make sure that god damn General gets fired."

"This way sir," the CID man said as Hank stood up and reluctantly followed him outside the tent.

About the time Hank exited the entrance to the tent he looked back and saw the nice-looking blonde sitting down in his seat and he was infuriated. Hank nevertheless went outside and followed the man wearing the suit to the General who was patiently waiting. Then he unloaded with his *quad barrel machine gun attitude.*

"General this is outrageous, I'm the director of MIT's physics department, and I see some woman was just put in my seat."

"What's your name?" General Short asked.

"Hank Rogers."

"Hank, I hate to be the bearer of bad news, but the Alien specifically requested that woman be seated there because they were talking yesterday and did not finish their conversation before, they all had to leave because their exhausted and need some rest."

"General, if you don't get me back in my seat immediately, I'm going to get you relieved."

"Hank, to be honest, I would love to be relieved about now. You have no idea what I'm going through."

"How soon will I get access to one of the Aliens, preferably one of those sitting up near the middle, whose most likely one of the Alien leaders?"

"Hank, we have not discussed with the Aliens how long they plan on being here, but something tells me they are not going away real soon and there should be ample opportunity for you to talk with them."

"Just when is that?"

"What I'm going to do when the Aliens leave again, I'm going to announce to all the scientists here we are going to hold raffles on seats, randomly drawn for tomorrow."

"Are you going to use that as some excuse for me not to sit up front? I waited nearly two hours there to get my chance to talk to the Aliens."

"You just won the first seat, your pick tomorrow."

"Well, that's better than the chaos you got going on now."

"Hank, these are dreadful times now, can you imagine what it may be like soon if this is divulged to the public?"

"General, the public has the right to know."

"That may be true, but would you take personal responsibility if the world collapses into utter chaos and people start killing each other in large numbers?"

"You can't say that's going to happen."

"You can't say that it will not happen when all of a sudden a lot of religious fanatics have their doctrine challenged by the arrival of these Aliens."

"Fine General, if I get the front row seat tomorrow like you promise I suppose I can wait a day."

"Thank you, Hank. I promise you will be rewarded by your patience."

~~~

Sophia Kuznetsov was delighted to get the honor of sitting in front of Metongy Zeugcha. She somehow sensed
~~~

the electricity he had for her and the attraction she had for Metongy Zeugcha was true as well.

"It's good to see you again Sophia Kuznetsov."

"Thank you Metongy Zeugcha, please just call me Sophia."

"Certainly, Sophia."

"Tell me Metongy, what was life like for you on Caro and what do you do for hobbies?"

"What do you mean by hobbies?" Metongy asked as even though he was fluent in English there were still a number of words he didn't use or practice."

"Hobbies mean activities you do for fun including participating in arts and crafts such as oil paintings, music, astrology, and other personal activities."

"What are oil paintings?"

Sophia suddenly realized there were several things the Aliens did not understand. She started taking some notes of materials she would have NASA bring out to share with the

Alien for their next visit if there was to be one.

The Alien today brought with him a small box that had a variety of things in it. He began sharing them with Sophia holding them up to the glass window that separated them.

Outside the tent and all around the new makeshift city General Short had constructed, including "portapoties" and air-conditioned bunk rooms and tents set up to feed the several thousand scientists that were now on site, were signs stating, "Photography is not permitted, any camera's will be confiscated."

Mimeographed and posted in many locations was notification:

"The Army has professional photographers to take pictures and if a researcher has a request (such as a picture of the shuttle), a picture would be taken, but serialized, stamped TOP Secret and the Army would deliver it to the institution if it had certified storage and tracking systems."

Any scientist who chose to get those photographs would soon regret taking custody, since what went with it was lifelong non-disclosure agreements and intrusive government oversight in their lives.

At this very moment, several scientists severely hated the photographic restrictions because the Alien started pulling pictures out of the box. He then held the picture up to the glass window separating him and Sophia and described the image.

"This is an aerial view of my city where I live, Preznium."

Several scientists crowded in, the circus like behavior was almost to the tipping point as General Short feared but hoped didn't happen. The Caro Alien City looked like something out of the future. A good science fiction author such as Isaac Asimov would quickly identify with such topography and technological innovation.

Sophia marveled at the picture of the Caro City, Preznium and asked, "How do you travel around your city?"

"See the long green objects on the streets?" Metongy asked.

"Yes?" Sophia responded.

"Those are Crawlers. They're our basic transportation. One

could say their like city transportation we observed here on earth, but they travel slower, approximately 15 miles per hour."

Sophia could see in the picture the Crawlers seemed to bend around corners and asked, "They are probably as long as a dozen busses tied together, and they seem to bend around corners?"

"Yes, they do, here's another picture." Metongy pulled out another picture he had taken using his "Zrapolater" which electronically sent the image to a printer mechanism which produced a very high definition on a sheet that had a Mylar like material providing excellent reflective surfaces.

In this picture Sophia saw people getting on and off the Crawler, there were almost 30 Caronians in the picture. This appeared as the heart of Caro society. *They all looked human, and despite the fact they didn't seem fashionable like Earth people, none were obese, and they all looked rather healthy.*

Another factor the picture conveyed was the air seemed clear and there were no signs of air pollution including scaring of buildings one would see in places like London,

Paris, Moscow, Philadelphia, Los Angeles, and Denver, where the smog was starting to get heavy.

Sophia quickly spotted the Crawler had no wheels and had leg looking objects below the car bodies and asked, "Why no wheels? Don't you use wheels on your planet?"

"Yes, we have wheels on our tube carts they rest on when at stations," then pulled out a picture of him getting off a Tube Train with 20 or more other people.

"How fast do these things go?"

"Do your measurements include miles and other measurements we use?"

"No, none of our measurement systems match anything you use on Earth; we just converted it to your equivalent measurements so you would understand the dimensions of things we discuss with you."

"How do you travel long distance? Do you travel long distance on these Tube Trains?"

"No those are only for inner city use, we use Atmospheric Gliders to travel to other cities," Metongy then pulled out a picture showing the glider on the end of the ramp launching.

"How fast do they go?"

"That Atmospheric Glider will go 7,000 miles in an hour."

"What other forms of transportation do you have?"

"We have several other surface transportation modes to go over water and land, such as our Hovercraft, but we also have these Skycars which are used by emergency services, law enforcement, and wealthy Caronians use them as well."

"How are they powered?"

"They fly by electric driven propulsion turbines."

"Do you have pictures of your home?"

"Yes, in fact I do. Here's pictures of the inside including the lab I built inside there to monitor your communications."

The home didn't look lavish and it didn't have pictures on the walls like seen on Earth, but it did have some interesting decorations that made the walls feel three dimensional.

"The men in this picture are all my assistants that worked with me for many years studying your language."

Sophia noticed one of the persons in the picture was sitting a couple feet away from Metongy. She then said, "This gentleman to your left appears to be one of those in the picture."

"Yes, that's Doctor Marlneiker, a brilliant mathematician who worked on my staff."

"Did anyone else travel with you that you knew well back home?"

"Yes, Doctor Provkovitev sitting directly on my right."

"Will you come back tomorrow?"

"Yes, we would like to come back again tomorrow and hear more about Earth, and I would like to particularly talk to you and learn more about you."

"I'm not important; don't waste your precious time talking about me when there are so many important things about Earth you might be more interested in."

"I should be interested in you in case the opportunity arises to take you back to Caro with me."

"That's never going to happen, I'm not going to leave

Earth, my parents and family are here, and I want to spend my life with them as much as possible."

"Perhaps then maybe I can stay on earth after the rest leave to go back to Caro."

"Don't be absurd, you wouldn't want to do that."

"We have so much to learn from each other, I would volunteer to stay if this planet requested that I did."

"I think you are teasing me."

"Sophia, I'm a scientist first and foremost, even though I might have personal desires and aspirations, for the advancement of science and the purpose of discovery and learning more about the universe around us, I would be willing to stay on earth to help you learn more about the Caro."

"Would Caro have to give you permission to stay?"

"Doctor Provkovitev is our ambassador to Earth, and I've sworn allegiance to carry out his instructions. If he either asked me to leave with the rest of the Caronians back to our planet or allowed me to stay here on Earth, I would carry out his wishes."

Overhearing what Metongy Zeugcha just stated, Doctor Provkovitev took the opportunity to weigh in on the discussion and said, "We have not made a determination that any such personnel exchange with planet Earth would be allowed but given the discretion the Planetary Security Service gave me, if it made sense for Doctor Metongy Zeugcha remain behind, I would give it due consideration."

Upon the conclusion of Doctor Provkovitev last statement, the crowd seemingly got more illuminated, and the discussions grew to a great crescendo and immediately people started formulating ideas and plans. This was truly an astonishing event. *"But was the world ready for it."*

<div align="center">~~~</div>

Chapter Thirty-Eight
The Exchange Begins

Part of the agreement each American scientist made before they were allowed into Area 51 included:

"Not attempting to access or discuss or photograph anything at Area 51 that did not directly pertain to this special conference. If they were accidently exposed to experimental aircraft or any other technological advancement, they were barred for life in discussing it."

They agreed to a conference to discuss whether disclosure should occur by secret ballot and if enough scientists that were invited voted to withhold any information associated with the conference, they were barred for life discussing it with any entity, unless the President wrote an executive order releasing their sequester of information surrounding this event.

No personal pictures were allowed, only official Army photographs would be allowed taken by Army photographers who would control the marking and registration of the image that could only be used in a limited amount of time and returned to the Army for destruct no later than the date assigned to the controlled item.

Army photographers involved in the Area 51 project Buffalo were restricted to ensuring all copies were sent to Fort Meade for certifiable destruction and under no circumstances were any form of copying allowed.

The next day Majestic 12 group which is the advisory panel to the President secretly met in Boston to discuss whether they would entertain allowing any of the Aliens to stay and the question of setting up a quarantine and eventual medical clearance to the Aliens to allow American scientists to have physical contact with the Aliens.

CIA director: "We have not yet determined they are safe to be allowed into the public here."

Bank President: "We certainly would have to get the person or persons to submit to some medical tests including blood work, XRAYS and such to verify they're not carrying a disease we can't control that might wipe out the human race."

Army General: "Will we be putting medical professionals at risk to exposure by doing the blood work and other medical examinations?"

Vannevar Bush: "We'll have to ask for volunteers who will have to be quarantined for a long period of time."

Air Force General: "If we build a medical habitat for the medical people and the Aliens, where would we put it?"

CIA Director: "Area 51 has to be the place."

Air Force General: "We still have a lot of classified projects going on at Area 51 that's going to be a problem."

Army General: "Why not set aside an area slightly away from the main complex where all this can be isolated but yet have a service road access to it."

CIA Director: "After the President approves the plan, we'll have to do some construction right away. I can have my DD/P boys Bissell and Barnes get in touch with EG&G

and have them build a facility, their cleared for Area 51."

Vannevar Bush: "Since we already have sector areas S-1, S-2 and S-3, we should designate this S-4.

Everyone currently present at the meeting, voted in agreement.

An hour later, Allen Dulles was on the SAAC-23 Jet flying to Andrews Air Force base where his Bell UH-1 Iroquois Helicopter sat, waiting to fly him to Langley. Per prior arrangement the chopper pilots were monitoring the frequency the Jet was using making final approach and started its turbine when the jet was 10 miles out on final approach.

The SAAC-23 came down on Runway 01R which was convenient since the end of the runway is where the hanger was located and the UH-1 was warming up. The Jet pulled up to the hanger moments later, stopped, Maryanne opened the jet's door, lowered the built-in stairs, and walked down and stood on the side and said, "Goodbye Allen, I hope you had a good flight."

"Yes Maryanne, as always appreciate your dedication."

He then walked 50 feet over to the waiting Helicopter and moments later it went vertical and headed for Langley. Waiting in the helicopter was Richard Bissell and Tracey Barnes who had just landed on the Super Constellation parked nearby that would be loaded up with some more scientists, medical professionals, and equipment, and after refueling would be heading back to Area 51.

By the time they got to Langley, Dulles had briefed them on the plan and Bissell and Barnes would be driving over to Crystal City that was just being built up by Hymen G. Rickover and EG&G along with a few Beltway Bandits hell bent on grabbing their fair share of defense contracts that were looming over the growing Vietnam conflict. Within weeks, thanks to John Cabot Lodge, sent to Vietnam by Kennedy, the Diem brothers would be dead, and the speculation these developers on the commercial real estate property would pay off handsomely. The only other Real Estate gamble in the USA that would pay out as much as Crystal City did eventually was Howard Hughes investments in the Las Vegas Strip.

Barnes, Bissell and three EG&G execs were on the SAAC-23

barely 2 hours later, heading for Area 51. General Short met them five hours later and looked at the aerial photographs EG&G brought with Richard Bissell and had provided with markings for the prospective S-4 site that would be rushed into being.

"Phase-1 will include temporary trailers and some tents to begin conducting some of the medical examinations."

"Power lines, water, phones, sewer hookups, etcetera, installed there?"

"We'll have to install generators and have water trucks and other temporary services until permanent installation is complete.

"Certainly, everything they need."

"Phase-2 we'll build structures using prefabricated buildings to expand the facilities."

"Phase-3 build permanent structures including a high rise building that will be mostly self-contained."

"How much will all this cost?"

"We expect you to give us a blank check, the EG&G guy

said with a smile."

"Let's all get in these cars and drive over to the proposed building site."

The men all jumped into the Air Force 1959 Plymouth station wagons with the wings in the back and drove over to the proposed S-4 area. This piece of property southwest of Groom Lake was a dry lakebed called Papoose Lake. The big hill between them would obscure them from the Groom Lake facility to keep each function isolated and compartmentalized from each other at the same time providing some physical protection for the Groom Lake personnel to insure they would not be infected by any disease the Aliens might bring with them.

No doubt weighing heavily on Allen Dulles was the fear of a mass extinction event if these Aliens were carrying some disease that humans were not immune.

The cars drove west around the hill and gradually on a counterclockwise direction eventually angled south to the Papoose Lake area.

The CIA men saw potential growth and the fear of running

out of room at Groom Lake was instantly eliminated.

The cars pulled up to the center east portion of Papoose Lake and the men got out of the cars and looked around.

"It looks kind of desolate here."

"That's why we like it, not even a buzzard can survive here without bringing in external food and water."

"During phase-1 we'll have to camouflage the facility, otherwise people from a distance might see the trailers and tents."

"Not a problem, Air Force has put in some rather neat tents that cover up large areas of Area 51 that from above look like a dry lake bed."

"Plus, we can tunnel into the hillside there and build vast underground facilities if we need too."

"Yes, it sure has a lot of growth potential."

"Wonder why the Groom Lake operators never considered building down here?"

"The Air Force wants to have a single control tower and

every aircraft on the ground in view. The hill is in the way."

"It's good they never figured it out, their loss is our gain."

"How do you figure?"

"The control tower could be up on that hill and they could see a lot further away."

"Well, they probably didn't figure on Groom Lake getting as big as it is now."

"Wait until the Vietnam War expands; they have no idea how big things can expand."

"Especially if China gets involved like they did in Korea."

"Did you guys see enough?"

"Sure did. Work starts tomorrow."

"That fast?"

"Certainly, that's why we call you Cash in Advance."

The men hopped back in the Plymouth Station Wagons and headed back to Groom Lake.

~~~
~~~

Chapter Thirty-Nine
A New Role

At about 04:00 a.m. Sophia Kuznetsov said to Metongy Zeugcha, "I've enjoyed talking with you, but I'm tired and need to get some rest and make a few phone calls, I'll see if I can get some things to share with you."

"Alright, I'll see you tomorrow evening."

Sophia got up and left and her seat was immediately taken by one of the other scientists who wanted to talk directly with Dr. Metongy Zeugcha.

Sophia went to a trailer NASA had just brought in which had power connections and an air conditioner. She did not have a shower or toilet there but at least she had a place to sleep, which she shared with a couple other women who worked for NASA in a variety of tasks, including typing via teletype to headquarters. By agreement, when they all went to bed for a few hours, the teletypes were turned off and there was no incoming because the machines were very noisy and prevented sleep. Before she turned off the lights and went to sleep, she typed out a request for a few books, a globe and other minor items she thought would be beneficial to communications with the Aliens.

The Caronians had left Area 51 before sunrise. It was all appropriate since the temperatures would be uncomfortable during the day. They had given General Short an idea of when they would be arriving later in the evening. It seemed to General Short the Aliens were almost instinctively aware of security and arrived and departed at practically the best possible times. That morning as they left, the briefing room cleared out, General Short ordered the tent roped off and prohibited anyone from entering. There really wasn't much need for people to be in there with the Aliens gone.

About 09:00 in the middle of a restful sleep Sophia Kuznetsov was quickly awaken when one of the typists named Sarah shook her and said, "You need to wake up Sophia. There are a couple CIA men outside the trailer that needed to talk with you."

It didn't take Sophia long to get ready since out in the desert away from anyone didn't require a person to dress up very much, so she slipped on some blue jeans, put on a light tee-shirt, and put her ponytail through a ball cap with a strap on the back, and walked out of the trailer to a command post set up as a message center. She then approached the Air Force Major who was in the shade under a large tarp installed to help keep everyone slightly cooler and out of direct sunlight.

"Excuse me major, I understand there are a couple CIA folks that want to talk with me?"

"Your name please?"

"Sophia Kuznetsov."

"Let me see, ah yes, the two CIA men said to stop by building 28 and they would talk to you over there."

"Who is it I'm meeting?"

"A gentleman by the name of Richard Bissell."

"Where's building 28?"

"See that big Aircraft Hangar over there?"

"Yes?"

"That's building 28, access door on the right side."

Sophia went to the building, found the door very easily since it had 2 armed guards on it.

"Excuse me; I need to see a man named Richard Bissell."

"And who are you?"

"Sophia Kuznetsov."

They could see Sophia had her NASA badge on clipped to the neck of the tee-shirt and suspected she was one of the "spooks" who worked in building 28.

"Just a minute please."

One of the Guards went inside the building and about 45 seconds later the guard and a well-dressed man wearing a suit, came outside.

"Sophia?"

"Yes."

"Come with me."

The well-dressed man led Sophia into building 28 around a barrier and in front of this strange looking jet were a couple desks that looked like they were hastily setup with some telephone lines and a Teletype currently spitting out a wad of paper.

The man on the phone said, "I'll call you back in a while Allen, she's here now."

Bissell hung up the phone, stood up and approached Sophia and held out his hand, "Hello, I'm Richard Bissell, deputy director of planning for the CIA, this is my assistant Tracey Barnes."

"Hello, I'm Sophia Kuznetsov, NASA; I work on the Mercury program and sometimes help out on the Apollo."

"Glad to meet you, Sophia Kuznetsov."

"Thank you, Mr. Bissell."

"I suppose you are wondering why we wanted to talk with you."

"Yes, what can I help you with?" Sophia responded in a very professional manner that a brilliant scientist would do.

"This Alien arrival certainly has turned the world upside down. The Alien yesterday making the statements he would consider remaining on earth has taken on a life of its own."

"That doesn't surprise me."

"The President was briefed and has given temporary approval for him or others that indicate they may want to remain here to become more educated on Earth and our society here."

"That's interesting, but how does that affect me."

"One thing occurred last night after you left and went to bed before the Aliens went back to their ship, the person you were conversing with, Metongy Zeugcha is one of their senior members and is the Caro chief scientist who first mastered the English language and is their chief communicator, indicated that when they come back again tonight, he wants your seat reserved so he can continue talking with you and has also requested you do a one on one with him."

"I would assume we would be separated by a protective barrier?"

"Certainly, we would want you fully protected."

"So that's why I'm here to discuss with you what you want me to say to the Alien?" Sophia Kuznetsov asked suddenly feeling the CIA was going to use her to manipulate the Alien in some way. She had heard some of the rumors surrounding the CIA and the wild nature of their operations in places like Greece, Cuba, Guatemala, Southeast Asia, and the Philippines.

"No, it's way beyond that. We had a psychologist near you last night observing you and the Alien and his report is the Alien is infatuated with you and if he does decide to remain behind, we are going to build a facility to house him, get him through a lengthy period of quarantine and medical checks before he can be cleared to be exposed to humans."

"What if he doesn't pass the quarantine and is a danger to this planet?"

"Unfortunately, the Alien would have to be destroyed."

"Don't you think you should tell him that before he commits to something that could be fatal?"

"We have."

"Just like that?"

"Yes."

"And what's in it for him?"

"He may have reasons to believe he would have time here to explore the people and planet and in discussions with the President and the Director of the CIA and several other officials. The Alien Metongy Zeugcha has stated they have agreed to take any Earth person back with them in an exchange."

"You are asking me to go back with them?" Sophia Kuznetsov asked as she was now super animated having experienced some of the machinations and nefarious activities that went on behind the scenes at NASA where imagery was more important than science and ethical moral values.

Sophia was also aware of some of the CIA activities that resulted from interactions between NASA and the CIA. The CIA had tendrils into the United States Air Force and NASA. The Army and the Navy had their own INTEL apparatus and were seemingly just as powerful as the CIA and stood their ground. But the Air Force and NASA were pushovers because they loved sucking on the CIA tit. The computers that went into the A12 spy plane that allowed fully automated operation allowing the CIA pilots to concentrate on flying, were developed for NASA's Gemini Space Program. The CIA confiscation of those micro-processors which were truly revolutionary in 1961 was just one of the many covert operations the DD/P boys at the CIA routinely performed. Sophia was now in great fear knowing how nasty the CIA bastards could get including forcing her on a trip to an Alien planet.

"Actually no, we'd prefer you stay here and be part of a program to help Doctor Metongy Zeugcha adapt and get some exposure to Earth. We expect in a few years from now the Caro would return bringing our people back and take him home or others that might initially stay here with him."

"Mr. Bissell, you probably know by now since you CIA guys have the means to fully check someone out, my involvement in the space program?"

"Yes, Doctor Kuznetsov, we are quite aware you are a contributing member of the design team for a couple of our space craft."

"I'm at the pentacle of my career now, why would I want to risk that and lose out on all that opportunity to be a high-tech babysitter?"

"Doctor Kuznetsov, we know of your contributions to Mercury and Apollo, but we believe your contributions here would be more meaningful."

"Mr. Bissell, let me be frank, how could be a liaison to these Aliens in any way contribute as much as I would be doing so by helping design our future space program?"

"There will be a gradual technology exchange. It will take someone with a highly advanced technical career such as you who can sift through the massive amount of data promised us to find items that would be most beneficial to Americans holding sole ownership."

"You mean keeping it away from the Russians?"

Richard Bissell gestured towards the A12 to his left side and said, "One of the reasons why we are forced to build this Jet is because our Russian adversaries create some of the most challenging scenarios for us. With some of this Alien technology, we can leapfrog ahead and be able to skip incremental development such as expensive aircraft like this A12 which the world doesn't know about."

"It sounds like you will remove me out of NASA whether I like it or not?"

"That's not true; we will just borrow you for a few years. You will remain on NASA payrolls and be subject to promotions just like anyone else. And if you facilitate spiral development by your activities with the Alien, I will assume your promotions would be automatic and in a dozen years your current boss will be working for you."

"I'm a team player of course but I'd rather continue on the space craft design and testing."

"There will be bigger and better space craft for you in the future. This activity almost guarantees you will be a major part in developing it since all the innovation and Alien secrets will pour through you."

"Have you made any promises to this Alien you might not be able to keep?"

"Absolutely not. He knows there is nothing implied and we simply said we would talk to you and get some feedback from you to see if you would entertain starting the project to get him medically cleared so he can enter the basic existence here on earth to provide him a better understanding of this planet, even though he's already studied us many years and already knows a lot about us."

"I need to talk with my boss, Mr. Black at NASA to see if he would agree to loan me to the CIA."

"We've already talked with Mr. Black, he's already approved your TDY, all you have to do is sign the orders request, and you will be effectively working for us today."

Richard Bissell reached over to the papers that had barely come off the facsimile machine just before Sophia walked in and handed them to her to sign.

Sophia was a fast reader and whipped through all 3 pages on the TDY request. Being sophisticated and around NASA a while she understood the professional damage, she would do to herself if she didn't "play ball."

Richard Bissell seeing, she didn't have any writing utensils handy quickly handed her an ink pen which she reluctantly used, signed the document, and handed it back.

Tracey Barnes then spoke up and said, "Miss Kuznetsov get some rest, the Aliens will be back no later than 20:00."

As soon as Sophia walked out the door at building 28, Tracey Barnes walked over to the facsimile machine and proceeded to send her order's request to NASA Headquarters where the personnel office was standing by to receive and process the document to cut Sophia a set of orders that would send her TDY for a couple years. Being on per diem for a couple years wasn't such a bad deal.

~~~
~~~

Chapter Forty
The New American Satellite

KGB official Alexander Nikolayevich Shelepin was about to fall on his sword. Khrushchev was getting increasingly irritated because things were going on in Area 51 and they were not getting any reports out of Shelepin that even slightly suggested what the activity was. Furthermore, he still was not able to explain the new American Satellite they only saw briefly that appeared to disappear.

Vladimir Yefimovich Semichastny would soon be tasked to take over from his mentor as Khrushchev got more desperate and the Cuban missile crisis loomed in the near future.

Shelepin's policy of providing KGB support to national liberation movements in Central America and Sub-Saharan Africa was adopted in the summer of 1961 by Khrushchev and Soviet Central Committee and included an aggressive policy of military support for African national liberation movements with Che Guevara, in co-operation with Ben Bella of Algeria, playing a leading role.

Shelepin left the KGB when he was promoted to the Central Committee Secretariat in November 1961 but still exercised control over the KGB, which his protégé Vladimir Yefimovich Semichastny had took over as leader.

Shelepin then became a First Deputy Prime Minister in 1962. He was a principal player in the coup against Khrushchev in October 1964, obviously influencing the KGB to support the conspirators. Shelepin probably expected to become First Secretary and *de facto* head of government when Khrushchev was overthrown.

The geostationary orbit of the Caro Interplanetary Transport did a lot to diminish Shelepin's pursuit of information. No doubt had it continued orbiting the planet, Russian Astronomers would easily find and track the huge spaceship had the orbits continued. Also, the civil wars Shelepin spawned and the lead up to the Cuban missile crisis distracted the Russians enough to where the Caronians spent all their time on earth exclusively with Americans.

But since scientists tend to have big mouths and have a hard time keeping secrets, there was suddenly interest by the KGB in some of the rumors circulating around on some of the campus they had infiltrated in Berkeley, Boston, and New York City.

Shelepin was going to get to the bottom of it because Khrushchev was now starting to get on his nerves and the growing tensions in Cuba were gradually making things worse that could ultimately lead to the big showdown.

~~~

By noon, Sophia was woken out of a nap by a knock on the trailer. It was an Air Force Major who informed her *she was being relocated to other facilities.* Someone else from NASA would be arriving and would take her place in the trailer as well as all her official NASA duties.

Virtually moments later, a female Air Force officer, Lieutenant O'Grady based on her name tag on her uniform said, "I've been sent over to help you get your personal belongings. You are being moved to a CIA enclosure that has increased security due to your role with the Aliens."
~~~

"These facilities here are good enough for me and there is a military guy outside providing an element of security. I don't think I need to relocate."

"I'm sorry Dr. Kuznetsov but this is a security matter. The CIA who I also work for even though I'm wearing a uniform, is very concerned about your security and they want you some place where they know they can protect you and isolate you from a growing number of people that have requested interviews with you."

"What you are really saying is they want to limit my communication with my peers and professionals that are here for this extraordinary event?"

"Doctor Kuznetsov, as a security specialist, I see the virtue in what the CIA has arranged. You soon will discover you now have a very important role, and we have to protect you."

"If this will help me get back to designing spacecraft in a few years, then I'm team player all the way."

"Thanks for being a team player, Doctor Kuznetsov, our missions sometimes get tough."

Sophia looked into Lieutenant O'Grady's eyes and with premature wrinkles and other indicators knew this woman had probably gone through some stress detailed to the CIA. Little did Sophia know Lieutenant O'Grady had several adventures where she ended up at Checkpoint Charlie that separated East and West Berlin. Her days as a Cryptologist at the American Embassy in Prague, Czechoslovakia was some of the worst days of her life. Especially the time she had to assist Tracey Barnes operating nearby in Hungary during the uprising in 1956.

Lieutenant O'Grady was there to give Sophia a ride and move all her personal belongings, but she also knew more about what was going on with Sophia than she let on. As soon as they loaded up the 1959 Plymouth Station Wagon, they drove a short distance on the other side of all the UFO enclosures to an area that looked kind of strange.

"It's a big tent that is camouflaged," Lieutenant O'Grady stated.

"I actually thought it was a hill until we got closer," Sophia Kuznetsov stated.

Under the large tent it felt like a different Climate. Actually, it was because the tent had a couple air conditioners that kept it cool and out of the direct sunlight.

"It comes with running water, toilets that flush, a real shower, private bathroom, etc. All assigned to you."

It was clear almost immediately the CIA had more funds than NASA to take care of their employee's comfort.

No sooner that she got her suitcase unpacked and was starting to relax and mentally prepare herself for this Alien meet, than someone knocked at the door. It was a couple women both carrying a several small suitcases.

"Hi, I'm Jane and this is Barbara, we are here to help do your makeup."

Barbara had a couple dresses not too much different than dresses Sophia would wear and explained, "We are your personal makeup artists, we will help you plan any public appearances."

"This is getting interesting," Sophia Kuznetsov said then reflected that she was slowly getting immersed into something she didn't bargain for. She was also sophisticated enough to realize rotten bastards at the CIA could hurt her badly if she wasn't a team player. In her own mind she realized more than ever, the Alien attraction to her led to all this. And now she was a pawn in a game of superpower efforts to collect the lion share of the technology out of the Aliens. Sophie had just become a CIA concubine. It was disgusting and it was pitiful, but it also put great fear in her in what her masters would ultimately expect out of her.

"You are a fine-looking woman Miss Kuznetsov, and probably do not need any makeup, but there are always reasons for everything."

Even though Sophia had been a PhD in aerospace for several years, she was still young having completed her master's degree at the age of 21 and PhD at the age of 23. Looks were deceiving. Even though she looked very young and quite beautiful, she was also a tough cookie on design issues and applied her mathematical genius to solving design issues including the pioneering of what would soon be considered primitive modal analysis of rocket bodies.

The Mercury space craft designed for a single astronaut was actually very advanced for its day, and the Mercury electronics were revolutionary including establishing the foundation for future space flights during the Gemini and Apollo missions. The Mercury spacecraft, America's first manned space vehicle, was designed, developed, and built by McDonnell Douglas Aircraft (Merged with Boeing many years later) in St. Louis. A total of 20 Mercury spacecraft were delivered to NASA, six of which carried astronauts into space between 1961 and 1963. Among Sophia's contributions included technology leading to advancements in autopilot, rate stabilization and control, and fly-by-wire systems.

While the 2 makeup artists performed their magic, Sophia transcended from a cute lady to a gorgeous creature that would humble mere mortals, let alone Caronians.

Clothes the CIA handpicked to accentuate her, added to the luster which no doubt would soon influence Doctor Metongy Zeugcha. Around 9:00 p.m. she was ready and there was a knock at the door to her private trailer which was nice and cool and comfortable and would never give a hint she was out in the middle of the hot desert during the day. She went to the door and Tracey Barnes was there and said, "I'm here to take you to the next meeting."

Tracey Barnes was a very handsome man. He always remained in good shape, though exposure to hot deserts in North Africa and the Tropics of Guatemala and winters of Hungary was starting to turn his boyish flamboyant looks into a leatherier complexion exhibiting someone who had experienced the rigors of life. If it were not for the fact, they had a mission to perform that would get in the way of any pursuit of a romantic tryst, Sophia now possessed the image that would just about push Tracey over the edge to join the pursuit. The CIA had done their magic on Sophia, and it would not be the last time they would do something like this to further their goals as their top spies were often pampered with similar applications.

Tracey Barnes and Sophia Kuznetsov got in the 1959 Plymouth station wagon with the engine running, air conditioner running, which was a rare component in cars at this time, since they added severely to the price of the automobile, most people would not spend the extra funds to include the feature. CIA had air conditioning in all their Area 51 automobiles.

The drive to the landing strip did not take long. The

number of white tents had increased in the past 12 hours. The Aliens were soon asked to split into 4 groups in separate tents so that multiple conversations could go on and better access to scientists with spread out seating arrangements.

When Metongy Zeugcha queried all the Caro during the day how many would consider staying on earth to study the people and the planet, understanding they would have to go through a quarantine period before they would be allowed to mix with the Earth people, he came up with an initial head count of 6 Caro including himself. Those six Caro were divided into tent #1 and tent #2, the remainder were divided into tent #3 and tent #4.

As promised the night before, Hank got a front row seat in tent #3 and the remainder of the seats was assigned based on reservations.

Metongy Zeugcha and Doctor Provkovitev were escorted into the Alien side of tent #1 by security men wearing bio hazard suits that would be burned in a decontamination cell after the Aliens left for the mother ship several hours later.

Sophia was seated in the middle next to Allen Dulles,

Tracey Barnes and Richard Bissell and they were surrounded by another 25 scientists in the tent which had limited and restricted access.

Doctor Metongy Zeugcha leading Doctor Provkovitev and Doctor Marlneiker walked directly to the glass screen and sat down in the student chair with desktop, paper pad and several sharpen pencils.

The transformation of Sophia Kuznetsov had a stimulating effect on Metongy Zeugcha. He had sudden eruption of emotions that had been rare in his life and not typical of any he experienced since his personal life had been inactive as he pursued his research during the 15 years prior to the Gamulin Mission. The desire to remain on Earth was now growing and his attraction to this Earth woman who ostensibly had clouded his common sense and impacted his rational thinking.

Doctor Provkovitev was also leaning on staying simply because of vast curiosity and the novelty of experiencing a strange place. In essence it would be like a 10-year government paid vacation where work wasn't really required, and he assumed he would be pampered and flowered with tangible activities that anyone might enjoy.

Sophia noticed a table was in the tent on the Alien side of the glass wall had several items. She quickly surmised the materials were some of the things she requested which included a dictionary, several books, magazines, a globe, a few maps, and a small box of pictures that appeared to be labeled.

"Doctor Metongy Zeugcha, if you look at the table to your right you will see some materials, we are giving you to take back to your ship and back to your planet that will help you study us."

"Thank you."

"There is also a phonograph with some albums that contained a variety of music."

"How does it work?"

"There should be some instructions inside the box."

"How is it powered?"

"The phonograph is battery powered; your engineers should be able to figure out how to build a power supply for when the batteries all run down."

Metongy Zeugcha then said, "We'll send for some protective covers to carry those materials onto our ship and our medical personnel will disinfect them before we look at them."

Allen Dulles then asked, "Have you made a decision as to whether any of the Caro is willing to remain on Earth in a personnel exchange?"

"Yes, we think six of us are willing to stay. How many Earth people are willing to travel back to Caro?"

"Right now, we have 12 scientists as volunteers willing to go back to Caro with your ship."

"We do not have the luxury of doing quarantine on board. Your volunteers will be immediately exposed to any of our Bio-Hazards, so they must understand up front, there will be a risk to them."

"I'm sure they will understand the risk. Which leads me to ask you, when will your volunteers staying be ready to start the quarantine process here on Earth?"

"I discussed this with the crew, and we have all unanimously came to the conclusion it would be best for everyone if we do the personnel exchange and our ship depart immediately back to Caro."

"We hate to see your ship leave so soon."

"We have already succeeded in the goals of our mission and it's most important that we get back to inform our leaders the validation of this discovery and thus plan for a future visit and possible technology exchange."

What Metongy Zeugcha was really thinking is they needed to get back with the proof of the aliens before the Clerics could possibly overthrow the government and prevent their return. They didn't want to return home to a hostile reception.

"That's a good idea. No doubt such actions will prevent people from having second thoughts and change their mind."

"I doubt the six Caro staying will change their mind."

"Some of the Earth people might, this situation has never occurred in all of human history before."

"Are the 12 individuals that would go with us here tonight?"

"Yes, they are, all unmarried people, no chance of breaking up Families."

"Then your government could take care of their personal affairs which means they could leave with the ship tonight?"

"Certainly, they all would be willing to leave tonight with you."

"Doctor Provkovitev will return to the ship now with the Caro who will be leaving and come back with special containers for the gifts you gave us, and a pilot who will take the 12 people up to the ship."

"Will your ship leave orbit then?"

"The Interplanetary Transport will almost be out of the solar system by morning."

Doctor Provkovitev then stood up and was soon escorted to Tents #3 and #4 and gathered the Caro who would be leaving the planet and returned to the shuttle. Several people outside observing the shuttle watched the Aliens depart, wondering what was going on, but were soon told some of the Aliens remained so the Q & A could continue.

In due time the shuttle returned with Provkovitev and the pilot, each carrying what would appear like a few modern-day trash bags and went into Tent #1. With Doctor Provkovitev guidance they picked up all he gifts and put them in the bags and sequentially carried them to the shuttle which raised great curiosity of the gathering crowd.

Names were called out and the 12 scientists who had volunteered to leave were escorted over to building 28 and put on a bus. The bus immediately left for the proposed S-4 area that would be the rendezvous so that crowds would not know the 12 scientists were leaving on the Alien ship.

Doctor Provkovitev retook his seat next to Metongy Zeugcha and continued with the interviews until after the last bag was loaded aboard the cargo bay of the shuttle. Director Dulles met Metongy Zeugcha a few minutes later by the entrance of the tent and explained where the shuttle would pick up the men a few miles southwest of Groom Lake, including maps and then stated:

"The bus would be the only thing out there now with lights on, would be easy for the shuttle to see."

Even though the pilot could speak English. Metongy Zeugcha briefed the pilot in Caro language to make sure there were no misunderstandings. Metongy Zeugcha and the Pilot bowed towards each other and then the pilot entered the shuttle where he soon flew it vertical out of sight. The Caro Shuttle then swung around counterclockwise and headed down to S-4 designated area and quickly found the bus stopped waiting for the shuttle. The shuttle landed, the pilot got out and approached the bus.

The driver opened the door and the 12 scientists which included 2 women who didn't bring much with them because it was not required, walked towards the Shuttle. Shortly the door on the Caro Shuttle shut with everyone onboard and it lifted off into Space and in what seemed a very brief time docked in the Caro Interplanetary Transport. As soon as the Shuttle Bay hatch indicated shut, the Cyclonic Inverters cut in and from Area 51 people on the ground looking out into space could suddenly see a bright light for a while that appeared to be moving and gradually faded out after an hour. The space pioneers started their voyage to Caro and the existence of this Alien Exchange program was then buried conceivably forever.

After several more hours of Q & A, the Aliens were led out to an area by the tents where a bus with a man in a bio suit pulled up. The Aliens got on and it drove off to an undisclosed location where brand new trailer houses had been brought in that had water, electricity, sewer connections and fully fitted out for long term stay.

The facility was surrounded by guards and eight-foot-tall barbed wire fence. Hence security at the initial S-4 facilities was extremely tight and evolved into what is now one of the most controversial locations in the United States including claims from Bob Lazar, and others that have since came forward to corroborate his claims. One of the more distinguished witnesses is a former Air Force SR-71 pilot [5.11.21SR-71 Blackbird Pilot Confirms Bob Lazar Story : UAP.News].

Metongy Zeugcha suggested to the 5 others staying on Earth with him, "We should proceed now and even with the fear of possible death by ingesting Alien food, get on with the program and if it kills us, we are ready to meet the end."

Doctor Provkovitev added, "Our lifelong goals have been fulfilled, so there should be no fear of dying."

To their pleasant surprise the food tasted good and none of them had too badly of a physical reaction though some did have diarrhea for a few days. Apparently after a few days their guts acquired the right bacterial flora, all their digestive issues ended.

The Caro were all men and had been away from society for well over a year, so another delay because of the quarantine was not a serious challenge. Nobody except for MJ-12 and CIA knew these Aliens remained. Metongy was delighted when his CIA contact Tracey Barnes indicated, "You will be seeing a lot of Sophia Kuznetsov."

~~~
~~~

Chapter Forty-One
The Sardukretchen Differentiator

On Caro, the Clerics were still in disarray over Cleric Zrebrek, and the **Sardukretchen's Temple remained empty for several months after it was announced** Zrebrek **had been arrested and convicted of conspiracy and attempted murder.** Pirsrgyo information was never released as it was determined his sabotage would cause the government a lot of grief should the public become aware of such treachery existed.

Cleric Gummartukchik always staying arm's length away from ever being implicated in any conspiracy because he always operated through other Clerics who swore their allegiance to the Sardukretchen's. Cleric Gummartukchik knew he had to prepare for the return of the Caro to silence them before they could ever breath a word of information concerning Earth to the public or the Planetary Security Service.

Cleric Gummartukchik **figured the Interplanetary Transporter would attempt contacting Caro when they returned back in range to communicate with the planet which most likely coincided with the point, they would start to get down to light speed or below and possibly after they started breaking to slow down as they entered the solar system. At this point in time, it was unknown what would happen if a spacecraft hit the denser hydrogen within the solar system traveling above light speed. Some calculations indicated it could severely damage the ship if not destroy it. Should such a disaster happen, the Cleric would be most happy. However, it's unlikely because the plan was to slow down before they reached that critical point.**

Cleric Gummartukchik needed advance warning of the approach. Nobody including the Planetary Security Service really knew for sure if or when the Interplanetary Transport would come back, or even be able to return. So many variables existed nobody could predict, and the first they would know the ship survived would be the initial communications upon return and approaching the solar system and the slow down point.

The only way the Sardukretchen's would be able to beat the Planetary Security Service would be to have their own Mass Differentiator to look for clues. The best place to have a Mass Differentiator would be side by side of an observatory. Cleric Gummartukchik wasted no time in arranging for an observatory be built near a mountain top just east of Preznium. The 15,000-foot peak was above the thick air and far enough away from the city where night lighting did not have a depilatory impact.

Within six months of the Interplanetary Transport departure, ground was broken on the Sardukretchen's Observatory, and a very secret building next to it housed the Sardukretchen's Mass Differentiator.

Ten months after Metongy Zeugcha's Gamulin Mission was on its way, the observatory started its initial operations. As the planet spun on its axis numerous night sky stars were photographed and analyzed, but each time they got near a point they could train the telescopes on the Gamulin solar system, all attention was devoted there. A couple months later the Sardukretchen Differentiator started operating and as expected as it pointed towards Earth which they could do 33% of the time due to orbit and positioning, the radio signals from earth were intercepted.

The Clerics did not have an Arithmetic Preconvolver or a scientist like Metongy Zeugcha capable of building and operating one. Sardukretchen Cleric's mathematicians were just as good as Ferdastad but without Arithmetic Preconvolver working on the small signals to clean them up, the electro-clarifier was never going to spit out the vast amount of data Ferdastad and Metongy Zeugcha accomplished before the Gamulin Mission commenced.

With the power and influence that Clerics had over society, it didn't take them long to reach out and find those that could develop technology that met or exceeded the Arithmetic Preconvolver. Within six months before the Interplanetary Transport return an ambitious plan by people motivated by material wealth and other factors started to produce results. Their determined and disciplined efforts paid off in ways nobody expected. Scientific analytical process and

Gummartukchik's perseverance gradually exposed real time information derived through algebraically designed algorithms.

The Sardukretchen's Differentiator gave much information in parallel that Planetary Security Service would obtain through the team now managed by Ferdastad. Should there be any Earth communications that exhibited an Alien arrival the Clerics would have it at the same time as the Planetary Security Service and if they were lucky even before, assuming the Interplanetary Transport would be signaling before absolute assurance of transmission quality to make sure Caro detected them on the inbound leg as early as possible to make sure their arrival was properly handled.

Since Planetary Security Service did not plan on returning Aliens, the ship would have to make contact well before arrival to make sure all the proper guidance would direct them and facilities provided for the Aliens, such as quarantine or any other considerations.

On the return trip, the Caro did DNA analysis of the Earth people who looked almost identical and one of the major wonders of the universe became understood. The persuasive DNA test results showed an almost close match, which articulated, the two widely separated societies either came from the same creator, which was the conventional viewpoint, or through galactic history they were widely separated due to some galactic event.

Clerics spies, saboteurs, and operatives were slowly organized, and possible acts were contemplated. One logical conclusion is the ship would most likely be put back in the Space Dock upon arrival for checks and repairs and possibly refitting for future missions, not only to the Gamulin System but possibly somewhere else. The possibilities were frightening to the Clerics, because of one question: "What if we find life on other planets besides Earth and Caro?"

The Clerics had no way of knowing that Doctor Provkovitev had negotiated a personnel exchange. If they had that knowledge the level of effort would far exceed what they were now doing. And it never crossed their mind that such activity could exist because the Interplanetary Transport was not designed for any passengers other than Caro, including isolation and protection from transmitting potentially extremely harmful germs and bacteria that might threaten society.

The Germ Card is something the Clerics would no doubt press should such discovery ever manifest. And because the ship returned quicker than the radio waves, the Interplanetary Transport would send most of the crew down in the two shuttles leaving only a skeletal crew for Space Docking operations.

Because the atmospheric controls aboard the Interplanetary Transport as well as the relative health of the 12 Americans, the close confinement for a year did not expose any diseases or serious medical conditions other than the aging process would continue regardless of their disposition in space.

~~~
~~~

Chapter Forty-Two
Quarantine

On Earth the Quarantine period lasted almost a year. With television sets, radio's, record players, and an exercise area next to the trailers allowed the Caronians to gradually get used to their new environment while quickly grasping the essence of what life was like on Earth.

Happiness prevailed until one fateful day. During October 22, 1962, at 7:00 pm EDT, when President Kennedy was suddenly on TV addressing the American Public. Since all broadcasts were interrupted on TV, Metongy Zeugcha suddenly observed President Kennedy delivering this nationwide televised address on all the major networks announcing the discovery of the nuclear missiles in Cuba 90 miles from America's shore.

The words were frightening. Metongy Zeugcha had by now discovered America and Russia now both had Hydrogen Bombs. A number of these weapons were no longer City Killers, they were now Country Killers. It would not take many of them to exterminate the Earth.

Area 51 Sector-4 was close enough to Groom Lake to hear aircraft activity and sometimes see them take off rapidly into the air. U2 spy planes with the long wings took off from Area 51 and flew down to Cuba and back delivering numerous pictures of the Soviet SS-4 missiles. Without operation "Boresight" and "SOSUS" the Soviets would have achieved the purpose of the grand plan and strategy KGB director Alexander Nikolayevich Shelepin had planned. And when Khrushchev was humiliated by Kennedy who shocked Khrushchev by informing him of **the location of every single Soviet Submarine in the world** that had been compromised by **BORESIGHT** and **SOSUS**, Vladimir Yefimovich Semichastny his protégée was then moved in as KGB director so that Shelepin could proceed to work on the ouster of Khrushchev for cowering to the

American President.

Even though Metongy Zeugcha was attracted to Sophia Kuznetsov and had designs towards her, the sudden shock that he was now marooned on a planet just about to be wiped out in a nuclear war made him feel like he made a terrible bad choice to remain on Earth.

Sophia Kuznetsov arrived shortly after the Kennedy speech because she knew the Aliens would see it and they would be alarmed if not terribly concerned they had stumbled into the beginning of a nuclear war. It was rather ironic that possibly the only survivors to Earth's potential nuclear holocaust were now traveling to an Alien planet.

Metongy Zeugcha watched intently Kennedy speaking, "It shall be the policy of this nation to regard any nuclear missile launched from Cuba against any nation in the Western Hemisphere as an attack by the Soviet Union on the United States, requiring a full retaliatory response upon the Soviet Union."

"Does this mean we are all going to die?" Metongy asked while Kennedy continued speaking.

"To halt this offensive buildup, a strict quarantine on all offensive military equipment under shipment to Cuba is being initiated. All ships of any kind bound for Cuba, from whatever nation or port, will, if found to contain cargoes of offensive weapons, be turned back. This quarantine will be extended, if needed, to other types of cargo and carriers. We are not at this time, however, denying the necessities of life as the Soviets attempted to do in their Berlin blockade of 1948."

Sophia tried to reassure the Aliens. "I'm sure everything will work out ok, each country has too much to lose by starting a nuclear war."

All day long jets were taking off at Area 51 including the A12 which created incredible loud vibrations as it went up. The U2 spy planes sent down to Cuba were also extremely loud taking off with afterburner.

It was obvious to Sophia all this extra noise from these surveillance aircraft coming and going all day long wasn't reassuring to the Aliens. They had never observed this density of aircraft operations nearby, especially when the U2 spy planes kicked in the afterburners to get up to altitude quickly.

Burning the extra fuel to get up in the air quickly was not a problem because the U2s would be air refueled over Tulsa Oklahoma by a new Boeing KC-135 Stratotanker on the way to Cuba and on the way back if necessary. This extended the aircraft's range from approximately 4,000 to 8,000 nautical miles (7,400 to 15,000 km) and extended its endurance to more than 14 hours. Sadly, a couple of those U2 spy planes would not return because Russians shot them down flying near Cuba.

This seemed like a very strange day to the Caronians, and when President Kennedy spoke about the Cuban Missile Crisis, the sensation was greatly intensified.

Part of the Psychological Warfare the Americans now performed on the Soviets included flying the A12 from Area 51 to Kadena Airbase in Japan and back, getting refueled on the way to and from. The last refueling over the Pacific Northeast of Hokkaido Japan gave the jet all the fuel it needed to buzz by Vladivostok then continue down and land at Kadena and be put in the hanger until it got dark again and they would return back to Area 51. The Soviet radars got a few hits on the plane because its radar cross section was not perfectly stealthily, at certain angles. The A12 noise taking off agitated the Aliens and it added to the stress and feeling of helplessness.

"When will this all end?" Metongy Zeugcha asked.

"I think people will come to their senses soon and this will be over with shortly," Sophia offered knowing Metongy appeared to exhibit great fear.

"What about your war with Japan, you deployed 3 nuclear weapons back then?"

"Only two were used attacking Japan, the third was the test bomb we detonated in the desert first."

"I see. Is that why it didn't seem to have the same yield as the next two actually dropped on Japan?"

"That's correct it was a much smaller bomb."

Metongy Zeugcha now knew his trip to Earth was far more

important than what he realized, because *if this planet ever developed Interplanetary Transports, the Caro would be at risk.*

The Cuban Missile Crisis situation escalated; Major Anderson's U-2 was shot down over Cuba just hours after Richard Bissell wished his good friend a safe flight. The Earth was not presenting a good image to the Aliens, but things would eventually get worse as the Vietnam War came about. The U-2 shoot down almost triggered the nuclear war.

A lot of scary events occurred which had the Aliens knew about would have greatly added to their fear and regret of being on Earth. But on October 28 after numerous and continuous lab tests the medical results showed conclusive evidence the Aliens were actually cleaner in many respects than Humans, the decision was to remove the quarantine. They were now free to mingle with the humans. It was an auspicious day in that Russia and America came to agreements on the end of the Cuban Missile Crisis.

The worlds' view is that Khrushchev backed down, and that was used by Alexander Nikolayevich Shelepin to remove Khrushchev from power. At the same time General Curtis Lemay had a differing opinion than the joint chiefs when he said, "The Cuban Missile Crisis was the greatest defeat in our history."

Anyone analyzing the poor agreement Kennedy made agreeing to pull Jupiter missiles out of Italy and Turkey while at the same time strengthening Castro's hand in Cuba tends to support LeMay's claim. Kennedy was also removed from power just before Khrushchev. And by that time Allen Dulles and Richard Bissell had been fired. Tracey Barnes survived a few more years, but he too fell on his sword when Lyndon Johnson's CIA director Richard Helms had Desmond Fitzgerald fire Tracey Barnes. The Aliens would never again see the three CIA men.

"Now that you are no longer in Quarantine, would you like to see some of America?" Sophia asked.

Still feeling somewhat bewildered over the Cuban Missile Crisis, Metongy Zeugcha was slow to respond as he felt his inner sanctum had been tested to its limits as nothing on Caro had ever seemed this grave before. Even the Clerics situation now seemed far more tolerable. Perhaps this mission was a huge mistake because now the Earth men knew about the Caro. If he had to do it all over again, he might have sided with the Sardukretchen's. But as he was soon to discover, that due to the strange space conditions, Earth would never receive signals from Caro. Knowing that would be comforting.

Sophia observing Metongy's radical departure from his prior jovial self knew the Cuban missile crisis was troubling him deeply and tried to snap him out of it and said, "We can go to Las Vegas and see some shows, do a little gambling, then plan to visit some other cities."

"I suppose that would be okay, I was just transfixed on this Cuba deal, I truly was scared."

"You are not alone; the world was scared."

"Even the Russians?"

"The Russians were particularly scared because it would have been worse than WWII which they never want to see again."

"Reasonableness prevailed this time, but what about the next time?"

"I think we came so close to the brink that everyone is soul searching."

"When will we go to Las Vegas?"

"We can leave in the early morning to avoid traveling when it's too hot at mid-day."

"What about the other Caro?"

"We have other activities planned for them. Doctor Provkovitev is going to be invited to Washington DC to visit the Pentagon. Doctor Marlneiker is going to be taken to an educational institution MIT. The others are going to be taken down to Cape Canaveral to watch one of our space craft launches."

"Is there any reason why we can't just leave now and go?"

"We are going to provide you with some identity and brief you on how you should act."

"I already have an identity, I'm Metongy Zeugcha."

"I'm sorry Metongy; the world does not know you are here. The decision was made to hide your identity because the government is fearful that if the public knew we have Aliens living on this planet there would be mass hysteria and lose control."

"You Americans are starting to sound like the Cleric on my planet."

"I'm sorry but the public is not prepared to deal with your arrival."

"What about all the scientists that I saw in the tents when we arrived."

"They're all scientists, sworn to secrecy and would go to prison if they divulged your arrival."

Metongy Zeugcha was starting to feel more and more anxiety. The combination of the Cuban Missile Crisis and the secrecy of his being were overwhelming. If it were not for the fact this beautiful Earthling was so nice to him and seemingly encouraging him, he wasn't sure he could cope and survive.

Two of the three CIA men were no longer in position to help Sophia and soon the third would be gone. Their departure from the immediate activities seemed to make this entire operation questionable. Sophia was now just living day to day wondering when the big ax would come down on it all. She had also become quite intertwined with the DD/P folks and knew quite a bit more about operations than normal CIA or NASA employees, was well aware it would not be out of the question for the CIA to whack these Aliens to permanently hide the fact they arrived. They also questioned whether the Aliens would come back in a dozen or so years like they promised.

Even though Sophia still had some perks, the constant make-up jobs and psychological operation to more or less seduce this Alien were now behind her with Allen Dulles departure. She preferred to dress up more plainly with less makeup and Metongy Zeugcha preferred her when she was more natural. *Earth women were far vainer than Caro. Perhaps it was due to more overcrowding on Caro, or the fact they were more advanced may reduce such desires?*

The seemingly dishonest methods of fake I.D. and subterfuge he was asked to carry out didn't set well with Metongy's moral and ethical values. This was just one more thing that made his desire to stay less and less. *It was almost unbearable sitting here getting briefed by the CIA man concerning his I.D. and his fake family that was all made up in the event he ran into difficulties and was separated.*

Special phone numbers were sewn into his clothes so in a panic all he had to do is call from a telephone which he was now very capable of using after much time in Quarantine, he learned to use. All he had to do is tell the operator it was a collect call, and she would patch him through. CIA had people 7/24 ready to answer those emergency numbers.

That evening just as he was feeling drudgery, Sophia surprised him when she suddenly showed up with a bag full of groceries and said, "Tonight is your lucky night."

"Why is that?"

"I'm going to cook you a meal." Sophia said as she thought the mere activity would be a useful distraction.

Sophia knew everything that was in his kitchen in his trailer as the CIA was very careful in making sure every specific item the program manager determined should be there to support the Aliens was delivered.

In a reasonable amount of time the private meal was served, and they sat down together which turned out to be their very first meal together. It marked a special event.

Sophia could tell Metongy was calming down a bit and now the TV was considerably more benign. Part of the reason was Kennedy secretly pleaded with the network officials at CBS, ABC, and NBC to calm down the airways and give people a rest from the Cuban Missile Crisis for a few days. Normal programming was resumed. Ed Sullivan show, Jackie Gleason and the Honeymooners, Lawrence Welk and a variety of other popular shows were now on in place of the constant news cycle concerning the Cuban Missile Crisis.

Sophia watched intently as Metongy grabbed his first bite with the fork and tasted the food. Sophia was a fantastic cook. Her Russian mother had taught her well when she was a girl in grade school and because her family was very close, she was always getting cooking tips from her mother.

The food was unlike anything Metongy had in his lifetime. Sitting there eating and looking at this beautiful woman who made it for him suddenly shifted his spirits. The music on the Ed Sullivan show playing while they were eating added to the ambience. Had Sophia thought more about it she might have brought a candle, but whether she could have got one in time is another question.

After the meal and a little more TV, Sophia insisted on washing the dishes and when she was all done, she said, "I'm sorry Metongy but I need to go back to where I live and do a few things and get ready for tomorrow and get some decent sleep so that I can get up early in the morning."

"Sophia, thank you very much for the meal, it was very special to me."

"You are welcome Metongy, I'm glad you liked it."

~~~
~~~

Chapter Forty-Three
Road Trip

The next morning only the two of them got in the Plymouth station wagon with Sophia driving and they scooted off the base and down what would later be named the "Extra Terrestrial Hiway" and made their way down Hiway 93 and on into Vegas which had just starting to build a few Casinos on the strip.

Frank Sinatra and the Rat Pack shows and time in the swimming pool and a little gambling on CIA money and a few other activities seemed to distract Metongy really well to the point he blocked out all thoughts of the Cuban Missile Crisis or the loneliness he felt while he and his Caro colleagues were in Quarantine.

The Sands Hotel Casino operators thought it was kind of strange *the man and woman had separate hotel rooms*. And the surveillance they spotted on the two left them with the notion something nefarious was going on. Some of the hotel security people met up with several FBI agents whom they knew, so they understood this really was indeed some serious surveillance. However, the FBI seemed to leave the couple alone.

The next day Sophia said to Metongy, "We are going to the airport and fly to Las Angeles, going to show you a major city and a theme park."

"Okay, that sounds interesting. What is a theme park?"

Sophia then explained to Metongy what a theme park was and the various aspects of Disneyland which would give Metongy ample time to observe up close society having fun at such an event.

"What will happen to the car?"

"Another agent will drive the car back to Papoose Lake at Area 51, S-4."

They both got into a taxi and drove to McCarran Airport and were soon seated on a TWA Convair 880 four engine jet which seemed like it didn't take long to get to Los Angeles where they were met curb side by a company driver who dropped them off at Disneyland in about 25 minutes.

"I thought I would show you where a lot of people take their Families for entertainment."

The amusement park had a number of fun rides and lots of good things to eat. An ice cream cone was excellent. The association with Mickey Mouse further isolated any thoughts on the Cuban Missile Crisis. Metongy thought it was interesting that nobody seemed to remember or care that a nuclear holocaust was narrowly avoided. As Sophia predicted, life moved on.

The novelty of the steam engine train circling Disneyland interested Metongy quite a bit. Then he saw the Monorail and thought, *this would be better than a Crawler and it sure goes a lot faster.*

When they walked by the waterfront and saw the steamboat and the sailing ship, Sophia had to explain them to him. And when they walked past the submarine ride, she explained how they worked and the nuclear-powered submarines that shot Polaris Missiles. Unfortunately, Sophia didn't realize she caused Metongy to suddenly feel some of the emotions he just escaped from observing the Cuban Missile Crisis on round the clock coverage by American TV Networks.

Metongy started thinking, *"The submarines would most likely have been in a war had it started."*

They spent the night in Anaheim and in the morning, Sophia suggested, "Us take the train down to San Diego, we can go visit San Diego Zoo and Balboa Park."

"Alright," Metongy said smiling and interested in observing more of this planet. However, he already determined when the Caro came back in a few years he would leave this planet behind. It turned out not to be what he expected.

The "company" driver took them to Los Angeles Union Station.

The landmark station slowly was losing its relevance as people were shifting to air transportation, but there were 3 major railroads serving the station and at the time they walked out to the train platform waiting for their train down to San Diego that would be arriving in a couple minutes. A Southern Pacific passenger train was one track over in one direction and a Union Pacific City of Los Angeles train one track over on the other direction. Within moments the Santa Fe train they would board slowly backed into the terminal.

This regional train had left Santa Barbara early that morning and would have them down to San Diego in less than 2 hours. As soon as the train stopped, several passengers got off and Sophia led Metongy to car #3 which was indicated on their ticket. They quickly found their seats and in 15 minutes the train slowly started pulling out of the terminal. Metongy felt very comfortable and far more luxurious than the Crawlers or Tube Trains back on Caro. The train seemed to be moving very slow and Metongy thought San Diego must not be very far away if they were going so slow.

The further they got away from the station the more the train sped up. To some extent the experience was thrilling because Metongy got to peer out and see a lot of humanity. The train passed crossings that cars were patiently waiting and in some cases automobiles and trucks on roads paralleling the tracks either passed by or were maintaining a slightly different speed than the train while the train sped up.

Metongy marveled at the vast number of automobiles.

People on Caro would be amazed that Earth people had so vast number of private transportation vehicles.

Houses and buildings were often close to the tracks. *Those people must be lucky they can see all the trains going by every day,* Metongy thought.

Some homes had very well-maintained yards; others indicated a lack of personal pride. In due time the size and scale of Los Angeles became apparent. Caro cities were high density and relied on high rise buildings. There were few if any small homes like he witnessed. Only the clerics and the wealthy lived in homes that small with private yards.

As the train slowly edged out of Los Angeles it soon started passing farms. The Orange trees were spread out in large amounts. Metongy was quite interested in the trees with the large fruits hanging and asked, "What are those Trees?"

"Those are Orange trees."

After a while the farms were behind them and they were suddenly traveling along the coast. The vast Pacific Ocean suddenly sprang into view which left quite an impression with Metongy.

"That looks like a large body of water."

"Yes, the Pacific Ocean takes up more than ¼ of the surface of the planet."

Off to the distance perhaps two miles off the coast, Metongy saw a formation of ships and one huge ship in particular was in the middle of the group. They were all painted gray and had large numbers on them.

"What are those ships?"

"Those are Navy ships. The large one in the middle is an aircraft carrier."

"Why does it carry aircraft?"

"An Aircraft Carrier is like a sea borne tactical air base. It actually launches the aircraft that fly to targets in the event of war."

"Were they used in the Cuban Missile Crisis?"

"Yes, they were deployed to the vicinity of Cuba to carry out the embargo of restricting any ships delivering weapons."

"What kind of weapons do the aircraft that deploy from an aircraft carrier deploy?"

"They can drop any kind of bomb."

"Does that include nuclear weapons?"

"The purpose of an American Aircraft Carrier is to project power. Since there is a lot at stake, its most likely the Pentagon would use them to their full potential. If that included deploying nuclear weapons, the Pentagon would authorize it if it were necessary."

Metongy suddenly had a sudden lapse into melancholy as he quickly realized these humans were quite capable of destroying themselves quickly.

"Can they deliver Hydrogen bombs to a target?"

"Had the Cuban Missile Crisis elevated to an all-out war, most of the Aircraft Carriers would not have survived very long, but before their demise, it's conceivable they would have launched aircraft carrying hydrogen bombs and the Russians would quickly have regretted starting the conflict."

"How far can these aircraft fly?"

"It's my opinion that most of the pilots flying those aircraft realized they would not have an aircraft carrier to fly back to, would assume it would be a one-way trip, a suicide mission. As such if they made a one-way trip, since hydrogen bombs are relatively small, they would have fuel to allow them to fly several thousand miles. Any target we wanted to hit would be within their reach."

The incredible power and danger these ships imposed added to Metongy's worst nightmare, a planet he was now marooned on could conceivably destroy itself in the matter of hours. Coming to Earth now seemed like a huge mistake because the Earth people now knew where Caro existed. Metongy sadly felt, *I just made Caro a target.*"

The sunlight was coming from the East as it was morning which added greatly to the enjoyment looking out to the west. In due time, they saw campers and people on surfboards. The visual imagery of people enjoying the water sports helped in many ways to diminish the negative psychology created when Metongy looked at the Naval Vessels.

"Do you have ships like that on Caro?"

"No, we do not have such huge bodies of water. All our major areas that contain water are about one tenth the sizes. Also, any of our craft that go out on the water are Hovercraft."

"What is a Caro Hovercraft like?"

Metongy knowing that Sophia had a notebook and pencils with her said, "Let me see your notebook, I'll draw you a little picture of what they appear like."

Metongy was an excellent artist and drew a very nice replica of a Caronian Hovercraft. The following day when Sophia gave the picture to her CIA associate, it was soon sent via facsimile to the Pentagon and the Commander of Naval Operations was looking at the picture.

Within hours, the National Research Development Corporation sponsored a full-scale development of a craft that looked much like the drawing. The NRDC placed a contract with Saunders-Roe for the development of what would soon eclipse the SR-N1 which they had previously produced in 1958. Now a full military version as feasible as Metongy's drawing solved some of the major issues the current designs exhibited.

A short while later the train passed by an area that had flower fields. The sight enthralled Metongy as it provided imagery he never seen before.

The coastal Hiway appeared jammed with cars next to the train tracks; the congestion seemed to get worse the closer their passenger train got to San Diego.

Before long they went past an odd-looking series of buildings. "What are those?"

"That's a horse racetrack."

About that time Metongy observed a person on top of some huge creature and he asked, "What is that animal the human is on?"

"That's a horse; they ride them in the races that go on here."

Soon the train went inland and slowed down going up a hill and as they rounded the hill Metongy was suddenly surprised when a Military Jet took off from the Miramar Air Base and passed near the train. The aircraft seemed very loud, and they could hear it on the train.

"What kind of an aircraft is that?"

"That's a military aircraft; it's the type that flies off the ship's you saw earlier."

Soon the train sped up as it headed down a hill and were passing by a park like bay area. There were many homes now in this area and they passed by a busy intersection. Soon they passed by an area of large buildings and Metongy could see several aircraft.

"What are those aircraft?"

"Some of them are military, some are civilian."

"Are the aircraft there to defend the city?"

"No, they're manufactured here by a company named General Dynamics."

35 years later at the end of the cold war and after BRAC (Base Relocation and Closure) those former General Dynamics [Convair] buildings were torn down, and all such manufacturing of military aircraft and helicopters ceased. Across the Runway on Harbor

Drive was Teledyne Corporation heavily involved in military helicopter manufacturing. None of that Military Aerospace exists any longer in San Diego. The sprawling former General Dynamics Convair site out in Kearny Mesa is now Condo's and businesses. The old General Dynamics and Missile Park that had their own miniature railroad that employee Families could ride on the train (similar to Balboa Park) is now gone and replaced by commercial enterprises.

About that time, Metongy saw a plane taking off from the airport, it was a DC-8 a four-engine jet with a name, "United Airlines" on the side of it.

"Is that a military jet?"

"No that's a civilian passenger jet."

Metongy then thought, *that must be like a lot of the numerous aircraft they were tracking on the Interplanetary Transport.*

In a while the train slowed and came to a stop.

"Okay, we get off here."

Metongy followed Sophia off the train. On top of the building, he could see a big sign, "SANTA FE."

As soon as he got off the train, and walked towards the train station, another train started leaving the station. The two General Motors [EMD] built F9 diesel locomotives painted red on the front of the cab with a silver cab body increased its noise level as it appeared to be accelerating. The vibrations coming off the locomotive had an interesting sound to it which conveyed the notion of power, rich in harmonics. By the time they walked into the station the train departing was gone.

Metongy followed Sophia out the door and there was a yellow car sitting there they approached. The cab driver opened the door and Sophia said, "Get in; we are going to go in this vehicle."

The car soon pulled out after the driver shut their door and hopped in.

"Where do you want to go?" The cab driver asked.

"Take us to the San Diego Zoo, please." Sophia replied.

The car didn't drive very far before it made a left turn onto Broadway Street and drove for several blocks. The buildings were taller here, but nothing like Caro.

"What are these buildings like compared to Caro?" Sophia asked.

"Our buildings are about 10 times taller, and our streets are narrower."

As they passed a bus, Sophia asked, "Do you have transportation for the public like these busses?"

"No, our Crawlers are ten times longer and do not have wheels."

"I remember the picture you showed me when you first arrived. They must be impressive machines."

Soon the taxi turned left and crossed over a bridge and passed by Balboa Naval Hospital painted pink and were in a park like area.

The Taxi passed by a Ferris wheel and made a left turn. It soon passed by a scale model train that people were riding on and then on to the front entrance of the

Zoo.

Sophia paid the Taxi $2.00 which included the tip and the taxi driver then got out of the driver's seat and walked over and opened the cab door for the couple who quickly got out and proceeded to the Zoo entrance.

The cost for the ticket to the Zoo for each of them was $1.50; they soon were inside walking around looking at all the strange animals.

This was a strange sensation for Metongy because Caro had no Zoo's. Any wild animal caught there would quickly be eaten by anyone that caught them. Most of the planet was void of wild animals and only a few reserves existed where scientists were attempting to restore the wildlife population.

Metongy was slightly depressed from observing all the air pollution especially up in Los Angeles, but San Diego air was a lot cleaner and the park like appearance of the area was more appealing than where they came from. Even Disneyland had too much air pollution.

"Are these rare animals?"

"No, they exist in large numbers around the planet."

"If they have large numbers, what makes them so special to have on exhibit here?"

"Most of the people who live in America cannot see these animals. They come from other areas of the planet."

"It seems rather inhumane having them locked up here. It's almost like a jail for animals."

"I suppose you are right, but it's the only way, anyone in this city could ever see the animals, plus they are treated better and fed better here than they would be in the wild."

"Why do you say that?"

"In the wild some of these animals would be eating the others."

"I suppose that's a negative."

"Plus, areas go through periods of drought where they do not get rain, and the animals die from lack of food and water."

After walking about an hour or two, Sophia felt she was getting thirsty and said, "Why don't we get some food and drink."

"Alright."

Sophia led Metongy into a Zoo restaurant where they had hamburgers, French fries, and a Coca-Cola drink.

After the meal, Sophia said, "Us walk over to Balboa Park and look around; there are some nice buildings and museums over there."

They left the San Diego Zoo, walked back out to Park Boulevard, then continued on until they saw the waterfall and walked past it. A short distance was the Natural History Museum which Sophia thought would be good for Metongy to see to understand a little how this planet had formed.

The displays were rather remarkable. Some of the skeletons showcased showed huge ancient animals.

"These animals no longer exist?"

"No, they disappeared millions of years ago."

"What happened to them?"

"Some scientists believe a large asteroid hit the planet that caused a huge explosion and changed weather conditions that killed them all."

After a while it appeared that Metongy had seen all he was interested in, so Sophia suggested, "Why don't we go over to the art museum."

"Visiting an Art Museum sounds good."

They walked a block past some beautiful architecture and past a duck pond which had a building at the end of it that looked rather strange.

"What's in that building with the strange shape to it?"

"It's a display of plants and trees, a type of Botanical exhibit."

"Maybe we can go there after the Art Museum?"

"Sure, if that would please you."

The two entered the Balboa Park Art Museum and the main entrance had some impressive works which caught Metongy's attention very quickly.

"These Art works are absolutely beautiful. Are they rare?"

"Yes, quite a few of them are 200 and 300 or more years of age. The masters who created them are long gone."

"How many paintings are there here?"

"The Art Museum has 3 floors and has many paintings."

"Where did all these paintings come from?"

"Many of them were from masters donated or loaned. If you look at the little cards under the paintings it describes who donated them and who the artist is."

"I see, that's very generous of them," Metongy thought and realized there was little of such generosity on Caro. These Earthy people certainly have complexities he never realized.

After looking at the first-floor paintings, Metongy said, "We have nothing like this on Caro."

Those comments struck Sophia who suddenly thought, *life on that planet must be void of a lot of things we take for granted.*

Soon they climbed the stairs and looked at many more

paintings which had color and definition that transfixed Metongy and drove his consciousness to new realizations. Even though Earth was perilously in danger of self-destruction, it had subtle differences that transcended life on Caro. *Without the fear of nuclear annihilation, most Caronians would prefer living on this planet.*

The art exhibits were extraordinary all the way up through the 3rd floor. The paintings left an impression on Metongy that he would always have. If Earth could somehow figure out how to eliminate war and nuclear weapons it would be an ideal place to live. Metongy familiar with Caro history understood vividly that since Caro's fought the Tauceti for 150,000 years, it could be a very long time before such peace could be obtained. *But what if Aliens from a hostile planet suddenly appeared? The countdown for peace and reconciliation could then be extended another 150,000 years or indefinitely.*

"Okay, us go to the Botanical Gardens," Metongy said, and Sophia acknowledged as they started down the staircase and soon headed towards the Gardens.

As they walked up the pathway by the duck pond there were a number of beautiful ducks floating around. Other ducks were walking along the shoreline showing no fear of the humans. Metongy was rather astonished that wild animals had no fear of the humans.

"Why are those birds not afraid of humans?"

"Because they see them every day and the humans feed them."

Inside the Botanical Gardens a screen canopy to keep out birds and animals was apparent. Metongy quickly noticed there were orchids and flowering plants with fabulous colors and images.

"Are these plants native to the area?"

"No, almost all of them were brought in from some distances."

"Just like the animals at the Zoo?"

"Precisely. The only place most San Diegan's can see these plants are here in the Balboa Park Botanical Gardens."

"What kinds of plants do people have in their homes?"

"They have a variety of plants, many of which are nothing

as exotic as the plant species you see here. Over there are Orchids. Some women have Orchids in their homes. It changes all the time as new fads erupt."

"What do you mean by fad?"

"It means something becomes popular and people copy the activity, which might be selection of clothes, plants for the home, the way they cut their hair, just human nature in general."

"What do you plan to do next?"

"When we get done here, we can get a TAXI and go on a site seeing tour."

"Alright."

In about 15 minutes they had seen much of what they wanted in the Botanical Gardens, and Sophia led them out of the area back to the Zoo where a line of taxi's waited for passengers. They approached a cab driver who opened the door for them, and they got in.

"Where do you want to go?"

"We want a taxi tour of San Diego; take us down by the

beach areas and some nice houses."

"Sure."

The cabbie drove down the short distance to Park Boulevard and made a right turn, drove on down to Broadway and made a right turn.

"This is the heart of the city."

The trolley tracks still ran down the center of Broadway, but no trolleys were operating.

"Where are all the Trolley's?" Sophia asked the cab driver.

"They have been discontinued for a few years. Private automobiles killed the Trolley industry."

They passed a new high rise building under construction then drove past the Greyhound Bus building and across the street was a Continental Bus company building.

"It looks like those bus stations are conveniently located near to the Railroad Passenger station," Sophie noted.

"Yea, there is no passenger trains heading East out of San Diego, they have to take the bus. Also, people that need to go to Escondido and beyond, must take a bus if they don't own a car," the cab driver responded.

Soon the taxi turned right on Harbor Boulevard, passed by a couple hotels, County administration building under construction and the waterfront.

Several fishing boats were in port and Sophia asked, "What do those boats fish for?"

"Those are Tuna boats."

"What's Tuna?" Metongy asked.

"It's a really nice fish, a lot of Americans love to eat Tuna."

"And the Japanese love to eat it raw?" The driver added thinking about sushi when he spent time in Japan in the Navy.

As the taxi continued along Harbor Boulevard soon was parallel with the Airport as a silver Boeing 707 jet was landing with the name American on the side.

"Is that another passenger jet?"

"Yes."

"Do you have a lot of Jets?"

"Yes, increasing every day, probably one every half hour."

"Does Caro have aircraft like passenger Jet Airliners?"

"No, we have atmospheric gliders that get launched on ramps and go a lot faster."

"How many people fly in the atmospheric gliders?"

"The larger models carry over 3000 Caro."

After a while they passed the Naval Training Center where they saw many recruits in formation marching along.

"What are those people doing?"

"They're training for the military."

"That's probably like our Planetary Security Service, but we no longer have wars. Our Planetary Security Service are now more or less just a police force."

The car turned left onto Scott Street and went past quite a few fishing boats.

"You can hire these guys to take you out on a day trip if you want to go fishing for big fish," the Cab driver said.

Metongy looked at some of the big fish hanging up that were being weighed and sold to individuals, then said, "Wow those are huge, how much do they weigh?"

"The Bonita there may weigh up to 10 pounds or so but the other fish like the big Tuna may weigh over 100 pounds. Atlantic Tuna can weigh up to 1500 pounds. A lot of Tuna the Japanese use for sushi weigh 250 pounds."

"What's sushi?" Metongy asked.

"The Japanese cut small pieces of the meat and put them on rice balls and put a little wasabi which is a hot spicy substance and you eat it with pickled ginger that supposedly prevents you from getting sick."

"Maybe in the future we can go on a fishing trip."

The cab then turned right went a block up to Rosecrans Street, made another right then a couple blocks later turned left on Nimitz Boulevard and continued.

The houses up on the hillside were apparently owned by affluent people, the size and decorations definitely stood out. The car continued and went across a bridge and then after a few twists and turns ended up next to the beach where a roller coaster and an amusement park stood.

"This is the Mission Beach area; you can have fun here."

"This looks like a mini-Disneyland."

"It is a lot smaller and doesn't have the large number of attractions that Disneyland has."

The Taxi turned right on Mission Bolevard and continued on. Eventually they saw a pier sticking out and a lot of tourists seemed to be there. The cab turned onto a side street that went right down to the beach. There were a lot of people out on the beach having fun. Women were almost naked! Metongy was shocked.

"On Caro we never saw anything like this!"

Sophia smiled knowing the cab driver had no idea what they were talking about.

A while later the road suddenly curved left then right again, and the cab was suddenly in La Jolla. The houses had impressive landscaping here.

"There is nothing like this on Caro. You Earth people really live-in extravaganza."

The cab driver was beginning to think the guy in the back was a weirdo. But he didn't care because he was making a lot of money driving them around. The woman was eye candy, so he didn't mind the fact he got a good look at her through the rear-view mirror.

The car snaked around La Jolla while Metongy Zeugcha took it all in. The buildings and the architecture had such pleasant appearances. The people were well dressed and healthy looking. Eventually they drove up a hill and soon the Cab driver took a side road and said, "This is the Scripps Institution of Oceanography, one of the most important research centers in America. It's been here since 1903."

The cab driver eventually got back up to the top of the hill and continued down a main road and said, "This is a new University of California. It's only been here a couple years." New buildings were apparent, and more were being built.

The cab made its way down the coastal hiway where it went past a community and the driver said, "This is Del Mar."

After they got through town he went to an open area and

Metongy quickly noticed the structure they saw on the train, as the driver said, "This is the Del Mar racetrack."

"Can we pull over and see some of those animals."

"You mean the horses."

"Certainly."

The car pulled up to the racetrack, they all got out of the car right when a jockey on a horse passed by close. Metongy was thrilled to see the animal up close. From the parking spot they could see the ponies running.

"They have some excellent races here."

It was getting close to sundown and Sophia realizing they needed to get a room for the night said, "Let's get in the cab, we are going to the Hotel Del Coronado and get a room for the night.

It took the Taxi about 25 minutes in traffic to get to the ferry downtown to cross over to Coronado Island. They pulled up to the Hotel, and the driver got out and opened the door in the front entrance.

After paying the Taxi $20 plus tip, Sophia led Metongy

into the wonderful, decorated hotel and walked up to the counter and said, "I have reservations for 2 rooms."

The receptionists asked her name, and right after Sophia responded, handed her a set of keys. The room was already paid for by the Cash in Advance people.

The porter asked, "Do you have any luggage?"

"No, it will be delivered later."

"Alright we'll be here to take it up to your rooms when it arrives."

As it turned out, Sophia had given the agency a rough plan and they knew she would be traveling to San Diego and at her request booked the reservations for the Hotel Del Coronado. With CIA efficiency, luggage was flown down to San Diego and while Sophia and Metongy were at dinner a while later the luggage entered their prospective rooms.

The Hotel Del Coronado had exclusive dining for the guests and people who were well off, enjoyed the fabulous meals prepared by world class chefs. Just like many other nights, a pianist played a grand piano and during a 30-minute break, a violinist went from table to table playing lovely melodies. When the violinist was near their table, he was performing an adaptation of a violin sonata composed by the late composer Giuseppe Martucci, added to the ambience. [G. Martucci - Sonata Op. 22 (Tranzillo - Pone) - YouTube]

The candlelight flickering illuminated Sophia's face giving it a soft casual and endearing appearance. She was susceptible to human emotions like any other woman, and it Metongy's appearance was quite compelling. His facial features and flawless body allowed him not only to fit his clothes really well, but he had that distinct Hollywood jaw and a smile that radiated in ways that effected women. There was a sense of mystique as well as mystery that seemed to invigorate Sophia's feelings towards him. His soft and gentle mannerisms, unassuming and forever polite laid a foundation that made it easy for Sophia to work with him.

The fact he was much more educated in physics, mathematics and Earth's electronics were still in the model T stage compared to the Caronians, could have easily given Metongy reason to be condescending or opinionated. But none of that ever surfaced as he always displayed a genuine level of curiosity as well as respect.

Tonight, as Metongy gazed into Sophia's eyes the look seemed quite different than he previously experienced. Likewise, Sophia's female intuition sensed a rather remarkable change in him. Metongy, though appreciative of Sophia's beauty, did not use that as a basis for any unrequited manifestation of emotions that now grew in him. The lure and the attraction were unmistakable. On the surface the awkwardness of this relationship seemed like it would be virtually impossible to experience anything other than the informal visit ostensibly to introduce Metongy to American culture and society.

Metongy had never experienced wine before, perhaps his body was ill prepared to deal with it, the effects obviously had an impact even though his few sips had no measure of consumption anyone would consider significant. The beautiful music, the candlelight flickering on Sophia's face then suddenly the violinist stopping right at their table, playing an incredible Giuseppe Martucci piece followed by a Brahms solo precipitated the exponential growth in desires, lust, and attraction towards Sophia. Metongy's conclusion seemed to indicate a Caroing like influence that could alter the fabric of his being.

Sophia's dress was nowhere as exotic as the many wealthy women sitting in the surrounding tables, but none of them had the demure everlasting beauty. Hence the magnification she created added to the allure not only Metongy experienced, but several gentlemen nearby also enjoyed the presence of her beauty.

The sounds of the music resonated long after the violinist left the table and resumed his performance near other tables. The food, wine, Sophia's beauty, and the music combined to create an intoxicating sensation.

As soon as the meal was finished, Sophia asked Metongy, "Would you like to go for a walk along the beach?"

"Sure, why not."

They soon left the restaurant and walked out to a lovely

stretch of beach. The sounds of the small waves crashing onto the shoreline created and everlasting memory. It was slightly cold, and Sophia said, "I'm kind of cold would you mind if I walk close with you?"

"Sure."

Metongy could feel Sophia's, shivers as she pulled close to his warm body and the walked down the beach after sunset that left behind an azure sky that was giving way to the purple that slowly painted the evening.

Sophia's physical touch stimulated Metongy more and more. The half glass of wine would not do much to an Earth person, but for someone like Metongy who had never experienced it before, that chemical process and the emotions that were building up in the past week created a temporal anomaly and a reduction of restraint that Metongy usually exhibited that would be counterproductive towards a romantic transcendence.

They were alone on the beach with the sound drugging his consciousness that now overflowed with emotion when he suddenly turned and faced Sophia. Caro did not kiss and would consider it highly irrational behavior. But having lived in isolation on Earth for a while, watching movies and TV shows, Metongy felt the desire to attempt what these Earthy people did when they displayed the emotion that romance creates.

He embraced Sophia and kissed her. At first Sophia felt a little surprised, and even though she might have developed a subtle attraction towards Metongy would most likely not make any assumptions or attempts to explore the essence of her feelings. Caught off guard Sophia didn't know how to respond, but the sensation it gave her left no doubt in her mind she was experiencing some element of gratification. That growing sensation in her caused her to reciprocate and in a sharp moment, the kiss expanded mutually with intensity.

Perhaps it was the excitement of kissing an Alien, Sophia didn't know why the feelings were pouring out of her in caldrons of passion. This compassionate embrace lingered as the gentle waves rolled in synchronizing the moment with oscillations of energy release.

Sophia had never been with a man before. Her scientific

and academic life demanded too much of her to set aside time for personal gratification. Falling in love with an Alien as the first man in her life as an idealistic person could never seem to find inner peace until this moment. It was almost if the weight of the world was suddenly lifted off her shoulders. Even though her life had been focused on the development of space and travel to the stars, the seemingly impossible was happening. This spontaneous eruption of passions had an element of spirituality because just like Einstein once said, "God leaves nothing to chance."

Metongy's affection gave an uncharacteristically authentic kindness as he never asked for anything and never assumed anything as well. Sophia was open-minded, but she also was not a fool. Her mother trained her well and gave her a lesson on human nature and men most specifically. She knew all the signs and traits of genuine motivations created by emotional appeal and not the quest for quick gratification. This was more than simple curiosity. Sophia's knowledgeable and personal experience with Metongy having evaluated him constantly since arrival defined his essence and exposed the critical parts of his personality. Sophia knew this was real and not synthetic, though complicated.

~~~
~~~

Chapter Forty-Four
Doctor Provkovitev at the Pentagon

About the time of the splendid euphoria between Sophia and Metongy, Doctor Provkovitev was ushered into the Joint Chiefs where they could size him up personally. The fact he arrived in a peaceful manner, not making any demands or suggestions clearly demonstrated integrity and empathetic reasoning one would expect out of an ambassador. Director Bazion had seen those qualities in this man and knew this would be an extraordinary challenge. Just getting to Earth alive was a huge, calculated risk.

The reception by the Earth people was another gamble. There were many unexplained questions, yet some alarming details came to light in the Cuban Missile Crisis. The Interplanetary Transport detected the radio broadcasts associated with the November 22, 1955, Soviet's detonation of their first megaton-range hydrogen bomb. It would be weeks from now before those radio waves reached Caro. Obviously, Director Bazion would realize the significance of this development. Should Earth be able to develop their own Interplanetary Transport and somehow figure out how to build their own Cyclonic Inverter, they would pose a severe risk to the Caronians.

Doctor Provkovitev's diplomatic abilities would be challenged more than anything else he did in his lifetime including the one-year trip to get to Earth.

"Tell me Doctor Provkovitev, how does your power plant work that got your spaceship here so fast and violate the laws of physics on traveling faster than the speed of light?" General Curtis LeMay asked.

"General, I'm a diplomat and not an engineer. I leave the engineering details to the technical guys."

"You were not at least curious as to how it works?"

"General, a man in your position knows there is enormous

risk in enterprises such as traveling in space to the unknown. Our entire trip was based on theory and no facts. It seemed better to me to compartmentalize my knowledge and facts and avoid exposure to a lot of things I didn't want to worry about."

"It's hard to believe you don't even know the slightest detail on how such incredible propulsion systems work?"

"General, I have more important things to think about that are far more pressing to me than how a Cyclonic Inverter works."

"What could that be?"

"General Curtis LeMay, here on Earth from what I've read while in Quarantine thanks to all the information your government provided me, it's not a pleasant thought to be marooned on a planet that just came really close to nuclear annihilation," Doktor Provkovitev stated in a clearer professional tone to convey the seriousness of his comments.

"Doktor Provkovitev, you are not marooned. The agreement is your Caro Interplanetary Transport will come back in approximately a dozen years and pick you up."

"That may not be of much use to me if I'm in a city that just got incinerated by the Russian new CZAR bomb."

"Is that your main problem?"

"No sir, when I return to Caro, I will have to face the Clerics like anyone else. I fear they may try to silence me or anyone else that returns to Caro from Earth visits."

"Why would your Clerics want to do that?"

"General LeMay, think about what it would be like if your Priests, Rabbi's, Ayatollah's, Monks, and Protestant Preachers all got together and formed a uniform organization that permeated all of society and do not want the public to know or believe life exists on any other planets."

"Doctor Provkovitev, do you have problems with Caro Clerics?"

"Our world is now unified and globalized after 150,000 years of fighting. The Clerics are the political remnants of the Tauceti. Three/fourths of the planet is Caro. The Clerics are attempting to maintain power and control and managed to assert themselves even though the Tauceti were neutralized in the final Tauceti War #4. Some believe they are part of a secret society that eventually wants to restore Tauceti rule and if they make that move it could trigger a civil war and break apart the globalization and world unity."

"Since you have so many problems on Caro, why did you agree to stay here?"

"Had I known you were going to have the Cuban Missile Crisis, I would have recommended nobody stay, and when our Interplanetary Transport returns, I will recommend we all leave and not come back."

"Why is that?"

"We have enough problems of our own on Caro. I fear we can't solve our own problems and dealing with Earth's problems is just a distraction."

"Suppose your Caro Interplanetary Transport does not come back in 12 years. What will you do?"

"I will remain a diplomat first and foremost. As such you should realize I can't choose sides. Your government and Moscow need to work things out on your own. But what I can do is warn you what happened to my own planet where we easily wiped out half the population and with as much as was lost, we are a long way away from completely rebuilding."

"Doctor Provkovitev, you are not a technical person then?"

"General LeMay, our society isn't designed like your world. My expertise covers several areas where your scientists and medical professions are more specialized."

"And how does that work?"

"Well for instance, I could qualify as a medical doctor, psychiatrist, politician, and pharmaceutical researcher here on earth."

"Do you think you could improve our medicines?"

"Sure, we could probably advance your medical field 1000 years, but we can't because you haven't figured out how to do population control yet. If we interfered and extended everyone's lives on Earth 50 to 100 years, then you would end up with excessive congestion and quality of life would shrink."

"I see. So, you are not really interested in helping us."

"General, I'm the diplomat, the official designated

ambassador from Caro. I represent our entire population. I'm here strictly in the ambassador role. I didn't plan on staying but after we examined your invitation, we decided for the good of establishing friendly relations between planets, we would sacrifice ourselves and stay, that's why we are here."

"Will any of the other Caronians that are here help us?"

"It's strictly up to them and what is in their conscience. They have to make the moral decision and weigh the consequence of their actions."

"What if, some of the Caro decide to permanently stay on Earth and not go back?"

"Again, that's their decision which I chose to not interfere with. If we are marooned here for 12 years, it's only human nature that some might develop a taste for the lifestyle here and chose to not go back."

"Doctor Provkovitev, is what you are saying, you would not prevent them from remaining and force them to return to Caro?"

"No, absolutely not. I would not interfere in their decisions, nor would I offer advice on leaving or staying because I do not want to be responsible for their happiness."

"Why would that occur?"

"General just suppose one of the Caro that remained here meets a woman and starts a family, I doubt they would be willing to abandon the family to go back to Caro and it's unlikely we could permit them to bring their family back. Nor do I believe the Clerics would tolerate them bringing back Earth people in my lifetime."

"Doktor Provkovitev, suppose you did bring back a dozen earth people that are part of their Families, what would become of them?"

"I have no doubt the Clerics would do everything in their power to eliminate them very quickly and hide the fact they ever arrived."

"Sounds like your Clerics are devious and cunning people."

"Their no different than what you have had here on Earth. I have read up on the Christians, the Knights Templar's, the Crusades, the Inquisitions during my stay in Quarantine. In essence we have a lot in common."

"Well Doctor Provkovitev I appreciate you visiting us and setting the record straight."

"Thank you for inviting me to visit the Pentagon, General LeMay."

"Tell me Doctor, what do you think of America, setting aside the negatives we already discussed such as nuclear weapons, Cuban Missile Crisis, and the other major international events?"

"General LeMay, our planet is probably 5 times more populated. Some our animals and plants are now extinct, others are becoming extinct. We are attempting to restore it all, but it will take time. About 75 centuries ago we started rebuilding from the last major Tauceti conflict. It may take us another 75 centuries to fully recover."

"Do people live better off in Caro?"

"Caro is more of a synthesized and far more crowded world. We've experienced far more than Earth and have destroyed ourselves many times over. The food and many of the products we use are all synthesized. Rarely is any of it fresh or real like what you have on earth. Your basic diet for the poor would be a luxury on Caro. But the people are used to it, that's all they know."

"We have better transportation and cleaner air. You have more water and natural resources."

"That must in some ways show our planet is not so bad," General LeMay responded in a slight confrontational tone.

"We can travel to other stars. You haven't even got to your moon yet."

"It's obvious there is a big difference between our societies, hopefully we can learn from you while you are here to make this a better world."

~~~
~~~

Chapter Forty-Five
Cape Canaveral

Three other Caronians arrived at Cape Canaveral aboard the CIA's Lockheed Super Constellation. They were schooled on how to dress and how to act before they arrived at the space center wearing suits and ties. None of the NASA people really knew who they were, and they were escorted by high-ranking NASA officials who played a double role working for the CIA in the Corona space craft and currently working on KH-4 system that would soon launch.

Spanish explorer Juan Ponce de León visited Cape Canaveral in 1513. Until the 1950's the cape was a nothing more than barren and sandy scrubland. Because of the hostilities on the Korean Peninsula and the predictable war, in 1950, missile testing began at Cape Canaveral. NASA was formed in 1958 and the space agency chose

Cape Canaveral for its Space Research and Exploration. It was officially renamed Cape Kennedy from 1963 to 1973.

Nearby Port Canaveral is one of the busiest cruise ports in the world, and the Cape Canaveral Lighthouse is located at the Cape. The city of Cape Canaveral lies just south of the Port Canaveral District. Human remains uncovered show humans have occupied the area for at least 12,000 years.

The first rocket launched at the Cape was a German V-2 rocket named Bumper 8 from Launch Complex 3 on 24 July 1950. It was a very happy but somber day for Wernher Magnus Maximilian Freiherr von Braun (23 March 1912 – 16 June 1977), who was the lead of German rocket designer. On 6 February 1959, the first successful test firing of a Titan Intercontinental Ballistic Missile was conducted at Cape Canaveral.

Most Americans are unaware of the Minute Man III activity at that area. On Dec. 14, 1970, the last unarmed Minuteman III (LGM-30G) was launched from Cape Canaveral, Florida (formerly Cape Kennedy). Future ICBM launches moved to Vandenberg AFB, California, where they continue today. All NASA Mercury and Gemini space flights were launched from Cape Canaveral, as were Apollo flights using the Saturn rockets.

These Caronians were slated to watch the final Mercury launch scheduled for May 15, 1963 and get a dog and pony show of the Gemini that would launch a year later. They soon arrived at Launch Complex 14 in a Ford station wagon from the air terminal to where the large Mercury Atlas 9 rocket, christened "Faith 7" was in the final assembly stages on the launch pad. The Astronaut scheduled to fly the mission Gordon Cooper was on hand to meet them. Gordon was one of the few astronauts who received the special briefing and the only person besides the CIA/NASA guides who knew they were extra-terrestrial beings.

Because top NASA and CIA executives wanted to get some feedback from the Aliens, they temporarily cleared out the facility of all the workers so the conversations could go on without divulging the essence of Alien visitors while the Q&A session unfolded.

They gathered around a space craft mockup that was in an enclosed area next to the pad where engineers and scientists could make measurements and do emergency assessment analysis before attempting to modify the capsule if required. Hence whatever was deemed required to be done, got accomplished on the mockup first so risk of damaging the craft was minimized when the actual corrective actions occurred. The Aliens peered into the tiny space craft and could not help but to have a slight condescension because the size and scale compared to their huge Interplanetary Transport was a quantum difference. Not knowing anything about the craft they asked a few simple questions like: "Where are the ship's computers?"

"The Mercury spacecraft does not have an on-board computer, instead we rely on all computation for re-entry to be calculated by computers on the ground, with their results (retrofire times and firing attitude) then transmitted to the spacecraft by radio while in flight," Gordon responded.

"Where are the computers to fly this ship?"

"All computer systems used in the Mercury space program to control the spacecraft are housed in the Goddard Space flight NASA facilities on Earth."

"Where's that at?"

"Goddard Space Flight Center is located approximately 6.5 miles (10.5 km) northeast of Washington, D.C. in Greenbelt, Maryland, United States."

The Caronian Aliens were just down from a quick tour of Washington DC knew where the city was and how it looked.

"What are the computers like?"

"We wouldn't know what your computers are like; these are probably quite inferior but the initial computers for the early flights were the IBM 701 computers. After several launches, we upgraded to the 709 series sometimes referred to as the 7090."

"How big is the computer?"

"With all the peripherals it takes up a good size room."

Having some current understanding of the American currency and relatively what some things cost, one of the Aliens asked: "How much does one of these computers cost?"

"When the center was first built, the monthly rental for a 701 unit was approximately $8,000. "

"What's the architecture of the computer like?"

"The system uses vacuum tube logic circuitry and electrostatic storage, consisting of 72 Williams tubes with a capacity of 1024 bits each, giving a total memory of 2048 words of 36 bits each. Each of the 72 Williams tubes is 3 inches in diameter. Memory could be expanded to a maximum of 4096 words of 36 bits by the addition of a second set of 72 William's tubes or (later) by replacing the entire memory with magnetic core memory. The William's tube memory and later core memory we upgraded to has a memory cycle time of 12 microseconds."

"The Williams tube memory required periodic refreshing, requires the insertion of refresh cycles into the 701's timing. An addition operation required five 12-microsecond cycles, two of which were refresh cycles, while a multiplication or division operation required 38 cycles (456 microseconds)."

"Instructions are 18 bits long, single address:

Sign (1 bit) - Whole word (-) or Half word (+) operand

address

Opcode (5 bits) - 32 instructions

Address (12 bits) - 4096 Half word addresses

"Numbers were either 36 bits or 18 bits long, signed magnitude, fixed point.

"The IBM 701 had only two programmer accessible registers:

The accumulator was 38 bits long (adding two overflow bits).

The multiplier/quotient was 36 bits long.

"Anweisungen sind 18 Bit lang, einzelne Adresse:

Vorzeichen (1 Bit) - Operandenadresse für ganzes Wort (-) oder halbes Wort (+)

Opcode (5 Bit) - 32 Anweisungen

Adresse (12 Bit) - 4096 Halbwortadressen

"Do you plan on putting computers on space craft?"

"Our Gemini space craft is the first astronaut-carrying

spacecraft that includes an onboard computer, *the Gemini Guidance Computer*, to facilitate management and control of mission maneuvers. This computer, sometimes called the Gemini Spacecraft On-Board Computer (OBC), is very similar to the Saturn Launch Vehicle Digital Computer we are building for the Apollo Program which will allow us to land on the moon."

"How big is the Gemini Guidance Computer?"

"The Gemini Guidance Computer weighs 58.98 pounds (26.75 kg)."

"Does it have more memory than previous computers?"

"Its core memory has 4096 addresses, each containing a 39-bit word composed of three 13-bit "syllables". All numeric data is 26-bit two's-complement integers (sometimes used as fixed-point numbers), either stored in the first two syllables of a word or in the accumulator. Instructions (always with a 4-bit opcode and 9 bits of operand) could go in any syllable."

NASA officials thought it was time to learn about alien computers (data terminals).

"What are the computers like on your Caro space craft?"

"We don't have computers; we have data terminals and data cubes."

"How is the computational processing accomplished?"

"It's all done in the data terminals."

"What is the data cube capacity?"

"It's always increasing; the ones we took for this mission hold many Terra Bytes of information."

"How do the systems work if you don't have computers?"

"Data terminals run everything. All the processing power we need is in data terminals."

"How many data terminals do you have on your interplanetary transport spacecraft?"

"Each crew member has their own data terminal for personal use. The pilot, co-pilot, mission specialist, engineers, and various functions have operational data terminals which do all the processing necessary to support their activity."

"How about your shuttle craft, does it have data terminals?"

"The pilot and co-pilot in the shuttle have data terminals, plus there are data terminals to facilitate maintenance and simulation."

"Why does it have simulation?"

"So that crews can keep proficient in flying the shuttle while on long trips without having to actually go on real shuttle flights."

"Does your ship also have simulators?"

"Yes definitely. In fact, prior to launch out of the Space Dock we ran the simulators for a couple months to improve crew member's efficiency."

"What do the simulators do in terms of crew training?"

"It provides realistic displays for all our sensors and visual indications."

"You don't look through windows?"

"No, at our speeds we can't have windows we only have cameras to look outside."

"How do you get the information from the cameras to

displays?"

"The cameras and other equipment can send data either with electrical signals or with light transmissions through special harnesses."

"What are the data terminal display's like?"

"The data terminal displays can be built as large as we want, but for the most part they're about the size of the entire control panel of your space craft."

"And for personal use?"

"Yes, each crew member has their own private room which has a data terminal in it where they can use it to study or look at information from the ship's cameras to look at stars and other planets."

"Are these the same size as the others you mentioned?"

"They are typically twice the screen size as the Television sets, we were given to watch when we were in Quarantine at Area-51."

"That seems kind of large for personal use."

"On Earth, you have movies and television. We have something like that and each crew member can watch all that on their personal data terminal."

~~~
~~~

Chapter Forty-Six
Caro Clairvoyance

The Sardukretchen Differentiator was in full operation just watching Earth, but the Clerics were intensely waiting for the Interplanetary Transport to show up so they could carry out appropriate plans.

The Planetary Security Service plans for the Interplanetary Transport return that Clerics obtained through another recruit, conveyed the Interplanetary Transport would dock at the Space Dock upon return. For the most part the Space Dock was evacuated for almost a year and a half. There was no point in leaving anyone up there and maintain all the essential life support systems since the dock was empty and there was nothing to do.

In anticipation of the Interplanetary Transport return, 6 months prior, a skeleton crew was sent up to restart systems and gradually bring online the entire Space Dock facilities. The Cover over the dock which provides airtight environment so people could work without space suits on had been shut after the Interplanetary Transport was launched on the mission and pressurized. Monitoring systems that sent telemetry data back to the surface of the Caro planet showed measurements on all vital aspects including Space Dock air pressure and the status of the fusion reactor that was in reduced capacity with a single pump and electric generator running for "hotel" power as to avoid running off batteries and motor generators. All those systems were monitored at the control center that was part of the complex that houses the Interplanetary Transport 3D Mockup and Simulator.

There had been some talk of building a second Interplanetary Transport in the event the first one developed a serious problem and called for help. Unfortunately, they would have to send the request for help near Earth or some place that transmitted through the space convergence zone; otherwise, it would never make it to the Caro planet. Since there were so many dead zones where emergency help requests would never make it to Caro, the decision was to hold off on producing another ship for the time being.

The Clerics armed with the fact the ship would enter the Space Dock upon return, gave them one opportunity to take out the crew and eyewitnesses before any Alien information could make it down to the surface of the Caro planet.

Their Sardukretchen Clerics began recruitments started the same day the Caro Interplanetary Transport deployed to the Gamulin Star System.

Cleric Mersevard replaced Cleric Zrebrek as Gummartukchik's right hand man, when Zrebrek was arrested. The Sardukretchen's Temple always had vast numbers of visitors. Some of the worshipers were devout Sardukretchen's and willing participants in any type of program the Clerics designed, and they went to great lengths to recruit useful idiots and people they could manipulate. Accordingly, there were always targets of opportunity. There were many issues of political, financial, religious, and societal woes that drove people into the arms of the Clerics. The Clerics who were impeccable record keepers maintained vast databases to facilitate knowing who's who in the zoo.

Portions of the Sardukretchen relational databases included fields of friends and relatives and associates of strong members and characteristics of kinds of work, hobbies, or tangible impact to society they bring. With the speed of modern data terminals, it did not take long to search the huge world-wide database to find breadcrumbs leading to the specialization they sought. As an example, if the Sardukretchen Clerics searched on Space Dock, within minutes they would find everyone associated with work on the Space Dock in the database and at what capacity were they involved in.

Then it was just a matter of recruiting them. Some of the recruitments were by adverse actions. Others were philosophical influences or emotional appeal. Cleric Mersevard was nothing like Zrebrek who actually retained some element of moral and ethical values. Mersevard another Cleric Gummartukchik protégée would not allow anything to get in his way. There was virtually nothing he would not do including blackmail, seduction, murder, kidnapping, or illegal financial activities. Bribing public officials was just the cost of doing business as far as he was concerned.

Gummartukchik laid out the groundwork for the campaign to prevent any knowledge of Earth to get back to Director Bazion, which meant destroying the Interplanetary Transport before crew members could disembark for Quarantine.

Metongy Zeugcha's clairvoyance was the only thing that stood in the way of the Clerics achieving their goals. Those special instructions to the Chief Pilot who remained aboard the Interplanetary Transport the entire mission along with his Co-pilot were not known to the rest of the crew, and for good reason. Metongy even though not returning with the crew and remaining behind on Earth expected the Clerics to move the Chess Pieces. Should the Clerics succeed in winning this battle, Metongy Zeugcha, Doctor Provkovitev, and the four other Caronians would remain marooned on Earth for the rest of their lives. At the present time it didn't seem to matter to Metongy Zeugcha because of his transcendence into an Earthly relationship with Sophia Kuznetsov, but he still wanted the option of going home one day in the future. He truly hoped the Chief Pilot would accept his recommendations and carry them out. The Pilot would of course wait till the fateful final minutes before making that decision. A lot was at stake.

~~~

Doctor Marlneiker was left behind in Washington DC as word went through the NASA director President Kennedy wanted to meet with one of the Aliens. President Kennedy was just interested in seeing what they looked like and was told they could actually speak English since they had studied it for a while. The reason why they picked Marlneiker is he had spent the most time with Metongy Zeugcha at his secret lab for 15 years studying Earth radio intercepts. Doctor Provkovitev was still with the Joint Chiefs and would not be available for a couple more days, so based on Metongy Zeugcha's recommendation it came down to Marlneiker being the first Alien to meet a world leader from Earth.

President Kennedy was still mildly shell shocked from the Cuban Missile Crisis and had it not been for "Dr. Feel-good," Doctor Max Jacobson, it's unlikely he would have
~~~

been physically ready to meet Marlneiker.

"Mr. President, this is Doctor Marlneiker, one of the Caronians that was left behind in the personnel exchange."

President Kennedy got up from his desk in the oval office smiling and walked around to greet Marlneiker. Even though the Caro never shook hands, part of the indoctrination on Earth behaviors, Marlneiker knew instinctively, this would be a classical meeting in many countries and when Kennedy held out his hand, Marlneiker firmly grasped it and smiled.

"It is a pleasure to meet you Mr. President."

"Would you like to sit down?" Kennedy held out his hand in the direction of the comfortable sofa directly across from a special chair Kennedy had at the end of a coffee table, which was the Commander in Chief's chair, nobody was allowed to sit in, except for the President, just like the ship's captain chair in the Officers "Wardroom" of a Naval Vessel.

"Thank you," Marlneiker responded and then approached the sofa and set down as Kennedy then sat in his CINC chair.

"Tell me Mr. Marlneiker, how long did it take your ship to get here from your planet?"

"Mr. President, based on an Earth Calendar it took around a year."

"How far away is your planet?"

"Mr. President, My Planet Caro in the Tauceti Solar System is seven light years away from your planet Earth."

"But that kind of violates Einstein's formulas of E=MC squared don't you think?"

"During our Quarantine period I studied Einstein's equations. I'm a mathematician. He made some glaring mistakes partly because he and earth do not understand the inner fabric of space. However, for about 90% of cases his formulas are correct, but the other 10% is where he is wrong."

"In what ways is he wrong?"

"As an example, time stops in the middle of a black hole and at the event horizon it can be measured to slow down."

"Did you actually measure it?"

"We did that thanks to pulsars that we photographed. We measured particles of light shooting at high speed while we were dissecting the event horizon of the black hole in the center of our galaxy."

"Tell me, how did you go faster than the speed of light?"

"Mr. President, it was due to a couple factors."

"Such as?"

"We have the Cyclonic Inverter which increases efficiency and thrust as our ship approaches light speed."

"What's a Cyclonic Inverter?"

"It's our main propulsion system, Mr. President."

"How does it work?"

"Mr. President, that's a states secret and none of the crew members were trained or allowed to know how it works."

"Why is that?"

"Mr. President, during our training prior to this mission we were denied knowledge of that technology. Our leaders explained the reason why we were not allowed to know the physics behind the Cyclone Inverters is that they are concerned that if we had that knowledge were to be captured by some evil leader in the Galaxy who wanted that capability and could manage to capture us, we would lose control of the technology. Our leaders do not want the exceptional ability of the Cyclone Inverters scattered through the galaxy in the event there are hostile civilizations out there that could one day become a threat to Caro as a result."

"Do you view America as a potential hostile nation?"

"That possibility has yet remained to be determined."

"Why do you say that?"

"We had the opportunity to observe all the news programs while in quarantine during the Cuban Missile Crisis, a short while ago. You came very close to use nuclear weapons to destroy each other that would have confirmed you are a hostile race of intelligent beings."

"What are your feelings about the Cuban Missile Crisis? Were we right in those regards?"

"Mr. President, it's not my job to judge you to determine if what you do is right or wrong. What the Earth ultimately does is none of Caro's business."

"Do you view the actions I took were appropriate?"

"Quite on the contrary, it's a universal understanding among all the Caro who remained on Earth, we felt the possibility of being marooned and possibly killed because of it. I suddenly had regrets staying here instead of returning to my world with the crew. Had the ship not already left, I think all 6 of us Caro would have left, and none would have remained."

"Now that you are here, will you help us develop technology?"

"Any technology transfer we give, which can't be much because we did not leave behind a data terminal, has to be shared with the entire planet. We can't give it to just the United States of America."

"But it's the Soviet Union and China that's evil, you will be doing the world a favor by not giving them advanced technology."

"I'm sorry Mr. President, that's our guidance from our superiors."

"Let me ask you this question, does it seem our technology

is on par with what the Caro have?"

"Mr. President, there are a number of wonderful innovations we see on Earth, but 3 areas I think we are way ahead of you are:

"In numerical processing: You guys call them computers; we use data terminals. Your computers are terribly inferior to our data terminals."

In transportation you use jets; we use atmospheric gliders that fly 10 times faster. Your trains only go 100 miles per hour. Our Tube trains run 300 miles per hour.

"In weapons, you have nuclear weapons as your chief weapon. We use lasers and other things."

"We have lasers too."

"Our lasers are ten thousand times stronger, capable of shooting down any object in the air around Earth."

"Do you fight with those weapons?"

"No, all war on our planet ended more than eight centuries ago when the planet unified."

"Maybe one day Earth can be like that too and have no more wars."

"We hope, but it's unlikely."

"Why do you say that?"

"Caro used to be just like Earth. It took us 150,000 years to end war."

"That sounds horrible."

"It is and the last war killed nearly half of the planet."

"What are your religions like?"

"Very much like what you have here on earth. I was curious and read the Christian Bible. It could have been written by one of our Clerics."

"Does your religion have similar covenants and circumstances?"

"Caro Sardukretchen Clerics have a different story, but we have essentially the same perspective."

"In 12 years when your Interplanetary Transport comes back with our 12 scientists returning, will you go home to the Caro planet then?"

"If I'm still alive, sure. It's my home and I have no desire to live and die on this planet."

"How about the other Caro people who stayed behind?"

"Twelve years is a long time, much can change by then, I suppose we really will not know until the time comes for them to make their decisions, all I know is I want to go back to Caro, live out my life there, and possibly start a family."

"What if you meet a woman here and fall in love?"

"Anything is certainly possible, but I'm sure I will want to go home."

"How about the American Scientists we sent to Caro, do you think they will all want to come back?"

"That's a good question. It's possible some of them might want to stay because they will live two or three times longer there due to lack of pollution, a healthier diet, and better medical technology."

"What are the major differences with your medical technology compared to what we have on Earth?"

"Caro medical science use Robotic Surgery, different types of medications you do not have, as well as Three-Dimensional Imaging Systems to allow better diagnosis and treatments."

The President said, "I have one more question, then I must say goodbye to you because I have a number of things I must attend to." Marilyn Monroe was on his mind.

"I've thought it would be best for humanity if I disclose the presence of you Caronians, how do you feel about us telling the entire planet you are here?"

"Sir, that's your call. We can't make decisions for this planet. We are here strictly as your guests and do not wish to influence your decisions in any manner."

"Thank you, Doctor Marlneiker, your comments were very informative."

"Thank you for inviting me Mr. President," Marlneiker stated as he stood up, was escorted out of the Oval Office and out of the White House to the helicopter pad where an Army Bell UH-1 Iroquois helicopter with 2 CIA pilots were doing their final check lists in preparation for takeoff.

In a short while, Marlneiker was back at Langley where the CIA was attempting to seduce him and the others to get them to cooperate on technology exchanges.

The next morning Sophia took Metongy down to the beach. The water was cold the weather was typical for a San Diego beach day, and the beach was nice as the waves were not too big. It definitely was not surfing waves like over at Ocean Beach or La Jolla Wind and Sea Beach, but the solitude was nice. There weren't many people on the beach, which was okay with them since Metongy had never gone to a beach before because large bodies of water didn't exist on his planet and the bodies that did exist were off limits because they were part of the critical water supply. The only vessels allowed on Caro bodies of water were registered Hovercraft mainly because the perimeters of the bodies of water were usually full of plant life and made it almost impossible to get around any other way. Any Caro who went to the Florida everglades would feel at home.

Metongy was feeling both euphoria and melancholy at the same time. His sojourn into a surreal romantic embrace with Sophia the night before crossed boundaries he had never crossed in his life before. Their lack of experience was good for each other because they both knew they were special to the other person.

The hotel furnished bathing matts and towels they could sunbathe out in front of the hotel and swim if they desired. They were sitting there, and the most horrible thing suddenly happened. Strange creatures walked out of the water, appearing to be holding some type of weapons and were wearing face guards, and a strange breathing apparatus.

Metongy almost panicked. It almost appeared those creatures were coming directly at him!

He looked at Sophia and all she did was smile as if she had no care in the world. Without her strength and forbearance, he might have panicked and got up and ran to find cover someplace. He felt ridiculous being fully exposed on the beach!

As terror was gripping his heart and he was suddenly regretting once again remaining on Earth suddenly, those creatures stopped, pulled off their masks and seemed confused until some military guys in uniforms suddenly appeared out of nowhere and seemed to approach them and hollered instructions and insults.

"Okay you dog faces, line up!" One of them yelled.

Soon they pulled off their frog feat and they all marched over the sand southwards.

Suddenly no longer feeling frightened, Metongy gained the strength to ask Sophia: "What's that all about?"

"Those guys are frogmen."

"What do they do?"

"Their part of Naval Special Forces, they swim ashore from boats out at sea to conduct guerilla warfare and special operations."

"What were they doing here?"

"I think they missed their mark when they swam ashore and got a little too far north. That's why their officers were out there redirecting them."

"Were those real weapons they were carrying?"

"Most likely."

"How do they work?"

"Do you have guns on Caro?"

"What's a gun?"

It took about 15 minutes for Sophia to describe guns, and then she discovered something strange as Metongy stated, "There are no guns on Caro."

Metongy went on to say, "There are some ancient relics a few collectors like myself have, including illegal ammunition."

While they were sunbathing and taking walks along the beach, Metongy now getting deeply involved with Sophia, asked about her family.

"My parents live in New York City. I have a brother that lives in Chicago."

"How about your family, Metongy?"

"My father died a few years ago, my mother died right afterwards from a broken heart."

"I'm so sorry."

"They lived a long happy life that was fulfilled."

"How long do Caro live?"

"I'm not sure how long they could last on this planet with the pollution, especially Los Angeles, but we typically live 150 earth years."

"New York is our largest City; would you like to go there and meet my parents?"

"Yes, I would enjoy that very much."

"Ok, I'll make arrangements and we can go there tomorrow."

In a few minutes a couple guys in suits approached them and one of them said, "Sophia Kuznetsov?"

"Yes?"

"We would like to have a word with you."

Sophia knew they were probably agency personnel said, "Sure," then turned towards Metongy and said, "I'll be right back, this is probably work related."

The men walked Sophia far enough away where they were

out of hearing range of anyone then began.

"We got a little concerned last night when your Alien friend didn't go back to his hotel room."

"He was with me."

"Where the hell were you?"

"In my room."

"What the hell…."

Sophia cut them off before they went any further and said, "It's none of your god damn business, it was a private matter."

"We'll have to report this to the director and pull you off the case."

"Do what you have to do, but my Alien friend probably isn't going to like it."

"We'll see about that."

"Also, just so you know, I'm going to New York tomorrow."

"That's not in the itinerary."

"Well, it is now because I need to go tell my mother I might be pregnant."

Sophia had an evil grin because she knew she just upset the applecart and decided she might as well bury them now with her next comment, "And Metongy will be coming with me to meet his future in-laws."

"You can't be serious."

"I have enough money to pay for our air fare, in case the agency doesn't wish to cover the expenses of me babysitting Aliens."

"You are off the case as of now."

"Okay, I resign, have a nice life."

Sophia steamed and turned back and walked to Metongy and said to him, "We have a change of plans now. The agency is being a pain in the ass, so we are going to travel today instead of tomorrow; us go back to the room and pack."

Jack, who Tracey Barnes never liked was a hot head and pushy. Tracey tried to instill in him that subtlety in their business was essential. Otherwise, they ended up having to pay out too much Cash in Advance.

Jack went back to his hotel room and called Langley reporting what just transpired. Tracey was on shaky ground since Bissell and Allen Dulles had been fired, and every former enemy they had now set their sights on Tracey. Eventually LBJ's appointee, Helms would eventually get rid of Tracey who actually succeeded in getting things done and replaced him with Jack who ultimately made a disaster out of Vietnam. It should be noted that many years later Helms was found floating down the Potamac. That's how the spy business works.

Sophia knew time was at an essence and informed Metongy, "Just put on your clothes you had on earlier. Get your identification and leave everything else alone. The FBI or CIA surveillance will simply think we are going somewhere for a meal and entertainment since it's around noon."

They then left the hotel and walked out front and asked the sentry to hail a taxi, which arrived one minute later from around the corner.

"Where do you want to go?"

"To the airport."

"We got 10 minutes to reach the ferry, or we have to wait an hour or so, I hope we don't run into traffic."

Timing was perfect. Jack and his assistant Ben were slow on their heels and didn't figure out the two had skipped out until they asked the bellhop if they had seen a man and woman that fit the description.

"Yea, they just left in a taxi about 5 minutes ago."

Jack turned to his partner Ben and said, "Us go."

It took them almost a minute and half to get to the parking lot, got in their rental car, and headed to the most logical place, the ferry as the couple would most likely be heading for downtown San Diego.

"What if they are attempting to leave?"

"She's not that dumb to piss off the CIA."

"Well, she's a woman and I think you pissed her off."

As soon as they got down at the ferry, Jack banged his

fist on the steering wheel as the Ferry was halfway already across from the bay.

Sophia asked the cab driver, "What airlines have a lot of flights to Los Angeles?"

"Pacific Southwest Airlines has a lot of commuter flights up there, mostly prop jobs, leaving about every half hour."

"Ok take us there."

"Sure, they have their own terminal."

The ferry docked not far from the airport. As soon as the Taxi got off the Ferry it was at the airport in 5 minutes.

Sophia and Metongy walked up to the airline counter and Sophia said, I would like 2 tickets to the next flight to Los Angeles."

"No problem, that will be $40, we got plenty of room."

"Any luggage?"

"No."

"Going up there for the day? Need a return ticket?"

"We'll take the train back," Sophia lied to throw off anyone looking for her.

About the time the cab got back to the Ferry it was ready to leave to go back across the channel to Coronado. Jacks' rental car was on the other side, and he was steaming wondering where they went. Several people were sent to the hotel to look out for the couple, hoping they just went on a joy ride.

Jack said, "We might as well go back to the Hotel, there is no telling where the two went."

Jack's partner Ben who was far more rational than Jack suggested, "We should talk to the taxi driver if he comes back and find out where he took them."

"Good idea."

The four propeller Pacific Southwest Airlines Lockheed L-188 Electra aircraft was soon airborne and in 45 minutes landed at Los Angeles International Airport (LAX). Pacific Southwest was at terminal 6 right next to United. Sophia instinctively led Metongy to the United Airlines ticket counter and said to the ticket agent, "We would like 2 tickets to New York."

"That will be $145 each coach or $300 first class."

"We'll take coach class seats."

After the money was exchanged the airline attendant handed them the boarding passes for La Guardia.

"Any luggage?"

"No."

The airline employee thought it was more Hollywood types by the way they were dressed as she watched them walk towards their gate.

About the time they boarded the DC-8 Airliner, Jack's partner approached the cab driver who just pulled up and asked, "Excuse me, did you take a couple from the hotel recently, a good-looking blond with a man in a blue shirt and nice hair cut?"

"Sure did."

"Where about did you take them?"

"To the airport."

"Which terminal?"

"Are you writing a book or something?"

Jacks partner Ben reached in his pocket and pulled out some $20 "Cash in Advance" and said, "Does this help your memory?"

"Sure does, took them to the Pacific Southwest Airlines terminal."

"Thanks."

Ben, immediately ran for Jack and found him and said, "I know where they went."

"Where?"

"To the Airport."

"Grab that FBI guy Jerry, we might need his assistance."

Ben went up to the 2nd floor knocked on the door to room 205. A man in a suit answered, "Yes what's up?"

"Jack says he needs your help. I think we are going to the airport."

Shortly the 3 men were in Jack's rental car again and stuck missing the Ferry boat by another 2 minutes; all he could do is swear.

By the time Jack, Ben, and the FBI agent got to PSA terminal the United Jet flying to New York was already over Denver.

Jack's rental car pulled up to the curb right next to the PSA terminal got out and was walking in the terminal when a police officer approached and said, "Sir, you can't leave your car parked there."

The FBI man pulled out his badge showing it to the police officer and said, "FBI, watch the car for us."

The three men continued into the terminal and walked up to the counter. At the time there was just one airlines ticket agent since it was a lull in the day.

The FBI agent whipped out his badge and said to the agent, "I'm with the FBI, we need to ask you some questions."

The airline ticket agent was a little shocked at first, the last thing she ever expected today was an FBI agent walking up and throwing out his badge asking questions.

"Approximately two hours ago a blonde lady named Sophia Kuznetsov and a man named Rex Gordan (Metongy's CIA undercover name) were here and purchased a ticket, where did they fly too?"

Let me check the reservations. The attendant typed into the teletype the name and hit an inquiry and soon got a printout. "They flew to Los Angeles."

Jack was upset and knew Sophia Kuznetsova and Rex Gordan were probably heading to New York under different jurisdiction and the FBI guys in New York can be pricks and seldom cooperated with the CIA. In fact, the New York FBI office detested the CIA, and considered them lawless rouges.

Jack had another problem, Sophia got along with Tracey Barnes and Jack realized he might have just blown his career. Jack though survived because Helms enjoyed surrounding himself with incompetents so that nobody would outshine him. That's primarily one of the reasons Helms fired Tracey Barnes in 1966.

When the plane landed in New York, there were agents at the terminal waiting for Sophia and Rex Gordan. As they started to walk to a taxi at the curb one of the agents approached Sophia and recognized her from the facsimile just sent an hour ago and said, "Excuse me Sophia, I need to talk with you."

"Who do you work for?"

"I'm with the FBI here in New York."

"Am I being arrested?"

"No, we just want to know what your intentions are."

"You can tell your handlers some asshole in the CIA named Jack mistreated me in San Diego and forced me to resign from NASA and the CIA, I will officially send in my resignation papers next week."

"Fine and dandy but Rex Gordan must come with us."

"He's not interested in going with you, he and I are going to my mother's house so unless you want to arrest me and explain all this to a judge who might be interested in whom he really is, I suggest you leave us alone."

The shrewd FBI agent knew better than to escalate the situation, just because Jack is a *flaming asshole* doesn't mean he needs to be one. And he knew Jack well from past run-ins.

"Okay Sophia, go visit your mother, hopefully calmer heads will prevail soon. Here's my business card if you want to call me and talk."

Sophia looked at special agent Kevin Jones business card and replied, "Thank you Kevin, I'll give you a call in a couple days. I'm sure the agency can tell you precisely where my mother lives since they know everything about me."

Kevin walked over to the Cab, opened the door for Sophia and said, "Here's your Taxi, stay safe."

"Thank you."

Sophia and Metongy hopped in the cab and drove off.

About 12 hours later, Jack was in Tracey Barnes office, who was temporarily DD/P working for a Temporary CIA director awaiting Helm's congressional confirmation.

"What possessed you to be an asshole and screw this up?"

"Well, Sophia kept the Alien out all night and apparently was EFFING his brains out."

"She's not that kind of girl."

"How the hell do you know that?"

"Well Jack, you sure as hell don't know and I'm going to

put some statements in your record disciplining you. You just blew this operation because you're an arrogant prick and always wanting to pull a John Wayne routine."

"That's your opinion."

"Until further orders, Jack, I don't want you near Sophia or the Alien. Now pack your shit, I'm sending you someplace where they need a guy like you."

"Yea where's that?"

«Vietnam. »

~~~
~~~

Chapter Forty-Seven
Home Sweet Home

The cab pulled up in front of Sophia's parents' home. It really was going to be a situation, they didn't have any clothes, her apartment was far away in Georgetown in DC and all Metongy's meager possessions were out in a trailer at Area 51.

The good news is since her brother and she were gone, their bedrooms were empty.

"Hello mother, let me introduce you to my friend Rex Gordon."

Her mother could take one look at Sophia and realize this was a special man in her life. Her heart was suddenly filled with joy.

"Glad to meet you Mrs. Kuznetsov."

"I had no idea we would be expecting you, Sophia."

"It's a strange story and I'd rather not get into it now and I need to use your phone and make a couple phone calls."

"It's right where it usually is by my recliner and the sofa on the telephone stand."

"Thanks mother."

Sophia knew Tracey Barnes phone number by heart. She also had known Bissell's until he was fired, and she feared Barnes would be the next head to fall as Kennedy appeared to be going crazy over firing people over Bay of Pigs fiasco which Kennedy screwed up when he pulled back the jet fighters because he lost his nerve which resulted in the B25's getting slaughtered by the MIG's the Soviets were flying with Cuban markings. And then the Cuban missile crisis hit, and Kennedy now was even more unpredictable.

The phone rang. Sophia recognized the voice when he said "Hello."

"This is Sophia, just wanted to call you and give you my side of the story and offer my resignation."

"I will not accept your resignation; we still need you on

the team."

"I can't work around people like Jack who's too dam pushy."

"Don't worry about Jack, I'm sending his ass to Vietnam where he can have some real sweet times."

"I needed to visit my mother; it is very important."

"You need some time off, and I understand you have Rex Gordan with you."

"Yes, he wants to meet my family."

"Things going well with Rex?"

"Very well, he's enjoying life."

"That's good to hear."

"Tracey, can you do me a favor?"

"Sure. What can I help you with?"

"That loose cannon Jack forced us to leave abruptly, we didn't check out of the hotel and all our belongings are still there."

"Not a problem, your belongings will all be sent to you immediately."

"Thank you."

"Do you think you will be back a week from now?"

"Yes, I want to stop off at my Georgetown apartment before I go into the office."

"Sure, I understand."

~~~
~~~

Chapter Forty-Eight
Return to Caro

The Caro Interplanetary Transport started signaling at the location they thought they lost Caro communications on their outbound passage.

The Planetary Security Service Mass Differentiators did not detect the signals for nearly a week. The Sardukretchen Differentiator a much newer design utilizing the up-to-date state of the art, had slightly more sensitivity managed to detect the signals. Once that occurred the telescope started looking in that direction. The pulsing light that pulsed every few minutes appeared like a twinkling star to the naked eye. The Clerics now had a jump on the Planetary Security Service.

The trip for the Americans was quite an ordeal for some and not much of a challenge for others. The food was bland and without any prior training and familiarity, a crash program was put in place because some human needs were extraordinarily crucial since space craft did not have normal bathrooms in them. Earth people had never spent a lot of time in space, so all of this was new to the 12 volunteers.

People do not really know how they're going to react to a strange environment. The Aliens naturally gravitated towards the use of their own Caro language and often had to remind themselves the Americans had no idea what they were saying, hence had to make an asserted effort to speak English in front of the Earth people as much as possible.

The food could be rated as bland to terrible. This worked out really well for Hank Rogers who was Obese at the beginning of the trip. His weight loss was so profound the Caronians thought he was ill, and the ship's doctor spent a considerable amount of time diagnosing a non-problem. Hank routinely told the doctor, "I'm losing weight because I do not like the garbage you are feeding us."

The doctor who was light on English was delighted when he was told the Earth people had provided a paper dictionary in the numerous gifts. The ship's captain who looked over the manifest decided they would suspend the quarantine after a month when none of the Caro showed any signs of illness and the dictionary was immediately given to the doctor. When the doctor looked up the word garbage, he was mildly offended by Hanks's terminology of the food they were provided, which was actually better than what most Caronians had back on the planet where much of it was synthesized from yeasts and mushroom like plants.

Eventually the Earth people grew more accustomed to the Caronian diet, and the complaints subsided around the midpoint of the trip. Hank shrank so much that a crew member who had a collateral function of ship's tailor swung into action to make Hank new clothes. Out of what he brought aboard which wasn't much. They were led to believe all their clothes and necessities would be provided by the Caro, so there was no need to bring along much of their personal items. Those that ignored that advice were the smart ones because when they reached Caro, any item they brought with them was priceless and would make the person immensely wealthy in relative terms.

Not all of the Earth people adapted well to space travel. Low gravity affects people in different ways, some of them in very bad ways. None of them had gone through proper psychological screening and relying on the fact they were all PhD's was a poor choice of measure. The two who took it the hardest had to be sedated during much of the trip, to the point the ship's doctor worried his supply of sedatives would not last the trip and the men might go mad and must be restrained for the final leg of the trip. The doctor with the help of one of the Americans that was a chemist eventually came up with a formula where they were able to manufacture synthetics that mixed with the dwindling sedatives on board lasted barely long enough to get them to the planet. Once on the planet and in open air in a place resembling a sanatorium on Earth, the men snapped out of it.

How two men with claustrophobia got put on the spaceship showed how unprepared they were to attempt such a personnel swap. In 12 years the agreed upon return trip would have to deal with these two men if they were ever to return home. As it turns out one of them opted out not to return, the other died from natural causes.

The days soon passed where they were single digits away from returning to Caro. The Space Dock and Habitat was fully manned. The Interplanetary Transport ship was ordered to dock and a careful quarantine was planned to be set up in the Space Dock.

The Pilot and Co-pilot were alone in the control room when final planning for arrival and docking now underwent careful considerations and deliberations.

"I've made a decision on how to conduct the arrival."

"It should be cut and dry, Caro wants us to enter the Space Dock and quarantine will be established there until we all get medical clearances."

"I had long discussions with Metongy Zeugcha and he

fears the Clerics will somehow destroy us before we can get back on the planet and claim this trip was just a hoax."

"Come on you can't be serious?"

"Do you know about the third Cyclonic Inverter?"

"No. What happened?"

"It was destroyed by a Cleric Saboteur as they tried everything in their power to prevent the mission."

"How do you know this?"

"Special briefing from Planetary Security Service. That information is privileged; do not discuss it with anyone."

"That's almost 2 years ago; nothing seems out of order on the planet based on all the communications we've just received."

"We'll be sitting ducks in the Space Dock."

"What can we do? We surely can't all take shuttles down to Nimbocratus. Someone needs to remain aboard the Interplanetary Transport until it's docked."

"I've been on the ship almost two years, another few extra

months will not affect me much, I can remain onboard since the ship is mostly automated, and we really do not need much of a crew onboard."

"You do not plan on taking the Interplanetary Transport into the Space Dock?"

"No."

"Why?"

"We have people we left on Earth we need to eventually go back for and return with them. If we allow this ship to be destroyed by the Clerics, they would be marooned there for the rest of their lives."

"I could think of far worse places to be, especially in cramped Caro Cities."

"Well as bad is it is in some cities, it's their home and their lifestyle. Earth is just an assignment. We owe it to them to bring them home one day."

"You realize you will be in serious trouble?"

"After you guys all leave, I can take the ship a lot of places, there will be enough food left on board for me to last several years."

"Understand, so where do we go and how do we get there?"

"Planetary Security Service will most like try to take over the Shuttles and fly them remotely. I'm going to disable remote control on both shuttles. They will have to fly via internal data terminals. That way the rest of you can return to Caro."

"Where in Caro will we go? The Planetary Security Service will be very angry with us."

"We primarily need to get you to the planet and make a presence the Clerics can't stop. My suggestion is you land the shuttles at the former Interplanetary Transport construction site. They can easily set up quarantine there."

"What about the rest of the crew, some of them know you have orders to arrive at the Space Dock?"

"We'll have a meeting. I'll give them the option to remain with me indefinitely or take the shuttles down to the planet immediately."

"You know they could send shuttles back up and attempt to board."

"But they can't get the hatches open; I'll have all external links severed. Plus, I can take a short galactic joy ride, while they are stewing."

Metongy Zeugcha's clairvoyance predicted the Clerics actions almost to a great degree of accuracy.

~~~

Fearing their past failures, the Clerics using their relational data base eventually recruited two space workers that would spend time in the Space Dock clearing out all the residual helium from their fusion reactors and Cyclonic Inverter maintenance. Neither of the saboteurs knew of the other, as their deep cells were fully compartmentalized.

Within a week of arrival, the sabotage was fully in place. An escape plan was built around scheduled shuttle flights to deliver required men and materials to the Space Dock. The saboteurs were schedule to return to the planet's surface on those scheduled flights and upon launch from the Space Dock they would initiate timers that would detonate the
~~~

bombs, destroying the crew and the ship and killing the space travel program. Metongy, Doctor Provkovitev, Marlneiker, and the other three were destined to be marooned on Earth forever. There would be no proof anyone went to the Earth and Bazion would soon be dispatched by Cleric Gummartukchik.

~~~

Colonel Gujane established her base camp at the Interplanetary Transport Construction site where they had bivouacked nearly 2 years before during the pre-launch period of the Gamulin Mission.

A third of the Battalion was already up on the Space Dock, looking for bombs and anything out of the ordinary.

~~~

The Caro Interplanetary Transport pilot called the crew together and they met in the spacious control room so that he did not have to leave it.

"The reason why I have called you all together is we have a change in our arrival plans."

"Is there a delay?" One of the worried crewmembers asked.

"No actually some of you will be leaving earlier than planned."

"Did Planetary Security Service come up with a new plan?"

"No, I did."

The men were now fully alert and somewhat surprised.

"Some of you are aware there was attempted sabotage on the ship prior to us leaving on the mission. We can't be fully sure there will not be more attempts."

"We are landing on the Space Dock; shouldn't we be fairly safe there?"

"I'm not going to land on the Space Dock any time soon. The ship will remain in space until further notice."

"What about the crew?"

"The crew will be taken immediately to the planet's surface as we approach the Space Dock as I want you men to be sure and get home safely."

The pilot then explained the process they would follow:

"I want all the Earth people divided into the two shuttles they will be the first to arrive at the planet and will be accompanied by six Caronians in each. I also want their artifacts they have brought with them, books and materials loaded aboard those 2 shuttle flights to make sure we get proof of Earth to the planet's surface."

"It will be a complicated arrival, and I will ask the pilots of both shuttles to remain onboard and come back and pick up the rest of the crew except for myself and one volunteer."

"I'll stay Captain," the Co-pilot offered.

"No, I want you to go to the planet's surface and be my spokesperson and explain why I'm violating Planetary Security Service orders."

Hank Rogers a transformed person who felt slightly invigorated suddenly spoke up, "I know I'm not one of your crew members, but I will volunteer to stay with you Captain."

"Doctor Roger's that will not be necessary. Actually, I prefer you go down to the planet surface so that you can answer a lot of questions about Earth I'm sure the Caronians will ask."

Nobody on the crew was about to fight the Captain on disobeying Planetary Security Service orders. Everyone except he and the Co-pilot had enough of space and to get down to the planet right away instead of languishing on the Space Dock in quarantine for a year was all right by them!

One half hour to docking when the Interplanetary Transport reached Caro Orbit the first group was in the shuttles and as soon as the transport was directly above the Great Hefoxia Desert, the pilot directed them, "Shuttle one, commence launch."

"Commence launch in progress," the Shuttle crew reported. Soon the shuttle was separated from the Interplanetary Transport and moving towards the planet.

"Shuttle two, commence launch."

Shuttle two followed shuttle one from a safe distance and with its planned arrival position locked into the navigation system and outside links disabled, headed a safe distance behind Shuttle one.

It didn't take long for Planetary Security Service to discover the Interplanetary Transport had disgorged its shuttles in violation of their operational orders.

"Transport, this is Planetary Security Service headquarters, what's going on?"

"We have sent part of the crew to the planet with 12 Earth people to prevent them from being destroyed in case the Space Dock is booby trapped."

"Transport, we have many Rapid Deployment Troops on the Space Dock, you are safe to land there. Recall your shuttles."

"Too late they should be landing any moment."

Bazion who was shortly in the Planetary Security Service Control Center in his building asked, "Where are they landing?"

"Looks like the shuttles are landing in the Great Hefoxia Desert, next to the Interplanetary Transport Construction Site."

"Isn't that place shut down?"

"Yes, it is, but the Rapid Deployment Force set up camp there to support the Space Dock operation."

"Alright, inform the Rapid Deployment Force to isolate everyone that is arriving, until we get a quarantine habitat set up for them."

Bazion was very disturbed a ship's captain was violating his orders, a formal Court Martial and later execution was in order.

About the time Planetary Security Service headquarters contacted Colonel Gujane, she observed the shuttles come down and land almost 200 yards away from their camp.

Soon it all started to get interesting as Colonel Gujane suddenly received a communication from the Space Dock.

"Colonel Gujane, we have just discovered a bomb with a timer that appears to have one hour to detonation!"

With only one Rapid Deployment Force shuttle available, most of her troops were doomed, they would probably all perish. Then she figured out her next move.

"Get all those people except the pilots out of the shuttles

and place them in the first couple of barracks and keep everyone away from them and mark it with bio-hazard signs. Tell the pilots not to leave; I have a new mission for them."

"At least I can get more troops off the Space Dock before it blows," Colonel Gujane explained.

Colonel Gujane walked over to the shuttles and told the pilots the dilemma. "We need to get as many rapid deployment force personnel off the space dock, as soon as possible."

"May I make a suggestion Colonel?"

"What do you have in mind?"

"We could ferry your troops over to the Interplanetary Transport as a temporary measure to get them out of harm's way, there is plenty room there and that way we can get them all off by not having to make trips to and from the planet which eats up too much time."

"Excellent idea, go ahead and proceed to the Space Dock."

The two saboteurs were all smug in their knowledge it was

too late for anyone to stop the bombs as they were on the only shuttle now entering Caro atmosphere when suddenly, their pilot was directed to land at the Interplanetary Transport Construction site deep within the Great Hefoxia Desert.

"I wonder what that's all about?" one of the saboteur's asked the other one sitting next to him. Neither one of them knew the other guy was in the same business as their cells were compartmentalized and knew nothing of the other.

"We have some Rapid Deployment Force guys on board, maybe that's their base and we are dropping them off?"

"I got transportation waiting for me at Nimbocratus, I have an atmospheric glider to catch, or I'm stuck there another day," the first saboteur said feeling suddenly disturbed he would be delayed in picking up his credits and the good times those credits would provide him.

Colonel Gujane contacted Planetary Security Service Headquarters to explain the situation and what actions she had taken and has her communicator contact the Space Dock and prepare the troops to evacuate as best as possible and instead of pumping down to ½ pound per square inch to save the air, they would equalize it right away since it was all going to blow anyways.

The pilot of the Interplanetary Transport was notified of what was going on and to expect almost one third of an RDF battalion aboard his ship was asked to approach the Space Dock at a safe distance so the shuttle flights could be sped up by eliminating distance and time between flights.

The Great Space Dock Evacuation as it would later be recorded in history, unfolded with military precision and speed. The Transport Captain likewise followed the common-sense approach and instead of wasting precious time pumping down near a vacuum to save air, quickly equalized it to space losing the air which could be delivered at a later date, if required.

One of the last troops to be evacuated was stationed by the bomb they knew of reporting how much time was left as the shuttle operations continued.

During the evacuation there were periods of time when they calculated they would run out of time and the last group would not make it when the pilot figured out what they had to do:

"In the remaining flights, crowd them aboard. One person sitting on someone else's lap in every seat except the pilot."

In doing so they sped up the evacuation. The last few shuttle flights were heavily overstuffed to the point people had problems breathing as the CO_2 levels rose quick and the shuttles disgorged their passengers just in time before they would start passing out. With the air exchange to the shuttle bays during the offloading process, enough air was exchanged to make the next flight possible.

10 minutes were showing up on the bomb timer as the shuttle came in to pick up the remaining personnel. The Rapid Deployment Force soldier took one last look at the timer going below 10 minutes and quickly headed for the shuttle. He didn't even bother sealing the compartments behind him since he knew they were all going to blow anyways. The rest of the shuttle was waiting on him knowing how much time they had and were highly spooked and nervous and wanted the hell out of there!

"I'm the last man out! Let's go!"

The young man found that he really had to squeeze into it and practically lay down on 4 people who were sitting on someone else's lap.

The shuttle operator initiated the equalization, dumping it all to space watching the air pressure slowly drop as he looked at the chronometer showing about four minutes before it was going to blow!

The pilot on the Interplanetary Transport also wanted to get room between him and the Space Dock and would kick in the Cyclonic Inverters as soon as the shuttle docked, and hatches closed. The RDF guys would get a rare chance to see some of the solar system because it would force them out of orbit and they would have to then re-enter orbit, so he might as well give them a quick tour of another planet that was famous for its rings that was inhabited but not that far away.

With three minutes left the shuttle activated the electromagnetic pullers and was coming into the shuttle bay. At two minutes the shuttle hatches were closing when the pilot initiated the Cyclonic inverters. By the time the shuttle hatch shut, they were already up to 20% power and the RDF guys felt G forces like they never felt before. Since the two bombs were not synchronized the pilot had no way of knowing another bomb would detonate a minute earlier. The ship was getting space between them and the Space Dock when suddenly, they felt the shockwave rumble through the Interplanetary Transport. They were not damaged, but it's safe to say a few RDF guys had to soon change their underwear.

Bazion was extremely angry when he was suddenly told: "The Space Dock just blew. It's gone!"

People on the ground could see the explosion in space especially on the dark side of the planet. The Clerics had finally gone too far.

Bazion had no proof initially, but he didn't care.

Cleric Gummartukchik was all smiles getting reports from the planetary news briefs he watched in the room with a dozen other Clerics on the data terminal. There were claps and cheers. They had succeeded! The Earth business and the Interplanetary Transport were finished. They finally won!

Then information started flowing in that slowly became disturbing.

"We have not been able to make contact with the saboteurs. Nobody has heard from them."

"Did they make it off the Space Dock, not that it matters?"

"I'm sure they did, they should have left on schedule two hours ago."

"What are the people at Nimbocratus saying?"

"They have not seen any shuttles for almost four hours."

Colonel Gujane didn't know what to do with all the civilians that were sent down on the shuttles before the emergency and had them all get on the Hovercraft to send them over to the Tube Train entrance two miles away when unexpectedly, she received a communicator call from Planetary Security Service headquarters. It was Bazion himself!

"Colonel Gujane this is Director Bazion."

"Hello director, what can I do for you?"

"Where are all the people that came down on the shuttle from the Space Dock?"

"They are all here, getting ready to send them over to

the Tube Train entrance so they can get transportation at Yarneos Air Transportation Center."

"Colonel, detain all of those people immediately, put armed guards on them. I'm sending over some interrogators to debrief each one of them. They are not to leave your site until further orders directly from me."

"Understand director Bazion."

As soon as Bazion hung up, Colonel Gujane yelled, "Major Finkster, get all those civilians off the Hovercraft and bring them over here immediately."

Just before the operator was to hit the switch to turn on the turbos to get the Hovercraft moving to the train station, Major Finkster said, "Shut it down, everyone get off the Hovercraft and follow me."

Finkster led the twenty Caronians around to Colonel Gujane where she addressed them, "I'm sorry but you are all going to have to wait here for a while. Major, put all of these people in barracks number four and place armed guards on it, none of them are to leave the barracks until further orders."

"Right away Colonel."

Bazion's people then contacted Colonel Gujane and had her pull the identities on all of the people that came down on the shuttles and they started examining them. The Earth People and crew members of the Interplanetary Transport were simply stuck because of Quarantine requirements. The others were a different matter.

Bazion also was a smart user of relational databases. He had his experts on the data terminals searching for any possible Sardukretchen involvement and most specifically if they could ascertain any of them that had Sardukretchen Temple activity.

Five names popped up on the search criteria, and those individuals were singled out and immediately picked up by Planetary Security Services agents on an atmospheric glider sent in and flown back to Preznium to Planetary Security Services headquarters. The two saboteurs were members of the 5 that had been detained and transported.

Once at Planetary Security Service headquarters they were separated and fiercely interrogated. The Clerics had no idea their two men had already been turned by the expert interrogators and just as in the Pirsrgyo case, Bazion had them out of Planetary Security Service headquarters and in a safe house long before Cleric Gummartukchik had any clues they had even been arrested.

~~~
~~~

Chapter Forty-Nine
Arrest!

As time went by the satisfaction of destroying the Space Dock was slowly eroded as the World-Wide News (WWN) reports on their data terminals were giving a special report. The government just announced 12 Earth Beings from the Gamulin Star System 7 light years away had just arrived on Caro and were undergoing Quarantine at a secret location! The news reports showed images of the Earth Aliens who looked remarkably like Caro.

Gummartukchik was holding an emergency meeting strategizing with his disciples on how to find out where the Earth people were being held so he could deal with them and find out what happened to the Interplanetary Transport.

A Cleric walked into the room and said, "Your Excellency Gummartukchik, there is a half dozen Planetary Security Services Skycars landing in the driveway!"

Gummartukchik suddenly alarmed wondered what he should do thinking, *"Maybe their coming for me."*

Cleric Gummartukchik said, "Don't tell them I'm here," and got up and started heading for the Botanical Gardens where he would hide out.

Six of the Skycars landed as planned, but the other 4 remained airborne as vertical scouts watching the compound in the event Gummartukchik or any of his associates would attempt to escape. It did not take long for them to spot Gummartukchik with very capable Planetary Security Service video tracker equipment that had built in facial recognition software.

As Gummartukchik and a couple associates walked briskly into the Botanical Gardens their coordinates were relayed to the other sky cars and a couple of the skycars on the ground were then sent back up in the air and directed to land in the open picnic area that Zrebrek had often used to seduce Zurella Myco.

Other Planetary Security Service men who got out of the Skycars followed Gummartukchik and his men down the pathway though the Botanical Gardens. Gummartukchik did have a special getaway tunnel; unfortunately, he was boxed in and would never make it. There suddenly were 2 Planetary Security Service men in front of him blocking his path.

Gummartukchik looked behind; the Planetary Security Service men were approaching very briskly. He had no choice; he took out his blaster hidden in his cloak and as an expert shooter knew it would not be a challenge to knock out the two Planetary Security Service agents blocking his path. Bazion observing in one of the Skycars overhead saw the gunfire exchange and Gummartukchik shoot and kill his two agents that was the final straw. Bazion on the controls armed the Planetary Security Service Devastator System and put the tracker on Gummartukchik, then activated fire.

The 12-barrel gun capable of shooting 12,000 rounds a minute sliced into Gummartukchik. His associates that were with him were severely wounded by the ricochets. Suddenly they were all lying on the ground with Cleric Gummartukchik in a big pool of blood.

~~~
~~~

It was a somber day at the Sardukretchen's Temple. Mersevard was anxious because members of his two cells that just blew up the Space Dock had not reported in and when he tried to call Gummartukchik just then there was no answer, nor was Gummartukchik's associates answering.

Mersevard's sermon was kind of lackluster. The congregation was not too impressed with his performance today and for some reason it appeared he was not on his game plan.

The four Skycars, landed in the open spots next to the Temple. Men immediately exited and surrounded the Temple.

Bazion, Chomvik, and a few more of his most trusted men suddenly walked into the Temple right in the middle of the sermon.

Mersevard became slightly agitated as he observed several of the Planetary Security Service agents walk down the outer isles and even more agitated as they had the audacity to step behind him in the very spiritual realm of the Cleric's space in the Temple. His sanctity was being violated and the crowd was suddenly making strange noises when abruptly one of those who just arrived said, "Ladies and gentlemen, the service is now over please exit the Temple immediately."

"You have no right being in here damaging the fabric of this service!" Mersevard exclaimed.

"And you have no right blowing up Space Dock!" Bazion countered while the congregation started slowly to get up and start leaving as they looked around and saw a spooky sudden appearance of people surrounding them.

As the congregation arrived at the door, Planetary Security Services members there ushered them out the doors signaling to the guards outside to let them pass. This process was quickly repeated many times over until the Temple was empty except for Mersevard, Bazion, and the Planetary Security Services agents.

"I'm afraid you will have to come with us."

"Cleric Gummartukchik will have his way with you!"

"He can't, he's dead," Bazion said nonchalantly.

Bazion then nodded to the men behind Mersevard quickly

moved forward before Mersevard could react and put on hand restraints. They then led him out a side door that opened to about 30 feet away from their Skycars.

~~~
~~~

Chapter Fifty
Caro and Earth

The Earth people eventually completed their quarantine. The entire Caro planet was stunned as the WWN had numerous interviews. Unlike the Clerics predicted, there was no mass chaos. The people seemed to relish the notion they were not alone in the universe and the Earth people seemed so idealistic.

Bazion noted to his assistants, "12 years will sneak up on us quickly and we need to immediately set in motion the construction of another Space Dock."

It took 10 years to get another Space Dock up into geosynchronous orbit. Since technology greatly expanded because of Earth ideas and other ways to solve problems they would not otherwise correct, they determined a new ship would also be built. The original Interplanetary Transport was put in orbiting mothballs and shut down.

A new crew was formed, none of the originals would go back, nor did they desire to, especially because two years in space was not a real enjoyable experience.

Only Eight Americans wanted to go back to Earth. Two had died and two had started Families on Caro including Hank Rogers who was now thin, slim, and racy with a beautiful Caronian wife that eclipsed just about any beauty queen back home.

The launch date arrived and this time there was no fear of Clerical interference. The Americans were eager to see planet Earth again and grateful it would only require a year to get there.

It has been widely speculated President John F. Kennedy was assassinated because he wrote and executive order directing the CIA to disclose to the public information on the Caronian Exchange.

When Allen Dulles was called by Bissell and said, "Turn on the TV, they just shot Kennedy," he was truly shocked. He had no special love for Kennedy after being fired because he refused to release information on the Caronian Exchange and when the Caronians seemed to disappear, most of which because they feared for their lives and privacy, he told Tracey Barnes the last man standing, "Don't ever divulge to the public where they went."

Thanks to the fake I.D. the CIA had given Metongy, (aka Rex Gordan) he was able to get a job and work. Because his identity they manufactured showed an undergraduate degree, he easily applied for and received a Master's Degree at MIT and soon afterwards a PhD.

Metongy and Sophia Kuznetsov were married and before long there were a couple little Gordon's running around and Sophia suddenly became a domestic engineer.

In 12 years, their lives flourished, the kids were wonderful, Rex was loved by Sophia's parents and because he had such a brilliant mind picked up Yiddish quickly. While out in public when they wanted to speak privately without people knowing what they were saying, Rex and his father-in-law often spoke in Yiddish.

~~~

Caro-2 Interplanetary Transport slowed down as it
~~~

passed by Saturn and was soon traveling one quarter light speed. The Captain looked at the communicator and said, "Commence communicating with Earth, we need to announce our arrival."

None of the original crew came back, but they were well trained by members of the original crew and wondered how they would be received.

"Do you expect they have new technology the six Caro left behind explained to them?"

"We'll find out soon. Metongy Zeugcha was a distinguished scientist, if he chose to share with Earth what he knew about a lot of things, then Earth may have advanced rapidly."

The communicator began speaking the call signs the original Interplanetary Transport had been advised to use: "Square this is Triangle attempting to contact you."

"It will take 10 minutes for those signals to reach Earth, based on our present location."

"Expect to get reply in 20 minutes if they hear us."

Richard Nixon was in the throes of Watergate. The nation

was in a stupor and sour mood. NASA had not heard from the Caronians for 12 years and wondered if they had made it back to the Caro planet alive. Then one day, the people at SETI (search for extra-terrestrial intelligence) started receiving some strange signals. Their antennae indicated the signals were coming from outer space. But the signals contained English spoken words: "Square this is Triangle attempting to contact you."

The main researcher at SETI Jeremy Brown contacted his good friend at NASA, Doctor Holloway and informed him about it.

"We have detected these signals coming from space, 'Square this is Triangle attempting to contact you."

"Probably some pranksters on Earth fooling with your antenna."

"It's not possible, we have multiple antennas."

"Well, its UHF there is no reason why anyone from space would be sending voice signals via UHF."

"Ok Doctor Holloway, have some of your guys at NASA point an antenna towards the Orion Star system and see what you get."

Later that day Doctor Holloway was having lunch with one of his associates and they joked about Jeremy Browns comments.

"I might just put an antenna up in that direction just for the heck of it," the associate said and later actually did.

Shortly Doctor Holloway received a phone call, "We have received a few of those triangle and square communiques, I think you need to take Jeremy Brown's comments serious."

Soon Holloway was in the lab looking over the receipts of the messages coming in. Out of sheer luck one of the scientists who happened to be at Area 51 12 years prior said, "Their due to be back about now."

NASA immediately informed appropriate officials in the CIA about this significant event and in a short period of time they tracked down Metongy and Sophia.

~~~

Metongy Zeugcha (aka Rex Gordon) had earphones
~~~

on plugged into his stereo which he often used to listen to Earth Classical music which he enjoyed playing quite often. As Metongy rested in his leather recliner, listening to the lovely performance of Charles Villiers Stanford - Piano Concerto No.2 in C-minor, Op.126 [Charles Villiers Stanford - Piano Concerto No.2 in C-minor, Op.126 (1911) - YouTube], the doorbell rang. Since it was the weekend the Gordon family wasn't expecting anyone but, on weekends friends did pop in now and then.

Sophia knew Rex had headphones on was reclined and most likely in dreamland, so she walked over to answer the doorbell. Looking through the security eye piece she spotted two men outside with suits on. Instantly she was alarmed as they smelled CIA.

This was not a pleasant moment for Sophia because she knew when the Cash in Advance boys visited you on a Saturday, that usually meant something important. She had already lived enough drama in her life and after retiring from NASA/CIA the last thing in the world she wanted was government affiliation or the government demanding any more of Metongy's time.

Sophia reluctantly opened the door.

As soon as the CIA men had direct visual on Sophia and they knew her quite well from all the surveillance they had on her, one of them said, "Hello, Sophia Gordon?"

"Yes, who are you and what do you want?"

"I'm Mike McCall and this is Bradly Liddy, we are from the CIA DD/P's office, and we need to talk to you and Rex about Caro visitors."

If there was any moment in Sophia's life where her personal psychology was tested, it was now, because instinctively she knew it was about time for the Caro to return. To say she wasn't the least frightened about the implications to her and her family was an understatement.

Sophia knew she had to deal with this just like all the other crisis that was bestowed upon her from the very day the Caro first landed more than a dozen years ago. With all her superhuman effort she retained her composure and did the only rational thing to do at the moment.

"Please come in, I'm sure Rex would like to hear about this."

Sophia held the door open and Mike and Bradly who walked in the Gordon home and followed Sophia 20 steps into the family room adjacent to the front-living room of their home.

Rex was not sleeping, but he was in a different mental state thanks to the tapestry of the crescendo's that Charles Villiers Stanford - Piano Concerto offered. When he looked up and saw the men in suits standing next to Sophia, he knew this was probably not going to be a pleasant meeting.

Mike McCall was evidently the senior CIA man present and initiated the discourse.

"Metongy, "the Caro have returned."

Metongy knew one thing for certain, only a few people in the world knew his real name and they were all associated with NASA or the CIA and a few in the FBI.

"I kind of felt in the back of my mind to expect them any

time soon."

"Just as they promised, they are back."

"Are they bringing American Scientists back?"

"Yes, they are scheduled to come down at S4 in Area 51 in the same location where you were Quarantined. A new Quarantine facility is being put together now."

Metongy made a request, "I would like to be taken to Area 51 with my wife and kids to see the Caronians."

"I'm sure the agency had that in mind. Prepare your family for a short trip and we'll be back in two hours to take you to your transportation."

The CIA men then left the Rex Gordon home and Metongy and Sophia looked into each other's eyes. This would be the ultimate test for their marriage.

Within hours Metongy, Sophia and their family were flown by a CIA Lear Jet from San Jose to Area-51. It was a somber experience.

What soon unfolded was a tumultuous experience as now decision time was coming for Metongy. He now had a family, wife and two children ages 9 and 11 whom he had grown very fond of. The family was very close, his wife Sophia not only was his best friend, but his life now orbited around her. He had no idea what love was until he met Sophia, and now it was the foundation of his existence.

"Do you want to go back with the Caronians?"

"I want to go back to Caro but yet I don't want to leave my family."

A much older Maryanne very sympathetic to the family and nearing her retirement fulfilled her role as the CIA's plane's conductor was standing next to them as they prepared to takeoff. Metongy realizing the choice he must make felt awkward he didn't have any writing materials and asked Maryanne, "Do you have something I can write a letter on?"

"Certainly, I have notepads and envelopes." She then walked over to a cabinet and grabbed a new notepad, envelope and an ink pen.

"Here you go." Maryanne said as she handed Metongy the writing materials.

It was a fateful day that Metongy seemed to think would never happen as the Caro were long overdue. But now here they were back abruptly, and he had to make what could be heart breaking decisions.

Since Metongy was planning on not returning to Caro and he had no relatives left there since his parents passed away, he was giving his residence to Ferdastad who could keep it as a laboratory or sell it for the proceeds so that he and Zurella could move into a much nicer home. He was also leaving all his possessions to Ferdastad including his credits to help him pay to keep the lab running if he so chose.

Metongy had developed a very negative mental framework towards Earth during the Vietnam War. He had not lived during the times the Caro fought the Tauceti's but the more he watched the TV coverage of Walter Cronkite and others the more he realized he made a terrible decision staying on earth. If it were not for the love of his family, the decision would be easy to get off this planet.

But now he had a couple of little "Gordon's" in the family. As much as he wanted to leave this evil planet that left scars in his heart all those years watching the Vietnam War and all the negatives that unfolded, his children were priceless to him.

When the Caro Interplanetary Transport finally arrived again and the shuttle landed at the secret location S-4 at Area 51, he was told bluntly by the Caro who arrived, "We would not probably sanction another trip for 50 to 100 years due to internal problems unfolding as the Tauceti had once again raised their ugly heads with the demise of the Clerics," and that "If you went back to Caro, it would most likely be a one-way trip."

In discussions with Sophia and the children, it became rather apparent what their intentions were.

"Maybe we can all go to Caro?" Metongy asked in almost a hopeful manner.

"The children would soon miss Earth as much as you miss Caro. Their grandparents, friends, and relatives are all here. They can have a natural life here. If you take them to Caro, think about what they might possibly be subjected to."

Metongy suddenly remembering life on Caro knew deep in his heart his children would be viewed as freaks and could never live a normal Caro life. It was almost a non-starter for them to go to Caro.

"Traveling in space is very dangerous, there is a possibility we might not make it," Sophia a space craft designer reiterated.

"That's true."

"Plus, we may never be able to return. The children would never be able to see their relatives again and would never know what happened to earth."

"We can get information about the Earth while in Caro."

"But it would not be the same as living here. Plus, as you said, it's what happened seven years prior."

Fear and sorrow gripped Metongy's heart; his decision to never go back to Caro was now laid before him. His beautiful wife and kids just about tore his heart out when he looked at them when he had to make that fateful decision.

Because of Watergate, Vietnam War, Cuban Missile Crisis, Cold War, and a variety of other issues, NASA plainly informed the Caronians, "You cannot stay long. America was too fragile to explain all the omissions about aliens and you must leave before it becomes a public spectacle." An immediate decision had to be made; there is no allowance for time to consider the decision.

The Interplanetary Transport Captain and several crew members were behind a temporary glass barrier that had microphones and speakers set up so they could hear and observe each other. This scene reminded Metongy of when he first arrived.

The ship's Captain said, "I understand the dilemma you faced and since four Americans didn't come back from Caro, it was natural that a couple Caronians would decide to stay on Earth as well."

Doctor Provkovitev, who married a Japanese wife, also brought to Area 51 and standing beside Metongy talking with the Captain stated, "I've decided I will not be leaving Earth."

The four others had all decided to return to Caro and were led to the shuttle where they promptly entered and waited for immediate departure.

Metongy's children were old enough to understand they could never discuss this with anyone and were very glad the ship's Captain explained who his father really was: "The man who first discovered the original signals from Earth."

They all exited the tent, the Caro walked over to the side of the shuttle and the group walked up to the yellow police tape that marked a barrier for everyone to remain away from.

The Caronians said goodbye to Metongy who had tears going down his face as he now knew he would never see Caro again.

Metongy now only a few feet away from the Captain asked for a special favor, "Would you please give this letter to my good friend Ferdastad and give my regards to Director Bazion."

He handed the letter which was in a small plastic bag and would be zapped with microwave energy with the rest of the artifacts they carried when they returned to the ship to kill any germs.

The Shuttle then launched and the final exposure to Earth

was done. The Caronians never did come back, nor did anyone ever obtain any information on what happened to the Caro who simply vanished.

Once again Earth was alone in the Universe.

Paul D. Escudero

San Diego, CA, 2021

Author Notes:

This book is fiction no living person is depicted in this book. A few historical names were used to paint the era. They have real stories of their own, quite remarkable. But they in no way are implied to have engaged in any of the fiction in this book. But one never knows unless they research what really happened in their lives. Hopefully they will not be forgotten for the sacrifices they made in real life.

This first part of the author notes is my comments about my concern about UFO's and what is now starting to emerge. My concerns are for mankind and the entire human race.

Leaked Navy video appears to show UFO off California should have been a wakeup call.

My speculation is the military is about ready to ask Congress for an additional $100 Billion in United States

Space Force Funding.

The way it works in DC, you can't go asking for big bucks for military expenditures unless you have a perceived Threat.

Logically one would have to conclude its either a funding ploy or, the Aliens have finally become so aggressive we are in a pickle.

If it is the second reason, the government bureaucrats who control policy only have themselves to blame.

Assuming that Roswell New Mexico UFO crash in 1947 and the Aztec New Mexico crash in 1948 were real, the government didn't do themselves any service by covering it up.

If those crashes really happened the people in charge made some very bad choices, because we wasted 75 years preparing to deal with Aliens. If those crashes really happened, an honest government would have weighed all the factors and came to the conclusion it was time to get together with Russia, Great Britain, France, Germany and other technology advanced countries and deal with it on a global measure, because how could they possibly know the Aliens intentions?

As a science fiction author when I create these Novels, I look at various sides to the story that I create.

Using logic and taking emotion and bias out of the equation, a rational thinker would have to conclude, based on probabilities, if there is an Alien race visiting planet Earth, there has to be others. We are not alone in this galaxy, the Aliens visiting us are also not alone.

Aliens by logic also have enemies. They too have surveillance on them. It would only make sense. And if a ship that came here from the Serpo planet ostensibly in the 1960's, who's to say some of Serpo's enemies didn't follow them here to figure out why they were going long distance and for what reason? Then suddenly you have 2 Alien races now surveying the planet.

I hate to be the bearer of bad news to some of you.

Just like in my books (how did I know this?) some of these Alien planets are probably over-populated. Worse than New Delhi or a few cities of China. For that matter even in

America we have population densities in New York and Los Angeles with cities like Houston not far behind.

Alien visitors also may need certain natural resources like Uranium and Plutonium. You can make Plutonium out of Uranium, but you at least need Uranium in order to create the Plutonium.

What would an advance Alien race use plutonium for? No doubt they have wonderful fusion reactors that operate off plutonium. They too probably need to build hydrogen bombs for their own defenses.

We also have rare Earth materials. In essence Earth due to our primitive technology is the low hanging fruit.

My speculation is that if this process of Aliens following other Aliens to this planet, eventually we'll get some Aliens who are interested in either plunder or shifting 50 Billion people to this planet to deal with their own severe overcrowding.

There are numerous other scenarios one can conclude as well.

Now here's the punch line if you will. **If there is merit in**

my speculation guess what›s going to happen next?

More Aliens will be arriving more often, and the bad ones will be even more aggressive.

What if one of these Alien races decides to make Earth one of their far-off garrisons for galactic defenses?

We are pushovers, all we got to shoot at them are spitballs.

Dishonest governments have a tendency to paint themselves in a corner.

The United States government has painted itself into a corner on the Alien issue.

There really is only one solution now:

It's a come to Jesus' moment and they need to come out and admit all the Alien details they have such as Roswell, Aztec, Serpo, Dr. Reed's Alien, and a few other things they currently attempt covering up.

The longer they wait to reach that come to Jesus' moment the harder it will be for this planet to deal with Aliens who are coming here to pick the low hanging fruit.

Concerning this novel and what's behind it.

Planet Earth has been sending out radio waves almost 120 years. On December 12, 1901, Guglielmo Marconi successfully sent the first radio transmission across the Atlantic Ocean. There were not a lot of signals then, but they slowly increased, just like I crafted in the early part of the Story when Metongy Zeugcha first got involved in receiving Earth signals.

The Thesis of the book is:

"What if they hear us before we hear them?"

As discussed with some brilliant scientists I've met, radio signals have severe attenuation in space because there is not much of a medium to carry them. That's one of the reasons why we do not receive many signals from space unless they are of extreme wavelength. We would not receive Alien signals of any significant levels to detect with Earth primitive equipment unless they get close. That is why you do not hear scientists claiming they received radio signals from Aliens. The signals just can't get here.

But what if there is a convergence zone in space somewhere that recombines the signal, and we receive it or the Aliens receive our signals?

Our early radio transmissions were relatively low frequency (long wavelengths). They have a better chance of getting somewhere than newer modern transmissions. But on the otherhand if Aliens have very sensitive receivers with a receiver sensitivity of -220 dB/V/Hz they might be able to receive those highly attenuated signals. Or if they send robotic probes in this direction, they will get close enough to detect the signals.

Now think about this: Why is it the Aliens didn't start showing up in any significant numbers until 1947?

What happened in 1945? Just like in the book, we produced 3 nuclear explosions.

Nuclear explosions give off a huge energy blast including photons. Photon's do not attenuate in space, they simply spread so it appears they attenuate. But when you have a fireball with the amount of light a star gives off that suddenly leaves a planet, smart Aliens a long distance away know what that is. Nuclear explosions in the galaxy are nothing new. Mars was wiped out by 2 gigantic nuclear explosions as described by Doctor Brandenburg. If you have not read his books or looked at his videos, I highly suggest you do.

What I'm leading to is a nuclear explosion coming from a planet, gives off a unique spectral signature. Advanced Aliens know it came from a nuclear explosion.

What's happened since 1945?

Above ground nuclear explosions. Also, America did 5 space nuclear explosions which I mention in one of my other books. No atmosphere to block the photons leaving a space nuclear explosion. Far off Aliens might get a signature leading them to believe some sort of space war was going on.

US detonated a nuclear weapon 9th July, 1962 about 240 miles into the sky. It was named Starfish Prime. This nuclear blast in Space had an explosive yield of 1.45 megatons.

5 orbital nuclear explosions were carried out by the US during the Cold War. The Pentagon did this study the effects of nuclear weapons in outer space and high altitudes. The warheads after being detonated gave off heat and light along with high number of X and gamma rays. The effects of the blasts were felt thousands of kilometers from New Zealand to Hawaii.

An electromagnetic field was generated above the earth and was bigger in size than what scientists were anticipating, the beginning of EMP weapons. Aircraft experienced electrical surges, aircraft lights were blown and a giant aurora bloomed in the sky.

And now: The Counter-electronics High Power Microwave Advanced Missile Project (CHAMP) is a joint concept technology demonstration led by the Air Force Research Laboratory, Directed Energy Directorate at Kirtland Air Force Base to develop an air-launched directed-energy weapon capable of incapacitating or damaging electronic systems by means of an EMP (electromagnetic pulse).

Results of those 5 space nuclear detonations is why the Champ missile is viable and the Russians and the Chinese fear it because they don't know their vulnerabilities as the cause and effect are far too complicated for any rational person to come to grips with. More Aliens started arriving after we tested the Champ missile. See a connection there?

America and the Soviet Union did above ground nuclear tests until we signed the test ban treaty.

It takes Aliens a while to get here depending on where they came from. We exploded atomic bombs in 1945 and two years later, Gray Aliens arrived and two of their space craft crashed at Roswell (not just one, yes there was two of them).

According to some sources we obtained at least one living Alien from those crashes. Then the following year another crashed at Aztec, New Mexico and we found 18 dead Aliens in that spaceship.

There has been great effort to call the Aztec crash a hoax as part of the coverup.

Eventually when the government has that come to Jesus' moment, they will have to eventually admit the Aztec crash happened and how many people they hurt in the cover-up.

With the recent aggressive behavior of the Aliens around U.S. Navy ships that has been admitted by the Pentagon, that come to Jesus' moment is now.

In this book some of the terms such as Cyclonic Inverters, Space Dock, Space Shuttle Craft, 160 mile per hour Hovercraft, Skycars, and 300 mile per Hour Tube Trains will most likely one day manifest. And now we see where a lot of things Isaac Asimov wrote about in the 1950's is happening today. Case in point in one of his book people no longer had physical meetings, all communications and interactions was on a computer display like terminal. Look what the internet has done to us. A lot of my friends have only internet communications or cell phone text messages to me.

In case you are wondering who would read my books? GRU, FSB, MSS, MI6, and even the Artificial Intelligence at the CIA most likely do. Just think its people like me now indirectly programming those CIA Artificial Intelligence networks. Kind of scarry isn't it? What's even more scarry is how I'm reprogramming the mindset of Chinese, Japanese, Russians, and others. The pollination of ideas has irrevocably occurred. That's why from this day forward you need to think: "Is Science Fiction and Aliens important things to be aware of?"

I hope you enjoyed the book.
Paul D. Escudero
San Diego California 2022

www.ingramcontent.com/pod-product-compliance
Lightning Source LLC
Chambersburg PA
CBHW060740210726
48292CB00012B/34